I0635540

Special thanks to:

Amanda Kay Smith, Anij Fallows, Azia MacManus, Burning Spear Comix, Carl W Bishop, Catherine Leja, Chris Call, Christine Gourley, Collin David, Courtney Cannon, Damion and Cathy Gilzean, Daniel Groves, Dave Baxter, DeWayne Copeland, Earl Hall, Elizabeth Nohelty Romano, Emerson Kasak, Erin Congdon, Jake Schroeder, Jason Crase, Jeff Lewis, Jimbo, John Mead, Joshua Bowers, Katrina Roets, Ken Reich, Kimberly Lucia, Laura Reed, Mark Byzewski, Mark Hill, Massimo Piras, Matthew Johnson, Michael H Bullington, Nick Smith, Nikres, Odile Purcell O'Byrne, Paul Rose Jr., Peter Anders, Rob Fowler, Rob Steinberger, Sammy G., scantrontb, Schreuka, Scott Kilburn, Shannon Carlin, Sherry Mock, SwordFirey, Talinda Willard, Thomas Werner, Venron, and Walter Weiss.

Invasion

By:

Russell Nohelty

Edited by:

Amy Cissell and Chris Barnes

Cover by:

Paramita Bhattacharjee

Invasion

First edition. August 6, 2019.

Written by Russell Nohelty

Book 1
"Infiltration"

Chapter 1

Joshy Carter didn't much like the idea of spending his summer traveling across the country with his parents. Not that he had much going on back home. He'd never had much success making friends, so there was nobody to miss. Still, his room had his PlayStation and his sleep—his precious, precious sleep—and solitude.

On the road there was nothing except for his family, his sister, and—

"The open road, Joshy!" his father, Bill, said. "There's nothing like it."

"Actually, there are tons of things like it. There's nothing literally everywhere. This is the part I hate in video games. Endless nothingness until you reach a town. At least in games, you can fast travel. Can't do that here, though. We gotta endure every excruciating second."

Josh folded his arms across his chest. "And I hate being called Joshy," he added. "I'm eighteen years old. I'm not a child anymore. Like literally, I am no longer a child in the eyes of the government, even. Pretty much everywhere, I am an adult by any measure of the word."

Joshy squeaked when he talked, and it made his mother Carole laugh. After all, that was the kind of child...adult...that Joshy was...the kind that people didn't fear. He was kind of meek, and frankly uninteresting. The only thing he cared about was playing Fortnite.

Joshy played all day and night, hardly leaving his room except to eat. He dreamed of being a professional video game player, which was the kind of thing that wasn't even possible a few years ago and now consumed the thoughts of millions.

"Would you lower the volume of that music," Joshy said, looking over at his sister blaring K Pop from her phone. "I can hear it all the way over here."

"Suck it up," Leslie said.

"You're gonna go deaf," he replied.

"That's future me's problem," she replied.

K Pop was a thing Leslie loved, so of course, it was stupid to Joshy. That didn't make it any less fun or catchy. Most people couldn't listen to it on repeat like she could, but to each their own. If Joshy could spend hours rotting his brain with computers, then Leslie could rot hers with Korean pop music. That was the American Way.

"This blows," Joshy said with a deep sigh. "America is boring."

While Joshy was dull and uninteresting, his sister was spectacular. Not only did she graduate two years early from high school and take an accelerated track at Stanford, but she was going to be the first in her family to graduate law school. If all went to plan, she would be the first in her family to be governor of California, too, though that would be true for most families.

"That's a horrible attitude, mister," his mother said to him. "You should take a second to stop and enjoy these little moments. I would have killed to go on a road trip with my parents as a child."

"That's a lie, and you know it, mom," Joshy scoffed. "Nobody has ever wanted to go on a road trip with their parents in the history of the universe."

Leslie raised her hand. "I did. I mean, I took time off from summer school to be here, so your point has been disproven inside this very car."

"You're a bit of a know-it-all, did you know that?" Joshy said. "It's really annoying."

The voice inside the GPS blared through the car before Joshy and Leslie had a chance to argue more. "In two miles, stay left on Interstate 15 North."

"We're getting close, Joshy!" his father exclaimed. "Can you smell it? Vegas baby! Vegas!!!"

"No," Joshy said. "Just no."

"I don't see why you think Joshy would be excited about Vegas," Leslie said. "It's not like he can drink or gamble."

"As long as the room has internet and AC, I'll be fine," Josh said.

*

While there were many outrageous hotels in Vegas, made up like New York City or a glass pyramid or the Venetian canals, their differences were generally aesthetic. Inside, they all performed the same functions. There was a casino area, a shopping area, a restaurant area, and then the hotel itself, which depending on where you were in Vegas took on a different look.

At the Elara, it meant elegant white marble everywhere. The Elara was a timeshare complex attached to the shopping center of the Planet Hollywood Resort and Casino. It didn't have a casino of its own and wasn't affiliated with Planet Hollywood, though it glommed onto its popularity. The Elara, much like David S. Pumpkins, was its own thing.

Bill Carter pulled his minivan up to the front of the hotel and stepped out of the car. His bones ached from five hours of driving, and his back cracked as he arched it.

A valet in a red vest and bright smile ran up to him. "Your keys, sir?"

Bill pulled his keys close to his chest. "No. I'm sorry. I'm going to…self-park."

"It's complimentary, my friend," the valet said with a smile. "There's no charge for valet."

Bill liked that idea. He was thrilled about it, actually. He never valeted his car in Los Angeles. After all, who had an extra $10 to pay the valet? Forget about it. But a free valet, well he could indulge in that. Those are the best types of splurges, Bill thought, the free kind.

"Quit talking with the valet and open the trunk!" Carole called to him, cranky from the long drive and ready to relax by the pool.

Bill reached into his car and pushed the button to open the trunk. He thought it was quite extravagant to buy a car where the trunk opened by itself, but it was included in the base model price, so who was he to argue?

Before the trunk finished opening, a bellboy pulled up a luggage carrier to the car and loaded a large suitcase onto the carrier. It was heavy, and the bellman struggled with the massive weight, but he didn't say anything, except to let out a soft grunt.

"I'm sorry," Carole said. "Do you want any help with that?"

"It's their job, mom," Joshy said with a scowl. "Let them do their job."

Joshy hadn't yet learned the concepts of compassion or empathy. That was something that solidified with time, work, and sacrifice, none of which were things Joshy ever had to deal with much in his privileged life.

"I'm fine, ma'am," the bellman said. "Please go to the front desk. I'll meet you there."

Joshy pulled a tattered backpack out of the trunk and flung it across his back. Then, he walked inside and up the escalator toward the front desk.

*

By the time Joshy's parents joined him in the lobby of the hotel, he was already halfway through his fifth level of Angry Birds. It insulted his skill to play casual games, but his Nintendo Switch had lost power halfway through the trip, and he'd forgotten his car charger at home, so he was stuck until he got into his room.

"About time!" Joshy said in a huff when his parents stepped off the escalator.

"You could have helped them unload the car," Leslie replied. "It would have gone a lot faster if you did."

"Sure," Joshy said, standing up. "But I can follow directions. He said to go to the lobby, so I went to the lobby."

Now, you have to imagine Joshy, an eighteen-year-old human male, saying this, with all the sarcasm of an eighteen-year-old human male, dripping with testosterone and filled with the kind of wisdom only a teenager could confidently show, devoid of any irony in the fact that he truly knew nothing.

Bill stepped up to the front desk and pleasantries were exchanged. Once the keys were given and the platitudes traded, Joshy and his family were on their way up to their room, a rather luxurious suite filled with nice beds, cozy towels, and the like.

"You and your sister get this room," Bill said, gesturing toward the room on their right as they walked into the suite.

There were two queen beds inside, and little else. Then, he pointed toward a much larger room across from them, beyond the couch and dining room table. "Your mother and I get that one."

"Not fair!" Joshy said, walking inside to see a kitchen, couch, and big screen TV mounted on the wall. "Why can't I have my own room?"

"Because life isn't fair," Leslie replied. "It's not like I'm happy about this either. You snore."

"Do not," Joshy argued, except he totally did. If he had any friends, they would all agree with Leslie.

"Well," Carole said with a smile. "I'm ready to do a little lounging around. Who wants to go down to the pool?"

"Sounds nice," Bill said, thumbing a wad of money in his wallet. He knew the odds of hitting it rich in Vegas were low, but that wasn't going to stop him from trying. "I'll come for a little bit. Then, I want to walk around."

"Not me," Leslie said. "I plan to lounge by the pool until dinner."

The doorbell to the room rang. Bill ran to the door to welcome in the bellman, who pulled his luggage carrier inside and took all their suitcases off it. Once he was done, he stood there, smiling, for a good ten seconds without saying a word. It was quite awkward.

"I think he wants you to tip him, hun," Carole said.

"Oh!" Bill replied. "I thought it was free. Isn't this free?"

"Yes, sir, technically."

Bill slapped the bellman on the shoulder. "Perfect! Then I'll see you again soon. Have a great day."

The bellman left, grumbling to himself. Bill was the third person in a row to stiff him. He hated his job and looked forward to the day he finished night school with a computer science degree. Nobody would stiff him then.

Chapter 2

Joshy didn't join his family at the pool when they filed out of the room. He wanted to get in some gaming first, so he plugged in his laptop and handily won three Fortnite battles. Then, he put on his swim trunks and went to the elevator that would take him down to the pool.

Joshy wasn't a fan of most elevators, and he didn't like this one any better. It was one of those fancy glass ones which looked down on the strip. He could see all the way down to Mandalay Bay at the bottom of the strip if he cared to look, which he didn't.

His suite was on the fifteenth floor, which meant that he risked running into humans thirteen times before he reached the bottom. Of all the things Joshy disliked, humans were at the top of the list. They were rude, annoying, and smelled horrible. He hated elevators because it meant being trapped with humans in an enclosed space, and that meant he might have to interact with one. It was bad enough that humans existed around him, but the thought of having to engage with them was a fate worse than death.

Luckily, nobody entered the elevator while Joshy rode down to the pool. He took the circuitous route around the lobby of the hotel and toward a side door guarded by a burly security guard. Thumping techno music echoed through the glass.

His family was already at the pool and had been for some time, but Joshy needed some alone time before he joined them. He needed the serenity only video games could bring. Playing video games relaxed him. That was what his family never understood about his passion. It was quite hard being Joshy, but when he played video games, all of that melted away, and he was able to be somebody else for a while.

Joshy's main problem was that he hated himself. He hated other people as well, but nobody as much as he hated himself. That was what stopped him from joining clubs, or flirting with girls, or existing like a normal human…he was always in his own way.

Of course, sometimes other people were in his way, too. In this instance, it was a tall, bearded, black man with a three-piece suit and rippling muscles who guarded the entrance to the pool area.

"I'm gonna need to see some ID," the guard told him.

"Why? I'm a guest at this hotel," Joshy said, pulling out his keycard.

"Gotta be twenty-one to use the pool."

"Really?" Joshy said, raising his voice half an octave. That kind of thing happened all the time. It wasn't the manliest thing in the universe, and it didn't make him seem older than his eighteen years.

"Yeah," the guard replied, holding up a clipboard. "Now, I'm really gonna need to see some ID."

Joshy hadn't cared much about using the pool when he left his room. He was doing so to placate his mother so she wouldn't nag him later about not hanging out with his family. He was ready to turn around and head back to his room, until a group of bikini-clad, bronzed women pushed passed him and into the pool area.

Joshy peered into the pool area, past the glass, and saw dozens of beautiful women dancing rhythmically, gyrating, and…well, it was enough to make Joshy believe that while most humans sucked, those particular humans were fine with him.

"Come on," he said, flinging his arms in the air. "I left it in my room, but I'm twenty-one, I promise I'm twenty-one."

The bouncer chuckled. "Yeah, and I'm Otis Redding. Get lost, kid."

Joshy couldn't believe that he was trying to get closer to his parents, but he desperately wanted to get into that pool. It wasn't enough to creepily stare at the bikini girls from the other side of the glass.

As the wheels started to turn in his head, Joshy watched his father stand up from his lounge chair, place his sunglasses in his pocket, and walk toward him.

"Look," Joshy said. "That's my dad right there. He's got a bad heart, and I need to give him his pills."

"Show 'em to me," the bouncer replied.

"Well, I don't have them on me!" Joshy said.

Joshy's father walked out of the pool and past the bouncer, smiling at him as he passed. Bill then made a beeline for the lobby that would lead him out of the hotel toward the casino. He had already wasted enough time on pleasantries, and now he needed to get down to business.

"Dad!" Joshy shouted.

Bill, startled, turned to him. "Oh, there you are, kid. I thought you were still upstairs."

"No. I'm trying to get into the pool," Joshy replied. "This guy won't let me in. Says you have to be twenty-one to get inside."

"To use a pool? That sounds stupid."

"Rules are rules," the bouncer replied. "I don't make the rules. I enforce 'em. We got a kiddie pool around back he can use."

"The Gestapo had rules, too!" Joshy replied, furious.

"Alright, alright," Joshy's father replied, grabbing his arm. "Wish you had used a little more of that knowledge in history class, last year. Maybe then you wouldn't have nearly flunked. You can come with me."

"What!" Joshy whined. "Come on, dad, I don't want to go with you. Do you see what's in there? Come on. Tell him that I can go in."

Bill looked through the glass toward the pool and saw the women dancing, the drinks flowing, and thought about how desperately he would have wanted to go inside if he were Joshy's age…and knew he couldn't let his son anywhere near that.

"Guard," he said. "My son is eighteen. Don't let him into that pool if you see him again."

"DAD!"

"Will do, sir," the guard said with a smile. "You can count on it."

"Come on," Bill said, pulling his son along. "You can ogle women later. That'll be about all you do when you get to be my age."

*

Outside of the Elara sat a strip of shops and restaurants that lined the "miracle mile," which was supposed to be a play on the Miracle Mile in Los Angeles, except that, well it didn't look like LA at all.

For instance, smack dab in front of the hotel there was a bar where you could buy premade margarita slushies. Nothing like that bar existed in Los Angeles. Plus, if you craned your neck up at the right place, you saw a ceiling lined with stars, which is something you would never see in the Miracle Mile in Los Angeles. Maybe Griffith Park, but not in the heart of Los Angeles. Then again, that wasn't really the point, was it? People didn't go to Planet Hollywood for the authentic experience. Vegas wasn't built on authenticity.

"Alright," Joshy's dad said when he got to the casino entrance. "Can you keep a secret?"

Joshy shook his head. "No. You know I can't keep a secret."

Bill grabbed his son tightly around the arms. "Well, I need you to try, son. I need you to try really hard, because I'm gonna do some things in that casino, and your mother can't know about it."

"What kind of things?"

"Just—" Bill stuttered. "Things. Okay. That's all you need to know."

Bill held the money in his pocket tightly. He wasn't used to holding over a thousand dollars in cash on his person. He feared it would be stolen, or worse, fall out onto the ground for some other lucky sucker to collect.

"You're scaring me, dad," Joshy said. "Not much, but a little."

"Don't worry about it. Look, I've got a system. Everybody's got a system, but I got a system, a real good one, okay?"

"Systems don't work, dad," Joshy said. "I've watched enough TV to know that."

"Yeah, but you haven't seen this one yet. Follow my lead, okay?" Bill said. "And stop being so negative."

Bill walked past the security guard and into the casino. Joshy sighed. He didn't know if his father was having a nervous breakdown, but he knew enough to know that a casino was a dangerous place to go nuts.

"Wait up, dad," Joshy replied.

Joshy barely took a step into the casino before a short, squat woman with cheap hair and long fingernails grabbed him. "No way, honey. Not today. You gotta be twenty-one to be on this floor."

Bill turned to Joshy, wanting to help his son, but less than he needed to gamble. So, he turned away, confident that Joshy could take care of himself, even though Joshy had never proved he could do so, not even one time in his pathetic life.

The security guard pulled Joshy out of the casino and plopped him down outside the casino entrance. "I'm watching you."

Joshy didn't know what to do. He couldn't find his mother and sister because they were at the pool, and he wasn't allowed to go with his dad into the casino. He was alone in Vegas. Then he realized, he was alone…in Vegas…and a devious smile crept across his face.

Chapter 3

It's a double-edged sword, being a teenager in Las Vegas. For one, you are in Las Vegas, the debauchery capital of America, and maybe the world... there were worse places in the darkest corners of the universe, but those places were not so open with their lurid offerings.

So, if you are a teenager in Vegas, you were in Vegas, which was good. On the other hand, you weren't twenty-one so you couldn't partake in all Vegas had to offer. Luckily, Vegas had been working to clean up its image, which meant there was plenty of all-ages fun for those who cared to look.

Joshy didn't care to look, of course. He wanted to drink, gamble, and cavort, and he was willing to walk up and down the strip for as long as needed to find somebody that would let him have a real Vegas experience. While in Planet Hollywood, as he walked around the shops, he saw no fewer than four places to buy alcohol and three to get a tattoo -- which he could technically get but would regret the next morning. But no, Joshy couldn't gamble, drink, or smoke weed. No matter how hard he tried, nobody in Planet Hollywood would budge on that, so Joshy had to take to the strip. It was a tough decision, to walk the strip or play video games in his room, but in the end, he figured he wouldn't be back to Vegas any time soon, so he should try to have fun, even for a little while.

The heat smacked against Joshy like a punch in the face as he pushed open the door to leave the shops and venture onto the strip. He lived in Los Angeles, so it wasn't as if heat was foreign to him, but that didn't make it any less oppressive when it crashed upon his frail body. Vegas hotels were kept rather cold to combat the oppressive heat, with the ancillary benefit of punishing people who left the safety of their buildings.

*

Joshy spent the next several hours walking the strip from casino to casino, trying, and failing, to satiate his urge to debauch himself. There's only so much trouble a human can get into in Vegas without money, alcohol, or a fake ID. Joshy had none of those things, and he didn't have the means to acquire them either, so he spent most of his time wandering around the strip aimlessly like a first level character trying to figure out the game mechanics of a new world.

He heard the gondola singers at the Venetian, walked through the tropical gardens in the Mirage, caught a horrible animatronic show about Greek gods at a fountain in Caesar's, watched an equally terrible pirate show at Treasure Island, and finally enthralled himself by staring at gallons of chocolate making their way through the largest chocolate fountain in the world at the Bellagio.

By the time he caught the seasonal decorations in the Bellagio's lobby, Joshy had walked almost ten miles up and down the strip, with nothing to show for it except some half-decent memories. He was exhausted, famished, and was ready to go home and take a shower.

He thought it was mildly weird that even after hours away from the hotel, nobody had called or texted him. Didn't they care he wasn't in his room? Or did they assume he'd found a place to hole up and play video games? He probably should have stayed in his room, but he'd been sure if he walked around long enough, something cool would happen; he'd been wrong.

The truth was that his family had not thought about him for hours because they were busy entertaining themselves.

His mother and sister were drunk, passed out by the pool. His sister had gotten so drunk, a DJ nearly convinced her to enter a wet t-shirt contest and almost got her mother to go along with it, but luckily, they fell asleep before the contest began, thus saving themselves an uncomfortable memory.

His father, meanwhile, had been at the blackjack table for six hours, losing every dollar he had and then some. He had already overdrawn their bank account and was working on the credit limit of his emergency credit card, but he knew that the system would work eventually. He should have known that the only people that got rich on systems were the ones that sold them to suckers like Bill. Poor Bill. He had so little joy in life and so few wins. He wanted a break, but he couldn't find one.

Of course, Joshy didn't know any of that as he walked down the sidewalk of the Bellagio. He knew he was ready to go back to his room.

As he reached the bottom of the driveway, the fountains in front of the Bellagio exploded in front of him, spouting their water dance, random and synchronized all at once. Tourists planned their entire days around watching the fountains dance at night, and the restaurants with a view of the show were some of the most popular in Vegas.

Joshy didn't know any of that, of course, because that kind of information took research, and he did none, and yet he lucked into the show anyway. There were few things as worthwhile to see for somebody with no money as the fountain show at the Bellagio.

He ambled down across the driveway to get a better look at the show. Water shot up from dozens of jets all throughout the fountain, which stretched nearly a whole football field along the length of the hotel. A smile crept across Joshy's cold, cynical face as he watched the water dance across the air. He felt like a child again.

He sat down on the lip of the fountain to rest his feet and craned his neck to see the fountain spurt into the air. He was enraptured enough to forget his burning stomach, but not enough to miss the soft voice that whispered on the breeze.

"Excuse me," the soft, feminine voice said. "Excuse me?"

The voice brought Joshy back to himself. He turned his eyes up to find the most heavenly face he had ever gazed upon.

Bright, blue eyes sparkled to highlight what Joshy could only describe as an angel walking on earth. She wore a pastel blue and yellow dress, with sandals that matched the yellow flower in her hair, and when she smiled at him, he went weak and nearly fell into the water behind him.

The girl reached out for him as he fell backwards and helped him balance on the edge of the fountain. "Oh my god," she said. "Are you okay?"

Joshy nodded. It was the most a girl without a blood relationship had talked to him outside of a mandatory school activity, ever, and all he could do was smile at her.

"Y-y-yes," he finally squeezed out.

"Are you sure?" she asked sweetly. Her breath smelt of cinnamon and cardamom that lingered on the air. He wanted to take a deep whiff but knew that would be exceedingly weird, even for him.

"Yes," he replied, standing wobbly on his shaky legs. "I'm fine."

"Good, good," she said. "I was wondering if you could take a picture of me. I've never been to Vegas before."

He nodded. "Yes, yes, of course."

She opened her tan purse and went for her phone, except when she pulled it up, it was dark. "Oh shit!" she exclaimed. "My phone is dead."

"That sucks!" Joshy said, looking down at his to make sure he had battery left. He had an extended battery charger for his phone so nothing like that could ever happen to him.

"Wait," she said. "You could take a picture of me and send it to me, right? That's not too much to ask, is it?"

Joshy shrugged, trying to be nonchalant, but the last time he got a girl's number was for a group project in English class. "I could do that."

"Great!" she said, moving Josh away from the fountain so he could get a good picture. "Take a couple. I never smile right the first time."

Joshy could not imagine her without a perfect smile, but he dutifully opened the camera app on his phone and brought it up to his face.

"Alright, smile!" Joshy said.

The girl gave a big, luscious smile, full of genuine happiness and joy. Josh snapped four pictures, two horizontal and two vertical.

"I think I got it," Joshy said.

The girl rushed up to him. "Let me see. Let me see."

She grabbed onto Joshy's shoulder and peeked over it as he swiped through the photos. Her smile grew with each picture he showed her. So did his, but mostly because her hair brushed his face and he smelt her perfume on the air.

"These are perfect! Here give me your phone."

Joshy handed his phone over to her. She opened the text app and selected the pictures, before putting in her number and sending the pictures to herself.

"Great! I should have it, but what's your number in case I don't get it later?"

A girl was asking for Joshy's number, and he didn't even remember what he said in response. His mouth jerked out ten numbers in an order that sounded right, and she wrote them down on her hand with a marker she pulled from her purse.

"Awesome. Now, if I don't get these tonight, I'm gonna call and yell at you, okay? Then we're gonna have to meet here and do it all over again."

Joshy almost hoped that the pictures wouldn't go through, but he nodded. "Okay."

And like that she was gone. Joshy looked down at his phone and saw that she'd entered her name in his contacts. Debra.

And that was how Joshy fell in love. Hard and immediately, like smashing into a wall at a hundred miles an hour. Except that he loved every minute of it.

Chapter 4

Falling in love is a lot like getting punched in the face. After falling in love, you walk around with your knees wobbly, in a daze, seeing stars. If you've fallen in love, you can barely remember your name let alone what day it is, and such was the case for Joshy as he stumbled back to his room after meeting Debra.

His steps felt loose under him, and his head was full of fog as he stumbled across the street toward Planet Hollywood. He didn't consciously remember where he was staying, but let his body lead him through muscle memory alone. He had a vague memory of walking through the shops around the casino and pressing the button for his room, but if you asked him later how he got into his bed, he wouldn't have been able to tell you.

He did, however, remember the door flinging open minutes after he returned to the room, and his sister barging inside. "Oh, there you are," she said, uninterested in the fact he had been gone for hours. "Get ready. We're going to dinner."

Food. At that moment, he remembered that he was starving. "How long—"

"Have you been up here all this time?" Leslie continued, putting in one of her pearl earrings at the mirror atop the dresser. "And where is dad?"

"Those are too many questions," Joshy replied. "Why would I know where dad is?"

Leslie cocked her head quizzically at Joshy. "Cuz we saw you walk off with him and haven't heard from either of you since. We assumed that you were together."

"Nope," he replied. "I have no idea where he is. Last time I saw him he was in the ca—never mind."

Leslie turned to him. She had a nose for dirt, and Joshy wasn't any better than his father at lying.

"No, don't stop. Finish that sentence. Where was he?"

Joshy stood up and skittered toward the bathroom. "Nothing. I'm gonna change."

Leslie blocked his path down the small hallway. She was spry like a cat, and her wicked smile widened as she smelt the fear escape Joshy's pores. "Come on, Josh. Tell me."

Leslie only called him Josh when she wanted something, as if he would forget all the thousands of times she called him Joshy much to his displeasure. The silly thing was, it usually worked, not because he forgot but because she was doggedly persistent.

"It's nothing. I saw him go to…the CAR!" Joshy realized that car could be the end of his previous sentence, and it made perfect sense. People went to their cars all the time.

"If he went to his car, why would you try to hide that from me?" Leslie asked. It was a good and valid question, and Joshy didn't have an answer for her.

"Because," Joshy started, not knowing how he would finish that sentence either. "He had a gift for mom, and I promised him I wouldn't spoil it."

Leslie stopped in her tracks. That was a valid answer to her question, and she hadn't prepared a follow-up, expecting him to break under her pressure like he always did. "You're lying to me."

Joshy smiled. "You'll never know."

"When he comes back without a gift, I will," she replied.

She was right, but that was future Joshy's problem. Leslie looked over at the clock. It was 8:30, and she wasn't ready to spend more time breaking him while her stomach growled so loudly. There was plenty of time to break him, later.

"Get dressed. We're going to a nice restaurant to celebrate the start of the trip, so try not to look like a hobo." Leslie went to the mirror to put on a fresh coat of lipstick. "And don't think we're done here."

*

A moment must be spent discussing the horrible luck that befell Bill while his son was falling in love. After losing almost all his money, Bill went on a bit of a winning streak. He clawed his way back to even, and even doubled it for a moment. He did what all the books said, and doubled his bet again and again, and he kept winning and winning. For a moment in time, Bill thought he might save his family, and if he had stopped while he was ahead, he might have even succeeded in doing so.

However, Bill never knew when to quit. He kept his job well after his bosses made it clear that they would turn the screws until he resigned. He kept dating Becky Ross in high school even months after he caught her cheating on him with Quint Collinsworth, and he kept doubling down even when he started losing again at blackjack, until he had lost everything and more.

Still, he had reached his daily cash advance limit on all his credit cards. So, when his son texted him that he needed to come back to the room because everybody was waiting for him to go to dinner, Bill had no choice but to return to his room with his heart sunk low. He would have to try his luck the next day and hope he could turn it around.

A second text from Joshy told him to bring a present for his wife, and though he didn't understand it or have the money to spend, he did what he was told, and stopped off to get Carole a pair of modestly priced earrings.

*

Dinner that night was awkward. Both Carter men hid a secret they weren't comfortable sharing yet, if ever, so they deflected any conversation that would lead to their family finding out what each had done with their day.

"I love these earrings," Carole said, giving Bill a kiss.

Joshy looked over at his sister with a smirk. Leslie knew he had lied to her, but she also knew when to fold a losing hand. There would be plenty more battles to win in the future. Besides, she was enthusiastically enjoying her steak and wine. Both she and her mother were having a lovely time.

Bill hadn't unclenched his butt cheeks since sitting down; he fretted about whether or not the credit card would clear with every bite his family took of their expensive steaks. He'd called the credit card company to discuss upping the credit limit, but since he'd already called to raise the limit three times in the same month, they told him it would be put under review.

Meanwhile, Joshy couldn't think about anything but Debra. His phone showed him that the pictures he sent her hadn't been delivered yet, which meant either Debra gave him the wrong number, which wasn't likely, or that she hadn't turned on her phone yet, which seemed even less likely. Joshy lived on his phone all hours of the day and night, so the thought that somebody wouldn't do the same didn't make any sense to him.

Yet, there he was, faced with those two realities, and all he could do was stare at the pictures he'd taken of Debra, falling more and more in love with each passing second.

"Hey!" Carole said across the table. "Could you put the phone away already? Your steak is getting cold."

Carole enjoyed eating out at nice restaurants, but she didn't like food going to waste. She knew her husband hated his job but worked hard at it all the same because that was what you did when you had two children and a mortgage.

Carole also worked hard, but her real estate business hadn't taken off as she hoped. She spent so much money on her license and advertising giving it the old college try, but the truth was, she hated people as much as the rest of her family—except Leslie, who was the family's lone extrovert— and real estate was almost exclusively about talking to people.

It was the same with every business she tried. They always failed—not because she wasn't smart enough, but because, well, she hated talking to people, learning about them, and putting a smile on her face. She was born with resting bitch face before that had a name, and she was too old to care about changing to please people.

"I'm sorry," Joshy said. "I'm...not hungry."

He lied. He desperately wanted to eat more, but he couldn't take his eyes off the screen. Any second Debra would get his pictures, and she would surely thank him. He had to be ready to reply, and it meant going through hundreds of possible messages until he found the perfect one. Right now, he debated between "No problem" and "You're welcome."

They sounded like two completely innocuous phrases, but they meant quite different things. No problem made him sound aloof and cool. You're welcome made him sound warm and endearing. Which person would she like better? He didn't know, and it was making him sick, even as the sweet smell of beef permeated his nose.

"Just do it, alright?" Leslie said. "This is not a cheap meal. Look at dad over there. Those aren't the meat sweats. Those are the 'This dinner is expensive, so you better enjoy it' sweats."

Bill didn't even hear her. He was really having the "My card is going to be declined" sweats.

"Fine," Joshy said putting down his phone and taking a bite of the delicious steak in front of him. However, he said it as if Leslie were telling him to eat broccoli or something, which she would never do. Broccoli was rabbit food. It was the food that her food ate, as she liked to say.

As Joshy chewed his steak, he felt a sudden rush of energy spike through his body. A deep, low, contented sigh escaped his lips, and for a moment, he forgot about Debra and focused on the meat.

It didn't last long, though, because as he chewed his phone buzzed. He swallowed prematurely and grabbed the food, meat juice running down his hand. He swiped open the phone and saw the text from Debra.

"These are great! Thanks so much! See you around!"

See you around? What did that even mean? He didn't know how long he was going to have to keep her attention, so he stopped thinking and started typing.

"Maybe. Will you be in Vegas long?"

Ahhh!!!! He screamed deep from his soul into his head. That was so stupid, but there they were, three little dots to show she was typing. What was she typing? Why wasn't she sending? What was taking her so long...

Then it came.

"No. Heading to the Hoover Dam tomorrow, then onto the Grand Canyon."

Josh popped his head up from his phone. "Hey," he said. "Can we go to the Hoover Dam tomorrow?"

Chapter 5

Surprisingly, after dinner Bill's credit card processed without a problem. When he looked at his statement later in the night, it turned out that the credit card company had raised his limit ten thousand dollars, which he took as an act of mercy, but was merely an act of capitalism. It meant, though, that Joshy and his family could continue their sojourn in relative ignorance of their financial strife.

It also meant that Bill could afford the rest of the trip, and happily agreed with his wife to take the family to the Hoover Dam the following afternoon, after they got through a timeshare presentation, of course, an obligatory formality in exchange for getting a free room.

"But I really want to go in the morning!" Joshy complained.

"I'm sorry," Carole replied. "It's not possible. We made a commitment to go to this presentation, and in this family, we honor our commitments."

Commitments were the worst, thought Joshy as he sat in the timeshare presentation the next morning, across from an over-eager woman named Sally, who ended all of her sentences with an upward inflection, like she was asking a thousand questions an hour.

"How are you enjoying your stay?" Sally asked to start them off. "It's quite lovely, right? Aren't our timeshares the best?"

It was common knowledge that timeshare presentations were a lost cause and nobody bought timeshares. Except there were thousands of timeshare buyers every year, and dozens of companies which sold and maintained timeshares, which went against logic.

"I know what you're thinking," Sally said, without waiting for a response to her previous question. "Timeshares seem great, but aren't they a little pricey? Well, you're not wrong, but I want you to think of this as part of your retirement savings. We call it a 401R. Once you pay off the initial investment, you have it forever, which means you can vacation for the rest of your life, and pass it on to your family, too, so they can enjoy it long into the future."

Joshy figured there must be hypnosis involved to force people into buying a property they could only use once a year. Or maybe they drugged the watered-down coffee. The truth, though, was much tamer, he finally decided, and involved badgering people with questions and confusing them until they signed on the dotted line, regretting their decision every day afterward.

"Now, I know you're not going to buy today, right?" Sally asked, already knowing the answer to her own question. "However, can I tell you that the absolute best time to buy is the first time you talk to us. Your deal will never be better than it is today."

"That's nice," Bill said with a courteous smile, "but we…no."

"I hear you," Sally replied. "But I don't believe you. So many people have said that to me before, and oh gosh, they turned around eventually, when they saw the value of what we have to offer. We're practically giving these away today, compared to the price you'll pay later."

"We're not really timeshare people," Carole said.

"Well, nobody is a timeshare person until they become one," Sally said, and she was so chipper Joshy actually thought she was a robot. Nobody could possibly be that chipper at nine in the bloody morning.

"Can we move this along?" Joshy asked, scowling. He was only there for one reason, to get his parents through the presentation as fast as humanly possible. Timeshare presentations tended to be arduously long, and the longer he waited, the less chance he had of catching Debra at the Hoover Dam. If he had to sit through a boring presentation, visit a boring place, and didn't get to see Debra, well that would have been a fate worse than death.

"Well sure," Sally said. "An eager beaver, I see. Well, let me tell you a little bit about the property. It's been—"

"I have seen the property," Joshy said. "It's nice."

"Oh, I understand you have. Unfortunately, your parents are the only ones qualified to buy, though, so that was directed towards them. Come back in a couple years, when you build up some credit though, and I'd love to talk to you about your future, too, m'kay?"

"Actually," Bill said. "Look, we're really only doing this to go through the motions and get the free nights. So, whatever you can do to move this along would be lovely."

"I see," Sally said, losing her overly cheery smile and sneering at us. "And do you feel the same way, ma'am?"

Carole nodded. "There is nothing in the world that could convince me to buy a timeshare in Las Vegas."

"Oh, I know people say that," Sally said, putting back on her fake smile. "But the Elara has a lot of trading potential. You can use your points anywhere in the world."

Carole nodded. "We can barely afford to drive across the country, honey. We ain't seeing the world any time soon."

Bill was relieved that his wife said she wasn't interested, so he didn't have to dash her hopes on a dream he couldn't deliver to her.

"We have great resorts in America as well. Phoenix, Branson, Chicago, Orlando, DC, even New York City. Wouldn't you like to stay in New York City?"

"No," Bill replied. "It's oppressively loud and dirty."

The smile once again dropped from Sally's face. "Okay, so here's the deal. You can leave right now. If you do, you don't get to ever stay at our resorts again, and you have to leave the resort today. Or you can give me an extra hour of your time, we can chat patiently, have a lovely time, and you can stay an extra night, completely free, for hearing me talk."

"I vote leave!" Joshy said.

It's not that Joshy's vote didn't count, but it didn't count for much. After all, he wasn't paying for anything, so it was easy for him to burn his parent's money. Carole and Bill, however, looked at each other for a long time, with a knowing look that only two people who had been together for decades could have, and they didn't have to say a word.

"One hour," Carole said.

"No!" Joshy replied.

"One hour," Sally said, returning to her regular smile. "That's all I ask."

Bill looked down at his watch. "Fine, but I'm timing you."

"Super-duper," Sally said, sliding over some brochures to them. "Let's talk amenities."

*

Joshy had to literally pull his parents away from the timeshare presentation after another ninety minutes spent with Sally. They were both rabidly ready to buy a timeshare on the spot, and it was only Joshy's steadfast insistence about getting to the Hoover Dam that prevented them from signing away their lives to Sally and her super special sales skills.

Luckily, the Hoover Dam was less than an hour from Vegas, which meant that Joshy got there by noon. Plenty of time to camp out and find Debra. He didn't want to ask her when she would be at the Dam; it would seem desperate and pathetic to show up at the same time.

However, if he happened to be there and it "slipped his mind" that she would be there, it would be an impromptu and casual meeting, as if the universe wanted them to be together. The kind of shit women love, Joshy said, even though he actually had no idea what women wanted, which is why he'd been alone his entire life.

It was a gamble, he knew, to show up without talking to Debra, but at least if he didn't find her, he would have some pictures that he could show her to keep the conversation going, and at this point, that was all he wanted, another reason to keep the conversation going.

"So now what?" Leslie said, looking over the dam toward the chasm below. "Do we stand around all day, looking at pillars and concrete?"

It was a good question, and one Joshy wanted the answer to as well. Now that he was there, how could he be sure that he and Debra "happened to run into each other?"

"Now, we walk!" Joshy said, heading toward the walkway across the top of the facility. "Cuz that's what you do here, walk around and see things."

Joshy didn't know whether that was true, but he said it so confidently that his family believed him. Of course, that might have been because the heat zapped their energy and with it their ability to question him. Sometimes, it was easier to go along for the ride.

"I've never seen this kind of energy from you before, Joshy," Carole said. "At least not about anything that involved walking."

"Yeah," Bill replied. "Who knew you were so into damn dams?"

Bill couldn't have been happier that they'd visited a cheap place for the day. Sally had given them four free passes to the Dam for sitting through an extra thirty minutes of her presentation, and Bill was all too happy to not use his credit card.

Leslie, on the other hand, liked being out of the casino, doing something. She spent most of her time reading and studying when she wasn't organizing rallies or working on political campaigns, so it was nice to get out and think about nothing for a while. Soon, she would start her rise from student to Representative, and then Senator, so these were some of the last mindless things she was going to get to do for a long time, and she was determined to enjoy it.

*

Joshy walked up and down that stupid dam for hours, trying his best to feign excitement for rocks and concrete on the off chance that Debra would show up. It was dumb, but love and stupidity often went hand in hand. He hated excursions almost as much as he hated family road trips, but he was determined to hold out hope for Debra, even if she came late. Even as the sun crept over the horizon, he was still determined to wait for her. His family, on the other hand, wanted to leave. They'd wanted to go hours ago.

"Let's go, Joshy," Leslie said. "I'm tired! I need a nap!"

"One more time around," Joshy said. "Please!!!!"

"I'm sorry, Josh," his father said in a stern voice. "We need to go back now. We only have one more night, and I want to make the most of it. Your mother and I both do. I have big plans later."

Bill regretted his words when he said them. What Bill meant was that he wanted to gamble, but what Carole heard was that he wanted to take her out, which was something she hoped to do in Vegas that hadn't happened yet. The look of hope in his wife's eyes was too much to ignore though, and there would be time for gambling later after she was asleep.

"I wanted to take you to dinner," he said to Carole, trying to feign excitement. "Would you be my date?"

Carole smiled. They didn't have much time together anymore, with only the two of them, and the thought of a date nearly made Carole tear up. "Absolutely."

"Then we need to go," Bill said. "I need a shower."

"It's time we go back, sweetie," Carole said, turning to Joshy. "I'm never one to quell your enthusiasm for knowledge, but there's literally nothing else we could see here. We've been pacing back and forth all day. I'm bored, sweaty, and tired."

Joshy fought back his rage. It was three against one, so there was nothing he could do. They wanted to leave, and he wanted to stay. He would have stayed for the next week if it meant he could see Debra. However, it was clear that she arrived earlier in the day, and he missed his chance with her, which made him furious. Now, he would likely never see her again.

"Fine," he said. "One second."

Joshy pulled out his phone and took a selfie of himself with the dam in the background. He texted it to Debra.

"Look where we ended up today."

As he walked back to the family car, the three dots appeared at the bottom of the screen. After a breathless minute, Debra texted back.

"Bummer. We decided to stay in Vegas one more night and do the dam thing tomorrow! How was it?"

"Pretty boring. Lots of water being dammed."

"Lol. About what I expected. GTG. Sent you a friend request on Facebook. Hope you don't think that's too stalkerish! KIT!"

"Hey, freak!" Leslie shouted, breaking his concentration. "Hurry up! It's hot out here!"

He was halfway to the car before Joshy processed the sentence Debra wrote. She sent him a friend request. She sent him a friend request! And she sent it to him!

Joshy fumbled with his phone as he sat down in the back seat of the car and pulled up Facebook. There she was, Debra Thompson. He had never clicked confirm so hard on a friend request in all his life.

She sent him a friend request for a reason. There must have been a reason. Maybe she liked him, or maybe she didn't, but Joshy knew he had to make a bold move. She was staying in Vegas for one more night, and so was he. Maybe it really was fate bringing them together, or maybe at least that stupid timeshare presentation might be good for something after all.

He opened his text app one more time.

"Nice avatar," he wrote, referring to her profile picture petting a llama.

"Thanks. It was in Peru last year. They are so cute!"

"Looks it," Joshy stopped, scared to type the next words. However, against everything his gut told him, he

pressed on anyway. *"Listen, you are in town tonight, so am I. Last time ever, maybe…dinner?"*

He stared at the phone for five full minutes, and nothing happened. Nothing at all. No dots. No text. Nothing. He flipped open Facebook and make sure she didn't delete him because he was so lame.

No, they were still friends. She must not have hated him that much. She must have laughed herself unconscious. *That was a thing, right?* Joshy thought.

He flipped back to the messaging app, and there they were, the three dots, but they weren't bouncing like she was typing. It was as if she was stuck in thought, like she was trying to let him down gently.

It's okay, Joshy, you tried. You did your best. You don't deserve happiness maybe. But then it happened. She responded.

"Sure. Had to clear it with parents. Mirage. Lobby. 8pm?"

Joshy smiled so much on the rest of the ride home that Leslie thought he broke his face, but he didn't care. He had a date with an angel.

Chapter 6

"Do you want a tie?" Carole asked as she helped Joshy iron the black shirt he'd worn to dinner the night before. This was the first time he'd been on a date with a girl that wasn't a school function in, well, forever. There was one time in fifth grade where he had a play date with Lindsey Susserman, but that wasn't a real date either.

"No thanks, Mom," he replied. "I think ties, well, they look like you are trying too hard."

"Nonsense," Bill replied, knotting his tie from his bedroom. "They make you look like you care about the girl, and you do care about the girl, right?"

Carole was so excited for a date with Bill that he couldn't break her heart, even if he wanted to gamble instead. Besides, he loved his wife and wanted her to enjoy the finer things in life, even if he couldn't afford them.

"Enough to not wear a tie and scare her off, dad," Joshy replied. "Thanks anyway."

"Don't listen to your dad," Carole whispered to him. "Even if he is right."

Carole had goosebumps, honest to goodness real goosebumps, about her date with Bill. They hadn't been on a date, with only the two of them, since before Leslie went off to college, and it was about time that they had some time alone longer than a quickie.

She had the perfect dress picked out. It was classy, blue silk with a high neck. She bought it hoping she and Bill would go on a date at some point during the trip, but she hadn't expected to wear it, which is why she had to iron it after she got Joshy out the door.

"Fine, dad," Joshy replied. "I'll take the stupid tie. I'm not gonna wear it, though, unless she's really nicely dressed."

Bill shrugged. "No skin off my back whether you take one or not. I'm only saying, it really classes up the man." Bill stepped out into the living room and into the light. He was dressed in a nice suit, freshly shaved, and wearing a smile from ear to ear. When Carole saw him, she remembered why she married him in the first place.

"You look nice," Carole replied, finishing Joshy's shirt. "Now, take this. I have to go get ready."

She handed the shirt to Josh and skipped into the bedroom with the energy of a twelve-year-old, giving Bill a kiss as she passed him.

"And that is the power of the tie, son," he said.

"For somebody that's been married twenty years, maybe. Nobody I know wears ties, though."

"Have they been married for twenty years?"

Joshy shook his head. "No. They aren't even twenty."

"Well, that's why, buddy. Take it from me." Bill let out a sigh. "Do we need to talk about—anything—birds related?"

"What? No! It's a first date."

"A first date in Vegas, son. And you know what they say, what happens in Vegas stays in Vegas."

*

Joshy arrived at the lobby of the Mirage at precisely 7:38. It took him fifteen minutes to finish getting ready, and forty minutes to walk from Planet Hollywood to the Mirage on the other side of the strip. He wanted to take a cab because the heat was nearly unbearable, but his mother only gave him thirty dollars and told him to spend it all on Debra, which meant hoofing it.

When he arrived at the Mirage, he turned left at the sports book where old, sad, drunken men hoped to turn their lives around with the outcome of a sporting event and went straight into the bathroom. He had taken his shirt off halfway through his walk so he wouldn't sweat through it, and now it looked like a great idea because he had already sweat through his undershirt.

Joshy peeled off his undershirt and blew it dry under the hand dryer. He caught a glimpse of his white, concave chest and shuttered at the thought of what Debra would think if she saw it. Luckily, shirts hid gross bodies.

He threw his undershirt back on, then the black shirt that he had also chosen to cover up any sweat stains. Finally, he took the tie out of his slacks and thought long and hard about putting it on. After all, this was a date, but ties were awful. He decided against it, placed the tie back in his pants pocket and dabbed the sweat off his brow before he went back outside.

He walked to the front desk, even though she didn't mention where to meet him. If she wasn't on time, he could always look around the rest of the casino for her or text her. Luckily, a little light Facebook snooping showed that Debra was the same age as he was, so she couldn't go into the casino areas either.

Joshy didn't want to do too much Facebook stalking before his date. He could have looked up everything about Debra for the past ten years, but he thought it was better to learn it straight from her. What if he said something she hadn't told him or hadn't told anybody except in a Facebook post from five years ago? She would know he'd been snooping, and that would be a bad look for him.

No, it was better to not peek until at least after the first date. So, he refrained from reading anything except her about page, which revealed that she liked the Bleachers, Lovelytheband, The Killers, Alice Merton, and Kesha, and that she watched *The Good Place*, *Parks and Recreation*, *Lucifer*, and *Gravity Falls*, four of his favorite shows, and five of his favorite artists.

His mind raced as eight o'clock drew closer. Was he in the right place? Was she going to show up? How long until he admitted she'd stood him up?

Then, right before it turned eight o'clock, she rounded the corner from the elevator, and his fear melted away. She wore a pink sundress with white streaks in it, and a thin white headband that pulled her hair off her face. He couldn't think of a word that described her perfectly, but if he could've, the word would have been luminous. It was as if she radiated warmth out of her every pore, and her smile melted Joshy's heart as she walked toward him, her blue eyes staring deep into his soul.

"Oh good!" she said. "I thought I was going to be the first one. I hope you weren't waiting long."
He had been waiting exactly eighteen minutes, fourteen seconds, but of course, he lied, because that's what you do when somebody asks you a question like that, and you don't want them to feel bad. Besides, what did "long" mean, anyway?

"Not long," he said, voice cracking.

Debra chuckled under her breath as she reached in and gave him a light hug. Marigolds. Joshy smelt marigolds on her skin as he hugged her back and was immediately taken back to memories of running through fields at his grandfather's house when he was a small child.

"Good," she said, pulling back. "Now, where are we going? I don't know if you know this, but we can't really get in many places here. My parents are having a blast, but I've been mostly in my room playing video games."

A smile crept over Joshy's face. "Video games, you say? I have an idea."

*

There was an old video arcade in the mall next to the Mirage, full of quarter video games from the 80's which wouldn't break the bank to play. Joshy hadn't been to an arcade in years, and his eyes lit up when he started playing Rampage with Debra, but the most amazing thing was that Debra's eyes lit up, too.

"I always like to play the wolf thing," Debra said when she took the controls

"You mean Ralph?" Joshy said. "But nobody likes Ralph."

Debra nodded. "That's why I like to play him, because everyone else thinks he's garbage."

The longer Joshy knew Debra, the more he fell in love. At first, it was the kind of puppy love that made his stomach float, but as they talked across their first hours together, playing old games like Centipede and Frogger, his infatuation grew, hardened, and emulsified into the real thing.

Eventually though, after two hours, he reached into his pocket and pulled out his last quarter. He didn't want the night to end, but he didn't have any way to keep it going, either.

"I have a confession to make," Joshy said, sighing as he walked away from the arcade.

"Oh no. You're my fool, aren't you?"

"No, that's Dave Grohl."

Debra replied. "You're a Cylon, then. I knew it. This whole time I was talking to a robot. How can you live with yourself?"

Joshy burst out laughing. He couldn't help himself. Debra wasn't cute funny. She was funny funny. He hadn't expected her to be funny.

"No," he said. "Worse. I only have one quarter left."

"In the whole world?" Debra said.

He nodded. "I'm afraid so. In the whole world."

She smiled at him and held up her purse. "Luckily, I came prepared for the possibility that you might be a deadbeat."

She went through her purse and pulled out a black wallet with an anarchy symbol on it. "So, I think I have enough in here for some pretty shitty pizza. You in?"

Joshy smiled. "That's my favorite kind."

Chapter 7

Finding cheap pizza in Vegas was easy. For every high roller, there were a hundred average shlubs that needed something to swallow down after losing their rent money, which was why every casino had, next to the five-star restaurants and ritzy nightclubs, at least one crappy little pizza place where you could get a slice without breaking the bank.

It didn't take long for Joshy and Debra to hole up in a crappy pizzeria inside the Venetian with a slice and a soda. It wasn't the flashiest date ever, but Joshy didn't mind, and Debra was having a great time. Joshy, despite all his failings, was killing it.

"So, okay, first concert?" Joshy asked.

"You're going to think I'm so lame, but Panic! At the Disco."

"Really? No way. I figured it would be something obscure, like Metric, back before Scott Pilgrim."

"Are you kidding? No. I didn't get into Metric until after Scott Pilgrim when they blew up."

Joshy took a bite of his pizza. "Well, at least you know what Scott Pilgrim is. Most people haven't even watched the movie."

"Are you kidding? I own the comics, the old original black and white AND the color reprints."

"Okay, respect, but do you have anything else from Bryan O'Malley?"

"I have BOTH Seconds and Lost at Sea, along with every issue of Snotgirl. Are you really testing my geek cred?"

"No," Joshy replied. "I don't know how to act around girls, and this is all I have to talk about." He took another bite of pizza. "I never liked Lost at Sea."

Debra shrugged. "It wasn't his best work, but you can see him working out what would become Scott Pilgrim as he drew it. There's a lot of similar stuff, kind of like Faith Erin Hicks with War at Ellsmere."

"Are you kidding me?" Joshy said with a smile. "That is like one of my all-time favorite graphic novels."

"Well duh, you can't really be an OG Faith Erin Hicks fangirl if you don't know her original works. I mean, her stuff is great now, but you can see the wheels turning on her style all the way back to those first books."

"Yeah, I miss when Oni had a house style. Like, you could pick up an Oni book and know it was an Oni book."

"Dude, that was SLG, not Oni."

"Are you sure?"

"One hundred percent."

"Oh, well my point still stands. I wish Oni still had that house style they popularized."

Debra sighed. "People grow Joshy, so do companies. Would you rather some other company publish Six Guns, really? You can't expect a company to keep putting out the same books for their whole life. That would be boring, wouldn't it?"

Debra got a bit heated as she took a sip of her soda. Joshy had never seen somebody get so worked up about something so trivial before, except for himself, of course.

"I guess so. I kinda just want more Scott Pilgrim, really."

"There's only one Scott Pilgrim, Josh. There will only be one ever. That's what makes it so magical."

She called him Josh like he wasn't a child. She had done it all night, but he never grew tired of it. Everybody else in his life knew him as Joshy, but she never knew him as a child. To her, he came into the world fully formed, like an adult kinda human.

After taking one final bite, Joshy threw down his pizza without eating the crust. "I'm so full."

"Aren't you gonna eat that?" Debra asked, disgusted.

"No. I don't eat the crust," Joshy said.

"You humans," Debra said, shaking her heads. "May I?"

Joshy nodded. "Sure, but it's got my saliva on it."

Debra smiled. "I don't mind."

Even Joshy, dense as he was, knew that was a sign, and the sides of his lips curled up as he watched Debra eat his pizza crust.

*

Joshy and Debra took the long way back to the Mirage, luxuriating in every step. They knew it might be the last time they saw each other for a long while, maybe ever.

"I wish I didn't live in Detroit, you know?" she said, sighing as the neon lights of Vegas flashed above her.

Debra crept her fingers around Joshy's as they stood for the light to change. Across the street, the Mirage loomed large, and every step they took meant it was closer to saying goodbye, a fate that neither of them wanted.

"What is there to even do in Detroit?" Joshy asked as the light finally changed, and they stepped onto the crosswalk.

"It's pretty close to Chicago, and there are a ton of cool bands and comic book people. Motor City Comic Con is one of the oldest conventions in the county, and Caliber Comics is there too, so you get a lot of cool indie comics coming through, and Chicago is a super literate town, so there are great things to see and do down there. You should come out in the next couple months, and I'll show you around."

Joshy was taken aback. Debra had invited him to come out and visit him. This was something he hadn't expected. He thought he would have to cozy up to her for several months before he got an invitation.

"Yeah," he said. "That would be cool. I mean, money and all makes it hard."

"I know," Debra replied. "But I'm saying it's pretty cool and you're pretty cool. So, I think you would enjoy it."

"Yeah, and if you are ever in Los Angeles—"

Debra chuckled. "I don't think so."

"What's wrong with LA?" Joshy asked as he stepped onto the curb in front of the Mirage. "I love it there."

"It's a shithole, Josh. Seriously, it's like living in a third world country. What is up with your roads, man?"

"Umm…fourteen million people live there, so there's a little more wear and tear than Detroit."

"Yeah? And the whole thing looks like it was designed by a drunken monkey. I mean you've got highways that lead nowhere."

"Hello, first highway system in the country. You're gonna have some growing pains, and maybe other cities should be thanking Los Angeles for paving the way."

"That's funny, paving, cuz roads. Fine, but I don't think I could live in a city that is so...devoid of culture."

Josh stopped. "That's total crap. There are all sorts of cultural things in Los Angeles. The Broad, LACMA, The Getty, The Skirball Center, Disney Concert Hall, Griffith Observatory. The Museum of Death. Los Angeles is filled with cool places to see, it's that—"

Joshy didn't have a chance to finish his sentence, because as he was talking Debra kissed him, hard and deep. He collapsed into her like he had always only seen in old movies. His knees buckled, and his eyes closed. Heat rose off his lips, which at first started as a pleasant sensation, but as they stayed connected, the heat grew in intensity until it singed his lips.

Joshy opened his eyes and saw Debra staring back at him, her eyes no longer the rich blue he remembered, but a flaming blue as if her eyes burned with the fire of the sun. Debra must have seen the fear in Joshy's eyes because she broke off the kiss.

"I'm—I'm sorry—" Debra trailed off as she made a beeline for the front door.

"What was that?" Joshy yelled after her, but she disappeared through the doors. He wanted to follow, but his legs wobbled under him as if the last ounces of his energy zapped out of him. It was all he could do to crawl over to a stoop and sit down and watch the fake volcano in front of the Mirage erupt in front of him as a fire erupted in his soul.

*

Joshy didn't want to go back to his hotel. He wanted to follow Debra back up to her room and figure out what was going on, but by the time he was able to walk again, it was half an hour later, and he'd promised his parents he would be home at a reasonable time, not Vegas reasonable either; actually reasonable.

As he walked home, he fantasized about the kiss he'd shared with Debra. That was his first real kiss, so he didn't know how it was supposed to work, but he was rather sure his lips shouldn't have felt like they were on fire, and while eyes might be the windows into your soul, he was quite sure that Debra's shouldn't have blazed like an inferno when they locked lips.

But maybe, that was how it was supposed to be, Joshy thought. Now that the date was over, he scrolled through Debra's Facebook page looking for any clue about what happened, and she seemed...so normal.

She played soccer and basketball. She ran track. She wrote for the school newspaper. She had friends and family. There were pictures of her winning awards, hanging out at parties, eating with her family. There were pictures of Christmas, Thanksgiving, and all the major holidays going back years. It wasn't like she was some zombie succubus who appeared in Vegas to eat him, right? She was a real human.

Of course, a zombie succubus with magical powers could easily make a Facebook page with magical properties or something. No, that sounded stupid, even for Joshy who was prone to conspiratorial thinking.

He was halfway back to the hotel when his sister texted him. "GET BACK HERE NOW."

He replied. "WHY?"

But Leslie didn't answer. That was her way. She issued commands and didn't have time to explain herself when people questioned her. Still, Joshy did what he was told and picked up his pace, nearly running by the time he got to the street corner near the Elara.

*

Joshy heard the screaming before he opened the door to the room. He had never heard his mother scream so loudly before.

"That's your excuse?!" Carole shouted. "You thought it would be better if we didn't know, if I didn't know?"

"I wanted—" Bill replied, cowering on the couch.

"No!" Carole screamed. "You don't get to talk. You get to listen, cuz you're the one that screwed up here, Bill, not me."

Leslie pulled Joshy into their room and closed the door. "Dude, you have no idea."

"What's happening out there?" Joshy said, flinging his arm toward the door.

"Mom and dad got back from dinner. Everything was fine. I heard them kissing. I closed the door. And then this happened."

Joshy poked his head out the door. Carole was no longer screaming, but crying, sobbing into her hands. Bill tensed up, wanting to touch his wife, but knowing she was disgusted with him.

"She started screaming for no reason?"

"I don't know," Leslie said, shaking her head. "I could barely hear anything until she started yelling out of the blue."

What happened was this: during their drunken make-out session, Bill tossed a wad of money on the dresser of his bedroom—a cash advance from his recently upped credit limit—and Carole questioned where it came from, as she had every right to do. It's not normal for a middle-class man to have a wad of thousands in his pocket.

Bill said something stupid trying to cover up the truth, which failed to fool Carole, and that stupid thing led to the unraveling of one lie, which led to another lie, which led to another lie, and eventually, Bill confessed his desperate situation to his wife.

It was worse than Carole ever could have imagined. Bill explained that he'd lost his job and was disastrously close to losing the family home. He'd survived on credit cards for the last six months, taking out more and more as he needed them, and paying one off with another. He had been gambling in a foolish attempt to break even, but instead fell further into debt.

He planned the family's trip across the country so that they could have one good memory to look back on when his house of cards came crashing down on him. It was the most selfish thing Carole had ever heard in her life.

As you can imagine, Bill's revelations made Carole a bit—miffed would be an understatement—she went apoplectic. Carole wasn't known for her wild mood swings or violent outbursts, so watching her freak out terrified her children.

Joshy didn't even have time to enjoy his first kiss before he had to deal with the looming doom of his family.

"We should go out there," Joshy whispered. "Maybe we can help."

"Are you kidding me?" Leslie said. "I've never seen mom like that. Let dad handle it."

"You've seen dad, right? He's not the most emotionally sensitive person in the world."

"And you are?" Leslie scoffed.

"Better than him. Besides, she's not mad at us."

"Yet," Leslie said. "Who knows what happens if we go out there?"

They didn't have a chance to leave their room to calm things down before Carole rushed out of the suite and slammed the door, sobbing as she went. Bill didn't attempt to follow. Instead, he sat down with his head between his hands and cried.

"Mom or dad?" Joshy asked.

"Do I have to choose?" Leslie replied. "I don't wish either of them on either of us."

Joshy nodded. "Yeah, you have to choose."

"Then, I guess I pick dad," Leslie replied. "Cuz at least he's here."

"Fine. I'll chase down mom, wherever she is."

Joshy rushed out of the room, forgetting his keycard and his lovely, weird date in the process, at least for a moment. Not many things could make him bury the memory of Debra, but he knew that his mother needed him, and he had to do what he had to do to help her.

Chapter 8

It didn't take long for Joshy to find his mother. After leaving the hotel, smack in front of him was a walk-up bar where you could buy margarita slushies by the yard. He thought it was weird that they didn't judge booze by the ounce in Vegas, but he let that thought go quickly when he saw his mother sitting at one of the tables trying to drink a yard of frozen margarita in a single gulp.

"Mom!" Joshy shouted, running over her and grabbing the yardstick full of booze, which was almost half gone already. He didn't know how many ounces that was, but drinking more than a foot of booze was never a good idea.

"Joshy!" she said, slurring her words. "You're here!"

"Come on," he said, picking her up. Her body was limp as a noodle. "Let's get you some coffee."

If there was something that Vegas had in spades, it was stimulants to keep people up and going, gambling and spending money all night long. Joshy didn't have to drag his mother more than a hundred feet — or thirty-three margaritas — before he found a Starbucks and walked inside, laying his mother on a bench near the front. He got a coffee for each of them with money he scrounged from his mother's purse, making sure his was decaf, and hers was double caffeinated.

"Do you know how much I gave up for your father?" she asked, taking a sip. She was getting drunker by the minute as the booze took hold of her brain. Joshy hoped he could counteract the effects with plenty of caffeine.

"No, mom," Joshy said, taking a sip. "How much?"

"I coulda been a nurse. Did you know that? Almost finished my degree and everything, but I gave it up for those big, brown eyes."

"It hasn't been all bad, has it?"

Carole smiled. "No, Joshy. It hasn't been bad at all. I got the two of you out of it, and I really, really loved that man, for a time."

"You still love him," Joshy said, taking another sip. "Don't you?"

"I don't know," Carole said. "He lied to me, right to my face, for a long time. He said he had a job he didn't have, and he spent our money, all our money, and more, behind my back. He decimated our credit. How can I ever trust him again?"

This was the first time Joshy saw that his mother was, in fact, a human being, and not a woman who materialized with the sole purpose of birthing him. He often complained that others didn't see him for who he was, but he was as bad as them. He always thought that his mother was some sort of superwoman, who was invulnerable to pain, perfect in every way.

"It's not like he cheated on you," Joshy said with another sip. It wasn't a good thing to say, but it was the best he could come up with. Joshy wasn't good at tough conversations.

"This is worse! Cheating, maybe I could forgive, but this… He destroyed everything we built. Your sister's going to be crushed when she hears."

"Why?" he asked.

"Think about it," she replied, looking into her coffee before taking a long sip.

Joshy did think about it. The wheels in his brain turned and chugged until eventually, a light bulb went off in his brain.

"You're not going to be able to pay for her college anymore."

"We're not going to be able to pay for her college anymore," Carole said with a nod.

"That means...you can't pay for my college either."

Carole snickered. "Do you even want to go to college, Joshy?"

"I don't know," he said. "I would like to have the option."

"Well, I'm afraid you're on your own, just like she is now. Poor Leslie. We wanted her to get out of school without any debt. Unfortunately, it doesn't look like I'm going to be able to say that about either of us, not anymore."

"You can turn it all around, though, ma. I know you can."

Carole smiled at him. "My poor, sweet boy. How naive you are. Not everything has a happy ending, my love."

"Does...that mean we're going home then?" Joshy asked. Yesterday, he would have been happy to pack it all in and go home, but now...he didn't want to go. Not like this.

Carole sighed. "Well, I've been thinking, and it sure doesn't look good for us, you know, but if your dad is right, and we're in as bad a shape as we're in, it's not like we're gonna even notice another couple hundred here or a thousand there."

"So...we can keep going?" Joshy asked, puzzled.

Carole looked him deep in the eyes. Joshy never realized how her green eyes splintered out and exploded into a nebula of different colors.

"For the sake of our marriage, Joshy," Carole said with a stone face. "I think we have to keep going. Because if I'm not forced to be around that man, I might never see him again."

Joshy had never heard his mother speak that pointedly or directly to him in all his life. She always kept a stiff upper lip, but now, in her weakest moment, Joshy saw his mother at her most vulnerable. He wanted to take care of her, protect her, but he didn't know how, or if he could help at all.

"I don't know if we'll finish this trip," Carole said, before a long swig of coffee. "But we won't get anywhere back home. I'm not even sure there will be a home to return to when this is all said and done."

They sat in silence for the next hour as Joshy fed her coffee, and Carole watched the people walk past.

*

There was no talking the following morning as they sat around the breakfast table, either. The Carters ate in silence, all glaring at Bill with hate in their eyes. He knew he deserved it, but it still hurt to watch those he loved vilify him. He did a good enough job vilifying himself.

"Where should we go next?" Bill said, trailing off at the end.

"Well," Joshy replied. "Since we have no money, I was thinking we could go to the Grand Canyon. It's cheap, close, and maybe looking at a giant hole in the ground will make us feel better."

"Not likely," Leslie snarled back.

She was already crying in bed by the time Joshy brought his mother back and laid her on the couch. He wanted to sleep, but his sister needed him, and Joshy could be selfless for a couple more minutes until he retreated into himself again to recharge.

"Did…she…tell you…there's…no…money…" Leslie heaved out through fits of bawling.

Joshy nodded. "She did, and that they can't pay for college. I'm so sorry, Les."

"I…don't…under…stand…
I…did…everything…right!" she sobbed into her pillow.

"I know, Les, but I guess that doesn't really matter, right? What did Picard say? It is possible to commit no mistakes and still lose."

"I…hate…him!"

"Picard, or dad?"

"BOTH!" she shouted. Joshy wasn't helping the situation at all, so he sat on his sister's bed and stroked her hair as she cried herself to sleep. What had started as a magical night turned into a nightmare.

The next morning, back at the breakfast table, Carole nursed a wicked hangover. The older you got, the more water you needed to drink to keep yourself hydrated, and she had nothing except coffee, which dehydrates you, and a lot of liquor, so she was feeling her hangover in every ounce of her body. Her pain tamped down her anger at her husband, but that was only temporary. When she recovered, the fire in her belly would return.

"I suppose the Grand Canyon is fine," Carole moaned. "At least it wastes a day."

"It doesn't really get us much further across the country," Bill said, before realizing that wasn't really the point. "But I'm sure it will be fine. After all, we have time."

"Yeah," Leslie said. "All the time in the world, now that none of us have anything to do!"

No matter which way you sliced it, Bill really screwed the pooch, and there was nothing he could do but accept his lot in life and hope that, with time, it turned around for the better. After all, time healed all wounds, no matter how deep the gash.

*

The Grand Canyon was the best-known hole in the country, maybe the world. That was what Joshy thought at least when he finally got there and realized that staring at a hole in the ground wasn't all that special. He couldn't believe that he helped choose two excursions that he hated, all for a girl who he wasn't likely to find anyway.

However, his family's vacation was about more than that now. He needed his family to stay together, and if this vacation from Hell needed to continue forever so they could mend their broken hearts, then so be it. He would do his part to suck it up and put on a good face.

"This is majestic, isn't it?" Leslie asked without a hint of irony. "I really needed this, Joshy. Seriously, it helps."

"How?" Joshy said, flippantly. "It's a big, friggin' hole."

"Do you see that down there?" Leslie asked, pointing to the river at the bottom of the Grand Canyon that was so big it was impossible to miss.

"You mean the huge river? Yeah, I can see it."

"Once, a long time ago, it was a little stream, slamming up against the continental shelf, until it burrowed through a little bit at a time, and eventually, it created this. Nature really can do anything. And if a little, stupid river can bend rock to its will, there's hope for me yet."

"Ugh, you are so positive," Joshy said. "It makes me sick."

"I mean, it's going to be hard, for sure, but I can take out student loans, and if my dad doesn't have a job, maybe there are even scholarships. I could run a fundraising drive. I mean, I would have to possibly take a semester off, but then I could reapply to all my student loans with Dad's horrible credit, and maybe they'll take pity on me."

"Is that a thing school's do, often? Take pity on people?"

"Are you kidding? They do it all the time. Hardship scholarships are totally a thing. I've been protesting and marching for more financial aid in the last two years. They are totally a thing, and the dean is actually coming around to the idea. Who knew it would help me out?"

"You realize you're insufferable when you're like this, right?"

"You would rather me be crying?"

Joshy didn't say anything, but he didn't know which he would rather have. Both versions of Leslie were rather insufferable, truth be told, but at least the other one sobbed into her pillow instead of screamed inspirational speeches over canyons.

Still, he couldn't help but smile; he liked to see his sister happy, and there was no doubt that his sister was happier now than she was last night, which was a massive improvement already. Maybe there was hope for his family yet, he thought, even though he was likely kidding himself.

"I'm glad you can look on the bright side of this," Joshy said.

"It's better than looking at no side of this, like you," Leslie replied. "What are you, a robot?"

"I—I'm sorry. I'm a bit distracted. I wasn't ready for two huge things to happen on the same night. I mean, that stuff with dad was huge, but it's not the only thing on my mind."

Joshy hadn't talked about Debra since he'd returned from his date. He didn't know what to say, and even if he could talk about it, he didn't want to distract from the monumental bombshell his father dropped the previous night.

"What was the oth—oh my god—your date. I didn't even remember. Damn, that's really selfish of me."

"Yeah, well, I don't think either of us have a lock on selfish, you know? It's not like I've even begun to process everything that dad did to us. I can't even believe it, honestly. At least Debra, I can believe that, because I watched it happen."

"So that's her name...Debra?" Leslie said with a playful twang in her tone. "What was she like?"

"She...god...I feel real bad thinking so much about this...but she's awesome, and she's perfect...and I loved hanging out with her..." he trailed off at the end.

"But...?"

"You're gonna think this is weird," Josh said, skittishly.

"I already think you're weird, Josh, so spill it."

"She kissed me..."

"That's awes—"

"And when she kissed me, my mouth got all hot, and when I looked into her eyes, they looked like they were on fire."

Leslie waved it off as if it was nothing. "You're seeing things...because you're so in looove."

Joshy shook his head. "No, I'm not. It was really weird. That's why I said we should come here; she said she'd be here, today."

"Are you stalking her? Josh, that's creepy."

"I'm not stalking her. I want answers. She ran off after it happened, and I couldn't—I want to know why I felt what I felt, and she's the only one who can tell me."

Leslie thought for a minute. "Do you know where she's staying?"

Joshy nodded. "I'm not proud of it, but I looked at her Facebook feed. She got here a couple hours ago. They're staying at the campground, site fifteen. Man, I know too much information about her, right?"

Leslie shrugged. "No. It's actually kind of sweet, like a movie. Then I guess that's where we're going tonight, huh? We need to make sure you two meet up, at least something good can blossom from this horribleness."

Chapter 9

Joshy's family hated camping. They didn't own tents, or sleeping bags, or anything that would bring them closer to nature, nor did they have any interest in making memories camping, so they had no interest in buying any of those things, either.

Luckily, the campgrounds at the Grand Canyon had not only camping but also glamping, which was all the rage with the yuppie crowd. It's kind of like camping if you were doing it at a five-star resort. It was only after hearing about the full list of amenities that Carole agreed to stay there instead of a hotel.

"But I thought we were trying to save money," Bill began to protest.

Carole looked at him side-eyed. "Oh, now you care about that kind of stuff? All you need to do is drive and pay. It's my turn to burn through money for a while."

Carole pinched every penny and counted every coupon for years. If she was even a dollar over budget Bill would nag her mercilessly until she felt terrible. That might have been the worst part of this whole situation for Carole. The betrayal was terrible, but the years of oppressive guilt might have been worse.

It was always a struggle to get any money out of Bill. Carole never forgot how she had to beg for money to get her realtor's license.

"We don't have the money to go chasing after every one of your dreams," Bill said repeatedly for months until he finally relented but not before unleashing a torrent of guilt on her.

That was her lot for over twenty years. It was always her dreams that were put on hold for Bill's career, as if her needs didn't matter at all. The truth of the matter was that she would have welcomed having to lead the household, for even a moment, and been the breadwinner, but Bill robbed her of that as he drained their bank account in the process. Carole didn't know if she could ever forgive Bill for depriving her of a moment to shine.

*

Joshy had to admit the luxury campgrounds next to the Grand Canyon were lovely. He had his own queen bed and a bathroom that he only had to share with his sister. It was almost better than home.

His family stopped off at Trader Joe's on the way to the campground and got tilapia, marshmallows, chocolate, and graham crackers so they could cook at the campsite. It wasn't long before life started to feel normal again as the whole family looked up at the stars surrounded by other families who were cooking dinner like them. It was as if last night never happened, at least for a moment.

"This was a good idea, Joshy," his father said with a smile, forgetting his failures for a second. "Us, out among the stars. I never would have thought of it."

Joshy smiled. "Well, I wouldn't have thought of it either. It was all Leslie's idea."

"I think we all had our part to play," Leslie replied, taking a burning marshmallow off the fire and blowing on it. "But it turned out alright."

"It's turned out alright today," Carole said. "Who knows what tomorrow will bring, but tonight is okay."

Joshy shrugged. He certainly didn't know what would happen tomorrow, but he knew it was almost two miles to hike from the glamp grounds to campsite fifteen which was well on the other side of the campground. He needed to start soon if he hoped to get back before morning.

Joshy leaned over to his sister. "Are you okay here while I—"

Leslie cut him off. "Of course. Do what you have to do, find the girl, but don't get lost, okay. There are all sorts of wolves and stuff out there."

Joshy's eyes went wide. "Really?"

Leslie shrugged her shoulders. "I don't know. Probably."

*

Wolves, Joshy thought to himself. *Was Debra really worth being eaten by wolves?* He didn't have to think about it for more than half a second before he knew the answer was yes. After all, she was the first girl to ever kiss him, to ever like him, and she ran off on him. He had to know if it was something he did or if it was something she did, or it would eat him alive for the rest of his life.

It's not like he could text her, either. He thought of that and decided against it. If he sent a text, there were too many ways for her to avoid him. She could unfriend him, she could mute him, or she could...ignore him. It was hard to ignore somebody in person, especially when they've tracked you down across state lines, which was a ridiculous thing to do, but people do ridiculous things when they are young and in love.

It was the kind of thing that Joshy saw on television and in movies all the time; the young, dashing protagonist went to win back the girl even after she ran away and told him to buzz off. Had he been raised by better parents and less television, he would have known that the thing he was doing was wrong, but as it stood, he was raised by television and thus thought it was perfectly normal, nay required, to find the love of his young, stupid life. Poor Joshy, and his stupid, stupid thoughts.

The ground was uneven and the terrain loose and hard to grip as Joshy made his way up a steep hill toward the campsite. When he reached the top, he looked out over the entire campgrounds. Yellow, ambient light speckled the darkness across the park, but Joshy was drawn to a dim blue light in the distance that twinkled and danced through the woods.

At first, Joshy thought it was a firefly, but he hadn't seen any since his trip to Nashville sophomore year. Besides, there were no other lightning bugs inside the park. No, this was something different, and though his body told him to move the other way, he couldn't help but walk toward the light.

A melodic hum grew with each step he took toward the light until he and the light were moving in time to the same melody, as if he were engaged in an effortless dance he didn't want to end.

Joshy finally reached the clearing where the blue light danced. He hugged a tree and peeked around it. The longer he looked, the more the light took the form of a human. First, a leg extended out beyond the light, then two arms twirling on either side of it.

He realized the hum was actually originating from a mouth. The longer he stared at the mouth, the more a face came into focus. Two bright blue eyes and a nose formed above the mouth and two ears on either side. Then, a wisp of hair fell into the face of the light, and its luminous arm brushed it away, revealing the face of the girl he loved; Debra.

But it was impossible; Debra wasn't light. She wasn't an aura. She was flesh and blood. He held her in her arms and tasted the cinnamon on her lips as she kissed him.

And then it made sense. It made sense how he could have—

No— he lost it. He thought he had an idea, but it fluttered out of his brain. Nothing made sense, not to him, not to how he saw reality. Humans looked like humans, after all, not beams of light, and he was certain that Debra was human, as sure as he was in his father— no — his mother's— no— and at that moment he realized that nothing he ever believed to be true was, so there was every chance that Debra was not what she claimed to be either, and she truly was a beam of light, which would have likely made her a figment of his imagination.

He should have run away. Every bone in his body told him to run, but he couldn't move. As different as she looked, she also looked the same, like he remembered her, though bluer than she had been before.

Joshy summoned all his nerve and stepped into the clearing. His heart slammed against his chest at a thousand beats a minute as he pursed his lips to speak. *Stop you fool*, his brain told him again and again, but he couldn't. He had to talk to her. He had to know.

"Debra?" he said quietly.

The light shot up straight as an arrow and whirled around until it faced Joshy. Debra's blue face turned from joy to horror as she realized who stood in front of her.

"Josh?" she whispered back. "What are you doing here?"

That was the moment that Josh's brain broke, and he fell backwards, unconscious, with only a blue light's glowing arms to save him from harm.

Chapter 10

Joshy's eyes fluttered open. When they focused, he was in a place he didn't recognize. It wasn't the woods. No, it certainly wasn't that. He was inside the cabin of an RV. A pot of half-drunk coffee sat on the kitchenette counter. Behind him, through a curtain, sat a bed with crumpled sheets, another, smaller bed laid over the driving cab in the front.

"Where—?" Joshy started, rubbing his aching head. "What happened?"

What happened, of course, was something that Joshy remembered in the moments after he said it. He met, and fell in love with, a blue streak of light that was not human. He didn't know what it was, but he knew that humans couldn't turn into blue streaks of light.

"We can't leave him here," A whiny male voice shouted from outside the cabin walls.

"Why not, dad? Do you really think anybody's gonna believe him?" That was Debra's voice. Joshy would recognize it anywhere. A tingle ran up his spine.

"I know you like this boy," a comforting female voice said from outside. "But I'm afraid your father is right. What happens if he tells someone? You're friends on Facebook for god's sake."

"You're talking about kidnapping, mom," Debra replied in a snarky tone reserved for teens talking to their parents. "People have wild alien encounter stories all the time, and nobody believes them, except for tabloids. Besides, in a couple months it's not even gonna matter, right?"

Alien? Joshy thought. *Was that what Debra was? An alien?*

Debra's father sighed. "We want you to be safe, Deb. This was a careless mistake, and you're not known for being careless."

"You really expect me to have a plan for when a boy I met in Vegas wanders through the woods and sees me dancing by myself? That is a contingency plan you expected me to make?"

"We expect you to be prepared for every contingency," her mother scoffed. "That is the price of living on this planet."

Joshy needed to stand before he fainted again. How much information was he expected to intake, after all, before his brain cracked in half? The girl he loved was an alien. Her parents wanted to kidnap him. Plus, the girl he loved was an alien. AN ALIEN! It was all too much for him to comprehend.

Joshy grabbed the side door of the RV and was surprised it wasn't locked. For a family that cared so much about contingencies and safety, it seemed like a careless mistake. The door to the RV creaked open, and Debra's family, none of them blue streaks at the moment, turned to him with frightened eyes. Even in the dim lighting from the camper's awning, Joshy registered the surprise on their faces.

"Debra!" her father yelled. "You were supposed to lock the door!"

"I'm sorry. I didn't think he would be up for a while, but here he is, I guess. Josh, these are my parents, Veronica and Darryl. Mom, dad, this is the boy you want to kidnap."

"Debra!" her mother chided. "Don't say it like that."

"Oh, so saying it some other way would change how horrible of an idea it is, huh?"

"Don't talk back to your mother!" Darryl reproved her, even though he couldn't rightfully think of anything she did wrong, per se. It was the kind of thing parents said to their children, hoping that a harsh tone would shut them up.

"It's nice to meet you," Joshy said waving at them. "Please don't kidnap me."

It was the please that made them all laugh. Darryl was slim, tall, and bony. His laugh was more of a titter than a howl. Veronica, on the other hand, with her pear shape and round head, guffawed loudly enough for half the campground to hear.

"Keep it down," Darryl whispered to his wife.

"Don't tell me what to do," Veronica replied. "Besides, that was funny. Debra, you never told me he was funny."

"Wasn't trying to be funny," Joshy replied, timidly. "I'm trying not to get kidnapped and taken up in a big spaceship to some planet far away."

Darryl could barely hold him his laughter. "We are not those kinds of aliens."

"There are different kinds of aliens?" Joshy replied.

"Loads," Debra said, gently. "There are so many different kinds."

"So," Joshy started. "What kind of aliens are you?"

"The kind that wants to keep their secret," Veronica said. "Are you the type of human that can keep a secret?"

Josh shook his head. "No. I'm not."

Debra slapped herself on the forehead. "Couldn't you lie and say you were?"

"I'm no good at that either."

"At least he's honest," Veronica said. "Stupid, but honest."

"Yeah," Debra said, smiling. "I liked that about him."

"Liked?"

Debra dug her nails deep into Joshy's arm. "Can I see you for a second, alone?"

*

Debra pulled Joshy away from her parents with a hard-enough yank that he was sure she'd dislocated his shoulder for a good minute. "What are you doing here?" Debra whispered angrily.

"I wanted to see you," Joshy replied, nursing his shoulder as the feeling came back to his fingers. "You ran away—"

"I ran away because I didn't want to see you anymore. Because I didn't want to tell you I was an alien!"

"Well, I know that now!" Joshy screamed.

"Be quiet," Debra said. "Why didn't you text me?"

"I figured you wouldn't text me back."

"And you would've been right," Debra replied, stamping her foot on the ground. "Because I didn't want to involve you in this stuff. My— you know what, you're acting like a real creep. Are you a creep?"

"No," Joshy said. "I mean, I don't think so."

"Play it back over in your head, Josh. Tell me what you would think if you were me."

Joshy didn't want to do what she said but decided it was easier than arguing. When he played back the last two days, he realized that he was...kind of a creep and that maybe Debra was right.

"Wow," Joshy said when he was done. "That does not look good for me, does it?"

"No," Debra said. "It does not. If you had stayed away, I could have protected you from all this, and you wouldn't have been any wiser, but now—"

"Now what—" Joshy said. "Now you're going to kidnap me?"

"Keep your voice down," Debra said. "We're not— I don't know what we're doing with you, but you should have stayed away."

"I wanted to see you again," Joshy said. "I know I screwed that up, but I wanted an explanation."

"Well, now you have one," Debra growled. "Feel any better?"

Joshy didn't feel any better as Debra pulled him back to her parents. There was a knot in his stomach that grew with each passing second. It wasn't even about him being kidnapped. No, it was about how over the line he had been in dealing with the girl he professed to love.

"No," Joshy said. "I don't. I'm sorry, Debra. Really. I didn't..."

"You didn't what?" Debra said, whipping back to him.

"I didn't think," he replied. "I wanted what I wanted. I didn't even think about what you wanted."

"No," Debra said. "You didn't. Now we gotta fix it."

Joshy wanted to ask if they were okay, but he feared he'd irreparably damaged his relationship with the girl of his dreams. It didn't even occur to him that he might not live to see tomorrow, which should've been what he was more worried about at that very moment.

Chapter 11

Meanwhile, half a campground away, Leslie had taken out her contacts and laid down in her overly extravagant queen bed. She didn't know how much they paid for their glamp ground, but whatever it was, it was worth it because the bed was like sleeping on a cloud.

"Goodnight, Leslie!" Carole shouted from outside the tent.

"Night, Mom," she replied.

"Goodnight, Joshy!" Bill said.

Leslie panicked. For the last hour, she'd explained Joshy's disappearance by telling them that he was in the bathroom, but he couldn't be in the bathroom all night. She couldn't talk like him, or speak like him, and if she did, they would know she was covering for him. She had to hope that her parents weren't the type to be parents and check on their children. Unfortunately, Leslie knew all too well that that was the exact kind of parents they were.

"Joshy!" Bill hollered. "I said goodnight. You can be mad at me son, but we're still a family."

Go away, Leslie thought. *Please go away. Don't be a father and check up on your son. It's okay to be negligent every once and a while.* But Bill was not negligent, at least not then. He brushed open the flap of the tent and stepped inside.

"We aren't rude in this house, mis—" Bill noticed that Joshy was not in his bed. "Where is Joshy?"

"Still…in the bathroom?" Leslie replied.

Bill looked at her side-eyed, in that way that only parents could look at their children. In the way that told

Leslie that no matter what she did, she was going to be in trouble, so she might as well come clean.

"Okay, fine. He's gone."

"What do you mean, 'gone'?"

"He went to see about a girl." Bill looked at her blankly. "Haven't you ever seen Good Will Hunting? Ugh with this family."

"He met a girl, here, already? I didn't know he had so much game."

"No," Leslie replied. "This is the same girl from Vegas. She's staying here as well."

"That's quite the coincidence."

Carole pulled open the flap and walked inside next to Bill. "What's going on in here?"

"Apparently, the girl Joshy met in Vegas is here," Bill said. "And he is out with her right now."

"That's quite the coincidence," Carole said.

"It's not a coincidence. He knew she'd be here. So, he got us to come here. He wanted to find her again and see her one last time. I helped. I thought it was romantic."

"Romantic?" Carole said, shaking her head. "He sounds like a stalker. You helped your brother stalk this girl?"

"What?" Leslie said. "He's not a stalker. He's doing what people do in every romantic comedy forever."

"Yeah," Bill said. "That's stalking. Where is he now?"

"I dunno," Leslie said in a huff.

"Young lady," Carole said sternly in that voice a mother used to force her children to open up. "Don't lie to me. I've had quite enough of that lately."

"Fine," Leslie said. "Campsite fifteen. That's where he's going. I guess he's probably gotten there by now, if he didn't get eaten by wolves."

"Don't be an idiot, Les," Carole said. "There are no wolves in the Grand Canyon. Coyotes sure, but they're scavengers."

"Dear," Bill said. "I think we're quite a bit off topic. We need to get going before Joshy does something stupid."

Bill and Carole ran out of the tent. Leslie jumped out of bed to join them. She texted Joshy as she threw on a light jacket, but she didn't know that at that moment he was unconscious in Debra's RV.

*

"That was a foolish thing you did, Leslie," Bill said from the driver's seat of their car. Carole wouldn't agree with him verbally, but she did so in spirit. Carole was still seething at Bill, but she couldn't disagree with him on that point.

"Turn right here!" Carole said as the headlights flashed on a picket sign with directions to each campsite. Campsite fifteen should be up ahead."

Traversing the campground by van took only a couple of minutes, while it had taken Joshy over an hour. Back at Debra's RV, Joshy was waking up and pushing open the door to the camper, but of course, the rest of the family didn't know that. They thought they might be in time to stop Joshy from doing anything stupid, even though they knew the depths of Joshy's idiocy all too well.

Bill pulled into campsite fifteen slowly. Most of the lights from the trailers and tents were dark. However, there was one in the back which remained on, and two figures talked under the awning. As he pulled to a stop, a young girl pulled a silhouette of a young man back under the awning with them. It was too dark to see, and his eyesight was too bad to make out exactly, but it looked like Joshy.

"There he is!" Carole shouted, pointing at the silhouette. "Oh no. He's already found them. I hope they aren't going to press charges."

"Press charges?" Leslie said. "Why would they do that?"

"Harassment is a crime, Leslie."

"He's not a harasser. He's just…Joshy."

"Everybody is somebody's son," Carole said. "It was a really stupid thing you did, helping him. I expected more from you."

Leslie wanted to argue, but there were bigger things to worry about at the moment. Leslie slid open the side door as her parents stepped out of the car. They didn't know it, but they couldn't have picked a better time to show up and save Joshy's life.

*

"Sorry about that," Debra said, pulling Joshy forward. "I needed to talk to Josh alone, but I think we're all good now. Aren't we?"

"I think so," Joshy agreed.

"We have decided not to kidnap you," Darryl said with a smile.

"Oh, that's go—"

"It's much too much effort, you see," Veronica continued. "We figure we can toss you down a ditch and leave you for the coyotes."

"MOM!" Debra replied. "That's horrible."

"Well, we have to do something, dear," Veronica said.

"Can't I just unfriend him on Facebook, or like deactivate my account, and then we can move?"

"That sounds inconvenient," Darryl replied. "No, he was wandering through the woods at night, and he fell. We didn't even see him. It's a very clean story."

"I want to be clear that I hate this plan," Joshy said.

"Me too," Debra replied.

"Good. Two against two. I guess we don't go forward with it then."

Darryl chuckled again. "This isn't a democracy, Josh, and even if it were, prisoners do not get a vote."

Darryl took a step toward him, but before Joshy could scream, three new figures appeared under the awning.

"Josh!" Bill hollered. "Is that you?"

"Dad!" Joshy yelled, rushing towards him. "I have never been so happy to see you."

He wrapped his arms around his parents and looked at his sister in the eyes and mouthed, "Thank you." She had literally saved his life, and she didn't even know it.

"You must be Debra," Carole said, extending her hand. "We've heard almost nothing about you."

Debra shook Carole's hand. "Yes, Joshy hasn't said much about you either. These are my parents, Darryl and Veronica."

Carole shook hands with both of them, firmly. "So nice to meet you. I'm Carole, Joshy's mom, and that's Bill and Leslie, his father and sister."

"Very nice to meet you all," Darryl said dryly.

"Well," Veronica whispered to him. "I guess we can't kill him now, can we?"

"No," Darryl replied. "I suppose other arrangements must be made." Darryl pulled Joshy close to him. "If you say anything, we'll have to kill your family, too. We wouldn't want that, now would we?"

No, Josh thought, shaking his head. *We wouldn't want that.*

Chapter 12

Darryl picked up six bottles of water from a large cooler and walked them over to the group, dispensing them to everyone in both families. Joshy sat in silence, worried, eyeing Debra, who didn't look much happier. Meanwhile, Bill, Leslie, and Carole smiled, ignorant to the truth. However, there was a fear behind their eyes that Joshy would be sent to prison.

"So, we have a bit of a problem," Darryl said. "A mighty big bit of a problem."

"How is that?" Bill said.

"Well, your son ambled through the woods and startled my poor daughter. That's a pretty shitty thing to do if you ask me."

"Very shitty," Veronica added. "And illegal, as you both probably know."

"Why?" Carole said. "Do we look like stalkerish types? Oh god, do we?"

Veronica smiled and shook her head. "No, I mean you did raise a son to be one, but I meant you are old enough to know some things about some things, and I assumed that is one of those things. Am I wrong?"

Carole took a long, relieved breath. "No. You aren't wrong. Well, my daughter seems to think it was all about love, but she watches too many movies."

Darryl grumbled under his breath. "Well, it's not romantic, is it? No. It's creepy. And we can't have that kind of thing happening around here."

"I understand," Bill said. "And I promise you that my son's going to have a talking to when we get back to camp."

"Is that enough though?" Darryl said. "I mean, my gut says we should call the police and let them handle it."

"No!" Leslie shouted out. "Look, this was partially my fault. I egged him on. I was the one that convinced the family to come here. Please, don't send my brother to jail because of something stupid. I'd never be able to live with myself."

"And your clear conscience is more important than my daughter's health and safety?"

"Of course not, but you can't actually think he's gonna harm anybody. I mean look at him. He's Joshy."

"Well," Veronica said. "We don't know what to believe. After all, you seem like nice people, but you raised the kind of kid who tracked my daughter across state lines."

"Where do you live?" Carole asked. "I know it's a weird question, given the situation, but please, humor me."

"Detroit," Darryl offered hesitantly.

"Good," Carole said. "We live in Los Angeles. That's half a country apart. Once we leave this trailer park, we'll never see you again, I promise you that."

Darryl stood and started to pace. "I have an idea. It's not the best idea, but it's not the worst either, not by a long shot. Let your boy stay here tonight, under my supervision. Let me get to know him a bit. Meanwhile, my daughter…well, I'm sure you have a bed free, don't you?"

"We do?" Bill asked, somehow both asking a question and making a statement at the same time. "This is very odd."

"Well, I know," Darryl said, scratching his head. "But this is a very odd situation, you see, and I'm not sure what else to do. I'm not ready to let him go, but I also like you folks, and don't wanna go ruining your boy's life without cause."

Debra stood up and pulled her dad away from the group. "What are you doing? I don't want to go with them. I want to put this behind me."

"I know you do," Darryl said. "Thing is, I can't let Josh leave and risk him talking to them about us until I have more time to think, and I can't have them running off either. I'm in a bind, and this is the best we can do for now, okay?"

Debra dropped her eyes, worried. "I don't know why you can't let it go."

"Hey," Darryl said, raising his daughter's face to meet hers. "You brought this on yourself. I'm just cleaning up your mess. Now, do what you're told, and we can fix this tomorrow."

Darryl turned back to the group. "Sorry about that. You know, my lovely daughter had a great idea. Tomorrow, we're headed to the Four Corners National Park. That's at the Arizona line. How about we caravan there, and when we hit the state line, I'll give you back your boy and we'll be on our way, assuming he doesn't cause any mischief before then. Sound good?"

Neither Bill nor Carole knew how to answer the questions posed to them. Darryl's proposal sounded horrible to everybody involved, but they also didn't want to risk their son's future when they could as easily go along with his plan. After all, they were headed in that direction, and it wasn't like they were the ones in the wrong.

"And you're not going to hurt him?" Bill asked, standing.

"Sir, there is only one miscreant in this group, and it's your son. Besides, I'm offering up my daughter in return, which I think is more than fair."

Bill hesitantly stuck out his hand before Carole pulled it away. "This is crazy! You can't do this, Bill."

"Do you have a better idea?" he asked, head turning from Carole to Leslie. "Either of you?"

Leslie shook her head. "I think this sucks, but all my ideas seem to suck today, so I don't have anything better."

"What about you?" Bill asked Carole. "I know you don't trust me right now, but can you at least try?"

Carole thought for a minute. When she let go of Bill's hand, it wasn't because she suddenly trusted Bill again. It was because she didn't have a better plan, and she wanted to pass the buck if anything went wrong.

"Fine," Carole said. "But this is on you."

Bill extended his hand, and Darryl shook it firmly and for far too long. Darryl liked the Earth custom of handshakes, which he didn't get on his own planet, and thoroughly enjoyed them every chance he got.

"Excellent. So, meet here bright and early at seven am, and we'll get on the road."

"We look forward to it," Bill said through gritted teeth, easing his grip and pulling his hand away. When he looked down, his palm was red and sore. Darryl, though slight of build, had quite the grip.

*

Debra enjoyed glamping a fair bit more than sleeping in a cramped camper. Her father had told her it was good practice for traveling the galaxy, and that compared to a spaceship, an RV was a mansion. This did not make her feel any better about the idea of interstellar travel.

"This is weird, right?" Leslie asked as she laid in bed. "I mean this is really weird."

"This whole day has been weird," Debra confessed, getting into bed. "I mean, everything has been weird for a while, but this day has been bizarre."

"Can I ask you something?" Leslie asked, turning over.

"I can't stop you, even if I wanted to," Debra said.

"Did you...like my brother?"

Debra smiled. "I did like him. He was nice, and sweet, and funny. We liked all the same stuff. I kissed him. Did he tell you that?"

"I think he mentioned it."

"I regret it now. If I hadn't kissed him, none of this would have happened."

"I'm sorry. All, well not all, but some of this was my fault."

"I suppose some of it was my fault, too."

"Can I ask you another question?" Leslie said.

"I still can't stop you."

"Do you still like my brother? After all this?"

Debra smiled. "I am uncertain, which I suppose, given the circumstances is the best answer he, or you, could hope for."

Leslie laid back down in bed. "I suppose so. Hey, don't kill me tonight, okay?"

Debra smiled, closing her eyes. "You either."

*

"I can't believe we left him there!" Carole shouted from inside her tent.

"And what were we going to do?" Bill replied, flinging his arms in the air. "Punch them out and take Joshy back ourselves?"

"That wasn't even on the table. Why wasn't that at least on the table?"

Bill sighed. "Look, I don't like it either." He went over to comfort his wife, but Carole bristled at his touch.

"I'm not ready, Bill," Carole said.

Bill threw up his hands. "I know. I was…hoping…"

Carole turned around and hopped into her queen bed next to Bill's. "You can't hope your way out of this mess. If you have to hope for something, hope that Joshy is safe."

That may have been true, but Bill didn't know any other way to handle the situation. He couldn't fix it. He couldn't take it back. The only thing he had left was hope. If he didn't have hope, he didn't have anything.

*

"We aren't the bad kind of aliens, Josh," Darryl said as he walked into the trailer after him.

"I don't know about that. You are kidnapping me."

"Am I?" Darryl asked. "Seems to me like your parents are letting you go, and you came willingly. Not much of a kidnapping to me."

"I only came with you cuz you were gonna kill my family if I didn't."

Veronica shrugged. "Kill is a strong word."

"It's the word he used," Joshy said pointing to Darryl.

"Only because there wasn't time to explain the plan to you. It's far too nuanced to whisper in your ear."

"And what is your plan?" Joshy asked, folding his arms.

"There is a neurology lab at the Four Corners National Park that can wipe your mind lickety-split. Then, you'll forget us, the last few days, and be on your way."

"So, you're not going to kill me?" Joshy asked.

"Not unless you annoy me," Darryl replied with a deadpan look on his face.

Joshy had to admit forgetting the past few days would be a blessing in disguise. He would forget his regrettable actions, his mother would forget all about his father's massive debt, and Leslie would forget that she couldn't afford college anymore. Maybe they could go back to being a family again, if only for a little while.

The problem with that, of course, was that he would also forget Debra in the process, and he never wanted to forget her.

"I know you like my daughter," Darryl said. "But the truth is you've only known Debra for a couple of days. You don't even know if you love her, or if you lust after her. It's not like you've been married for a decade or something."

"You'll find somebody else, somebody better," Veronica said. "Besides, it's not like we're going to be here for that much longer anyway. None of us are."

Veronica bit her lip as if she'd revealed a big secret. Darryl narrowed his eyes in his wife's direction, which only incriminated her further.

"What does that mean?" Joshy said. "Where are you going?"

"Cool it, Ronnie," Darryl said.

"Oh, what does it matter? We're gonna wipe his mind tomorrow anyway. Plus, I've got his phone, and…I mean what harm can it do?"

"Fine," Darryl said. "But I don't like it."

"You don't like anything," Veronica said, sitting next to Joshy. "Do you know how many aliens are on this planet right now?"

"I don't know, like fifty?" Joshy said, confused.

"Fifty!" Darryl said. "I wish."

"No," Veronica continued, shaking her head. "Millions. Hundreds of millions in fact. They're everywhere."

"No way!" Joshy replied. "I would know all about something like that."

"No, you wouldn't," Darryl said. "You humans are stupid. Very, very stupid."

"Excuse me?"

"You evolved from monkeys," Darryl replied. "Nuff said. That's not winning the genetic lottery. Humans are irrational, prone to anger, and they aren't that smart. It's all the flaws in your genetic code. You were a mistake."

"Oh, and I suppose you were made from a dinosaur or something."

"No, we evolved from the proto-carbon molecules that formed when our world did, like almost every other species in the cosmos. That means we have no limit to our evolution, because we are made from the universe, and the universe is limitless."

"And there are millions of you on Earth?" Joshy asked, leaning back in his chair.

"Yes, and unfortunately, many species. Ours are peaceful, and only seek to explore. However, there are others, much more dangerous, which look to conquer."

"That's crazy!" Joshy said. "Who would want to conquer us?"

"The Globorians, for one. They have plotted to overthrow Earth and enslave your planet for a hundred years. They have infiltrated every inch of your planet."

"So, there are Globorians here, right now, plotting to take over the world?"

"No," Veronica replied. "They have already taken it over. Look at all your world leaders, all of your state houses, all throughout the republic you love so much. Ever wonder why every politician acts against the interests of their people so often? Ever wonder how they keep getting elected? That is the Globorians' plotting, and they have finally succeeded. It is only a matter of months before their ships land and they carry out their invasion plans."

"Wait!" Joshy exclaimed. "If that's true, then why aren't you telling everybody?"

"Who is there to tell? Everyone in power is Globorian. All we can do is enjoy one last trip across this country before we depart forever."

"So, you're leaving us to fend for ourselves."

Veronica and Darryl looked at each other and then back at Joshy. They responded in unison. "Yes, that is exactly what we're doing."

Chapter 13

It should be noted that Globorians are a blight on the galaxy and have been since the moment they evolved from the proto-carbon. Most species, like Debra's Thimberians, were peaceful. Some explored solar systems for the sheer fun of it. Others dedicated themselves to science and research. Only a select few focused on war, and it ruined the galaxy for everyone else.

Since some species believed in never-ending war, it meant that every alien race had to practice some measure of self-defense, or at the very least, partner with a species that did. The fact that Debra's species had to think about war for even one minute meant that it was less time devoted to researching new species, which was their true purpose. Thimberians were never so happy as when they were studying the effects different species had on the universe.

Of course, that was what attracted Darryl to Earth in the first place. He heard that not only was there a savage form of monkey that evolved to communicate, but they also ran the world, and this was something he and his wife had to see to believe. When they arrived, they were stunned to see that not only did humans practice exploration and science, but they also seemed to be obsessed with war.

Usually, alien species were an expert in one of those things, which is what made Globorians even sadder. There was not one ounce of happiness in their pitiful bones. All they thought about was war. Humans, however, were different. They had the capacity for both great love and hate, often within seconds of each other.

This was why Earth was such a popular destination for so many alien species. It had something for everyone. It had primitive scientific practices to study, large, vast plains to explore, and for the Globorians, it had endless war. Of course, because of their numerous interests, humans were an expert on none of those things, which is why it was so easy for aliens to fool humans and live among them, and how they would be so easy to enslave.

*

The next morning, the Carters packed up their car and drove over to the Thompsons' campsite. By the time Bill pulled into the site, Darryl was waving at him, ready to go, as if he had been waiting up all night. *Note: He had been waiting up all night.* Joshy got a couple hours of sleep on the hard, uncomfortable couch in the camper, even if he had woken up with a stiff neck.

Debra, on the other hand, had slept like a dream. Her bed was pillow soft, unlike the camper she had been stuck living in for the past couple of weeks.

Darryl poured Bill a cup of campfire brewed coffee and brought it to him in the van. "Nice night?"

"No," Bill replied, taking the coffee. "To be honest, I didn't sleep well knowing my son was here with you."

"Interesting. How about you, honey?" Darryl asked, looking past him to Debra, who sat in the back seat.

"I slept really well. We should have tried those glamp grounds; that bed was heaven."

"I know, right!" Leslie said, excitedly. Sometime in the night, Leslie and Debra had become friends. It seemed that sleeping in the same room, not even the same bed, had a way of making friends from strangers, at least in this case.

"Where's my son?" Carole asked in a stern tone. Bill might be willing to be chummy with Darryl, but she had no interest in playing nicely with him.

"He's inside. He's fine. He's got a kink in his neck, so Veronica is helping him work it out."

"Prove it," she replied.

"Surely," Darryl said, turning toward the camper. "Ronnie! Can you bring our friend out here?"

Less than a minute later, Veronica opened the door, and Joshy ambled outside, rubbing his neck. "Hi, Mom! Sorry, my neck is sore. Veronica was helping me work it out. Her hands are like magic."

Veronica's hands were literally like magic. Her species was known throughout the galaxy for their ability to heal the sick and weary. It wasn't a skill Veronica had much experience using recently, since she had to live in secret, so she welcomed the chance to use her powers again, if only for a moment.

"See," Darryl said. "I told you. We're not the enemy here because there is no enemy, only two families caught in a tough situation."

"A situation brought on by you," Leslie mumbled.

"Hey!" Debra said from the back seat. "Let's not forget it was your brother who followed me here."

"You're right," Leslie said, followed by a long pause. "What a mess."

"Yes," Darryl said. "However, it is a mess that we are working our way through. How do you feel back there, honey? Are you okay to ride with them?"

"I'd rather not," Debra said. "No offense, but the camper is way nicer than this car."

"I'll bet it is," Leslie replied.

"Oh my god," Debra said excitedly. "You should totally see it."

"I have an idea," Darryl said. "How about Debra and Leslie ride with my wife in the camper, and I'll ride here, with you."

"That sounds terrible, no way you're going to have both of our children in that thing."

"No!" Leslie said. "That sounds fun. Besides, what are they gonna do? You'll be behind them the whole time. I'm sick of this car. It smells like feet. Plus, then I can keep an eye on Joshy and make sure he's alright."

"I don't—" Bill began to say.

"I'm not a child. I've been away at college for years, and I'm fine. I'll be fine."

"Well, then," Darryl said. "I guess that works for everybody then. Why don't you two scoot out of the backseat, and Carole, do you mind giving up the front? I have these long dancer's legs, and they get cramped in the back."

At that moment, Carole's look could have killed him, if her gaze could kill, which it couldn't, at least not in this sector of the galaxy, and not a Thimberian. That would be crazy.

*

"Is it bumpy back there?" Veronica asked from the driver's seat of the camper as she piloted the RV down Route 160 toward the Four Corners Monument.

"No," Leslie replied. "It's nice back here."

"Smooth as silk they told us at the dealership," Veronica replied. "It was supposed to be our retirement present, but we splurged early."

"Why?" Leslie replied, but Veronica didn't answer. She pretended she didn't hear, but the truth was she couldn't tell Leslie the real reason. Everybody else in the RV knew the reason though. The Globorians were invading in a matter of weeks, and there was nothing they could do to stop it.

Leslie wished Veronica would talk to her. She wished anyone would talk to her. The back of the RV had been awkwardly silent for the better part of two hours, as Joshy and Debra caught each other's eyes every few minutes, then turned away from each other.

"I think you should both grow up," Leslie said. "'Course it's none of my business."

"You're right," Joshy said. "It's none of your business."

"Do you always talk to your sister like that?" Debra said. "It's no wonder you stalked me."

"I didn't stalk—" Joshy thought better of his words. "I didn't mean to stalk you, alright? And besides, that's the way siblings talk to each other. You would know that if you had any."

"I couldn't have a sibling," Debra said.

"Why?" Leslie said.

"It's complicated," Debra replied after a long silence.

Thimberians were careful when procreating. When adults joined with their partner, they each took half of their own genetic code and gave it to their child. They led a half-life after that, but they were also able to seed their DNA for a new generation, creating stronger and stronger Thimberians in the process. Each time they procreated, their lives were cut in half again, which was why Debra's parents chose to have only the one child. They loved their lives too much to have any more.

"I get that," Leslie said. "Dad got snipped after Joshy there. He must have known what he would unleash on the world."

"Shut up," Joshy said to Leslie, before turning to Debra. "See, she does it as well. Why don't you get on her?"

"I didn't kiss her," Debra replied. "I kissed you. Thus, I expect more from you, though I probably shouldn't, given the circumstances."

"You two kissed!" Veronica said. "Debbie, you never told me that."

"Don't call me that, mom," Debra scoffed. "And yes, regrettably, we kissed."

"Was it that bad?" Joshy asked.

Debra didn't respond, but Joshy saw a glimmer in her bright, blue eyes that made him hope that it wasn't all bad. Of course, that might have also been the sunlight shining in from the windshield.

"Do you mind if I say something?" Leslie asked. "I've taken three semesters of psych at school, and I think it might help."

"How much longer?" Debra shouted to her mother.

"About ninety minutes, give or take," Veronica replied. "Why? Do you have to pee?"

"No, unfortunately," Debra said, turning to Leslie. "I guess I have time. Go for it."

"It seems to me like you are projecting onto Josh because you know you'll never see him again, and it's easy to cut ties with him, especially now that he did something so stupid."

"Hey!" Joshy replied. "You told me it was romantic!"

"I did, and that was stupid of me. I know that now. So, what do you think?"

"I think," Debra said, giving a moment's reflection. "I think that what Josh did was stupid and that if I let it go, he'll be prone to doing something stupid again. After all, this is SO stupid that the chances he'll do something else stupid are really high. But you're right. I'll be gone in a couple months, so what's the point, even?"

Debra didn't catch what slipped out of her mouth until Leslie had processed it completely. "Where are you going?"

Debra shook her head and lowered her eyes. "It doesn't matter. It would never work out."

"I don't care about that," Joshy said. "Honestly, even if you were going to rip out my heart in two months, I would still want those two months."

Thimberians do not rip out people's hearts. Globorians might, especially if provoked. Joshy was lucky he wasn't screwing with one of them. He would never have survived this long. Debra was touched, though, by Joshy's words. She had not met many people on Earth who were worth her time, and it sucked that she met Joshy right before she left his planet forever.

"Really?" Debra asked.

He nodded. "Yeah. I know I don't have much of a say about whether we are together or not, and I know what I did was stupid, but it allowed me to spend more time with you, even awkwardly, so it wasn't so bad, you know?"

There were few things that Joshy could have said that would have melted Debra's frozen heart, but those words, in that order, worked. She smiled, slightly, and lifted her eyes to meet his gaze. "You know after this summer I'll be gone right? And it's not that convenient to see each other even now."

He nodded. "I don't care."

"And it's gonna hurt way more in two months than it does now. It's easier to pull off the band-aid now."

"He was never any good at that," Leslie said. "He usually wore them until they fell off naturally."

"Thank you, sis," Joshy said, sarcastically. "She's not wrong, though."

Debra slid her hands over to Joshy's sweaty palm. "And you won't do anything stupid like this again, right?"

"No," Joshy replied. "If I do something stupid, it will be for a totally different reason."

Debra smiled, even though she tried to remain stoic. "I'm serious. I'm not a thing, and you can't treat me like something you own. And it's not all about you, okay? I have my own stuff going on."

Joshy looked deep into Debra's eyes. "I swear to you that I will always treat you like a person."

Joshy didn't hear himself call her a person, but Debra did, and that was all she'd ever wanted since she landed on Earth.

"Thank you," Debra said. She leaned forward to kiss Joshy, but hesitated for a moment, hovering over his mouth.

"Are you going to kiss or what?" Leslie asked.

Debra pulled back. "I want to, but I'm scared. I don't want to hurt him…like last time."

Joshy smiled as he brought his hand to her face, stroking it gently. "I trust you."

Joshy managed to construct another perfect string of words, which broke through Debra's hesitation. She took a deep breath, leaned forward, and kissed Joshy. There was a moment of pensive hesitation as she waited for her powers to hurt him, but when they didn't, her shoulders untensed, and she fell into his arms.

Veronica saw it in the rear-view mirror and couldn't help but smile. She knew her daughter had a hard time on Earth and was glad she'd found something to occupy her time, even for a short while. Of course, it made wiping his family's brains even harder to stomach.

Chapter 14

Darryl called ahead to the mind-wiping facility at the Four Corners National Park. However, their facility was closed and had not been open for several months. Only a single guard staffed the facility to answer questions from wayward aliens. Luckily, the guard pointed Darryl to a facility in Roswell, New Mexico which could take the Carters on short notice. Now, he had to convince them to extend their ride one more day, and he would be done with them.

"This is kind of lame," Joshy said, standing on the Arizona side of the Four Corners monument, which was basically two metal lines that crossed each other on the ground. It was wholly unimpressive.

"I hear it's not even accurate," Debra said, holding Joshy's hand and standing on the New Mexico side of the line.

"I'm pretty sure we're all in New Mexico," Leslie added from the Utah side of the line.

"Who knew geography could be so cool, right kids?!" Darryl shouted from Colorado, where he and the rest of the parents stood. "Isn't this great?"

"No!" all three of the kids shouted together.

"What do they know?" Darryl said, turning to Bill. "So, listen, friend. We're supposed to get going now, right? Split up and never see each other again, but our kids are actually getting along. And our trip was surprisingly fun, wasn't it?"

Bill smiled. "It was not unfun."

Carole would not agree. Darryl and Bill spent the whole time talking about sports, which was a topic that Carole didn't care about at all, not even a little bit. Still, she did enjoy spending her Audible credit on George RR Martin's fourth *Game of Thrones* book, *A Feast for Crows*, which was sure to keep her busy for many hours to come, so at least something good came out of it.

"Well, I have a little secret stop to make in a town called Roswell, New Mexico. Ever hear of it?"

"Yeah!" Bill shouted. "I've always wanted to go there."

"Along the way we're going to see Meow Wolf in Santa Fe and the giant rattlesnake in Albuquerque. It's another day's drive, but if you're up for it, then I am too."

"Can we?" Bill turned to his wife. "Can we? Can we? Can we?"

"I don't know," Carole said.

"Well, you know who lives in Santa Fe, right?" Darryl said. "One Mister George RR Martin."

Carole smiled. "You have my attention."

"Maybe he's there, maybe he's not," Darryl shrugged. "But it's a sight you'll probably never see again. I mean how often will you visit New Mexico?"

Carole sighed. "Well, this trip has taken my mind off...things. Alright. I'm not riding with you two again, though. I'll go with Veronica and Leslie. You take the lovebirds, and we have a deal."

Veronica smiled at Carole. "Will you give us a minute?"

"Take your time."

"What are you trying to do here?" Veronica asked, pulling Darryl away from the other two. "This is a bad idea. We should let them go and take our chances."

Darryl looked back over at Debra, who was still holding Joshy's hand and whispering in his ear. "I know, but look at them. She actually looks happy, doesn't she?"

Veronica sighed. "She really does."

"Besides, there's another facility in Roswell. One more day isn't going to kill us, is it? Debra deserves some good memories here."

"Let's hope the Globorians don't invade early."

"Well, if they do then we won't have to wipe their memories, now will we? Cuz we'll all be dead."

Veronica watched as Debra and Joshy laughed together. "I have to admit, seeing them together... It's been nice to see her happy. Alright, fine. Let's do it."

Darryl turned back to Bill and Carole. "Looks like we have a deal."

*

Debra pulled Joshy under a glow-in-the-dark octopus hanging from the ceiling at Meow Wolf, through a hallway, and into a room where fake iridescent trees lined the walls on either side of the room. They had been exploring the interactive art space for over an hour, and every room had been weirder and more psychedelic than the last. It was totally Debra's and Joshy's jam.

Their families weren't quite as impressed with the experience, and so they walked ahead toward the gift shop. After all, Darryl and Veronica had been across the solar system and seen actual iridescent trees. Bill and Carole were not as much fun as they thought they were, it seemed, and trippy neon trees hadn't done it for them since back in the 70's when they listened to the Grateful Dead.

Debra and Joshy, however, were just the right frequency of odd to find the whole experience magical.

"Do you think this is what it's like, roaming the solar system?"

"I don't know," Joshy said, touching the branch of one of the neon painted trees. "You're the alien."

"I know I am," Debra replied. "Dad told me stories, but I've never been off the planet. I hope it's like this."

Joshy squeezed Debra's hand harder. "Are you excited to go?"

Debra squeezed his hand right back. "Not as excited as I was a week ago. Still, it should be fun. I mean, who doesn't want to explore other galaxies?"

"Me," Joshy said. "I like playing games in them and all, but doing stuff. That's not usually my jam."

"We're doing stuff right now, homie, and you seem to be liking it fine."

Joshy smiled. "That's because I'm with you."

It was so corny, Debra knew, but she couldn't help but smile and kiss Joshy. She wanted not to like him as much as she did, but she would be lying to herself if she didn't admit that he made her not want to leave Earth.

*

After they finished at Meow Wolf, the caravan stopped at George RR Martin's house. They parked outside the front gate for twenty minutes. However, when they didn't see anything move inside for over a half hour, they decided to soldier on. It wasn't worth wasting their day trying to catch a glimpse of the writer watering his plants, if that was even a thing that he did.

From Santa Fe, it was a short trip down the road to Albuquerque. Before getting to town, they stopped at the giant rock sculpture of a rattlesnake north of town. It wasn't as easy to find as they thought, and it took them circling back three times before they finally found it. At 400 feet long, the families felt a little stupid that it took them three tries to find it, but eventually, they filed out of their cars and into the hot desert sun. While the parents walked behind them, Debra and Joshy took off by themselves. It was hot, miserably so, but they couldn't stop holding each other's hands.

"Why do you think your body tried to hurt me the first time we kissed?" Joshy asked.

"I dunno," Debra replied. "My mom thinks it's because my body saw you as a foreign agent trying to hurt me, and wanted to fight you off. Now, it's created antibodies for itself, so you aren't a threat anymore."

"Has it ever happened before?" Joshy asked.

Debra chuckled. "You're the first boy I kissed, Josh."

"I find that hard to believe," Joshy replied. "I mean, look at you."

"I've been guarded my whole life," Debra said. "I didn't want to make any mistakes or reveal that I was an alien to anyone. With good reason, too. Look at what happened when I slipped up one time."

"Why did you, then?"

Debra sighed. "I wanted to have one real date before I left Earth for good, you know, and real dates end with a kiss. I figured it was safe to let down my guard in Vegas since I was never supposed to see you again."

"Yeah, that worked out real well, didn't it?"

Debra smiled. "Yes, it did. And besides, you're cute, in your way, and you know about comic books, which is all I could ask for, really."

"Well, that's nice," Joshy replied, not knowing what else to say. "I'm going to miss this."

"No, you won't," Debra said. "You won't even remember it, or me."

"Not consciously, maybe, but I'll remember it down in my soul, like muscle memory or something. I'll bet I won't be able to see a snake without getting sad, and I won't even know why."

"Can't we enjoy this, right now, and not think about that?"

"No," Joshy replied. "I've never enjoyed anything in my entire life. I am always thinking about the worst possible outcome. That's why I like video games. They let me get out of my own head."

"That's why I like books, actually," Debra replied. "I'm going to miss books. Mom said all I could have on the ship is a Kindle, but I like the feel of books. I'm gonna miss the smell of books, too."

"I'm going to miss the smell of you," Joshy said, sniffing the marigolds in her hair. "It's gonna happen tomorrow, isn't it?" Joshy asked, not stopping his gait. "That's when they're going to wipe my mind. This is the last day I'm going to have with you, isn't it?"

Debra looked up at him. "If I said no, would it make this any better?"

Joshy looked down at her. "Nothing could make this better."

Debra kissed him again. Getting his mind wiped would be hard for Joshy, but it would be much harder for her, because she would always have the memory of Joshy with her, forever, no matter where she went.

"There's a little base outside of Roswell," Debra said. "Aliens love it there. It's like their Disneyland. We're going there tomorrow morning. Dad will say he knows a secret base that he wants to show you. He'll knock on the door, and they'll come for you. It will be over before you know it. Don't fight them, okay? It will be okay. I promise. Trust me."

"I do trust you," Joshy said, kissing her lightly. "I just wish there was another way."

"Me too," she said.

*

That night, Veronica sat in her motel bed; the next day's activities weighed on her brain. She had spent two days with the Carters, and she liked them quite a bit. Carole was funny and sweet. She didn't talk a lot, but when she spoke, the words she said mattered. Joshy and Leslie, when they didn't bicker at each other, were good children, and Joshy was good for Debra. She found somebody that lit her up, and tomorrow he would forget she ever existed. It didn't seem fair. No, it wasn't fair.

Veronica felt the pangs of regret throughout dinner that night as Debra and Joshy talked to each other almost in a language all their own. Debra could barely eat she was laughing so hard, and when she wasn't laughing, her eyes were lit up with excitement. Veronica didn't understand *Reservoir Dogs* or *Johnny the Homicidal Maniac*, but Joshy did, and that mattered a lot to Debra.

Veronica once read about a philosophy which stated that when somebody you love died, a piece of you died too, because some of your memories were stored in that person. If that were true, then you literally placed a piece of your soul into them for safe keeping, and when they died, a piece of you was gone forever.

Veronica wondered, as she watched Darryl get ready for bed, if they were killing a piece of their daughter by wiping Joshy's memory of her. How could they live with themselves knowing their daughter's best memories of Earth would never be remembered by the person she made them with?

"Are we doing the right thing?" Veronica asked after emerging from her deep thoughts.

"Of course," Darryl said. "Not only does it protect us, but it also protects them. If anybody found out that they knew about aliens, they would never be safe again."

"Sure, I know you said that, but what about Debra? She looks happy. She is happy, and we are taking that away from her."

Darryl sat down at the edge of the bed. "Oh sweetheart, she will always have the memories of him, no matter where we go."

"Yes, but he won't have the memories of her."

Darryl scooted under the covers. "And thank god for that. They should all stay ignorant for the next couple of weeks. Then, it will all be over, and the Globorians will enact their pla—"

"Yes," Veronica nodded. "I've been thinking about that, too. This has been our home for eighteen years. Don't we owe it to them to tell them aliens are going to take over their planet in mere weeks?"

"What will that do?" Darryl asked. "They can't save themselves, the Globorian infiltration teams saw to that. All they would do is fight like idiots, and die like idiots. At least they can live, and so can we."

"But what kind of life, Darryl? As slaves? As prisoners?"

"Better than dying."

Veronica sighed. "Shouldn't that be their decision?"

Darryl thought about reading his book about space travel, but he decided he wanted to end his conversation with his wife more, so he flipped off the light. He knew she wanted to continue talking, but he couldn't think about it anymore. If he did, he might change his mind. After all, he liked Bill as much as Veronica liked Carole. He didn't want to wipe their memories any more than she did, but that wasn't a choice they could make. For everybody's benefit, the plan had to go as scheduled.

*

Joshy didn't want to go to bed. The weight of tomorrow dragged down his soul, and bed only brought it about faster. Instead, he chose to sit out by the pool below the motel where both families had decided to stay.

"Hey, bro!" Leslie said from the balcony outside her room. "I want to go to bed, chop chop."

Joshy wished he were as ignorant of the future as his sister. He had bit his tongue the whole trip because Darryl said it would be better for his family. There was no reason, he said, to tell them the truth and freak them out. That made sense to Joshy, and so he agreed to keep their secret until it was over.

"I'll be up later!" Joshy shouted. "Please, keep the light on for me."

"I can't sleep with the light on," Leslie shouted.

Just then, Debra opened the gate to the pool and walked inside. "Hi, Leslie."

"Oooooh," Leslie said. "Never mind. Alright, bro. Take your time."

Leslie walked into her room and closed the door. Debra sat down in a pool chair next to Joshy and stared into the blue water. Joshy scooted his chair toward her and leaned forward.

"This sucks," Joshy said.

"I know."

Joshy sighed. He placed his hand on Debra's. There was so much more to say, but instead, he wanted to look out and stare at the water with the girl he loved. Eventually, it would be tomorrow, and he would deal with that, then.

Chapter 15

The next morning, the Carters woke in jovial spirits. Bill and Carole even slept in the same bed the night before, though the thought of Bill's touch made Carole shiver in disgust. Still, there was something in the crisp, Albuquerque air that agreed with them.

The Thompsons, on the other hand, were not in high spirits. In fact, they were miserable. Neither Darryl or Veronica slept much during the night, and Debra stayed up until two am talking to Joshy before they both succumbed to exhaustion.

Mostly, though, the Carters were jovial because they didn't know what was about to happen to them, and the Thompsons were miserable because they did.

"So," Darryl said with a slow groan, as he swallowed a mouthful of oatmeal. "I have a surprise for you."

"A surprise," Bill said. "For us! You old so and so, you didn't have to do that."

"No," Darryl said with a fake grin. "I really did."

Darryl told them about the secret base that lots of people thought was Area 51, and that he had a contact on base that agreed to let them tour the place, as long as they agreed to keep it under their hat.

"That's fantastic," Bill said.

"I'm excited to see it," Veronica said. "Aren't you, Carole? It sounds so fun."

Even Carole, the most skeptical among them, agreed that it was a cool idea. Her friendship with Veronica was a slow burn, but eventually, it took, and she trusted her, or at least had begun to trust her.

After breakfast, Darryl, Veronica, Joshy, and Debra led the way in the RV toward the secret base which would wipe the Carters' memories. The Carters followed close behind in their van.

"I don't understand why you have to wipe their memories," Joshy said, looking up toward Darryl in the passenger's seat. "I'm the only one that knows anything."

"It's for your own good. What do you think would happen if you didn't know something they did? They would think you were broken or something. I'm telling you, this is the best way. All of you get a clean slate together."

"And what about letting me go?" Joshy replied. "I haven't said anything to anybody yet. I haven't even posted anything to Instagram or anything. And you still don't trust me?"

Darryl turned around. "You say that now, but what if you and Debra get into a fight, or what if you…"

He trailed off. He had to admit, the more he thought about it, the less important it seemed to get Joshy's mind wiped. Still, he had told the facility that he was on his way and the purpose of his mission. If he didn't show up, they would know something was wrong and work to correct the problem humans with extreme prejudice.

Even if Darryl stayed silent, it wouldn't take a rocket scientist to match Joshy and Debra together. Even if they unfriended each other on Facebook, which he knew they wouldn't do, their profile information was on the cloud, and the cloud was controlled by the Globorians and had been since the 80's.

It's too bad that the Inkarians couldn't see what the Globorians did with their beautiful wireless technology. They would be none too happy. The Globorians may have superior might, but they could still be wiped out by superior technology, if necessary. Unfortunately, Inkarians never ventured far from the center of the galaxy, and would never sojourn out to such a backwater planet as Earth.

*

The steps from the camper to the door of the bunker were some of the hardest of Darryl's life, and he had traveled to thirty-six star systems over his three hundred years. He always tried to keep the beings he observed at a distance, but he failed in this instance, which made him mix emotions with his logical reasoning.

Debra never understood that concept of compartmentalizing. She knew she wanted to fit in on Earth, the only home she had ever known. Darryl remembered that feeling, of course, since he was once a youth, oh so many years ago. She would learn with age, he thought, to forget those that she met, or she would go mad with the pain of her memories.

Becoming friends with those you observed led you to the predicament that Darryl was in at the current moment. He looked back at Bill, Carole, and Leslie standing with Joshy, Debra, and his Veronica. They were all so pleasant and polite. He liked them a lot. Proximity made the heart grow fonder, even for aliens, but that was something that Darryl could not afford at this moment. He had to follow through with his mission, for the good of his family.

"Are you almost done up there, Darryl?" Bill shouted. "Could you go a little faster? The sun is a bit hot out here."

Globorians built the base in the middle of the desert off an old dirt road that somebody had to know existed before they could find it. The sun was unusually hot that day, and it beat down mercilessly on the group. Darryl insisted they wait outside the cars, though. Then, it would be easier to round them up when the time came to say goodbye.

"Just a minute!" Darryl said.

Veronica pulled him aside after breakfast and pleaded with him to call off his plan. She begged him to leave the Carters alone, but Darryl was a stubborn alien, and he needed to follow through with everything he set out to do.

Darryl stepped up onto the wooden porch of the bunker. From the outside, the base looked like an old wood shack, warped from the sun. However, inside it was a state of the art facility built by the Globorians with Inkarian technology that they bartered for after the third Inkarian War nearly destroyed both societies.

Darryl took a deep breath and closed his eyes. *You can do it,* he told himself. *You can do it.* He didn't like the look Veronica gave him when he refused to yield, nor how Debra turned away from him crying when she begged him to leave the Carters alone.

These were the times that tried men's souls, he told himself. Somebody must do the unpopular thing. Someone had to be the stronger person. Debra and Veronica were ruled by their emotions and feelings for the Carters, and it blinded them to the right course of action, but the smart thing was looking out for his own. Good things didn't happen to aliens who divulged themselves to humans.

How long had he been standing at the front door? he asked himself. *Five minutes, at least.* They probably saw him on the cameras on either side of the door. There was no hiding now. Even if he wanted to turn back, he couldn't.

So, he knocked. The moment that he rapped his hand on the door, he knew he was making a mistake. He wanted to take it back, but it was already done. The door creaked open, and a voice called from the darkness.

"You Orsti Thimberian?" A smooth, silky voice asked

Darryl wanted to lie, but he couldn't. It would do him no good. How many others were planning to come today? "Yes. That's me."

A rocky, cracked hand pointed to the Carters, standing in the sun, trying to find some shade. "Those the four?"

Again, the urge to lie was great, but he fought it. This was the right thing for his family, and his family was the thing that mattered most in the world.

"Those are them. Carole and Bill are the parents. Leslie and Josh are the children."

"And the other two are yours?"

"Yes," Darryl said. "Also Thimberians. They're not to be harmed."

"Noted."

"You will make sure the Carters have good memories when you wipe their minds, right? I don't want them to have bad memories of their trip."

Two bloodshot brown eyes came into view, squinting at Darryl. "I don't know what you think we do here, but it's too close to the invasion to wipe minds anymore. We can't risk anybody saying anything, even you. I'm sorry. For all of you."

Darryl barely saw the gun raised to his chest or power turned on. He didn't see the laser fire into his chest and cut a hole in it. He turned to his family, and in the last moment before he exploded, he wished he had more time with them.

*

Debra didn't see her father explode, because she was talking to Joshy, but Veronica watched it first-hand. She saw the gun rise and a laser blow a hole through his chest.

Darryl went white, and then blue, and then exploded into a million pieces. In the last seconds of his life, she thought he mouthed "I love you," but she couldn't be sure. All she knew was that her husband, to whom she had been married for 278 years, was dead, a million particles floating in the ether.

"DARRYL!" Veronica screamed, reaching toward him with her long blue arms. She couldn't contain her corporeal form through all her grief, and Debra had to turn into a blue beam of light herself to catch up with her.

"Mom!!!!" The foundation of the house flipped up, and two dozen soldiers holding laser guns ran out from the basement. They were not beautiful like Debra, or human like Josh. Instead, they looked like red rocks, craggy and ugly, cracked from the sun. Debra had been told that this was what Globorians actually looked like, but she couldn't imagine how horrible it would be when she saw them in person. Each soldier carried a long rifle in their hands that lit up in a hundred different colors as they moved.

There wasn't time for Debra to think. She flung her hands out in front of her, and a giant pulse of light sent a shockwave away from her and toward the Globorians. Sand shot up all around them as they fell from the force.

"Get to the camper!" she shouted as the Globorians worked to right themselves.

The Carters had never seen anything like it before. Except for Joshy, they didn't even know there were such things as aliens. Luckily, Joshy kept a level head and pushed his family toward the camper.

"Move!" Joshy said, pushing his parents toward the camper.

"Mom!" Debra shouted. "Help them!"

Veronica stuffed down her grief and focused on the task at hand. She couldn't save her husband, but she could save her friends. She flew toward the Carters at top speed and wrapped the family up in her arms before picking them up and throwing them into the van.

More and more soldiers ascended from under the house. They shook the Earth as they moved, firing their laser cannons as they stomped forward until Debra could barely hold them back.

"Debra" Veronica shouted from the cab. "Let's go!"

Debra turned and flew to the camper which was already revving its engine. The minute she jumped aboard, the camper took off, leaving the Globorians behind them, firing at her and burning laser holes in the RV.

Debra flung her hands wide again, sending a shockwave toward Bill's car. It exploded on impact, blowing the Globorians back as the fire flew fifty feet in the air.

"My car!" Bill said.

Debra turned around, still shimmering blue, still as beautiful as the night Joshy found her in the woods.

"I'm sorry, Mr. Carter."

"What is going on here!?" Carole screeched at Debra as she held on for dear life.

"There's something we need to tell you," Joshy said before he stood up and wrapped Debra in his arms. The pain of her father hadn't hit her yet, but she had to suppress it, just for a little while, until she knew the Carters were safe.

Chapter 16

When they reached Roswell, Veronica pulled the car into a truck stop and parked. Before she turned to the Carters, she stopped glowing blue and put her human face back on.

"I'm sorry you had to see that," Veronica said.

"What the hell is going on here?!" Leslie shouted. "Rock people! Lasers! You two turning into blue streaks of light! And you blew up our car!"

Debra wiped her tears and turned to them. She closed her eyes. Slowly her human face came back, and she stopped glowing.

"I will tell you the truth," Debra said. "We're aliens. We've been here for nearly twenty years, but we are peaceful."

"Peaceful my ass!" Bill said. "You blew up my car!"

"Because we had to," Debra said. "To escape the Globorians."

"Globorians?" Joshy said. "Is that what those things were?"

"Yes," Veronica said. "They are a vile race of aliens bent on conquering the galaxy."

"There are multiple races of aliens?" Carole said.

"Hundreds," Veronica said. "Thousands, even. Surprise."

"And what was that place you took us to?" Leslie said. "Were they supposed to kill us all?"

"No," Debra said, shaking her head. "They were supposed to wipe your memory of us. It was to protect you.

Otherwise, you would have been in danger the rest of your lives."

"But why?" Leslie asked. "It's not like we even knew-"

She stopped her sentence when her eyes connected with Joshy's, and he quickly turned them away from her.

"You knew," Leslie said. "This whole time, you knew?"

"Not the whole time," he replied. "I've known since the Grand Canyon when they kidnapped me."

"You kidnapped my son!" Bill said.

"That's ridiculous!" Veronica said. "We kept him here under our watchful gaze, to make sure he didn't say anything stupid."

"That's not much better," Carole said.

"I know," Veronica replied. "But here is the truth. It will be not pleasant to hear, but it will be the truth. You can't go home. The Globorians are looking for you. They know who you are and think you are a threat to their plan. They will kill you on sight. We are your only chance to stay alive."

"Says you," Carole said. "The ones who kidnapped my son."

"Look," Debra said. "He's fine. He even liked most of it."

"I did like most of it," Joshy replied.

"Shut up, you," Leslie said, disgusted.

"What else aren't you telling us?" Bill asked.

Veronica sighed. "Your planet will be invaded by Globorians on Labor Day. They have infiltrated every seat of power in the world. They have spent the last hundred years slowly taking over every sector of the planet. They filled your Congress, your governors' mansions, and your police departments. When their homeworld gives the word, the battlecruisers will appear, and they will take over. It will not take long. You will be slaves. You will be killed. There is nothing you can do about it."

"That is a grim picture," Bill said. "If that's true, we have to warn everyone."

"It's no use," Debra said. "You can't stop them. If you try, they will destroy you."

"However," Veronica said, sighing. "We can help you."

"I think we've had enough of your help," Carole replied.

"Mom!" Joshy snapped. "Hear them out."

"We can get you off the planet before the invasion. We have a ship. We can drop you at the nearest habitable planet with life on it. It's not ideal, but at least you won't be slaves."

"And the rest of the world?" Joshy said.

"We can save you," Debra said. "That is all we can promise."

Bill sighed. "We're going to need some time."

*

The Carter family asked Debra and Veronica to leave the camper so they could talk. They were close to kicking Joshy out of the camper too, but Joshy mentioned that if his father could destroy their family credit and still get a vote, he should, too.

"Great," Carole mumbled. "What is with the men in this family?"

"Snakes," Leslie added. "Both of them."

They talked for over an hour, and then an hour more. However, finally, after a bitter and contentious fight, they settled on a resolution. Meanwhile, Debra mourned her father and Veronica for her lost love. There would be time to give a proper ceremony when they were further from Roswell, but for now, they had to keep level heads.

Joshy spoke for his family as they lined up around Debra and Veronica. "Are you telling the truth?"

Debra stood up and looked into his eyes. "I'm telling the truth. I swear to you."

"Then, we will go with you, but we have to tell the world first."

"That's...not possible," Debra replied.

Joshy grabbed Debra's hands. "There are aliens on Earth, and I'm dating one. Everything is possible. Promise me you'll try, and we'll go with you."

"Don't do us any favors," Veronica said.

"Mom!" Debra shouted, before turning back to him. "I promise, if there's a way to tell the world, we'll find it. This is a futile mission, though, you know that."

"Sure," Joshy said. "But that's my deal. Take it or leave it."

Debra smiled at Joshy's forthrightness and gave him a kiss. "I'll take it."

This was a stupid idea. One of the stupidest ideas in the entire universe, and she couldn't wait to see how it turned out.

Book 2

"Invasion"

Chapter 1

A week ago, Joshy Carter didn't know aliens existed. Two days ago, he thought there were only a few aliens on his planet. Then, he watched his girlfriend's father get disintegrated by a Globorian laser gun, and he found out that there are tons of different types of aliens, and they aren't all good, either.

It was a lot for poor Joshy to handle. He wasn't known for his ability to handle tough situations. That was why he liked video games so much. They allowed him his only respite from the awful responsibility of making important decisions, like whether to go to college or when to look for a job. In video games, Joshy was a decision-making machine, but he didn't much like them when his decisions had real-life consequences.

"Let's go," his father said to Joshy as he was making the final adjustments to the tie he was trying to get right in the camper mirror. "We're going to be late."

Joshy's father hadn't known about aliens until the moment Darryl exploded in front of him, and a hundred Globorians chased him across the desert. He certainly didn't know that his son was dating one, nor that in her true form, Debra was little more than a blue streak of light.

"I'll be there in a second," Joshy said, with a deep sigh. He had been trying to tie his tie for fifteen minutes and couldn't get it right.

Joshy didn't like funerals. That didn't make him special among humans. There were not many humans alive who enjoyed funerals. However, Joshy was unique in that in his eighteen years he had never before been to a funeral. Perhaps unique was the wrong word. Lucky would be more appropriate.

Most humans had to deal with death before they turned eighteen years old. However, Joshy's family members either died long before he was born or were still alive and healthy, which made Joshy abnormal in the human race, one of whose main functions was to eventually die. If Joshy had friends, it might have been possible that they would have had deaths in their family, but friendship was not something Joshy had, outside of his family and his new alien girlfriend.

Joshy and his family had been living with Debra and Veronica in their RV for the last two days since they'd been attacked by Globorians at an army base outside Roswell. The attack ended in Bill's car being blown up and Darryl being evaporated by a Globorian laser. It had been a tense situation for two aliens and four humans to live in such a small space, especially after such a traumatic event; familiarity bred contempt. However, there was nothing they could do about it, at least not at the moment.

Outside of the RV bathroom, Joshy's sister Leslie stood in a knee-length black dress, angrily tapping her foot. She did not like her current living situation at all. While she'd agreed to travel across the country with her family, she hadn't intended to be stuck in a camper with aliens, nor attend a funeral for one of them.

Still, it kept her mind off college and the crippling reality that her family could no longer pay for her schooling. Her father took that option away when he lost his job and nearly bankrupted them trying to pretend everything was okay.

"We've been waiting long enough," Leslie said. "What were you doing in there?"

"I can't really tie a tie," Joshy said. "I finally gave up."

"You're an eighteen-year-old man who can't tie a tie," Leslie said with a sigh. "You're hopeless."

"It's never come up before."

"Let's go," his father said, opening the side door to the camper. "Leave the tie. It's not important. We're going to be late."

Bill was happy that things were starting to feel normal with his family. After all, it had only been a week since he'd revealed to his wife that their life savings were spent, and they would likely lose their house. Carole was madder than he had ever seen her before, but the discovery of aliens and their impending need to escape Earth seemed to flush his transgressions to the back of her mind.

"About time," Carole said, as Joshy came out of the bathroom and tossed his tie back in his father's suitcase. "We've been waiting forever."

Carole was trying the best she could to process the fact that there were aliens, they were out to kill her, and that one of them had died. She felt as though her brain had melted two days ago and was now functioning with only a brain stem, on autopilot, until things calmed down.

The Carters had been on the run for two days, ever since the great rock monsters of the Globorian race chased them from a base outside of Roswell, New Mexico. Joshy's girlfriend Debra and her mother Veronica helped them escape, and she appreciated their hospitality as much as she resented it. Maybe Carole should have thanked them for saving her family's life. However, they were the reason her family was in harm's way to begin with, so she was conflicted.

Joshy pushed open the camper door. He led his family across the parking lot to the wood trail that would lead them up to the top of a hillside where Darryl's funeral would be held. There was nothing left of Debra's father to mourn, but she bought a little cross anyway to mark the solemn occasion. Debra held it in her hand as she stood at the bottom of the trail waiting for them.

"About time," Debra said. Maybe she should have been mad at him for taking his time, but she had no interest in what awaited her at the top of the hill.

Debra didn't mind having the Carters around, except that they smelled like humans, and as the days progressed without a shower that smell ripened until it was close to unbearable. Still, she felt responsible for their predicament and felt compelled to keep them safe. The Globorians wanted them dead, and if she left them to their own devices, they would be found and disintegrated within a day. Humans really were hopeless, even though she liked them quite a bit, especially Joshy.

Joshy wasn't much to look at, but he wasn't all that horrible either. He was plain, like vanilla ice cream. Some people love vanilla ice cream, but it doesn't win any awards because vanilla ice cream is just…kind of boring. Even though Debra was a beautiful alien who literally radiated sunlight and he was some shlub from Los Angeles, she liked him all the same.

"Are you ready?" Joshy said, walking up to Debra.

Debra shook her head. "Not at all."

Joshy clasped his fingers around hers and squeezed. "You only have to do this once, ever."

"Is that supposed to make me feel better?"

"I don't know. I'm not really good at knowing what to say, so I guess, yes? I mean—"

Joshy didn't have to finish before Debra kissed him. It wasn't a passionate kiss, or a particularly good one, but still, Joshy enjoyed it. He didn't have much comparison, having never had a girlfriend before, so pretty much any kiss was the best of his life.

When Debra broke off her kiss, she was crying. It had been happening since her father died. She tried to swallow her emotions, but they couldn't help but bubble up.

"Are you okay?" Joshy asked.

She shook her head and dug her head into Joshy's shirt. She sobbed into his shoulder as he cradled her in his arms. His family passed by him and walked up the trail where Veronica waited for them to begin the service. Try as she might, Debra couldn't move her legs to join them. Joshy didn't mind, though, if they were late. He could hold Debra all day.

*

Joshy and Debra took their time walking up the hill to the funeral, enjoying each other's company. The funeral would be a small affair, of course, consisting of the six of them. Debra had taken her father's death as well as could be expected, given the circumstances. Almost all Thimberians made it to at least five hundred years old while some even lived to be a thousand years old.

Which meant even in a short life, Debra had anticipated another two hundred years with her father. She expected to leave Earth with him and explore other galaxies. She expected to hear his stories over and over again, ad nauseum, outwardly complaining that she'd listened to his tales a hundred times while inwardly taking comfort in them and him.

But that never happened. Debra only knew her father for eighteen very short years of her exceedingly long life, and she was not ready to lose him. When parents aged, it became more likely that they would die, but at least there was time to prepare for it. That didn't make their death any easier, but at least a long life made it more bearable to lose them.

Debra didn't have any of that. She wished she could tell her father how much she loved him and how much she would miss him. It wouldn't have done anything to change his death, but at least it would have made her feel better about it.

"Can we stop here for a second?" Debra asking, listening to the crunch of the funeral procession as their feet stomped on the leaves in front of her.

"Sure," Joshy said, letting go of Debra's hand. "Anything."

Debra sighed, wiping the tears from her eyes. "This is so stupid. I don't understand why I have to go up there and grieve with everybody else. Dad isn't up there. He's in the ether. He's returned to the universe."

Thimberians believed that the universe created them and when they died their molecules returned to the universe to be used again. In this way, their beliefs were very much in line with Buddhism but without all the suffering at its center.

Joshy squeezed her shoulder. "We don't have to go. Your mother will understand."

Debra batted Joshy's hand away from her shoulder. "No, she won't. She won't understand anything."

"I mean, she understands something. This is her husband like it's your father."

"It's not the same," Debra said.

"You're right. It's probably harder for her," Joshy said with a gulp.

"What?!" Debra said, flinging out her hands to push him. "How can you say that?"

"Well, think about it. You knew him for eighteen years, but she knew him for hundreds, right? I mean, she built a life with him. She traveled the universe with him. She thought she would grow old with him, and now…he's dead."

Joshy wasn't good with words, but these socked Debra in the gut. "I'd never thought about it like that."

Joshy shrugged. "That's okay. Everybody's entitled to be selfish about this kind of stuff. If you want to bail, let's bail."

Debra wrapped her arms around Joshy and pushed forward. "No. I want to keep going."

Joshy started forward, enjoying Debra's shoulder pressed against his side. "Who do you think was the best death in comics?"

"Hmmm," Debra said. "Is it silly to say Superman? Cuz I still think Death of Superman was awesome."

"There are thousands of deaths in comics, especially in DC comics, and you picked the most cliché one of all time. I mean that death was literally tailor-made to get more readers."

"All deaths are like that, Josh. I mean, literally every death in comics was designed to get readers."

"What about Uncle Ben? That happened in the first issue of the comic."

"Yeah, as part of Spider-man's tragic back story…to help get readers. How many times has that been recreated in comics and in film? Like hundreds?"

"Sure, okay. Well, how about Barry Allen in Crisis? That may have been to get readers, but the Flash's death was a way better than Superman's."

"He ran really fast until he died. He died by running. Ugh. It makes me hate running"

"And that's why I will never run again. Running is dangerous, yo, and Barry Allen proved that fact for all time."

Debra smiled. "But he came back, too, and he saved a lot of lives by running. What about that, hot shot?"

"I choose to ignore that fact," Joshy replied.

There was a long silence as they continued to walk. Joshy felt Debra's chest heave against his arm. It wasn't long before he heard her sniffling, and then outright bawling against his arm. He didn't know what to do, but inadvertently, he was doing the exact right thing, by being there, and letting Debra grieve.

Chapter 2

Veronica stood at the top of the hill in Mark Twain National Forest outside of St. Louis. The city sprawled below them in the distance. There were thousands of people bustling through its streets, but here, in seclusion, Veronica was safe to take her true form, that of a blue beam of light that glittered and glowed. She was no more svelte in her original form than in her human one, and though she could stretch to any length, she preferred to be squat, round and close to the ground. Darryl, her husband, gods rest his soul, preferred her that way, too, because it was the way she was happiest.

When Debra finally reached the top of the hill, Veronica hugged her daughter, and together they pushed the white, wooden cross into the ground. For a moment, they cried as a family. Then, Debra pushed off the ground and stood with Joshy, leaving Veronica to carry on with the eulogy alone.

"My husband," Veronica said, letting out a deep breath before she started her eulogy. Debra and the Carter family looked back at her, standing in silence, waiting for her to continue. "Was the greatest being I ever knew. He was kind, and polite, and courteous. He loved so deeply that often I thought I would be suffocated by his affection, but I never complained, because I loved him as much. His love filled our home, and our lives. I was not so warm and welcoming before I met Darryl. I had been through a lot, and thrown up my own barriers, both literally and figuratively."

Veronica swallowed deeply. "Darryl didn't care that it took me time to open up. He was gentle and understanding. He knew my pain, and he let me cope in my own way. He made me better than I ever thought I could be without him.

I will think of him whenever I do good in the galaxy because that is what he wanted. He wanted to do good."

Debra couldn't control her emotions anymore, and as her mother spoke, she dropped her human facade and turned into a blue beam of light as well, collapsing into Joshy's arms. She had never heard her mother talk about her father with such passion before, and suddenly, she realized that her father was more than one thing. He was a complete being, with hopes and dreams that extended far beyond her life, and she wept because she would never know that person.

"I know that might sound weird," Veronica continued, turning her attention directly to Carole. "Coming from me, a woman you only know because my husband kidnapped your son, but it was always his hope that he was doing good and doing it for the right reasons. He had a strict code of ethics that followed him always, and he never broke that, even to his last moments."

Veronica dropped her luminous head. "Look what it got him, in the end."

Veronica collapsed in a crying fit, and Debra flew forward to catch her. Leaning against her shoulder, Debra dragged her mother toward the Carters and sat her on the ground where she could overlook the mountains.

"This sucks," Debra said, hovering in the air. "We don't even have a body or a molecule to send into the ether. My father evaporated into dust, right in front of our eyes, and it's okay to say that's not okay. I don't know if I'll ever be okay again, frankly, and that is also okay, I guess…but this really sucks, and I don't want to be here anymore. Can we please go get food now?"

*

On the way down the mountain, Leslie joined Debra and Joshy in the front of the pack as they hurried toward the camper. Bill and Carole held Veronica together as they walked behind their progeny. Debra couldn't deal with her mother, right now. She had to put herself together first, and she hoped her mother would understand that.

"Good speech," Leslie said. "It was very…Garden State of you."

"It's true, though," Debra said. "This whole thing just…sucks. We were supposed to be off-world in a couple of weeks, and you were supposed to be home…"

"Yeah," Leslie said. "I'm not actually sure being on the run with aliens is worse than being home right now."

"We're not even sure we have a home to go back to, honestly," Joshy added.

There was a relatively good chance that everything Joshy owned was out on the curb right now, except what he had in his backpack. However, that didn't matter, because soon they would be off-world as well since Veronica had offered to take them with her when they left the planet with Debra.

"What do you think it's like, being off-world?" Leslie said.

"I don't know," Debra replied. "I've never been to space before, but I hope it's as trippy as Meow Wolf, with neon plants and animals all over the place, including a ton we couldn't even imagine."

"I hope they have good schools on whatever planet we end up on," Leslie said.

"You would really go to school?" Joshy said. "You have a whole universe to explore, and you'd choose school?"

"Well yeah," Leslie replied. "I mean, how else are we gonna learn about our new planet's history without seeming like idiots."

"That sounds horrible," Joshy said. "I'm not doing that."

"There's a whole school for aliens," Debra said. "Whatever planet we end up on, you'll have to enroll and take at least the basic classes."

"Did you have to do that?" Joshy said.

Debra shook her head. "No, but this was my first planet. Mom and...Dad...did though. It's the only way they'll let you stay."

"Can't you just...sneak in?" Joshy asked.

"Sure," Debra said. "But any planet worth living on will have some sort of immigration policy. You don't want to be undocumented. Then, you have no rights."

"Fine," Joshy said. "I guess we're going to school."

Leslie tried to hide her grin, but she really loved school. She was sad there wasn't much time before she would be done with school forever, but now it made her happy that she had a whole new world to investigate. That would mean years more research. Leaving Earth was not a fun thought, but at least she had that to look forward to.

Bill, on the other hand, couldn't wait to leave Earth. He had screwed up his life enough that he would probably never recover, so if wiping the slate clean meant he could start over and his family wouldn't have to be saddled with his horrible decisions, he was all for it.

Carole didn't agree, of course. She had roots on Earth and leaving it wasn't like moving cities or even countries. Carole would never be able to see her friends again. She would never be able to see her cousins again. She would never be able to see her mother again…although, that last one didn't mean that much to her. In fact, never having to deal with her mother or her in-laws again almost made up for having to leave Earth.

"I miss my husband," Veronica said sadly as she stumbled down the hill, being held by Carole and Bill on either arm. "He was a good man. He didn't deserve to die."

"I know," Carole said, looking over at her own husband. Darryl's death made her appreciate her own husband more. She wasn't willing to forgive him for destroying their life, but at least she could admit she would miss him if he died, which was something. Not much of something, but a little something none the less.

*

Debra and Joshy sat away from their families as they ate their eggs and pancakes. It's not that they didn't like their families, it was just that they had plans that their families couldn't hear about; clandestine plans hatched in the dark of night.

"Are you sure about this?" Joshy asked, rubbing Debra's hand.

"No," Debra replied. "But I can't let my dad's death be in vain."

"You realize he was trying to wipe my family's memories, right?" Joshy asked. "I don't think he would be gung-ho about you revealing yourself to the world."

Debra took a bite of her pancakes. "Maybe not. But he would be gung-ho about me doing the right thing, and this is the right thing."

"Your life is never going to be the same again."

"My life will never be the same again no matter what I do," she said, raising her eyes to meet Joshy's. "That is a guarantee."

Joshy didn't know what else to say. It was his idea to show the world that Debra was an alien on Facebook Live, but he questioned whether it was the right move, even as she grew more and more adamant about doing it. Debra resisted his plan at first, but the more her mother fretted about being found out, the more Debra knew it was the right choice to make.

She knew her mother was looking out for her safety, but she had to look out for her adopted home. Unlike her mother, she had never known a world except for Earth, and she felt a deep bond with it. It was the planet she was born on, and the one where she'd watched her father die. Everything she had ever experienced was on Earth, and she couldn't let it be destroyed by the Globorians.

*

"Alright," Veronica said, pulling her car into park on a small suburban street. "Now remember, these are only family friends. They are doing us a favor taking all of us in for the night."

"If they're such good friends," Debra said. "Why didn't they come to Dad's funeral?"

Veronica looked up at her, tears in her eyes. "Because they couldn't okay? But they can do this for us. Maybe one night out of this camper will have you in better spirits."

Joshy couldn't wait to get out of the camper. It smelt of BO something fierce, and being in a confined space with his family put everyone on edge. The only thing that saved them from themselves was the thought that Darryl was dead, and their somber reflections kept them from lashing out at each other too much.

The families filed out of the camper and followed Veronica to the front door of the little, blue ranch house with white shutters. A welcome mat featuring a festive pumpkin sat in front of the red lacquered door.

Veronica rang the doorbell. "Remember, best behavior."

She didn't know who she was talking to, but it was a thing she felt she needed to say. The Carters were extremely polite and quiet during the car ride, almost scarily so, but their emotions were at a boiling point. They were monkeys, after all, and thus didn't have her capacity for internalizing emotions.

She had not known them long, and now she was introducing them to her dear friends, the Martins. She needed it to go well, and she needed the Carters to stay calm when they learned that her friends were aliens, too.

However, she had nothing to worry about with the Carters; they already assumed that any friend of an alien would be an alien, too. They hoped it was the friendly kind, preferably not ugly like the Globorians, either. That was a secondary concern, though, to not wanting Veronica's friends not ripping off their faces or trying to disintegrate them.

Chapter 3

"You're here!!!!!!" Maddie Martin screamed as she opened the door to her house and wrapped Veronica in a big hug. "I know you said you would be here, but now you're actually here! In the flesh, no less. Come in, come in, come in!"

Maddie waved the group inside. Maddie was larger than life in every way. She had huge hair, huge eyelashes, and a huge personality. She made huge gestures with her hands and laughed too loudly for polite company. She wore too much make-up and blathered on constantly. She was 100% extra, and Joshy loved it.

"And you must be the rest of the gang. Let me guess," Maddie said, pointing her finger at Debra. "You must be Deb. I haven't seen you since you were a little baby. You are still adorable, but a lot less blue than I remember."

Debra chuckled uncomfortably as Maddie wrapped her arms around her. "Yeah. The blue is still in there, though, below the surface."

Maddie patted Debra on the back with her long fingernails. "Sorry, sweetheart. They're still drying, but love!" Maddie kissed Debra on both cheeks, leaving lipstick behind when she pulled away from her.

"And you all," Maddie circled her fingers around Joshy and his family. "You must be the Carters. I'm gonna guess the older ones are Bill and Carole and the younger ones, well you must be Leslie and Joshy!"

"Josh," Joshy replied. He wasn't going to start a new relationship being called Joshy. "Please"

"Oh, I'm sorry. Josh. What a big man. Look at you. Come here!" Maddie lunged and flung her arms around Joshy. "You are a strong one, yes, you are."

She went on like that for five more minutes, greeting each member of Joshy's family in kind before she finally smiled and placed her hands on her hip. "We are gonna have so much fun." She turned her head upstairs. "Ted! Get down here."

"I'm busy!" a gruff voice replied. Ted hated guests, no matter who they were, because it meant he had to wear his human façade, and he hated humanity.

"I don't care! We have guests!!!"

"We'll have guests in fifteen minutes too!" Ted yelled. "Leave me be!"

Maddie smiled a sad smile. "You know what, he'll be along any minute, or he won't. Meanwhile, let's get you some food."

Veronica tried to tell her that they'd already eaten, but it was no use. Maddie was a force of nature, and it was easier to turn into the skid of her than to fight her.

*

Maddie made too much food, as was her custom. She loved to cook, and Ted usually liked to eat, so it was a match made in Heaven. She liked to talk, and he liked to listen, or at least not talk even if he was zoning out, which was fine with Maddie, as long as she had the floor. She didn't really care if people listened to her, as long as they were around to hear her talk and acknowledge her existence.

"So," Joshy said, eating a chicken wing even though he was super full. "What kind of alien are you?"

"Joshy!" Carole admonished. "That's rude."

Maddie laughed. "No. It's fine. Ted and I are Ayirian. We were born from the fire of the sun Ayir when it cast off its excess radiation ten million years ago."

"Ten million years?" Leslie said. "That's a long time. A lot longer than humanity's been around."

Maddie smiled. "Oh yes, we're one of the oldest races in the galaxy. We were ancient when the Thimberians were babies."

Maddie liked to hold that over Veronica's head. She wouldn't say that she was better than Veronica, or any other race, but she would think it loudly, and she would say words that implied she was better than everybody else, but she wouldn't flat out say it, because that would be rude.

"And yet," Veronica said with a smile. "Here we both are, on Earth, in the last days before the Globorian invasion."

"Yes," Maddie replied. "Unfortunately, Ted is upstairs fixing a piece of our ship that's been giving us trouble. We were supposed to be gone months ago, but we just…couldn't find the right part. I mean, do you know how hard it is to find an intergalactic ship part in this quadrant of the galaxy?"

Veronica laughed. "Yes, I do—"

But Maddie didn't listen to, or want, Veronica's answer. She kept on with her story. "I mean, we went to twenty different parts traders, but none of them had the right part, you know? It was crazy. We were about to give up, when Teddy saw the carburetor of a 1957 Chevy Bel Air on TV and thought that he could mold it to fit. Isn't that crazy?"

"It's definitely crazy," Debra said, putting down the last remnants of a hot dog. She wasn't hungry, but she would miss Earth food, especially American food, when she was off among the stars, so she wanted to get her fill while she could.

"And how long have you been on Earth?" Carole asked, nibbling on corn on the cob.

"Not long. A hundred years or so."

"And that's not long?" Bill asked.

"Well, when you live to be five thousand, a hundred years is barely anything, you know? Ayirians have some of the longest lifespans in the universe. Why, I'm barely a baby by my planet's standards."

"What is the best thing you've seen, then?" Leslie asked, pushing away her plate. "What planet do we have to see when we're out among the stars?"

"We?" Maddie said, confused.

"Yeah," Leslie replied. "We're going up there, too, into space. I'm actually really excited about it. I was bummed at first, but then I realized how awesome it will be to explore new civilizations, like Star Trek, and now I'm excited."

Maddie's eyes narrowed. "Quite."

Leslie didn't know it, but it was illegal for aliens to take Earth people off world for any reasons. It was part of the immigration agreement aliens signed before they were allowed to immigrate to Earth, and Veronica was about to violate it.

*

"It can't be done," Maddie said, cleaning up dinner with her mind by telekinetically bringing plates to the sink, where she animated a sponge that cleaned it for her.

"I know," Veronica said. "But they were there when my Darryl—they don't deserve to be captured and enslaved."

"None of these people on Earth do," Maddie replied. "However, that doesn't change the fact that we can't do anything about it. We signed a pact. If you defy it, no civilized star system will ever let you inside their borders."

Three of the Carters sat in the living room, watching The Good Place on television and laughing, as if nothing was wrong in the world, even though everything was wrong. Debra and Joshy sat outside, on the back porch, watching the lightning bugs fly by.

"It's not fair. Maybe if a planet doesn't accept refugees, they don't deserve to be visited."

"Is that what you really believe?" Maddie asked, her mind pulling more plates of the table and stuffing them in the dishwasher. "Get it together, Veronica. How many times have you given this advice the other way when an alien came and told you they were taking a human off-world?"

Veronica sighed. "Too many to count. But I was wrong then like you're wrong now. It's not a bad thing to help these people. They are good people."

"Maybe," Maddie replied. "But they aren't sophisticated enough for intergalactic travel. No human is. Look at you. You're a thousand times smarter than these monkeys, and even you couldn't keep your secret while you were here. What chance do they have of not being arrested as aliens and ruining it for the rest of us?"

"These humans might surprise you."

Maddie nodded. "They might, but they won't. At the end of the day, they still evolved from monkeys, which evolved from fish, and that means they will only be so smart. I'm sorry, but you can't do it. I'm telling you this as your friend. Bring them to the ship, and then abandon them there."

"That's cruel!" Veronica said, almost loud enough for the others to hear.

"It's not cruel," Maddie replied, putting the last of the dishes in the sink. "This is survival of the fittest, Veronica. You and I are fit to travel. They are not. Thus, we will survive, and they will not. Do the right thing, if not for you, then at least for Debra."

"How is abandoning them the right thing?"

"Because it's the right thing for the universe."

*

Joshy and Debra sat outside looking up at the stars until the rest of their family went to bed. The Carters slept on couches in the living room, while Veronica took the guest room upstairs. Once all the lights were finally off throughout the house, Debra took her head off Joshy's chest and stood up.

"I think they're asleep," Debra said with a whisper.

"Are you sure you want to do this?" Joshy said. "Once we do it, there is no turning back."

Debra nodded. "It's the only way, right? I mean, nobody is going to believe us otherwise."

Joshy nodded. "Hand me your phone. This is going to work better on your feed since they all know you."

Debra dug into her pocket and pulled out her phone. She swiped open the screen and opened the Facebook app. She typed, *I am an alien,* into the live video screen and handed it to Joshy.

"Alright," Debra said with a deep breath. "Go."

Joshy tapped the *Go Live* button at the bottom of the screen, and it counted down until Debra would be live. Then, the screen brightened, and her feed lit up. Joshy nodded and gave her the thumbs up.

"Hello friends, family, neighbors," she started. "I have never done live video before, but there is something you have to see."

Two people watched her feed, and then four, eight, twenty-four, and thirty. Likes popped on the right of the screen as she talked, and even more people joined the feed.

"I don't want you to freak out, but I am an alien. My parents came to Earth decades ago, and while I was born here, I am a Thimberian by DNA."

Debra closed her eyes, and her skin melted away, revealing the blue underneath. She shimmered and glistened in the moonlight, which amplified her glowing aura. On screen, fifty people now watched, hearts popping all over the screen, and typing bubbles started to form.

Where did you get that dope filter?

How did you do that?

Man, the effects on Facebook are awesome NOW!!!!

Josh typed back. *This is not an effect. I am really an alien.*

Twenty people liked it immediately, but he could tell by their laughing emojis they did not believe her.

"I chose to tell you now because by the end of the summer your planet will be invaded by Globorians. They have already taken over all important government posts. They control your military, your police, and every seat of power in the country, maybe the world. You will be enslaved if you do not stand up and fight back. Please share this as much as you can with as many people as you can."

Debra turned back into her human form as the feed ended. "How did we do?"

Joshy turned the phone to her. "I don't think you are going to like it."

Debra scrolled through two dozen comments that asked her about the filter she used, and twenty telling her what a great joke that it was. Seven people wanted to know when the show she pitched was coming out because they would totally watch it, and only three people shared it.

"They didn't believe me," Debra said.

The light flipped on from her mother's room, and Veronica glared down at her. She had never seen her mother so mad in all her life.

Chapter 4

"I can't believe you would put yourself in that kind of position!" Veronica screamed from the kitchen. Her yelling had woken up the rest of the house. Bill, Leslie, and Carole sat groggily around the kitchen table, glaring at Debra and Joshy for ruining their sleep and jeopardizing their lives.

"I'm sorry, mom, but we didn't think you were going to help us," Debra said, careful not to catch her mother's eyes.

"Of course, I wouldn't have helped you do something so stupid," Veronica said. "Now, give me your phone."

"MOM!" Debra said. "You're being irrational."

"And you're being ridiculous," Veronica said forcefully, holding out her hand.

Debra slammed the phone onto her mother's hand. Veronica forced Debra to give her fingerprint authentication on her phone. It only took a couple seconds for Veronica to open Debra's phone and delete the live video from her Facebook stream.

"There," Veronica said, placing the phone down. "Now, it doesn't matter. Aside from a few people on your feed, nobody will be the wiser."

"It's not like they believed us anyway," Joshy said. "Everybody thought it was a joke."

"Good," Carole replied.

"It's not good," Joshy said. "People need to know about this."

"I know they do," Bill said. "But there's a time and a place—"

"Yeah," Debra said. "You've said that a dozen times. We're going to be off-planet in a couple days, and there won't be a chance to help them after that. Don't you want to help them? Don't you even care?"

Veronica looked over at her friends. Maddie had made a compelling case for abandoning Joshy's family. So compelling that she decided that she wouldn't bring them along, but Veronica couldn't tell them yet. Debra would revolt. No, she had to get them as close to the landing site as possible. Then, she could make her move, reveal the truth, and force Debra into their ship before she could protest.

"Of course we care," Veronica replied. "We just want to do it the right way."

"There is no right way," Joshy replied. "There's only the way we're doing it. It's going to be messy. It's going to be ugly."

"It's easy for you to say that," Carole said. "You're a kid, but that's not how it works, kiddo. There's always a right way."

"This whole trip has been wrong way after wrong way," Debra said. "We weren't supposed to meet in Vegas. Joshy wasn't supposed to follow me to the Grand Canyon. We weren't supposed to travel across New Mexico together. None of this is the right way, and yet...here we are. Sometimes the wrong way can be beautiful, so beautiful that it can become the right way."

"No," Bill said. "Those are nice words, but that's all they are. We're trying to look out for your safety here."

"We have to tell people," Joshy said. "Before it's too late."

"We'll tell people when the time is right," Bill said. "And that is final."

*

Joshy listened to his parent's condescending speech until they talked themselves tired, then went upstairs to brush his teeth. He was about to switch from his upper canines to his lower when he saw Leslie's shadow flash past the door.

"What do you want?" he asked, before spitting out his toothpaste into the sink.

"Hey," Leslie said, leaning on the doorjamb. "I thought it was cool what you did."

"Yeah?" Joshy said. "Fat lot of good it did us."

"Yeah, because you are thinking too small. Check this out."

Leslie pulled out her phone and turned it to Joshy. On screen was a young couple sitting between two red ferns talking to each other. The video looked like crap, as if they were using a 1980s handicam to record themselves, but their feed was being seen by over a thousand people.

"What is this?" Joshy asked his sister.

"One of my favorite public access shows is filmed right here in St. Louis. They're always recording, and their station is only a few miles away. You get Debra on that show, and there's nothing that any of our parents can do about it."

"So, what, we're going to crash a TV station? Who's to say they'll even let us on?"

"I know Thom a little bit from my model UN days. I whooped him really good in a debate once. It was awesome. We still talk sometimes. He'll let Debra on air if you've got a compelling story, and you've got a compelling story."

"So what, like a thousand college kids are watching this right now? It's not really national news."

"Maybe not," Leslie replied. "But you have to start somewhere. Sometimes, they'll break something that gets picked up by bigger outlets, and this could be one of those things."

"It's a pretty good idea, I guess," Joshy said. "But if we go, you have to come with us."

"No way," Leslie said. "I'm not about to get in trouble for you."

"It's not for me, Les. It's for humanity."

Leslie grumbled under her breath. She knew Joshy was right. "I hate you."

"What's going on in here?" Debra asked as she walked into the bathroom. "Something nefarious I hope."

"Leslie has a halfway decent plan," Joshy replied. "It's a long shot, but it's the best shot we got."

"It's probably stupid," Les replied.

"Way to go, Les," Debra said. "Stupid plans are the best."

"I'm warning you that it's kinda dangerous," Leslie said. "And our parents will be pissed."

"They're already pissed at me and Josh. You can only be so pissed until you've reached max pissed. There are, at best, logarithmic gains in anger after that. Whatever it is, I say we go for it."

*

It took Leslie, Debra, and Joshy over an hour to walk the four miles to the public access station. They argued vigorously about stealing the camper, but in the end, none of them were comfortable driving something so large, so they decided to walk instead. Besides, it was a nice night, and they only had a couple of days left on Earth, so they might as well enjoy the night air while they could.

"I'm going to miss humidity," Debra said as she walked along the side of the road.

"That's a weird thing to miss," Leslie replied.

"Well, when you're cooped up in a spaceship for years flying from one planet to the next, you'll miss it, too."

"Wait, years?" Leslie said.

"Well, yeah," Debra replied. "A spaceship only goes so fast, Les. This isn't Star Trek where we can traverse star systems in hours."

Leslie hadn't realized that it might take years for them to reach another habitable planet. "What do you do on a spaceship for years?"

"I dunno," Debra replied. "I've never been on one. But that's why we have such long lives, at least that's what dad used to say, so we can waste some traveling between the stars."

"We don't have such long lives," Leslie replied. "I think our max life expectancy is 120 years."

"Well, we better make the next planet count then," Debra replied, stepping up on a curb and trying to balance herself.

"What if it isn't nice?" Leslie said. "What if we want to leave?"

"Well, you gotta factor that in, don't you? One reason we've been here so long is because my parents thought learning more about you was more important than spending a decade locked in a spaceship."

"A decade!" Leslie said. She clearly hadn't thought through the implications of space travel.

"Well, yeah. I mean, it's not like we have an Inkarian ship. Ours putters along a bit below light speed, but it'll get there eventually."

The Inkarians were the most advanced race in the galaxy, and the geniuses behind most of humanity's most famous inventions, including wireless technology and the hamburger. However, they never came to Earth to witness their technology in action because it was a backwater hamlet without any notable scientific minds, and they detested places like that. They did, however, barter their technology with other races.

In the case of Earth, Inkarians bartered with the Globorians, handing them all the tech necessary to enslave Earth and make it halfway livable for other races. However, Globorians were not very good at construction, which was why advances like nuclear fusion never became a reality, and why the CERN supercollider still hadn't produced the appropriate particles to make time travel possible. However, they were able to make tech function well enough to make drastic technological advances to the planet using Inkarian tech.

"So my parents will be over sixty when they get to another habitable planet?" Leslie asked, hopping up onto the curb.

"Well, yeah," Debra said, sticking her arms out as she wobbled to either side of the curb. "But sixty is the new forty, and space travel adds years to your life."

"What if you don't have that many years left? Do they chuck you out of a hatch and keep going?"

Debra shrugged. "I wish I knew, but this will be my first flight. I know more than you, but only by a fraction of a percentage."

Leslie nodded. That might have been true, but to her that fraction was everything. Until a couple days ago, she thought she would live her whole life on Earth, so the thought of traveling through space blew her mind.

*

The public access station Thom and his crew used was little more than a whitewashed warehouse with an antenna coming out of the roof. There was no fancy lobby or even sufficient lighting.

Debra, Joshy, and Leslie walked inside to the main studio, where a wall of monitors and two cameras were set up in front of a tiny set. Overhead lights shone on two chairs situated between two red ferns. Leslie's friend Thom and his co-host Phyllis sat on the chairs between the ferns, talking to each other.

"If you truly want to understand the value of late-stage capitalism," Thom said. "Look no further than Kellogg's."

Thom had big, coiffed hair, perfect for television, with a smile that showed his glistening white teeth every time he spoke. He wore a tailored blue suit and a red tie. Joshy was immediately jealous of his tie dimple and how perfectly it hung around his neck.

"Don't bring that trite late-stage capitalist nonsense up to me," Phyllis replied, shaking her long black hair as she talked. Phyllis wore thick red lipstick that accentuated every word from her mouth and a black pencil skirt that stopped right above her knee. "If the Communist Party hadn't expelled Trotsky and allowed his ideas to foment—"

"But that's the problem with socialism, isn't it?" Thom interjected. "Its ideals get corrupted by those in power because it relies on a rosy view of the world and that people are good at their core. Capitalism works because it takes people for what they are, narcissistic, mean, and ugly. That's why it will always work, because it accounts for the evil in people, unlike Communism."

A red light blinked over the stage, and Thom checked a clock on the wall. "Well, that looks like a commercial break. Come back, true believers. We'll be back in a moment."

A few seconds of silence were followed by a bell ringing in the studio. A loudspeaker boomed over them. "That's five. Stretch your legs if you need. Great work, Thom. You too, Phyllis."

Joshy looked over to see a bald man sitting behind the bay of video monitors, squinting as his fingers worked quickly over an audio board.

"Why does he always compliment you first?" Phyllis asked.

Thom shrugged. "I'm more insecure than you, and they know it."

Phyllis chucked. "Well, that's true."

"If you want me to talk to Ivan, I will," Thom said, pulling out his earpiece.

"You shouldn't have to talk to him. He should not be such a misogynist. I don't need some man fighting my battles."

"Whoa!" Thom said, throwing up his hands. "I'm not the enemy. And he can hear you, you know?"

"I know," Phyllis replied, flipping Ivan off. "He knows I hate him. Can we please fire him?"

Thom stood up and walked toward a table filled with snacks. "He's the best we can afford."

"Then we need a bigger budget," Phyllis replied, following behind him. "You don't actually believe that stuff you said about capitalism, do you?"

"Of course I do," Thom replied. "Every word."

Thom stuffed a quarter of a sandwich down his throat, and then looked up to see Leslie staring back at him. "Well, well, well. Look what the cat dragged in."

"Good to see you, Thom," Leslie said, shaking Thom's hand. "What's it been? Three years?"

"At least. Not since model UN in Wichita."

"Where I kicked your ass," Leslie said with a grin.

"Where you beat me, sure," Thom replied, overconfidently. "I don't know if I would call it an ass kicking."

"Losers never do," Leslie said, pointing to Debra and Joshy. "This is my brother, Joshy, and his girlfriend, Debra. Oh crap. Is it girlfriend?"

"I guess so," Debra said. "We've not really talked about it."

"It's girlfriend," Joshy replied, wrapping his fingers around hers tightly. "It's definitely girlfriend."

Thom was cuter than he'd looked on Leslie's phone screen, and Joshy was insecure about his tenuous and burgeoning relationship.

"I guess it's girlfriend then," Debra said, trying to remove her hand from Joshy's vice-like grip. "It's nice to meet you."

"You too," Thom replied. "What can I do for you guys? Not to be blunt, but I have about three minutes until I'm back on the air."

"Straight to the point," Leslie said. "I always liked that about you. Debra, do your thing."

"Are you sure?" Debra asked.

Leslie nodded. Debra looked over at Joshy. Suddenly, she was quite self-conscious about her alien form. She had never shown it to anybody but her family and Joshy's before.

"It's okay," Joshy said. "If my sister trusts him, you can too."

Leslie smiled. "Trust is such a funny word. I believe Thom is a capitalist and will see the financial benefit of helping you, that's for sure. Plus, he knows I'll kill him if he hurts you, and he's too smart and self-involved to cross me."

Thom cracked a smile. "That is the nicest thing you've said about me, ever. Honestly, it's kind of scaring me."

"Thom!" Phyllis said. "Get back up here, we're back on in a minute. You can talk to your adoring fans later."

"Be right there," Thom replied. "It's now or never guys. Do you have something to show me or not?"

Debra sighed. There was no turning back now. She closed her eyes, and her skin faded away. In the center of the studio, she started to glow blue, pulsating and vibrating brighter and brighter.

"Oh my god," Thom said, clasping his hand against his mouth.

"My friend here is an alien," Leslie said. "And we want to give you the exclusive. What do you say? Do you have time to put her on the air?"

"I think we can definitely fit her in," Phyllis said. "After the next commercial break."

"Perfect," Leslie said.

Chapter 5

"Do you need anything?" Phyllis asked as she dragged a third chair onto the stage. "We have some make-up over behind the stage if you want to powder yourself up. Frankly, it doesn't matter what you do, these lights make everybody seem like they have dark bags under their eyes."

"I think I'm fine," Debra said. "I'm not going to be in my…well, I won't need it, I don't think."

"The most important part is to be yourself," Thom said, placing a water cup on the glass coffee table in front of her. "Now, your name is Debra Thompson, right?"

"That's right," Debra replied, sitting down.

"And what about your alien name?"

"I only have one name," Debra replied. "I mean, I think I only have one name. I never really asked. Earth is the only home I've ever known."

"Only home you've ever known," Phyllis said, writing it on a scrap of paper. "That's good. That's great stuff. Okay, and what about your parents? Are they…aliens who were born on Earth, too?"

"No," Debra said. "They've been all around the galaxy, but they chose to have me here."

"Why?" Thom said.

"I don't know. I guess they liked it here. Aren't we supposed to do this question and answer thing on the air?"

"Of course, and we will," Phyllis said. "It's just, so exciting. We don't normally have studio guests, and this is a huge get for us, you know? We're a little overwhelmed."

"I'll bet," Debra said. "You just learned there are aliens in the world. That can't be easy."

"So, do you have some sort of message of peace or something?" Thom said. "Why are you coming on today? Why now?"

Debra sighed. "I really think this is the kind of thing that would be better explained on camera."

The loudspeaker boomed with Ivan's voice. "We're live in fifteen seconds."

"Well," Phyllis smiled. "You're about to get your chance."

The lights to the studio dimmed, except for the ones around the stage. Those intensified until Debra was sweating and could barely see past the front of the stage. She was no fan of heat, and this was nearly as unbearable as the scorching New Mexico sun.

"Welcome back!" Thom said as the red light blinked above the cameras. "We're not known for having guests on this show, but when our next guest showed up—"

"We had to have her on," Phyllis cut in. "Say hello to Debra Thompson from Michigan. I know she doesn't look like much now, but she's amazing. Welcome, Debra. Thanks for coming on."

"Thank you for having me," Debra replied, squinting at the stage lights glaring in her face.

"Now, let's get down to it," Thom said. "Why are you here today, Debbie? I can call you Debbie, right?"

"I...would prefer Debra."

"Fair enough," Thom replied. "Now, you're here with an amazing tale. Something that, frankly, until I saw it with my own eyes, was unbelievable. Wouldn't you say it's unbelievable, Phyllis?"

"Yes, I would say that if I were watching this program, and I saw what you are about to see, I would find it wholly unbelievable. And yet, it isn't, is it Debra?"

"I certainly don't think so, but that's because I live it every day. I've been this way since I was born, right here on Earth."

"And what is it that you were born as, Deb?" Thom replied in a compassionate tone.

"Well, Thom. I'm an alien."

"An illegal alien?" Phyllis asked. "Like from another country?"

"No, well I'm here legally and documented, but I'm not from another country. I was born right here. However, I'm not from here."

"That's very confusing," Thom said.

"I know…it's…my home is a planet called Thimber. It's about thirty light years or so from Earth. You don't know it, because our sun is small and you haven't studied that quadrant of the sky yet, but we know you."

"You're saying you're an alien," Phyllis said in a stern voice. "Like from another planet."

"That's right," Debra said.

"I find that a little hard to believe," Thom said, chuckling. "I mean you look so normal to me."

"Well, this isn't my true form. I don't look like this. I mean I do look like this, but it is only a skin I wear, like your Terminator."

"Wait, so this isn't what you look like?" Phyllis asked, feigning confusion. "Then what do you look like then?"

"Should I show you?" Debra replied, smiling slightly.

"Please," Thom said. "Now viewers, you must trust us that this is not special effects, or magic, or any sort of visual trickery. I have watched her transform with my own eyes, and even though I'm not an expert, I 100% believe this to be true. If you have ever believed us before, believe us now."

Debra stood. Her whole life had been building to this, she hadn't known it. The pressure weighed on her, causing her legs to wobble as she stood. She looked through the bright lights to find Joshy standing next to the camera. She smiled at him, and it looked as though he smiled back. She was about to out herself, and aliens, to the whole planet. The butterflies in her stomach fluttered mightily as she closed her eyes.

"Here you go," she said, as her skin disappeared, and she shimmered blue in the studio.

"That is incredible. It's like shaking up blue glitter in a tube of glow in the dark liquid, isn't it, Phyllis?"

"That is totally accurate," Phyllis said. "It reminds me of a lava lamp, Thom. Now, Debra, you swear this is not made up, but for our viewers who don't believe, what can you say to them to ease their minds?"

"There's not much to say," Debra said, hovering into the air. "I can tell you there are millions of aliens on your planet, from thousands of star systems, and that while I am peaceful, there are some who are not."

"Wait," Thom said, confused. "Are you saying there are other aliens who are here to do us harm?"

Debra took a deep breath. "That is exactly what I am saying. There is a race of aliens on your planet called the Globorians. They have been on your planet for over a hundred years, infiltrating every sector of your government, working their way up to positions of power. They have taken over your government, and in a few months, they will invade and take over everything, enslaving your planet and everyone on it. They have done it before, and they will do it again, unless you rise up to stop them, human and alien alike."

"How do you know that?" Phyllis said, surprised.

"Every alien knows it. We were given instructions to evacuate this planet by Labor Day, or risk being enslaved with the rest of you."

"Why didn't you say anything sooner?" Thom said. "If you are peaceful, that is?"

"By being here today, I risk my family being killed by the Globorians. We signed a treaty when we arrived here twenty years ago that we would not reveal ourselves. Now, I have betrayed that treaty, and risked my safety."

"Then why do it?" Phillis asked.

"Because this is the only home I've ever known," Debra said, looking directly at Joshy. "I have never lived anywhere else, and I love it here. You don't deserve Globorian rule."

"I call on my fellow aliens to stand up against the impending threat," Debra continued. "This planet is not perfect, but it is our home and the home of many we love. It does not have to be like this. We can give humanity a future."

Both Thom and Phyllis were silent for a minute as the red light blinked over the studio. "We…we…we have to take a break," Thom said with a deep swallow of his throat. "Stay tuned."

*

"That was incredible!" Thom said when they were finally off the air. "You were amazing. We're gonna be on every television in the country! We're finally going to be picked up nationally! This is so, so great."

Thom was excited, but Phyllis didn't share his exuberance. "That stuff you said...was it true?"

Debra solemnly nodded. "I'm afraid so."

Thom didn't quite register the words that Debra said, only that she said them. However, looking around the room, he realized nobody else was as happy as him. "What's the matter, guys? We got the scoop of the century. You should be happy!"

"Did you hear what she said?" Phyllis asked. "Like, do you ever hear anything?"

"What? She said she was an alien, and then she turned blue, and said there was a war coming."

"No," Phyllis said. "She said we've already been invaded; we didn't know it until now. She said in a couple of months we're going to be slaves."

"Yeah, but that won't happen, right? I mean, somebody will stop it."

"There is nobody to stop it," Debra said, dropping her eyes. "Everybody who could've stopped it is either dead or never existed."

"No," Thom said. "I mean, I know you paint a bleak picture, but that's hype for the television, right?"

Debra shook her head. "I only came on television because it was such a bleak picture."

Finally, it sunk into Thom's head, and his mood turned as somber as the rest of the people in the room. "Oh."

"There you go," Phyllis said. "Sorry, it takes him a while sometimes."

"What do we do now?" Joshy asked, stepping up to wrap Debra in a big hug.

"You've done your part," Phyllis replied. "Go home. We'll take it from here."

"So that's it?" Leslie asked.

"No," Thom said. "If this is really as big as you said…this is only the beginning."

"If we do our job right," Phyllis added. "This whole thing will become a media circus within the hour. And trust me, we are very good at riling up our base. If there's any way to make this a media circus, we'll do it."

*

The adrenaline ran high on the walk home from the station. Leslie twirled in the middle of the street as she walked in front of Joshy and Debra.

"We did something, man," Leslie said. "We really did something. My whole life all I've wanted to do was something important, and tonight we did that."

"Well, I think that Debra did most of it," Joshy said, kissing Debra on the forehead. "You were very brave."

"Sure, I mean she was the one on the camera," Leslie replied. "But like there are more people behind the scenes working for change. I learned that during Councilwoman Beaman's campaign. Just because you're not in front of the camera doesn't mean you aren't helping."

"Leslie's right," Debra said. "We wouldn't have even known about that show if not for her. I'm still not sure if we did the right thing."

"Are you kidding?" Leslie said, excitedly. "There are thousands of people who watch their show every night. I mean, young people, like us, who will share the shit out of it. You were so inspiring. I am so proud of you."

Debra smiled. "Thank you. I was not sure I could do it until I did it."

"I knew you could do it," Joshy said. "Of course, I think you can do anything."

Debra clasped her fingers around Joshy's. If Thom and Phyllis were right, and everything was about to change, she wanted to remember these last moments of serenity with him.

"What do you think is going to happen now?" Debra said.

"I think we're going to see a movement form," Leslie said. "I think we're going to see people stand up and question things."

Debra laughed. "Wow, Joshy is right, Les. You are very naive. It's like you don't watch the news at all."

"I do, though," Leslie said.

"Then you know this country never changes, for any reason. People think the news is full of lies."

"That's true in the short term," Leslie admitted. "It's just, you think that because somebody is winning the battle, it means they won the war. Civil rights were a long and slow battle with hundreds of fits and stops. So was woman's suffrage. Hell, we fought a world war to stop fascism. If you looked at the Nazis in 1939, they looked unstoppable. And yet, they lost a few years later. I guess I don't believe that the rhetoric winning now is the one that's gonna win when all is said and done. Just look back on who is on the winning side of history."

"Sure," Debra said. "But history is made by the winners. And unfortunately, the Globorians are going to win."

"That's where we differ," Leslie replied. "You think they are going to win because they're winning. I don't."

"How can you be so optimistic?" Joshy asked. "If what she said is true, then millions of Globorians are already here, ready to fight."

"It's simple," Leslie said. "If they were so sure they were going to win…they wouldn't care who knew they were coming. The fact they don't want you to say anything means there is a way to beat them."

"Wow," Debra said. "That is optimistic as hell."

Leslie shrugged. "There is one more thing."

"Go for it," Debra said.

"If the world has really been controlled by Globorians for a hundred years…it gives me some hope that humanity isn't that bad—like maybe we didn't screw it all up. Maybe there is some salvation for us yet."

Debra hadn't considered that, and the thought brought her hope for a moment. However, when they turned the corner to Maddie's house and saw a dozen news camera trucks shining lights down on the front door, their hope turned to fear. It was the media circus Phyllis promised, and she had thrust her family and friends smack dab into the middle of it.

Chapter 6

The sun was peeking over the horizon by the time Joshy,
Debra, and Leslie crept around the back of the house to
avoid the reporters and hopped over the fence into
Maddie's backyard. Inside the house, the adults were
huddled around the television, leaning into the TV to catch
every word they heard.

The only ones missing were Ted, who was upstairs
avoiding the commotion, and Veronica, who stood at the
front window sticking her head out to see the cavalcade of
reporters and shaking her head.

"Well," Debra said, looking back and forth between
Leslie and Joshy. "This is what we wanted, right?
Everybody is talking about us now."

The TV was turned to CNN, where Alisyn Camerota
and John Berman bantered back and forth. Under them, a
caption read "Are aliens real?" A picture of Debra, glowing
blue, flashed on screen as Debra made her way to the door.

"Yeah," Joshy replied. "I hope our parents don't hate us
now."

"They'll get over it if they do," Leslie said.

"And what if they don't?" Debra asked.

"They will," Leslie said, not very confident in the least.
"At least I think they will."

Debra slid open the back door to the house. As she did,
everybody turned to her. Instead, of anger, their eyes filled
with great relief as the stood and ran to her.

"Oh! Thank god you are alive," Carole said, running
over and wrapping Debra in a big hug. "All of you." Carole
pulled her children close to her and squeezed them so hard
their necks started to hurt. "Never do that again, okay?"

"They can't do it again," Bill said. "You can only make the dumbest decision of your lives once, after all."

"You're one to talk, dad," Leslie said in a huff. "How many dumb decisions did you make bankrupting this family?"

"Don't change the subject!" Bill replied.

"I'm just saying that people in glass houses shouldn't throw stones. Besides, we obviously didn't think it was a dumb idea. Otherwise, we wouldn't have done it."

"Of course you didn't," Maddie scoffed, turning from the TV. "Because you're idiots."

"We're not idiots!" Joshy retorted. "It had to be said."

"And what about me, Josh?" Maddie replied angrily. "Did you ever think about me, or my husband? This is going to come down on us. Did you ever think about what's going to happen to us now?"

"No," he said, as politely as possible. "I didn't. I was thinking about the millions of people we could help by warning them about the invasion. That's what was important. I'm sorry that you're in the middle of that."

"You're sorry!" Maddie said, stomping forward. "I ought to—"

Bill stepped between Maddie and his son. "That's enough. He's our son, and we'll deal with him."

"You humans are all the same," she growled, spinning on her heels and storming up the stairs.

"You did a very stupid thing," Bill said, ping-ponging his eyes between Joshy and Leslie. "But I am glad you are safe."

"We wanted to do the right thing," Leslie said, pushing away from her mother. "We wanted to do what we thought you would do."

Carole let go of them and wiped her eyes. "We never would have done that, because family is the most important thing."

"These people won't have families in a couple months," Debra said. "They'll be captured or worse. What about them?"

Carole sighed. "That's not our problem."

"No," Joshy replied. "It's not your problem. It is my problem."

"Mine too," Leslie replied.

Debra left the standoff between Joshy and his parents and walked across the house to find her mother. She hadn't left the front window since Debra walked into the house. She just kept staring out the window and shaking her head.

"Mom?"

"Fourteen camera crews," Veronica said. "There are fourteen camera crews out there. They're not all local news, either. CNN is out there and Al Jazeera. This is international news now, kiddo. You really know how to make a scene. You always did."

"I wish it hadn't come to this, mom," Debra said.

"Do you?" Veronica asked. "Are you sure a small piece of you doesn't revel in it?"

"Yes," Debra said, lowering her head. "I'm sorry this fell to me. I wish somebody else had said something, but they didn't. I've lived on Earth my entire life. Every single day I've breathed the same air as these people. I couldn't let them die or be captured. I'm not like you. I care about this planet."

"I care about this planet, too," Veronica said, turning from the window. "It's the planet that brought me you and where I lost my husband, but we are more than one planet."

"I'm not," Debra said. "Maybe one day I'll be more than one planet, but right now, I'm from here. This is my home, and I can't watch it be destroyed, not when I can help it."

"You CAN'T help them, Deb!" Veronica said. "That's the point. You can't do anything. All you did was put us all at risk."

"I'm sorry you feel that way," Debra said, turning away from her.

Veronica sighed. "But you've done it already, haven't you?"

"I have. I can't take it back, even if I wanted to," Debra said, gulping loudly. "And I don't want to take it back."

Veronica smiled a tense smile. "Then, I suppose we should talk about what you're going to do next."

*

An hour later, Debra stood at the front door gathering her thoughts. A half dozen more camera trucks had arrived since she got home, and more seemed to be coming every minute. Outside, Bill had constructed a podium so that Debra could make a statement. Two dozen microphones sat on top of it from news outlets from all over the world.

"I never wanted to be famous," Debra said to Joshy, who stood by her side, holding her hand.

"I never wanted to date somebody that was famous," Joshy replied.

"Bullshit," Leslie said from behind them. "You had the hugest crush on Cobie Smulders when you were younger."

"Alright, that one—"

"And Brie Larson. And Raven from the Teen Titans, too. I mean, you crushed on almost everyone."

"Alright," Joshy said. "I get the point."

Debra squeezed his hand tighter. "I get your point, though, too, Joshy."

"Really?" Leslie asked. "You're the only one. I guess that's why you're together."

Debra smiled. "That's one reason."

"You don't have to do this," Joshy said. "We can still go out the back and disappear."

"Oh no," Maddie replied, arms folded, standing at the bottom of the stairs. "She made her bed, and now she has to lie in it. You're paying to get our lawn redone too, so you know."

"Aren't you moving off planet?" Joshy asked.

"That's irrelevant. It's the principle of the thing."

"Fine," Joshy replied. "We'll pay for your stupid lawn."

"I know you will," Maddie said. "Now, go out there and get this over with."

Joshy turned to Debra. "You don't have to do this. We can run away."

"No, she's right," Debra said. "I can't turn back now. This is my moment. This is when we all stop hiding, and finally do something."

"I was very content doing exactly what I was doing," Maddie mumbled.

"I know," Debra replied. "That's the problem."

Veronica walked up to her daughter and put her hands on her shoulders. "As much as I hate to admit it, your father would be proud of you. He didn't always make the choices I agreed with, but he always made the choices he thought were right. You must get that from him."

"Thanks, mom," she said, wiping a tear from her cheek. "How do I look?"

Veronica gave her a hard look up and down, then smiled. "Ready."

Debra clasped her fingers around the door handle and took a deep breath. The knob turned slowly, and the moment it creaked open, shutters flashed on the other side. Reporters screamed over each other as she took her first step outside.

Debra took another deep breath, and the yell from the reporters fell away. She smelt the burning flashes mixed with wet dew from the grass. She stepped deliberately toward the podium. Every step felt like a million miles until she clasped her fingers on the sides of the wooden platform.

"Thank you for coming," Debra said. "I never expected—"

"Can you confirm you're an alien?" one of the reporters asked.

"Is this all a hoax?" another asked.

"How long have you been on Earth?" a shrill voice screamed.

"How many aliens are there?" someone bellowed.

Debra could feel her heartbeat inside her head as the anxiety built in her chest. Her ribcage tightened around her, and suddenly she couldn't breathe. She spun back to the house where she saw Joshy watching through the window, smiling at her. He mouthed "breathe" to her, and she took another deep breath.

With her breath, the chaos slowed down, and she grounded herself again. "I know you all have many questions. However, I am not here to answer them. I am here to make a statement. I hope that statement will answer your questions, but I understand it likely will not answer them all. My name is Debra Thompson, and I am an alien. I was not born on a far-off planet. I was born here, on Earth, in Michigan, to two loving parents. I have lived here my entire life. I had planned to live here longer. However, three months ago we were sent a letter stating that Earth will be placed under the control of the Globorians on Labor Day."

The reporters muttered to each other, but Debra kept going. "The Globorians are one of the few war-like races in the galaxy. We aliens are mostly peace-loving and kind. However, for the past one hundred years, the Globorians have infiltrated every sector of your planet, from your financial institutions to your emergency responders to your politicians. They have worked their way from the outermost rim of your society to the President of the United States."

"I know this is hard to believe. Frankly, were I not an alien and hadn't read the evacuation letter myself, I would not believe it, either. The news spooked my family enough that we made plans to flee Earth. However, I could not in good conscience leave this planet to its doom without warning you."

"What you do with this information is up to you. I do not know how to defeat the Globorians. In fact, my father lost his life to them a couple days ago. This is the time, though, to band together. Your world is under attack. The Globorians have worked very hard to pull you apart, into Red State and Blue State. Into Republican and Democrat. Into Europe and America. But you are all humans, and you will only be able to defeat this menace together, if you can defeat it at all."

Debra closed her eyes. "I know many of you do not believe anything unless you see it with your own eyes, so I will show you the proof you seek."

The skin melted off Debra's body, and she turned into a blue, shimmering alien. She opened her eyes and lifted off the ground. She clapped her hands together and sent a shockwave far into the sky.

"This is not a parlor trick," she said, rising over the podium and above the reporters who stood with mouths agape in front of her.

When she had slowly circled the reporters, she returned to the podium and gripped it tightly. "Thank you for your time. I hope this has been educational."

With that, Debra turned around, away from the questions being pelted at her by the assembled reporters. She flung open the door and slammed it closed behind her. She had done it, but she could no longer contain her emotions. She started to cry, sliding down the door as she did. Joshy rushed to her side, and she collapsed into his arms, spent.

The three families stood in silence, proud of what they'd witnessed. Even Maddie had to admit it was a feat of great bravery to be so stupid, even if she thought it was idiotic.

Chapter 7

"You did good out there," Joshy said, rubbing Debra's shoulders as she pressed herself against the door. Her blue light dimmed around her as she turned back into her human form.

"Josh is right," Veronica said. "You were great. That was a lot of pressure, and I'm very proud of you right now."

"Even though you are an idiot," Maddie replied from the stairs. "I have to admit, that was pretty cool."

"You're on TV, actually," Bill said, pointing behind him. "If you care to watch yourself."

"I can't stand myself on camera," Carole said. "But you look great."

Debra stood up, wiped the tears from her eyes, and walked to the television. As she did, Leslie grabbed the remote and turned it up. Debra watched the skin melt from her body before she rose into the air and hovered around the reporters.

Before she came back to the podium, the screen cut to a young, brown-haired Latina reporter, holding a microphone with the FOX logo on it.

"That was the scene moments ago as a self-proclaimed alien announced that we were all going to die. Back to you, Bob and Tina."

The television cut back to the studio, where a perfectly coiffed man with a square jaw and helmet hair sat next to a blonde anchor wearing too much make-up next to a graphic that said Aliens: Fact or Fiction?

"Well," Bob said, snickering under his breath. "I'll be honest. I never thought I would be discussing aliens on television, at least not seriously."

"I'll agree with you, Bob," Tina added. "I'm surprised our newsroom took this story so seriously. After all, right now all we have is one girl's statement. You would think that these Glimberdoms would have a statement of their own if they were real, wouldn't you?"

"You would think so," Bob replied, shaking his head. "It's a dark day in news when this is what we take as fact."

Tina placed his finger on her ear. "I'm hearing that the mayor of St. Louis has a statement. Let's go to it now."

"What's happening?" Debra said, turning around. "Why are they saying that horrible stuff?"

"The whole system is rigged," Maddie said. "They're not going to let you say whatever you want without consequences. Those little peons outside might not be Globorians, but the ones running the newsroom sure are, and this mayor…forget about it."

Debra turned back to the TV as a short, fat, sweaty, bald man came on the screen. The chyron under him read Richard Meltzer, Mayor of St. Louis.

"The idea that aliens exist on this planet is ridiculous. Not only that, but it insults our intelligence. If there have been aliens on this planet for over a hundred years, humanity would know. This…trickster is trying to convince you we aren't smart enough to know whether there are aliens among us. She said all our leaders are aliens. Now, I ask you. Do I look like an alien to you?"

Debra grabbed a pillow and threw it at the TV. "I hate them so much!"

"What did you expect?" Maddie asked, grabbing her shoulder. "That this would all change because you wanted it to? No. All you've done is put us all in danger. Like I said, you were brave but stupid."

"That's not what I wanted," Debra said, flinging up her hands in the air. "I wanted to help."

"You did help," Joshy said, walking forward.

"No, she didn't," Maddie said. "Because nobody can help. The Globorians have already won."

Veronica nodded. "She's right, sweetie. You tried, and that's admirable, but now it's time to go."

"What's that?" Leslie said, looking out the window toward the street.

The rest of the group ran toward the window to see a Humvee and two SWAT vans speeding down the street. The news vans had already started to abandon the front lawn, convinced the news story was over, by the time a dozen SWAT officers in full battle regalia stomped out of their cars carrying semi-automatic assault rifles.

"We have to go, now," Veronica said. "Like right now. Maybe we can escape out the back."

"No, wait!" Joshy said. "I have an idea."

"Your ideas are what got us into this mess in the first place!" Bill said, jabbing a finger towards Joshy.

"No! That was my plan!" Leslie said. "And frankly, I don't think we're going to get anywhere by running. They must have the place surrounded. Now, Joshy, what's your plan?"

"Veronica," Joshy said. "Is there any way to force aliens to take their true form?"

"Well, maybe, but we would need a really big sonic disrupter."

"How big?" Carole said.

Veronica looked over at Maddie. "I know your husband has something up there. He spends all day tinkering away. Tell me I'm wrong."

"He doesn't like to come downstairs," Maddie said. "He prefers it in the dark where he doesn't have to wear a mask. He doesn't like being disturbed."

"Ted!" Veronica hollered up the stairs. "Do you have a sonic disrupter up there big enough to force an alien to take its true form?"

"Sure!" Ted screamed back. "Three of them."

"Can you be a dear and bring them down?" Veronica asked.

"Do I have to put on my face?" Ted asked from upstairs.

"No!"

"Then I'll be right down."

There was rattling above them, and then a loud crash as Ted inched across the floor and oozed down the stairs. Ted didn't have any interest in pretending for humans, and Veronica knew it. He'd been forced to play the game for years, but now that he and Maddie were leaving Earth for good, he didn't have any need to leave the house or to deal with humanity at all.

"Hi, everyone," Ted said, raising a slimy, green tentacle. "Nice to see you."

Ted was not much more than a six-foot slug with a dozen tentacles for arms. His eyes stood above his head on big eyestalks that moved independently from each other.

His mouth puckered when he talked making his voice sounds squeaky and faint.

"I wish you would put on your face," Maddie said. "We have guests."

"And that's why I haven't come downstairs yet. This is my house. I shouldn't have to hide who I am in my own house."

"Ted!" Joshy said, pointing to the silver guns in his hands. "Are those the disrupters?"

Ted rolled his eyeballs and looked down at his tentacles, where he cradled three ray guns with big, metal sonic dishes at the front of them.

"Yup," Ted said. "I made them to expose other aliens for being hypocrites, but then...well, Maddie said doing so wouldn't be polite."

"Not just impolite, but against the law, too."

"Whose law?! The Globorians? Those guys are the worst!"

"You can fight about this later!" Bill said. "The SWAT team is advancing. Can we please come up with a plan?"

"Oh, I have a plan," Joshy said. "We're going to force the public to deal with aliens, whether they want to or not." Joshy walked forward and grabbed the ray guns from Ted's tentacles. He handed one to Debra and one to Leslie. "When this door opens, we fire at the SWAT team. There's no way there aren't Globorians in there."

"And if there's not?" Leslie asked.

"Then hopefully the sound will let us escape anyway," Joshy said. "But I really hope there are Globorians in there."

"Is there anything we need to know before using these things?" Debra asked.

Ted shook his head. "Nope. It's a simple point and click interface. Make sure to point it away from you."

"Alright," Joshy said. "Stay inside. When the cameras turn on the SWAT team, get ready to run toward the camper. Debra, open the door."

Debra nodded to Joshy and Leslie, who nodded back. They gripped the guns tightly in their hands as Debra flung open the door. Reporters shuffled back to their trucks, leaving big divots in the front lawn. A couple of the bigger names, like CNN, had already pulled away, but the local stations were still milling around.

"Hey!" Debra shouted as Joshy and Leslie stepped outside. "Watch this!"

Leslie pulled up her sonic disrupter to eye level and fired. A sonic blast erupted from the barrel of the gun and pulsed across the lawn until it hit four members of the SWAT team. They fell to their knees in pain.

"Help me!" Leslie said.

Joshy and Debra fired their blasters as well. The sound was so loud Debra lost her human form as she shook violently and turned into her natural blue shimmering one.

"It's working!" Debra said, emboldened by her inability to control her disguise. "Keep firing!!!"

Together they created a wall of sound which shook the neighborhood to its foundation. Windows shattered and car horns blared. Finally, after a minute Debra took her hands off the trigger. Joshy and Leslie followed suit.

"OW!!!" Joshy shouted. "I didn't think it would be so loud."

"Of course it was going to be loud," Debra said. "It's a sonic disrupter."

"Duh," Leslie added, agreeing.

"Look!" Debra said, pointing toward the SWAT team. Except, no longer was the team human. Instead, they were ugly, craggily rock monsters. Their hideous forms stretched the fabric of their suits as they rose to their feet and snarled at Debra.

"Those are your aliens, people," Debra said, pointing to the reporters, quite a few of whom were no longer human themselves. None of them were Globorians, but they ran the gamut from the tall and spindly to the plump and slimy. The few humans on the lawn looked around and screamed, having confirmed their worst fear—they were not alone in the galaxy.

The reporters grabbed their cameras and swung them toward the aliens. Meanwhile, Debra opened the door. "Mom! Let's go!"

One by one, the group filed past the SWAT team and into the camper as the reporters swarmed the newfound aliens and pounded them with a barrage of questions.

Chapter 8

The camper lumbered down the road as Veronica weaved in an out of traffic. The RV was not meant for such jostling. It felt like it was going to rip apart at the seams with each jerk of the wheel. Somehow, though, Veronica kept it on the road. She was a very skilled driver, having piloted her spaceship across the galaxy, but her white-knuckled evasion maneuvers wouldn't keep them safe forever. They needed to find safety…fast.

"Hold on!" Veronica shouted as she spun the wheel to make a hard-right turn.

This time, the camper jostled and tilted as the passengers inside slammed hard against the side of the camper. The extra weight was too much force for the truck to handle, and its center of gravity tipped too far for Veronica to control.

The camper slammed hard into a traffic pole and spun on its axis, shedding its decorative plating as the wood pole scraped against the side of the RV. Debra dropped her human form and wrapped the Carters in a protective cocoon of light as gravity bandied them to and fro around the cabin.

Veronica fought a good fight, but she couldn't keep the RV upright. It collapsed onto its side and skidded across the ground, slamming into cars as it came to an uneasy stop halfway down the street.

Veronica's head throbbed as she pushed herself off the ground and looked around the cabin. "Is everybody okay?"

Debra released the Carters from her protection, and they rolled through the cabin onto the ground. "I'm fine."

"I think so," Bill mumbled, woozily standing. "Carole, are you okay?"

"Miraculously, I think so," Carole said. "A little bruised, but otherwise fine. Kids?"

"Yeah, fine," Joshy said. "A sore shoulder, but I'm good."

"Me too," said Leslie.

"Good!" Debra said, floating into the air to unlock the door to the trailer. "Let's go, everybody."

"Ted," Maddie said. "Put on your face."

Ted's sluggish alien body oozed down the side of the camper. "But…Everybody knows there are aliens now. Do I have to wear my human skin?"

"I think you overestimate how many people watch the news. Please, do it."

"Fine," Ted said, slinking up the walls. Before he reached the outside, he folded into a long-haired hippie with bell bottoms and a bushy head of hair. His afro barely made it out of the cabin.

"Ugh," Maddie said. "I keep telling him to update his look, but he refuses. It's been a tough couple of decades living with that."

*

When all the passengers were finally out of the RV, they looked around at each other. They were battered and bruised, but otherwise none the worse for wear, which was a miracle.

"What now?" Joshy asked, nursing his tender elbow.

"I have a plan." Debra pointed at Maddie and Ted. "You need to get to your ship and off the planet. Mom, you, Bill, and Carole go with them. Make sure they get to their shuttle, and we'll meet you there."

"What are we going to do?" Leslie asked.

"My mom made a good point. Nobody cares about the news. However, if we can unmask their mayor as a Globorian, then they'll have to believe us."

"You want to kidnap the mayor?" Joshy said.

"No, I want to expose him for what he is," Debra said, pulling out her sonic disrupter. "Do you have a problem with that?"

"Not at all," Joshy said. "Simply curious."

"How about you?" she asked, turning to Leslie.

"I think it's batshit crazy, and I love it."

"This is a bad idea," Carole told her son. "I don't like it at all."

Joshy grabbed her mother's hand. "We're saving the world, mom. You probably won't like any of it."

Carole wanted to argue, but her head ached too much to put up a fight. "I'm sick of arguing with you when you're just gonna disobey us anyway, so...be safe, okay?"

"I can't promise that, mom," Joshy said.

"Then, at least don't get your sister killed."

Joshy nodded. "I'll try."

"Hey!" Leslie scolded. "I'm older than him. I should be making sure he doesn't die."

"Watch out for each other, alright?" Bill said.

"I swear I'll get them back safely, okay?" Debra said. "Count on it."

Debra made the promise knowing she might not be able to keep it, but it brought some comfort to Bill and Carole's faces. None of it transferred to Veronica though, who looked as worried as ever that her daughter was doing something stupid.

Still, she knew better than to stop her. "I'll see you soon."

"Wait," Maddie said. "Swipe your phone open and give it to me."

Debra didn't ask questions. She swiped open her phone and handed it to Maddie. "I'm going to need that back pretty quickly. The police will be here any second."

Maddie opened the GPS and typed in an address. Then, she handed it over to Debra. "When you're done, meet us there. We'll wait for you as long as possible before we leave."

"Thanks," Debra said, nodding.

Debra hugged her mother, then ran off past the smoldering wreckage of the camper and down an alleyway out of sight as Leslie and Joshy followed behind.

*

"What's your plan here?" Leslie asked as they squatted in an alleyway next to city hall. The building was tall and beautiful, like a gothic castle, as if it was transported from an ancient European town to St. Louis. "Are we just going up and bum rushing him? That seems like a bad plan."

"When the mayor comes out, we're going to shoot him with these disrupters and record it to show the world he's a Globorian. If they won't believe anything else, hopefully, they'll believe that."

"Oh," Leslie said, unimpressed. "So, we're basically going to bum rush him. Cool. Cool cool cool cool cool."

"This is all a bad plan," Joshy said. "Sorry, sweetheart."

"No, you're right," Debra said, nodding. "There are no good plans here. We are up against an unstoppable menace, and the best we can do is the best we can do."

"So we're clear. You, Joshy, and I are going to bum rush the mayor and try to shoot him with these sonic disrupters, hoping he's an alien?" Leslie asked.

Debra nodded. "Yup."

Leslie sighed. "Can you at least pretend it's a better plan than that?"

"Sorry," Debra said. "I'm all out of pretending today. Now, when the mayor comes out, we jump out, shoot him, turn him into a monster, and then get it all on video, okay?"

Joshy sighed. "Yup. We're definitely going to get arrested."

"Don't be so glum," Debra said. "We're only probably going to get arrested."

A few minutes later, three bodyguards dressed in black suits and dark sunglasses walked out of the city hall building, flanking the short, stocky mayor on either side. The guards were built like trucks, Debra thought, as she inched out of the alleyway onto the street. Joshy and Leslie started the phone recording and stepped out behind her.

The mayor strode briskly toward a black Lincoln Town car which waited at the end of a large traffic circle.

C"Now!" Debra screamed.

The three of them ran into the street and opened fire with their sonic disruptors. The sound weakened Debra's disguise, and she turned a bright, vibrant blue as the waves of sound traveled across the street and broke the windows of the Town Car. Its horn blared, and the mayor dropped to his knees, along with all of his bodyguards.

"Don't stop!!!" Debra yelled.

After a full minute, Debra released the trigger on the sonic disruptor and the noise dissipated. The mayor got to his feet first, groggy, but still very much human. *Impossible*, Debra thought. She'd been confident he was an alien, and yet, he didn't change.

However, the same wasn't true for his bodyguards. Each of them rose to their feet as beefy, bulky Globorians, ugly and craggy, and they were pissed off. They saw where the sound was coming from and rushed toward Debra.

Debra rose into the air and clapped her hands. A shockwave rang out across the street and crashed into the Globorians.

"Get the mayor!" Debra said.

Joshy and Leslie rushed across the street as the Globorians rose to their feet behind them. Leslie pulled open the door to the Town Car and pulled out the dazed Globorian driver. Joshy ran around the car to the sputtering mayor.

"What…" the mayor muttered. "What's happening?"

"Aliens, Mr. Mayor," Joshy said. "Come with me if you want to live." He smiled. "I always wanted to say that."

Joshy pulled the mayor to his feet and pushed him into the back seat of the car before he dove in after him. Leslie peeled out as Debra heaved one last shockwave and flew into the back of the vehicle with Joshy and the mayor.

*

"What are you doing working with Globorians?" Debra asked as Leslie sped down the street and turned into an alleyway.

"What are you doing being an alien?!" the mayor responded.

Leslie pulled into the basement of a parking garage and slammed the car into park. "Wait, did you know they were aliens?"

"What's it to you?" the mayor responded.

Joshy pulled out the sonic disruptor and pointed it at the mayor. "I'm the one with the gun."

The mayor scoffed. "That doesn't look like much of a gun to me."

"It will blow your eardrums out. Then try hearing things."

"Stop it!" Leslie said. "All of you. We're on the same team here."

"I'm not so sure about that," Debra scoffed.

"Mayor, did you know about the Globorians before we revealed them to you?"

"Of course not!" he replied. "I would never knowingly work with aliens. Disgusting."

"Hey," Debra sneered, glowing blue. "I'm right here."

"Yes," the mayor replied. "And you kidnapped me, which proves my point."

"Enough!" Leslie shouted. "We don't have much time."

"He started it," Debra scoffed.

Leslie scowled at the mayor. "So you're saying that you don't ever remember intentionally working with an alien before?"

"What kind of stupid question is that?" the mayor said. "I told you no thirty seconds ago!"

"After what we've seen," Joshy replied, "nothing is stupid anymore."

Debra took a deep breath. "Do you believe there are aliens now?"

The mayor turned to Debra and got a good look at her. "Well, my dear. I can't say I know what to believe."

Debra took her hand and placed it on the mayor's arm. Her hand wasn't smooth like a human's, but rough, like sand, and it shifted under her as she held him. She brought his hand up to her face and placed it on her cheek. Her skin was warm to the touch. He stroked her cheek, and it seemed to move and quake under his fingers.

"I am real, Mr. Mayor," Debra said. "There are millions more like me, and like those Globorians who guarded you."

"Amazing. I've never—never seen anything like it."

"I wish there was time for your amazement, but your city is in real danger. Your whole planet is in danger. We need your help. Nobody will believe us, but they will believe you."

"I-I-I don't know what to believe."

"Believe your own eyes. You don't have to believe us, but you saw your security staff turn into monsters. Those are Globorians, and they are everywhere. We have friends who can help you tell the truth, but you have to trust us."

"If I trust you," the mayor said. "My family will be in danger."

"This is bigger than your family, Mayor," Debra said. "I risked everything to help humanity because it is important to me. I am not even a human, but you are. You should be willing to risk at least as much as me."

The mayor sighed. "Fine. I will help you. After what I saw today, I don't know how I could not."

*

Leslie drove them to Thom's and Phyllis's studio. They were all too eager to put Mayor Meltzer on the air immediately. Ten minutes later, he was hurried through makeup and on the air, seated next to Thom.

"And that is why, my fellow citizens, I can say unequivocally that I was wrong earlier today," the mayor said, looking straight into the camera. "There are aliens, and they are everywhere. I don't know their plans, but if what Ms. Thompson told me is true, then we must prepare, together."

Thom turned to the camera after the mayor had stopped talking. "Powerful stuff. We'll be right back."

Phyllis was busy downloading the footage from Debra's phone as Thom talked. "This is incredible. You've given us so many scoops in one day. The journalism gods are smiling down on us."

"If the gods were smiling down on you," Debra replied, "then the Globorians wouldn't be here."

"Thank you so much for coming on, Mayor," Thom said, shaking his hand. "We've been trying to get you on this program for a long time. I wish it were under better circumstances, but at least we got you."

"You know they are going to come for him any minute," Joshy said to Phyllis.

Phyllis unhooked Debra's phone from her charger and handed it to her. "I know, but let us worry about that. Some things are more important than safety. This is more important. We'll do everything we can to get it out before they come, but now, you have to go."

Joshy shook Phyllis's hand. They both knew it was the last time they would see each other, and somehow, they were both okay with that.

*

Joshy pulled into the address Maddie gave Debra before they left the camper wreckage. It led them to an old abandoned warehouse. The floors were cracked and stained with oil. The walls were crumbling, and there were deep cracks in the drywall. The ceiling had caved in some time ago, and in the middle of the floor was a silver space ship like the one Joshy remembered from Flight of the Navigator.

Maddie and Ted polished the ship as Veronica, Bill, and Carole watched the Town Car with nervous anticipation. When the car door opened and their children stepped out, a wave of rapturous joy washed over them. Veronica ran up to Debra as she got out of the car and threw her arms around her. Bill and Carole did the same with Joshy and Leslie.

"We're so glad you're safe," Bill whispered.

"I told you I would bring them back safely," Debra said, deep in the embrace of her mother.

"Thank you," Carole said to her. "Just…thank you."

In the commotion, Maddie and Ted inched toward their ship's entrance. It was several more seconds until Joshy saw them.

"Thank you for waiting for us," he said.

"I'm…sorry," was all Maddie said in response, sadly and without making eye contact.

"Yes," Ted said. "We're very sorry."

"What do you—"

Joshy didn't have to finish his sentence before he heard the footsteps. Fifty SWAT officers descended on the building in full battle armor, pointing assault rifles at them as they sprinted forward.

"On the ground!" they shouted. "Everyone on the ground!!"

Joshy placed his hands on his head before he craned his neck to Maddie. "How could you?"

"They said if we wanted to leave, they had to get all of you," Maddie replied. "I'm sorry."

Ted pointed his sonic disrupter at Veronica and Debra, whose wounded eyes could barely focus on the weapon before Ted pulled the trigger and they fell to the floor. Moments later, they were all on the ground, surrounded by officers. Thick metal disruptor collars were snapped around Veronica and Debra's necks so they couldn't use their powers.

Debra and Joshy locked eyes for a moment, and then the butt of a gun smacked Joshy in the back of the head, and he faded into unconsciousness. He never even got the chance to tell Debra he loved her.

In the confusion, Maddie and Ted disappeared into their ship. They would be gone from Earth before the others were loaded into the vans and taken away.

Chapter 9

Maddie never wanted any trouble, so she didn't think twice about calling the Globorian embassy after a dozen reporters appeared on her front lawn, nor did she have any reservations about pleading with them to spare her and her husband, no matter the cost to the others. She didn't want to be a hero. She wanted to get her and her husband off the planet. Everything else was secondary to that concern.

What she didn't expect was for Debra and her friends to pull off a stunning escape from her house and take their camper on a high-speed joy ride around the city. Once that happened, she needed a new plan, which meant gathering everybody in a place for them to be easily arrested by the Globorians.

Maddie thought her plan would be foolproof, but then she also didn't think that Debra, Joshy, and Leslie would run off on a fool's errand. The Globorians told her they needed all the troublemakers gathered together in one place before they made an arrest, which meant that Maddie had to keep the rest of the group alive and unseen as they trekked to the warehouse where she docked her spaceship.

That was where the Globorians would spring their trap. They promised Maddie that if she delivered the group alive, she would be allowed to leave Earth without consequence. However, if she failed, then she would be treated as a traitor along with all the others.

All Maddie wanted to avoid was any consequences for her friends' actions. Her husband was already on a Globorian watch list for taking his disguise off in public, creating unregulated weapons, and complaining about the possibility of Globorian rule in chat rooms on the dark web. She couldn't be seen helping traitors to the Globorian Empire as well.

"I hope the kids are okay," Carole said as they trudged through a construction site toward Maddie's ship. Big piles of dirt were stacked high on either side of a giant hole in the ground.

"I'm sure they'll be fine," Bill said. "Leslie has a good head on her shoulders, and I trust Debra."

"What about Joshy?" Carole asked.

"He's in good hands at least," Bill said, smiling.

Carole couldn't help but laugh. Bill had a good sense of humor. It was one of the things that drew her to him in the first place. Carole worried a lot, and Bill was very good at cutting the tension when she got lost in her own thoughts.

"They're going to be fine," Veronica said. "I hope they are going to be fine."

"We should focus on ourselves right now," Maddie said, pulling herself to the top of a mound of dirt to find her bearings. "That's the Gateway Arch, so it should be that direction."

"Why don't you use your GPS?" Ted asked. "I always use the GPS."

Maddie didn't want to use her phone while the Globorians were tracking it. She didn't want to mess anything up and make them think she wasn't a team player. She was the ultimate team player.

"Listen to me for once, Ted, okay?" She sighed. "We wouldn't even be in this mess if you hadn't helped them escape."

"Yeah," Bill replied. "But if he didn't help us, we would have been arrested by now."

"Exactly," Ted said. "And who knows what the Globorians would do with us in custody, you know? You should be thanking me."

Maddie slid down the dirt mound and walked toward the chain link fence guarding the far side of the site. "I will never thank you for forcing me to traipse through dirt, Ted. Get over yourself."

She clasped her foot into the fence and lifted herself over. Ted followed, wishing he could use his tentacles to slither over the fence or take advantage of his lack of a spine to ooze through. Being a human was too much work.

"I don't know if I can do that," Carole said. "I'm not as spry as I used to be."

Bill bent down and interlaced his fingers together. "Here. I'll give you a boost."

Carole smiled. "Then how will you get over?"

"Don't take offense to this, but I'm in better shape than you."

"Are not!" Carole said playfully, even though she knew he was right.

"Do you want my help or not?"

Carole placed her foot into Bill's hand, and he lifted her up to the top of the fence. She swung her leg over and dropped down to the other side. Bill was a good man, Carole thought. He was misguided and foolish, but in his heart, he was a good man.

After she was over the gate, Bill struggled to place his foot through the chain links. He desperately wanted help but was too stubborn to ask for it. It was a common problem for Bill throughout his life. He often refused to ask for help even when he needed it the most.

"Here," Veronica said, pushing Bill's butt up the fence. "Don't fart on me."

Bill latched onto the top of the fence and pulled himself over. Then, after he was over, Veronica leapt onto the fence and crawled over like a pro, making both Bill and Carole look foolish in the process.

*

While the vacation was a travesty, Carole couldn't say that she completely hated it. After all, it had given her a way to connect with the man she once loved, instead of the asshole who stole her money. Now that they were leaving Earth, it seemed a trivial thing, money. However, it had never been about that. It had been about his betrayal of her trust.

She still saw flashes of the man she loved inside Bill's eyes and in the way he curled his fingers around hers. Even a couple days ago, she would have cringed at the thought of his touch, but as time went on, she started to miss it. Her mind lagged far behind her body in its desire to stay mad at a man who had been by her side for over twenty years.

She had read something somewhere about how love is accepting that somebody will betray you. They will disappoint you, and the true test of love is if you can forgive them.

At first, Carole thought it was a silly thing to think. However, as time went on, she started to realize that the people she loved most disappointed her constantly. She would have liked to see Leslie more, but she was always busy with school. She would have liked Joshy to have more motivation, but he never wanted to leave his room.

She mostly saw it in the man she loved. He had disappointed her before, sure, but this new betrayal was well beyond the pale. Now, however, they would soon embark on a new journey together. They would no longer be on this planet anymore, and she had to trust a man if she was going to travel the galaxy with him.

Otherwise, she would have to stay behind, or force him to do so, and she didn't want to doom either of them to live under the Globorian rule, so Carole, as she often did, decided to be the better person, and try desperately to see the best part of her husband, even in the worst circumstance of their lives.

*

Bill had pulled every trick out of his bag to impress upon Carole that he was still the man she'd once known, and he was happy that it was starting to work. A few days ago, she would have cringed at his touch, but now she let him wrap his fingers around hers. She still refused to touch him at night, or face him when they slept, but at least she had warmed to the idea of him existing, which was a step in the right direction.

Frankly, Bill thought, he got off easy. Forcing his family off the planet was the perfect reprieve from his disastrous situation. In the age of modern technology, there was nowhere on Earth to run where debtors could not find him, which meant the only place they could truly start over was on another planet.

It was not a perfect plan by any stretch. A much better one would have been not to get laid off, or to tell his wife about it immediately after he did. However, that ship had sailed, and all he could do was what he could do, and given the circumstance, he must admit, it was a pretty good option.

He was happier than he had been in months. A great burden had been lifted off his chest, and he seemed to be getting away with his transgressions. There would be consequences, of course, but for the first time in months, he was hopeful for the future, and a new start with his wife and family.

*

Veronica's guilt had weighed her down the whole walk from the camper to the warehouse. Her shoulder hurt and her legs were sore, but what really weighed on her soul was the guilt…the guilt of lying to her new friends. She was certain now that she could not bring the Carters with her when she and Debra left the planet. Not only was it against the rules, but it was also completely impractical.

Veronica and Debra were made of light particles. They could shrink or grow to fit any space, so being cramped into a small ship for nearly a decade until they reached another habitable planet would be fine for them.

However, the Carters were flesh and blood. They were the size they were, and that size was too big to fit comfortably in a small space ship for a decade, or even for one night.

Besides, she knew one thing about humans, and that was they stunk to high heaven. It must have been a holdover from their monkey ancestors, but being stuck anywhere with humans was utterly untenable, let alone for a decade…without a shower…on a small space ship. Thimberians didn't need a shower, because they didn't sweat, but humans did.

And they were loud. Not just loud, but aggressively loud. Veronica wanted to do the right thing, but not at the expense of her sanity.

Then, there was the question of food. Her spacecraft didn't have a kitchen. It had a small refrigerator for souvenirs, but not enough to keep humans fed for ten years or even one year. And how would they excrete their bodily fluids without a bathroom? On the floor of the ship? No thank you.

Debra had convinced her that bringing the Carters with them was the right move, but her daughter had never even seen their spaceship before, nor did she understand the complexity of interstellar travel. They would have to fuel up three times more often, and there weren't that many filling stations between Earth and the next habitable planet.

No, as much as she hated to admit it, it was more humane to leave the Carters on Earth to deal with whatever punishment the Globorians had for them than to take them off-world. At least they might survive on Earth. In space, they would be dead in a matter of days, and then Veronica would have to deal with dead human smell for the rest of the trip.

*

"What do you mean you're working with the Globorians?" Ted whispered as they walked behind the rest of the group. Maddie had pulled him back to let him in on the secret, assuming it might not go well. Ted was known to overreact to such things.

"I mean, I'm getting us off this planet, and you can thank me later."

"Thank you?" Ted said. "I'm closer to killing you."

"Fine," Maddie said, scoffing. "But do it later. And don't say anything. We'll be able to leave the planet scot-free after this if we play along. Don't you want that?"

Ted dropped his head. He liked his house guests well enough, but not enough to risk getting off the planet. He'd already fixed the ship with the carburetor he found, and it was now purring like a kitten. All he was waiting for was clearance from the Globorians for take-off.

"I don't like this, Maddie."

"You don't have to like it. You don't even have to do anything. Keep your mouth shut, and this will all be over soon."

Ted watched as Maddie, the woman he loved, walked toward her friends like nothing was wrong. The woman was cold as ice, but deep down that was one of the things he loved most about her. She would do anything to keep them safe.

*

The Globorians watched from across the street as Maddie pushed open the door to the warehouse and led her group inside. They had tracked her across the city, and now five dozen of their finest troops laid in wait for their attack. The dissidents stood no chance.

It would only be a matter of time before the enemies of Globor would be in their clutches. Once they were captured, the Globorians could begin the disinformation campaign, as they had dozens of times before. Then, this incident would all be behind them, and they could carry out the rest of their plans to conquer the third world dirtball that people called Earth.

Chapter 10

The Globorian SWAT team tied black hoods over Joshy, Leslie, and their parents' heads and stuffed them into the back of a black van. Joshy's thoughts, when they weren't about his own death, funneled back to Debra. *What would happen to her now? What would happen to him?*

The van ride jostled him back and forth for over an hour. He slammed into the other members of his family more than once as he was bumped around, which hurt his aching shoulder, but at least it meant they were still alive.

"I want you all to know," Bill said, shaky in his voice as they rumbled down the street. "That I love you all very much. Very much. I'm sorry we are here now, but I am glad we are here together."

"That's a lovely sentiment, dad," Leslie said. "I wish I wasn't here though. I wish none of us were here."

"Both lovely sentiments," Carole said. She reached out into the darkness and grabbed for Bill's hand. "I'm sure we'll be alright."

Of course, she was lying. She knew they would not be alright, but she put on a brave face anyway. That was what a mother did, after all. She wanted to cry. She wanted to scream. She wanted to lash out, but most of all, she wanted her children and husband to be safe. She didn't care much about what happened to her, as long as they survived.

"You don't have to tell us anything," a man with dark glasses said from the front of the van. "We have everything we need already. However, it's in your best interest to cooperate if you want to survive. Your choice, though."

If Joshy didn't need to help anybody, he wasn't going to do so, at least not intentionally. He played enough video games to know that once somebody gets what they want, they no longer had any use for you.

"No matter what you all do," Joshy said. "Don't tell them anything."

"Oh Joshy," Bill started.

"No," Leslie said. "He's right. It's the prisoner's dilemma. If none of us talk, then we might all go free. If one of us talks, it could save that person, but the rest will get a harsher punishment."

"Yes," Carole replied. "But isn't the right course of action to talk and save yourself in that situation? I remember you telling that to me once."

"Sure," Leslie said. "If you don't know or care about the other people, but we do. So, listen, they are going to try to break us, but we have to be strong. We can't say anything, no matter what they do, agreed?"

"I am sure there's a reasonable course—" Carole tried to utter.

"Just do it, mom," Joshy replied. "Whatever they try to get us to do, it's going to hurt Veronica and Debra. The only way we can help them right now is to shut up."

"Fine," Bill said. "But if I hear they've hurt you, Joshy, I don't know how I'll stay quiet. I will do anything to protect you and your sister."

"Remember I asked, okay?" Joshy said. "Please."

*

Joshy was the first person the man with the glasses brought into the interrogation room. The walls were a dull gray, and there was no furniture inside but a metal chair and table. Guards dragged Joshy into the claustrophobic room and chained him to the table. A single light bulb hung low over his head.

"I know you want to be brave," the man said. "But it's useless. We already know everything."

"I want a lawyer," Joshy said.

"See, now, that's where we're going to have a problem. We work outside the jurisdiction of the law, Joshy," the man said, pulling off his glasses. "I mean, technically we are the judge, jury, and executioners."

"Then you must have lawyers if you are all of that," Joshy said, not catching the man's eyes. "What's your name?"

"You can call me Guy, I suppose," the man said. "It's as good a name as any."

"I assume you're an alien, Guy?"

"We're not all aliens, Joshy. Some of us want to keep the peace."

Joshy craned his neck up. "If you're a human, how could you be working with the Globorians? They want to enslave us!"

"I wish it was that easy, kid. You don't know what you're up against."

"Sure I do. I'm up against a bunch of pissed off aliens and some cowardly humans who want to watch their planet get taken over by Globorians."

"You watch it, kid!" Guy screamed. "There is nothing I wouldn't do for this country. We have a very different definition about the right thing, is all. Do you know what kind of tech those aliens brought to us? Do you know how far we've leapt forward because of them? This place is a paradise now, compared to a hundred years ago. Why do you think that is?"

"Yeah, I don't want humanity to be imprisoned or killed. That's kind of my barometer."

"Your friend is exaggerating what's going to happen. They're not so bad, once you get to know them. If you do what they say, not much will change for you."

"Except that we'll be ruled over by aliens."

"Yeah, like humanity's been doing such a good job," Guy replied.

"Maybe not," Joshy said. "But at least it's our planet."

*

Joshy turned out to be tougher than Guy thought. He was nothing but a dead end and a waste of time. Next, he brought in Bill, who was much more scared of Guy than Joshy had been. Of course, Joshy had watched too many movies featuring rebellious types who overcame great odds to topple evil empires. He's been groomed since birth to be the rebellious sort in the face of adversity. Bill, on the other hand, grew up believing that the government, and those in power, should be respected. Even through the Vietnam War and Nixon's impeachment, he always believed that the government was there to work for the people.

"Bill," Guy said. "I've seen your financial history. It doesn't look good for you. Seriously, I don't see how you can ever pull yourself out of this hole without selling a kidney."

"I have two kidneys," Bill said, swallowing. The sweat glistened off his forehead. Guy used a tanning light in the room for maximum heat, and it was working to make Bill's throat dry. "I only need one."

"I could make this debt go away, Bill, with the snap of my fingers. You could go back to your life without owing anybody anything. Heck, I think there might even be an opening in our Los Angeles field office for somebody like you, if you cooperate."

Bill gulped again. "And what do you want me to do?"

"Convince your kid to go on camera and tell the world that aliens aren't real. It's not that hard Bill. It's just a little lie. You do that, and all of this...unpleasantness...it goes away. You have my word."

"So, you want me to turn on my son, then? That's the price of my soul?"

"You sold your soul long ago, Bill. I'm trying to help you reclaim some of it."

Bill gulped again. "No, thank you. I could never look my boy in the eyes again if I did that."

Guy scoffed. "I'm surprised you can look him in the eyes now after all you've done."

*

"What you're doing is illegal," Leslie sneered as Guy paced back and forth across the tiny room. "You can't keep us here. I'm a citizen of the United States. I have rights."

Guy smiled. "You would think that, huh? But you'd be surprised how much you can rewrite the rules of these United States without people noticing. Everything we're doing here is perfectly legal, in a way."

"I don't believe you."

"That's fine," Guy said. "You don't have to believe me, but please trust that without my help you'll never get out of this place alive. Heck, hardly anybody knows this place exists."

"I'd rather rot than help you."

Guy shrugged. "That's fine. You can rot. I don't mind. I have plenty of time. I'm not on a schedule or anything. Take all the time you want."

*

They didn't cuff Carole to the metal chair like they had the others. In fact, Guy was smiling when she came into the room, unlike the stoic face he'd presented to the rest of her family.

"Good to see you, Carole," Guy said.

"Thanks, I guess," Carole replied.

"Oh, I know your family told you to be strong, and that I was tough, but that's not true. I mean, I suppose I am tough in a way, but most of that was an act for the others. With you, I can be myself."

"I don't understand what's happening," Carole said, her eyes narrowing at Guy as he walked toward her.

"See, all of this was an act," Guy said, waving his hands. "All of it. We don't care about you or your family at all."

"Then why intimidate us?" Carole asked.

"I'll show you," Guy replied, rummaging through his pockets.

Guy pulled out his phone and opened it to his videos. On it, Debra sobbed. After a few seconds, she wiped her tears and swallowed.

"My fellow Americans. I have played a horrible prank on you. I told you there were aliens in this world, when in fact, that was a lie. It was an elaborate ruse conceived of by myself and two of my friends. We were immature and childish. I thought it would be funny, but it is anything but funny. I regret my decision. Please, forgive me. Once again, aliens are not real. I am not one, nor have I ever seen one in my life."

Guy closed his phone and put it back in his pocket. "It's beautiful, right? Gonna air on every major news channel in an hour, and this whole thing will be behind us."

"What about the mayor?" Carole said. "He sat on television and told everybody that aliens were real. Or the news stations? They have aliens on tape."

"Smoke and mirrors. Weather balloons. We'll come up with something. Politicians like power too much to mess with the order of things. He'll come around. And nobody trusts the news media. They'll believe it was a left-wing or a right-wing conspiracy to confuse them. Humanity is very easy to trick."

"How?" Carole said, tilting her head up. "How did you get Debra to help you?"

"Oh, it was easy," Guy said with a devilish smile. "We told them we were torturing you and kept rotating your family in here until she believed us. You might be strong, but we are excellent liars. Love really makes people do stupid things, doesn't it? You know that better than anybody, Carole."

"You're a monster."

"No, Carole. A monster would have beaten you to death a long time ago. I am trying to do my job," Guy said, sighing as he walked toward the door. "Anyway, you are free to go. You all are."

"And what about Debra and Veronica?" Carole asked, concerned.

"Best you not think about that too hard," Guy said. "And best you not discuss any of this with people outside your family. After all, we'll be watching you."

Chapter 11

Guy led Carole through the hall of a quaint police station and out into the waiting area. The walls were decorated with smiling police officers receiving medals and community events they sponsored. She even passed a wall filled with pictures from the station's softball league. It was not very intimidating at all.

"See, this isn't even a secure facility. It's a police station on the outskirts of St. Louis."

"Are Debra and Veronica here, too?" Carole asked, irritated.

"That's classified, ma'am, I'm afraid. However, your family is here. They're waiting for you by the reception desk."

Guy pushed open the wooden door in front of him, and Carole walked out into the waiting area where her family sat in uncomfortable chairs trying their best to stay awake. Carole broke down crying when she saw her children and husband.

"My babies," Carole said, running toward her children and wrapping them in a hug. "I'm so happy you are okay."

"Us too, mom," Leslie said. "We were so worried."

"Thank God you're okay," Bill said, kissing her on the forehead. "Do you have any idea why they let us go?"

Behind her, the television grew in volume. Carole looked over to see Guy holding the remote and waving at her. Carole turned around. On the screen, Debra was crying. It was the same video Guy had shown her before.

The whole family stood in silence as they watched Debra give her tearful speech. At the end, Joshy and Leslie were bawling as Bill looked on in horror.

"That's why they let us go," Carole said.

"Y'all have a good day, now," Guy said. "I went ahead and rented you a car to get you back to Los Angeles. I suggest you hurry home and stay there."

"We don't have a home to go home to," Bill said. "So, I think we'll be sticking around."

"Well, interestingly enough, my people finished calling all your debtors, and we wiped it all away for you. You now are debt free, courtesy of the Globorian Empire."

"Why would you do that?" Bill said. "We didn't help you."

"Yes, but we got what we needed anyway, like I said, and we couldn't have done it without you," Guy replied. "Consider it my gift to you, because you were all so helpful."

In that instant, all of Bill's money woes were fixed, and yet, instead of feeling unburdened, he felt…horrible.

*

"So we're going to leave them there and let who knows what happen to them?" Joshy asked as Bill pulled the blue Camry away from the police station.

Bill didn't like the idea of leaving Debra and Veronica behind any more than his son did, but he had a family to think about, and they had been given a new lease on life. Bill's debt was wiped clean, and they were forgiven all their sins from associating with Debra and Veronica.

If they kept their mouths shut, perhaps the Globorians would spare them during the invasion. If Bill tried to help again, who knew what would happen to them? It was a risk he couldn't take.

"There's nothing we can do for them now. We need to look after ourselves and prepare for what's to come."

Carole was equally happy to be out of debt, but the guilt of leaving Veronica and Debra to rot in prison, or worse, gnawed at her as they drove away from the police station. Still, she agreed with Bill that there was nothing they could do for their friends. If they tried any heroics, they would surely die or be arrested, and they were suddenly granted a new lease on life.

"This is stupid," Leslie said. "They are our friends."

Leslie knew the reason the Globorians wiped her father's slate clean was so that he would be too scared to fight them. Her father was now shackled by their generosity. She saw it every time a politician refused to speak out about a horrible corporation because the business was a massive donor to the candidate's reelection campaign.

The Globorians were smart, and they knew the best pressure was monetary. Her father would keep his mouth shut until it was too late. Once the Globorians invaded, there would be nothing to stop them, and Leslie knew it. However, she also knew there was nothing she could do to convince her dad to give back the money and do the right thing.

"I'm not going back to Los Angeles," Joshy said. "Even if you don't help me, I'm saving Debra."

"If you do that," Bill said. "You'll be dooming this family. Think about us for a second, Joshy. You haven't known this girl for very long. You've known us your entire life. Is it really worth risking our lives so you can save your girlfriend?"

Joshy grumbled to himself. "It's not about saving her. It's about doing the right thing."

"Come on, Joshy," Leslie said. "I'm on your side, but that's a little naive even for you."

Joshy knew his parents would never agree to help him, especially not now that all their financial problems were solved. Perhaps, if his father was still in debt, it would be a different story, but he wasn't.

Joshy's phone buzzed, and he pulled it out of his pocket. The notification read "Tara Zal wants to connect with you."

Joshy pulled open Facebook messenger and clicked on the accept request button. Tara Zal wrote: *I know you want to help Debra. We do too.*

A lump formed in Joshy's throat as his phone buzzed again. This time it read: *meet us here.*

Tara sent him a pin, and Joshy pulled it up on his GPS. The location was two miles southeast, past the Gateway Arch, across the river into East St. Louis, and above the downtown airport. His phone buzzed again: *Come quick. There isn't much time.*

Joshy looked out the windshield and saw the freeway overpass up ahead. Once his father reached the highway, Joshy would be trapped in the car for who knew how long. Luckily, the light turned red up ahead of them, and Bill had no choice but to slow down as cars zipped past.

"I'm sorry," Joshy said.

Joshy popped open the lock to the car and ran out into the street. His parents screamed after him, but he couldn't hear what they said. By the time their hollers reached his ears, he was down an alley and half a block away.

*

Joshy couldn't believe that he ran away from his family. He wasn't the kind of person to…do things. He was the kind of person who didn't do things. However, the last week had changed him; Debra had changed him. He would crawl over broken glass for her. He would fight a dragon for her. He would risk his life for her. If necessary, he would die for her.

He often laughed at the protagonists in video games who willingly risked their lives for a girl. While he loved Shadows of the Colossus, he could never imagine fighting twelve huge monsters in order to bring the girl he loved back from the dead, and yet, there he was, trudging across the Martin Luther King Bridge, Gateway Arch to his back, willing to risk any danger for the slim hope of saving the woman he loved.

Joshy was nearly across the river when he heard a car horn honk behind him. He turned to see his parent's blue Camry rental car speeding across the bridge toward him. Joshy took off like a bolt, but he was no match for the car, which skidded to a stop at the bottom of the bridge in front of him.

Bill ran out of the car and stormed up to Joshy. "Get in the car right now!"

"No!" Joshy said. "I'm not going anywhere with you."

Bill grabbed for Joshy but came up empty as the boy swerved to avoid him. "I'm not going to let you throw your life away like this."

"Don't you get it, Dad?" Joshy replied. "There's no life to go back to. This is all going away in a couple of months, and no matter what you think, or you say, it's not going to stop that."

"I know that, Joshy," Bill said. "But that…that doesn't change the fact that we can't help her. All you are going to do is get yourself hurt, or worse."

"That's my choice," Joshy replied. "I'm an adult."

"Dad!" Leslie said, stepping out of the car. "Joshy's right. It's his choice."

"He's making the wrong one," Bill said.

"No, dad," Leslie said. "You are. You have a second chance on life now, dad, and you're gonna go back to doing the same miserable thing. You have the chance to do something new. Something different. To really make a change."

"I am providing a life for the two of you," Bill replied. "That's my only job."

"You raised us right, dad," Joshy said. "You raised us to make our own choices. And I'm making the right one, even if you disagree with it. I don't care if I die, I can't let Debra…I don't even know what they'll do to her. If you can't understand that, I don't know how you can ever say you loved me."

Joshy bolted down the bridge, past his mother begging him to stop. Bill tried to run after him, but Leslie held him back. "It's over, dad. He made his choice. You have to accept it."

Bill collapsed into Leslie's arms. He simply wanted one moment to enjoy his family being saved, and before he could even breathe, they were broken apart again, and he was empty.

Chapter 12

Joshy realized that it was stupid to believe a complete stranger, but he had little other choice in the matter unless he intended to fight the Globorian army single-handedly, which would have been an even more horrible idea than believing a cryptic text message. The simple fact was that the mysterious figure behind the text was his best shot at saving Debra, and he had to pursue it, even if it led to his doom.

Joshy arrived at the run-down airplane hangar from Tara's GPS pin twenty minutes after running away from his family. He couldn't believe that his father was trying so hard to prevent him from doing the right thing.

He always looked up to his father as the moral compass of his family. It took him destroying their life savings to crack that façade, and now it lay in pieces, shattered. At least his meeting with his father did one thing. It assured him that he was on the right track. If his father thought it was the wrong move, Joshy was sure it was the right one.

As Joshy moved toward the rusted, dilapidated hangar, a golf cart sped across the tarmac toward him. A thick Latino man in an army uniform three sizes too small white-knuckled the steering wheel, bearing down on him.

"What are you doing here?" the man snarled as he slammed on the brakes in front of Joshy.

"I'm here to see Tara," Joshy replied. "She sent me a Facebook message."

"How does she know you?" the man replied.

"I was…am…the boyfriend of the alien who was captured. The one from the news. I helped her…come out to the world."

"Debra?" the man asked, suddenly interested. "The blue chick?"

Joshy nodded. "That's the one."

"She is fine," the man said, licking his lips. "You hit that?"

"Umm…that's not really…I'm not gonna answer that."

"Nope. You didn't hit that yet." The man leaned forward. "Once you go blue, though, it's always in you."

"Can you, like, tell me what's going on here?" Joshy asked, scratching his head.

The man patted the seat next to him. "I think I'll let Tara tell you about that. Hop in."

Joshy went around the cart and sat down. "You are very weird. Did you know that?"

"Boy," the man said. "You have no idea. I'm Randall. You can call me Randy if you want."

"Do you think we'll really get close enough that I need to remember your name?"

"God, I hope not. Johnny."

"It's Josh."

Randall pressed down on the pedal, and they lurched forward. "I don't care."

*

Randall drove them across the tarmac and into the ramshackle airport hangar. Joshy didn't know what he expected, but he certainly didn't think it would be completely empty of people, planes, or any equipment whatsoever.

Randall stopped the golf cart and pulled out a pistol from his waistband. "Now, are you sure you are who you say you are?"

"Of course, I am," Joshy said.

"Prove it to me," Randall said, lifting the gun to Joshy's temple.

"Or what, you'll shoot me?" Joshy asked.

Randall cocked his pistol. "Yup, or else I'll shoot you. You got that right."

Joshy pulled out his phone and swiped to the conversation he had with Tara. "What about this? This is her, isn't it?"

Randall looked down at the picture, unconvinced. "That don't mean shit. You can photoshop anything to look like anybody these days."

Joshy opened Facebook to Debra's profile. "Look, we are friends. Doesn't that mean anything?"

"No. People will accept anybody if they got enough friends in common."

Joshy sighed. "What do you want from me?"

"Something that proves you are who you say you are, and that you got a real relationship with that blue alien lady."

"Debra!" Joshy shouted. "Her name is Debra."

"Don't yell." Randall pressed the gun into Joshy's temple. "That's rude."

"Wait!" Joshy said. "Here." Joshy opened his phone and pulled up the first pictures he ever took of Debra, back outside the Bellagio, when life was still simple. "Here, look at this. I took this of her. I did that. Back in Vegas. Only two people have these pictures. Me and her."

Randall looked at the pictures. "She's cute. Your camera work ain't very good, though."

"Thanks for the critique, but she seemed to like it well enough. Can you put the gun away now?"

Randall squinted. "I dunno. There's still something about you I don't like. Probably safer to kill you."

"Jesus Christ," a deep female voice said behind Joshy. "Put the gun away, Randall. My goodness." Joshy turned to see a black haired, tan girl with a bomber jacket and glasses standing in front of the bathroom, drying her hands with a paper towel. "You can't threaten to kill everyone that comes here, Randall. I appreciate your aggressive security, but I'll vouch for this young man here."

"You're Tara," Joshy said.

"That's right. I'm Tara," she said, smiling. "You came quickly. I appreciate that. Welcome to the resistance."

*

Tara's head barely reached up to Joshy's naval, and he wasn't exactly tall. She powerwalked on her stubby legs in front of Joshy toward the far wall of the hangar, which was as barren as the other three, except for a shiny black door that stood out against the rest of the wall.

"I know this doesn't look impressive," Tara said. "But we're trying to be as secretive as possible. After all, what would it look like if hundreds of aliens roamed around this hangar? It would surely draw suspicion."

"Aliens," Joshy said. "Are you all aliens?"

Tara shook her head. "Not all of us. Some of us are human, like you, but most of us, like me and Randall over there, are aliens. Hell, he's a Globorian if you can believe it."

"A Globorian, are you crazy?" Joshy asked.

Tara pressed her hand against the black door, and it lit up with a hundred different colored lights that spun around her hand. "Easy, Josh. He doesn't like it when people raise their voice to me. He's very protective."

"Why would you bring a Globorian here? They're all trying to kill us."

"Whoa, Josh. That's a little bit racist. Sure, the government of Globor is trying to kill and enslave humanity, but each Globorian is as different as you or me, and this one happens to believe that the invasion is wrong. He actually thinks you humans are kind of cute, in your own way."

The black door slid open, and Tara walked into the darkness beyond it. Joshy didn't move. He felt as though he was going to faint. His knees buckled under him as he steadied himself against the wall of the hangar bay.

"You coming?" Tara asked.

"Yes," Joshy said with a faint nod. "This is all a lot to take in."

"Well, do it quickly. If we're going to save your girlfriend, we have to do it by nightfall."

"Where are you taking me?" Joshy asked, walking toward Tara.

"This elevator will take you down to my secret hangar, where we're preparing to strike back against the Globorian horde."

*

"You have to understand something about Globor," Tara said as they descended the black elevator. "It's a hostile place. The only thing Globorians respect is force. And humanity hasn't given any pushback to them for a hundred years, so the horde thinks you are weak, cowardly even."

"We're not cowards. We fight all the time."

"Globorians don't consider that fighting. Globorians send nuclear bombs at each other when one of them cuts in front of another one in traffic. Their war game is strong. So, the fact that you haven't ever punched them in the face shows that you are cowards."

"The man who arrested us said the Globorians gave us tech that helped advance our civilization. Is that true?"

"Yes. They've worked with your government going all the way back to Teddy Roosevelt. It's insane how corrupt your government officials are, did you know that?"

"I'm vaguely aware."

"The Globorians aren't smart, but they are ruthless, so when they saw all it took to sway your politicians was money, they were more than happy to oblige. Seriously, you must be one of the most short-sighted species I've ever met."

"And what are you then, if you're not human?"

"I am Inkarian, the longest-lived species in the galaxy, and creator of the wireless network you use today."

"Inkarian?" Joshy asked, puzzled. "I thought there were no Inkarians on Earth. Isn't our planet too far from the center of the galaxy for you to bother with us?"

"It is, and we aren't. However, as I mentioned, each alien is an individual, as different as you humans are from each other. I was a slave on my planet, bartered off to the Globorians after the third Inkarian war. I was a slave to their race for eons until I made my escape with the help of Randall."

"Randall the Globorian helped you?"

Tara nodded. "He was my first friend on this planet, maybe ever."

"If you escaped from them, why are you still here?" Joshy asked. "Why didn't you abandon Earth?"

"I was going to leave this planet, but I grew fond of it. Besides, I had nowhere to return to. For an Inkarian, when we are sold, we are bound to that new species forever. I was without a home, and so I spent my days trying to sabotage that which I had built. You may have heard of Chernobyl. That was mine."

"That was a horrible disaster. So many people killed."

"I'm not proud of it, but I did what I could to rebel against the Globorian invasion. After all, Globorians only respond to force. I thought for sure my sabotage would bring out the fight in you humans, but you are so easily manipulated to believe it was an accident. Without the support of humanity, no aliens would step forward to help you.

"Then, your Debra's speech changed everything. Suddenly, there was a conversation among humanity. There was a groundswell of rebellion among you, and it has grown bigger and bigger since she started it. What started as a slow trickle of recruits became a flood as the hours passed. However..."

"However what?"

"Her face was plastered all over the news this afternoon, saying she was lying. It has shaken our cause to the core. We must get her back, and she must become the face of our resistance, or it will crumble."

"It's not too late?"

"No," Tara said. "The time draws nigh, and we must move quickly, but it is not too late for your love or for your planet."

The black elevator door opened, and Joshy followed Tara out into the rafters of a massive underground base. Thousands of aliens in a dozen colors, sizes, and shapes marched around the hangar moving boxes filled with guns and grenades. Speckled among them, humans of every race and creed shuffled back and forth. Sitting in the middle of the hangar was a long, sleek silver ship being polished by a purple alien with long arms.

"Wow," Joshy said, stunned.

"Yes," Tara said. "We have an army like we've never had before, but it is still not enough. We need to give hope to humanity and aliens all over the world. It is only together we can rise up and—"

A Skype call came through on Tara's phone. She answered, and Randall's head popped up.

"What is it?" Tara asked.

"There's a problem," Randall replied. "You're gonna want to see this."

"Put it on camera."

Randall flipped the camera around and tracked a blue Camry driving straight toward him across the tarmac.

"Are we expecting any new visitors?" Tara asked.

"I'm never expecting anybody, ma'am."

"Bring them to me. Alive."

Joshy caught a glimpse of the tall man in the driver's seat and the woman in the passenger's. Then, he recognized the car.

"Please don't kill them," he said. "That's my family. I want to kill them myself for following me here."

Couldn't they leave well enough alone? They didn't have to agree with his decision, but at least he expected them to respect it. Now, he was pissed.

Chapter 13

Joshy was anxious the entire ride up the black elevator with Tara. He knew how itchy Randall's trigger finger was and hoped the oafish guard could follow directions. When they finally reached the top, Joshy ran out of the hangar toward the speck on the tarmac that was his parent's car. He had never run so fast in his whole life, and by the time he reached the car his side ached something fierce.

"What are you guys doing here?" Joshy asked, pressing his hand on the hood of his parent's car. "I told you I'm not going back with you."

Bill sat nervously in the driver's seat, hands in the air, with Randall's gun pressed against his temple. "We're not here to bring you back. We're here to help you."

"Help me?" Joshy said. "That doesn't sound like you."

"He's telling the truth," Carole replied from the passenger's seat. "Can you please get this nice man to stop pointing a gun at your father now?"

"Randall," Joshy said. "It's okay, they're cool."

Randall didn't move though. If anything, he stiffened up harder. "I don't take orders from you, Jimmy."

"That wasn't an—" Joshy started, before turning to Tara. "Can you please tell him?"

"It's alright," Tara said, walking up behind Joshy. "Randall, put the gun down."

"You sure, ma'am?" Randall said. "I don't like the look of the one in the back."

He was talking about Leslie, and honestly, he was right to be a little scared of her. If she had her way, she would have ripped his head right off, popping it like a zit.

"Yes, Randall," Tara said. "Stand down."

Randall dropped his arms and placed his pistol in his holster. Once he was relaxed, Joshy let out a deep sigh of relief.

"Why did you come here?" Joshy asked. "You could've been killed."

"Like your mother said, Joshy," Bill replied. "We're here to help you. Your mother and sister were very convincing. They said that if it mattered that much to you, we should honor that as a family and help you."

"I used much stronger words," Leslie said. "But I'll let him make me look more eloquent than I really am." Leslie got out of the car and wrapped her brother up in a big hug. "I'm not gonna let you do something stupid alone."

"It's good to see you, sis," Joshy said. "But you really shouldn't be here. This is really dangerous stuff."

"He makes a good point," Tara said, walking up to Leslie. "How did you even find him anyway?"

"We put a parental tracker on his phone after he ran off at the Grand Canyon," Carole said, lifting herself out of the car. "We called the phone company, and they told us exactly where he was."

"Wait," Tara said frantically. "Which phone company?"

"Sprint."

"Shit," Tara said, looking up into the sky. "Sprint is run by the Globorians. They heard every word, and now they know where Joshy is, which means they know where we are."

"I told you it was a bad idea to bring him here," Randall said. "He's gonna ruin everything."

"There," Tara said, pointing up to a tiny speck in the sky. "Does that look like an SR-72 to you?"

"What are you looking at?" Joshy said, staring up at what looked like nothing to him.

"I can't tell, Boss," Randall said, squinting. "But if it is, you have three, four minutes tops."

"What's going on here?" Bill asked.

"Get back in your car," Tara said. "Follow me. Throw your phones down and run them over."

"Wait a sec—"

"No questions!" Randall said, raising his gun. "Just do it!"

The Carters, Joshy included, threw down their phones and piled into the car. Tara hopped into the golf cart, and Randall gunned it toward the hangar with Bill following close behind, running over their phones along the way.

"Good to see you again, Dad," Joshy said from the front seat.

"Your new friend seems nice. Hostile, but nice."

"Well, she's an Inkarian. They are like that, probably. Or not. I don't know."

Randall pulled into the hangar and Bill skidded to a stop right behind her. "I hear them!"

"Get into the elevator," Tara said, placing her hand on the black door until it opened for them.

Joshy heard the whistle of an aircraft fly overhead. In its wake, fire exploded on the ground where they'd dropped their phones. It snaked their way toward them, explosion after explosion erupting as the heat closed in on the hangar.

"Napalm!" Randall screamed as he pushed Joshy into the elevator.

With them all inside, Tara pushed the doors closed as an explosion rocked the rafters above them. The elevator vibrated and shook as the hangar collapsed on top of them, leaving nothing but a heap of warped iron above them.

"Don't worry," Tara said. "This elevator was built to withstand the blast of a nuclear bomb. We'll be safe in here."

Bill, somehow, didn't believe they would be safe anywhere, not anymore, not after his family threw in their lot with Tara and whatever she was planning.

"You're lucky," Tara continued. "If you had been anywhere else, you would have been dead right now. The Globorians were counting on that. If they knew what was down here, they would have sent an army."

"What's down here?" Carole asked.

"An army," Randall said with a sly grin.

*

The black elevator slid open inside the underground base, and once again Joshy was on the rafters overlooking the sprawling hangar bay, but this time he was with his family. Truth be told, he wasn't happy about his family coming to help him. He was hoping they would be on their way home by now. Even though he appreciated their support, he wanted to spare them the grave danger they faced for joining the rebellion with him. Now, that was impossible.

"As I was telling your son until you rudely interrupted us," Tara started, walking across the metal rafters toward a set of stairs near the wall. "I have been on Earth for over one hundred years, a relic of a pact made between my people and the Globorians. Twenty years ago, I escaped my captors and built this hangar to leave Earth for good. However, once I finished my spaceship, I couldn't leave."

"What stopped you?" Carole asked, following Tara down the stairs.

"Humanity did," Tara replied, her boots stomping on the metal steps as she descended the stairs. "You are dumb and irrational, but you do not deserve Globorian rule. So, I worked to sabotage and undermine their plans at every turn."

"That's noble, I guess," Leslie said.

"It was a hard few decades, trying to recruit an army. For a long time, the only person to join me was Randall. He is my oldest friend."

"Tara is my only friend," Randall replied. "Most aliens don't trust Globorians."

"You're a Globorian?" Leslie asked, confused.

"Don't judge," Tara said. "Some of my best friends while I was imprisoned were Globorians. He's the one who helped me plan my escape. The only one."

"Maybe you didn't have that many friends after all," Bill said.

"Maybe that's true," Tara replied.

Bill followed Tara across the hangar. A red alien with fire hair dragged a cache of machine guns across the hangar floor in front of him.

"Why did it take so long for other aliens to join you?" Bill asked.

"Most aliens chose to go off-world instead of fight. It's not their war, after all. They weren't willing to risk their lives for a planet that wasn't theirs."

"Makes sense," Leslie said. "Most humans aren't willing to fight for a different country, let alone another planet."

"Exactly. However, something magical happened after Debra made her speech a couple days ago. Aliens started saying yes. They started showing up when I recruited them. Literally overnight, our forces grew tenfold. Now, we have the beginnings of an army, and we can actually do something with it."

"So all of this was in the last two days?" Carole asked.

"It's best not to think how fresh we are. I wanted more time to train, but if we don't save Debra tonight, there's no telling where she will end up. She nearly broke our cause with her last speech this afternoon. We're hanging by the thread of a needle, and if we don't get her back, this could all fall apart as quickly as it came together."

"What do we need to do?" Joshy said.

Tara pointed toward a cache of weapons. "Pick a weapon, figure out how to use it, and pray to the gods that luck is on our side."

*

Leslie and Joshy stood over a crate full of semi-automatic machine guns. Leslie couldn't will herself to pick one of them up. Joshy wasn't having much more luck with his own nerves. It was one thing to be brave in theory, but picking up one of the guns in front of him made joining a militant rebellion all too real.

"I didn't think this would be how I spent my summer vacation," Leslie said, shaking her head.

"Me neither," Joshy said. "I thought it would be a lot of boring road music, and trying to zone out while dad made corny jokes. I thought it would be torture, but I didn't think it would be war."

"Yeah, I figured the worse it would get was when dad made us play the license plate game."

Joshy sighed. "I wish that's what'd happened."

"I think we all do. None of us want to be in an intergalactic civil war, do we?"

"I mean, when you play it in a video game," Joshy replied. "It sounds like the most fun ever, but now, faced with the reality it, it's a lot less fun."

"Still, you kind of like the idea of being a hero, don't you?" Leslie teased. "I mean you have been playing those stupid games your whole life."

"Yeah…" Joshy said, trailing off. "I thought I would be better prepared for it than I am."

Leslie reached down and picked up a gun. She handed it to Joshy. "Well, take this weapon and go find the ammo marshal, soldier. The world is in your hands."

"What?" Joshy asked, taking the gun.

"Isn't that what your games say? I thought it'd be better if I sounded more like them."

"Oh," Joshy said, gripping the gun tightly. "It doesn't, but thanks anyway."

"Hey," Leslie said, grabbing him by the shoulder. "It's going to be okay."

Joshy faked a smile. "Sis, I've played enough games to know that it's never okay. We might win, but nothing's going to be okay about it. Some of these people are going to die, and they're not NPCs, not this time. They are real flesh and blood. You might die, mom or dad might die. Hell, I might die."

Leslie wrapped him in a big hug. "Don't think like that, okay? Please?"

"I'll try," Joshy said, wrapping his arms around his sister.

*

Joshy walked away from his sister and toward a pile of ammunition. His father was picking through the ammo, picking a box up and setting it down, puzzled and bewildered.

"Joshy," Bill said, confused. "I can't seem to find the ammo for an M-4. Do you know what it looks like?"

"It's the same as the M-16 ammo," Joshy said, picking up a box of M-16 bullets. "They're interchangeable in video games. Here you go."

"Thanks," Bill said, taking the box. "You know, I've never fired a gun before."

"Me either. I mean, in real life. The closest I got was in arcades, firing those big, fake, orange ones."

"I never thought it was a necessary life skill to have," Bill said. "I guess I was wrong."

"It sucks," Joshy said. "You know, I appreciated that you made us feel safe all those years. I never thought I would need to protect myself, and that made my life…nice. I think it was the right call, even given what we know now."

"Well, I certainly feel like a failure of a father right about now," Bill said, tearing up. "But thank you for saying that."

Joshy nodded. "I'm going to hug you now."

Bill opened his arms, and Joshy disappeared inside his father's arms. He knew it might be the last time he saw his father, and Bill knew it too, but neither of them wanted to say goodbye.

*

After finishing with his father, Joshy walked across the hangar toward his mother, who was seated on a bench near a shuttle bay door.

Carole hadn't chosen an M-4. She wanted something smaller and lighter, so she went with an Uzi. She sat on the bench trying to jam the bullets into the clip, but her hand kept slipping.

"Let me help you with that," Joshy said, sitting down next to her.

"Thanks," Carole replied. "I don't have the strength, or coordination, to load a gun."

Joshy pushed the bullet down until the spring gave, and the bullet slid in. By the second bullet, his finger hurt something fierce, but he didn't let it show on his face.

"This isn't easy, is it?" Joshy asked.

"None of this is easy," Carole replied.

"I appreciate you coming here," Joshy replied. "I know you don't agree with me, but thank you for supporting me."

"I will always support you," Carole said with a smile. "As long as I'm able." She placed her hand on Joshy's back and rubbed it like she had when he was sick as a child. "I would do anything for you and your sister. You know that, right?"

Joshy smiled. "I do, mom. And I love you for it."

"I love you, too, sweetie," Carole said. "Now, how many of these barrel thingies do I need? I picked up fifteen of them. Is that enough?"

Joshy looked behind him and saw fourteen magazines piled up behind her. He couldn't help but laugh. "Yes, I think that will be enough. Leave it to my mom to be the most prepared person in a battle."

"You don't want to run out of ammo. I've watched you play enough of those games to know that."

Joshy laid his head on his mother's shoulder. He wanted to grin, and he wanted to cry, but all he could do was look off into space with fear in his eyes.

"It will be okay, won't it, mom?"

Carole stroked Joshy's hair. "Of course. It will all be fine."

Neither of them believed that, but it brought comfort for Joshy to hear it, and for Carole to say it, so they allowed the lie to linger on the air.

*

"Alright, listen up!" Tara shouted in front of the group of several hundred aliens and humans, including the Carter family, all banded together in the middle of the hangar, holding guns, dressed in army fatigues, and scared out of their minds.

"This isn't going to be easy," Tara continued. "Our goal is to intercept a convoy of prisoners being led out of a detention facility at 2100 tonight. The convoy will be heavily guarded, and the Globorians will likely be ready for our attack. We're not ready, but we have to attack anyway."

A green-tailed reptile alien raised its hand. "If we're not ready then why are we attacking them now?"

"Two reasons. First, because Debra Thompson is on board that convoy, and she has been the beacon of hope for our movement the past few days. She is the reason many of you are here. However, her last communication hurt us badly. We need thousands more aliens from all around the world to join the cause if we stand a chance of beating back the Globorians, and her last tearful broadcast scared a lot of folks out of joining us. It put questions into the minds of many humans, and if they won't fight, aliens won't fight either. We need her back on our side, and we need her to be that beacon of hope again, or we will fail before we even begin."

"What's the other reason?" A dark-skinned woman with long, black hair asked.

"The other reason is that if the Globorians don't see us punch back, they will never take us seriously, and they will never halt their attack."

"Do you really think we can make them halt their invasion attempts with one attack?" A purple alien with a dozen tentacles protruding from its head asked.

"No, not one attack, but this will be one of many. If we succeed, hundreds more will join our cause, all over the world. This is the first attack, which is why it must be successful. If we can beat the Globorians tonight, it will give us hope for the future. Are you with me?"

The crowd exploded into thunderous applause. Once they died down, Tara continued, "Then get your assignments, and may the gods bless us and keep us."

Chapter 14

Joshy stood behind a concrete barricade at the end of an alleyway in the perfect position to attack the oncoming convoy when it turned the corner. It had taken them three hours to make their way through the sewers under St. Louis and set up their blockade.

If Tara's reports were correct, there would be a large semi-truck and four Humvees coming up the alley in a matter of moments. Tara's army had created roadblocks around the city to funnel the convoy into the narrowest alleyway in East St. Louis, which wouldn't allow them to escape during the attack.

"I have to admit," Leslie said from the other side of a concrete barricade. "This is pretty exhilarating. How does it compare to your video games?"

"There is no comparison," Joshy grumbled. "This is a million times more terrifying."

Joshy begged Tara to be at the front of the ambush with as much vigor as he pleaded for his family be on the rooftops where they would be safe.

He looked up to see his mother and father along the rooftops on either side of the alleyway where they wouldn't be in as much danger as the assault team. His sister, on the other hand, was very persuasive and talked her way onto the advance team at the frontline of the battle even after Tara gave out her assignments.

"I wish you would fall back a little bit," Joshy said. "You don't have to be right at the barrier. They're gonna be gunning for us."

"You can move to the back, too," Leslie said, pressing her rifle into her shoulder. "I'm your older sister, and I'm going to make sure you don't do anything stupid."

"We're all doing something stupid," Joshy replied.

"Hey!" Tara shouted, moving up to Joshy's position with the rest of the five-person team which would lead the assault and rescue Debra. "I put you on the front lines for a reason. Debra needs to see a friendly face when we open the trailer. That means you two. Neither of you get shot, at least not until you've done your part."

"I'll try," Joshy replied.

"Don't try," Tara replied. "Do."

Tara's phone beeped, and she looked down at it. "The convoy is pulling into the alley now. The scout team will close in from behind, take out the back two Humvees, and block off the exit. Our job is simple. Cover fire from the roof will allow us to get to the back of the van and rescue Debra. Once we've got her and the rest of the hostages, we get out and escape. Nobody gets hurt, okay? Say it."

"Nobody gets hurt," Joshy mumbled.

"Nobody gets hurt," Leslie repeated.

*

"I'm sorry," Bill said, aiming his gun down at the alleyway in front of Joshy, where the Globorian convoy was supposed to appear any moment. Carole stood on the roof on the opposite side of the alley, doing the same. The buildings were so close together, they could almost reach out and touch each other.

"This isn't really the time, Bill," Carole replied. "I'm trying to focus."

"There is never going to be a good time, my love," Bill said. "If we don't get through this, I want you to know one last time that I love you, and I'm sorry."

Carole looked up from her post and smiled. "I love you, too. Even with all that's happened, I'm glad you're in my life."

Bill smiled at her, and she smiled back. Then, he returned to his post, looking down the barrel of his gun, as he watched bright headlights illuminate the alley. A moment later, the hood of a black Humvee came into view.

"Good luck," Bill said. "I love you."

"You said that already," Carole said with a smile.

"I know," Bill replied. "I really meant it though."

"I love you, too," Carole replied, holding her Uzi out in front of her.

*

A black Humvee turned down the street toward them. A couple seconds later, a semi-truck rolled through the alley. Joshy heard more Humvees behind the semi, but the alley was too narrow to make them out.

"This is it," Tara said. She looked down as another text buzzed through. "The convoy is through the alley. Scout teams have blocked them in."

Tara stood up and raised her arms. When she dropped them, floodlights shone through the alley. A rocket launcher fired down behind the semi-truck, and two of the Humvees flew into the air, on fire.

"Now!" Tara shouted.

From the rooftops, suppressing fire rained down on the first Humvee. Tara ran forward with two other members of the advance team. Joshy and Leslie followed them, guns drawn.

"Nobody move!" Tara shouted as she moved up to the first truck. She looked inside, but she didn't find a

Globorian. Instead, she found a Thimberian, glowing a faint blue and tied to the steering wheel, crying.

"I'm sorry," it said. "I'm sorry."

"What happened?" Tara shouted.

Joshy and Leslie didn't care to wait and see what happened. They continued down the alley to the semi-truck behind it. The rest of the advance team fanned out in front of them, checking out the burning wreckage of the Humvees behind the semi-truck. From down the alleyway, another team advanced into the alley, pulling up the rear of the attack.

"Cover me," Joshy said.

He jumped onto the back of the truck and pulled the back gate open. Inside, there was only Debra, tied to a chair, surrounded by a mountain of C-4. A timer clicked down behind her from one minute down to fifty-nine seconds.

"Josh!" Debra shouted. "Run! It's a trap!"

More suppressing fire came from the rooftops, but the new rounds sounded different than the ones from the guns of his allies. Joshy turned to see bullets raining down from the rooftops across the street from where the scout team was set up behind him. In a hail of gunfire, half of the scout team fell to the ground dead in a matter of seconds. He watched two members of the advance team fall as well, their blood mixing with the oil from the burning Humvees.

"It's a trap!!!" Joshy shouted.

It was too late, though. Two bombers whizzed through the air, and before he could look up, bombs landed on the buildings on either side of the alleyway and rocked the truck back and forth.

"Mom! Dad!" Joshy shouted. "Leslie, go check on them!"

Leslie ran away as the gunfire turned from the alley toward the buildings above them. Dozens of Globorians rose from the buildings across the street and fired at the remaining rebellion fighters. Joshy returned fire before ducking back into the truck toward Debra.

"Josh!" Debra shouted. "Get out of here!!!"

"I'm not leaving you!" Joshy shouted. "This whole mission was about keeping you safe. If we can't do that, we've failed and risked all their lives for nothing."

"You're an idiot!" Debra screamed back as Joshy rushed toward her.

"Maybe," Joshy said, looking around at the mountain of C-4. "Do you have any idea how this thing is wired?"

"No," Debra said. "If you can get the collar off me, maybe I can dismantle it, though."

Joshy smashed the butt of his gun against the collar. The collar didn't budge. All it did was shock Debra and send her crashing to the ground.

"Ow!!!" Debra shouted, struggling to wriggle free. "Why would you do that?"

"I thought…I don't know what I thought!"

Tara rushed into the semi-truck. "We're getting killed out there! What are you two lovebirds doing?"

The timer ticked down below thirty seconds. "There's a bomb. I can't get her out."

"Move!" Tara said.

"What's going on?"

"This was all a trap. They knew we were coming. Somehow. They knew Debra would be the perfect bait. If we lose fewer than eighty percent of my men, it will be a miracle."

"How are my parents?"

Tara acted like she didn't hear him, and he didn't want to know the answer anyway. She ran forward and placed her hand on the side of the collar. A keypad opened on the side. She pressed a sequence of numbers and letters, and the collar fell off. As it did, Debra turned blue and rose into the air. Her body vibrated through the metal bracers that kept her locked down until she was free.

"Thanks!" Debra said.

"Don't thank me," Tara said, turning to the bullets pelting the back of the truck. "We're about to die."

Debra rushed forward and threw a shockwave at the Globorians across the street. The buildings cracked and bulged under the force of her blast. The buildings crumbled to the ground, and three squads of Globorians fell with it. Debra looked back at the timer, it was down to ten seconds.

"Let's go!" Debra shouted.

Debra rushed out of the truck. Tara and Joshy followed behind. They hopped down the gate and around the semi-truck. Globorian bullets fired behind them as they sped down the alley.

"Back to the sewers!" Tara said, sprinting through the hail of bullets. "Fall back!"

Joshy stepped over a body, barely breathing. He looked down and saw that it was his sister. She had two bullet holes through her shoulder.

"Sis," he cried, pulling her to her feet. "Don't die! Don't die!"

"There's no time," Debra replied, before seeing it was Leslie. "Les!"

Beeping blared from inside the truck indicating the timer had reached zero. Debra rushed forward and pulled Joshy toward the barricade. As she did, he lost his grip on Leslie. She opened her eyes for one second, and then the truck exploded, hurling her forward, along with Joshy and the others.

For a moment, there was peace through the violence. Then, Joshy opened his eyes to ringing in his ears. He looked over to see the semi-truck on fire, and his sister smoking in the flames in front of him.

"Les!!!" Joshy shouted. "No no no no no no no."

He ran over to her and patted out the flames. She was severely burned by the explosion, but somehow, she was still breathing. One of her arms and both her legs her had been amputated in the blast, but she could still talk, even though her breathing was labored.

"Josh," Leslie said. "Did we—did we win?"

Josh looked around at the explosion. The rooftops that once held his parents were on fire. Debris fell around them as Tara's few remaining troops fired at the Globorians. Dozens of bodies lay riddled and dead on the ground.

"Yeah, Les," he said, tears in his eyes. "We won."

"Hooray," Leslie said. "Then—it was worth—"

She couldn't talk anymore. The pain was too great. She winced.

"Stay with us, Les," Joshy said, bawling big, ugly tears. "We're going to save you."

Joshy looked up to see Debra, tears in her eyes. "We're going to save her, right, Debra? Tell me we're going to save her."

Debra couldn't speak. All she could do was cry. Tara, on the other hand, knew exactly what to do.

"Medic!!!" she shouted. "This one is still alive!"

Two yellow haired aliens sprinted forward and threw Leslie onto a makeshift stretcher. They didn't waste any time before encasing her in a blue protective bubble.

"She'll be in cryogenic suspension until we can look at her back at the base. If we can save her, we will," Tara promised. "Now, we have to go. Globorian reinforcements are coming any second. Get back to the sewers and get out of here."

"Come on, honey," Debra said. "There's nothing more we can do here."

Joshy knew she was right, so he let Debra pick him up from the ground. He hobbled over piles of bodies as he walked forward, across the barrier, toward their exit. As he did, he saw the charred face of his mother and the dead eyes of his father, laying on the ground in front of him.

"No!" Joshy shouted. "They were supposed to be safe!" He turned to Tara. "They were supposed to be safe!"

"I'm sorry!" Tara said. "That's the price of war."

"I've lost everything," Joshy said. "Everything!"

Debra squeezed his hand as she struggled to keep him upright. His legs were like wet noodles beneath him, but Debra kept him moving forward. She knew the feeling of grief well, and sadness filled her soul as she looked at the carnage that her rescue had brought. However, she knew they couldn't stop either. If they stopped, they would be dead.

"You had better be worth it," Tara said to her.

"I didn't ask to be saved," Debra said back to her.

Joshy looked back at his parents one last time before he disappeared down the sewer grates to escape. It was his fault for involving his family in his battle. They could have been halfway home by now. Even if the Globorians invaded, and they were enslaved, at least they would be alive.

Chapter 15

Joshy dragged himself through the sewers under St. Louis and back to Tara's base, defeated and broken-hearted. His parents were dead. His sister barely clung to life. All that he had in this world was Debra, who had never left his side for one second.

He couldn't help but feel that though he still had Debra, the price wasn't worth it. He exchanged one person he loved for three, and it was his fault that they were dead. It was all his fault. He wanted to cry. He wanted to scream, but he just felt...numb...as if he didn't have anything left in his body.

"I never said thank you," Debra said, as they sat on a bench inside the hangar. The same one Joshy and his mother once sat on together for a brief moment before the battle began. "Thank you so much for saving my life."

"It was nothing," Joshy said.

"No," Debra said. "It was everything."

"You're right. It was everything." Joshy nodded, lost in thought. "How did they know, Debra?" He said. "How did they know we were coming?"

"I don't know," Debra replied. "Maybe they overheard something."

"Maybe, but the only people who knew our plans were in this hangar," Joshy said, looking around the hangar at the hobbling and wounded survivors. It was hard to believe one of them was a traitor, and yet, that was the only possible explanation. "One of these people got my parents killed, and I'm going to find out who it was, Deb."

Debra squeezed his hand tighter. "I know you will."

She wanted to say something reassuring to him, but she had her own guilt monster to deal with. She was the reason not only Joshy's parents died, but everybody else in that alleyway, too. All of this was her fault.

"Come with me," Tara said, walking up to Joshy.

"I don't really feel like—" Joshy started.

"Just do it," Tara said. "Please. I think you will feel better after you see what I have to show you."

Joshy sighed and pulled himself up from the bench, letting go of Debra's hand in the process. Debra went to pull him back, but he moved his hand away.

"I'm going to do this alone," Joshy said. "I'll see you later."

It broke her heart, but she understood. She also had lost everything, so she knew how it felt. Her mother was still imprisoned by the Globorians, and Debra's escape endangered her mother's life. However, she couldn't tell that to Josh, not until the pain of his loss subsided a bit.

*

"We recorded the whole attack," Tara said walking across the hangar with Joshy. "Frankly, we hoped it would go better."

Tara brought Joshy to a computer terminal with thirty screens. A frog-like alien with long, pink hair looked up at the screen, licking its eye.

"Gor," Tara said. "Show him."

Gor pulled up the attack, and Joshy watched it all unfold on video again, reliving his horror. He watched the suppression fire. He watched the explosions. He watched his sister blow up. He watched his parents struggle for their last breath.

"How would this make me feel better?" Joshy asked, sick to his stomach.

"We uploaded it to the dark web a few minutes ago," Gor said. "It's already got a million hits, in less than an hour. Take a look at this."

Gor pulled up a video of a blue alien that looked like a salamander who was sitting in front of her computer screen watching the video. "This is awesome! Screw Globorians, man! Let's fight and take back this planet!"

Gor pulled up another video. This time, a slug alien with translucent green skin was on screen, smiling at the attack. "Viva la revolution!!!! My planet has lived under Globorian rule for too long!"

Gor pulled up a third video. A black woman with a tight afro smiled at the camera. "Screw those Globorians! You tell me where to be, and I'll be there!"

"I still don't get it," Joshy said.

Tara turned to Joshy. "Don't you see? People are responding to us. We've gotten thousands of requests from aliens and humans alike asking to join the cause in the past hour alone. Cells are forming in twenty cities right now, all around the world, and that's because of what we did tonight."

"But my parents are still dead, yes?" he replied.

Tara dropped her head. "Yes, Joshy, but look on the bright side. Your planet might be saved."

"And my sister?" Joshy asked as if he wasn't listening.

"She's...my robots are working on it. You can look if you want," Tara said, pointing to a medical room across the hangar. Inside a chamber covered by wall-to-wall glass, two white robotic arms worked on Leslie, trying to revive her.

"There's nothing we can do for her body," Tara said as Joshy walked toward the window to watch the robots work. "At least not her current body."

"But she could live?" Joshy asked.

"She could. I made great advancements in medicine while I was on this planet, but I kept some of my best secrets hidden from the Globorians, including my biggest advancements in robotics. If she lives, she will be a cyborg, more robot than human, like your Darth Vader. I actually came up with the idea after watching the prequel trilogy."

A small smile crept across Joshy's face. His sister might live. His sister might live after all. At least it was a glimmer of hope that he didn't have before.

"Does that make you feel any better?" Tara said.

"A little," Joshy replied.

"Good," Tara said. "Now come on, we have to record another video."

Tara took his hand and led him toward the middle of the hangar. A dozen different alien species were huddled in the center of the hangar.

"Alright, everybody, gather around," Tara screamed. "We need you all to gather in the center of the hangar."

"Why?" an alien with buck teeth and yellow eyes called out.

"We're recording a new video. Something that will bring hope to the whole world. You are going to be the extras." Tara turned to Debra. "And you're going to be the star."

"Me?" Debra said. "I don't know if I can do that."

"We didn't risk everything because we liked you, Debra. We did it because we need you to be the face of our movement. So, pardon me, but I don't give a damn what you think you can do. You're going to do it. We risked too much for you to have a choice."

"Fine," Debra replied. "I'll do it. I don't need the guilt trip."

Tara brought Joshy to the mass of other aliens gathering in a semi-circle at the center of the hangar. There were blue aliens that looked like snakes and pink aliens that looked like butterflies. There were aliens with wings and ones with long ears. There were even a couple humans who looked as out of place amongst the aliens as he did.

"You stand in the middle," Tara said to Debra.

"I-I don't know—"

"I do," Tara said, placing her hand on Debra's shoulder. "You're going to be brilliant."

Gor ambled over with a video camera and stack of poster-sized cue cards under its arm. Gor placed down the cards and set up the camera in front of the group. "We should be ready to go live. Are you sure you want to do this? It will take them less than a minute to trace the feed. I did the best I could with encryption, but live video is tricky."

"It doesn't matter. We can't stay here. If the Globorians know our plan, then we have to assume there's a traitor in our midst, or at least there was one. That means they likely know where we are, which means we have to move as soon as possible."

"Move where?" Joshy asked.

"That's need to know, given the circumstances. I have bases all around the world that I've been building since I decided not to leave Earth. We will move from base to base until we find the traitor or destroy the Globorians, whichever comes first."

"Do you really think we can win?" Joshy asked.

"I swear it," Tara replied.

Her confidence made Joshy feel better. His family was still splayed and broken, but at least the traitor would be brought to justice.

Tara turned to Debra. "All you have to do is read the cards that Gor made for you. This is going out on every television channel and live stream in the world. It will be translated into thirty languages simultaneously. If this doesn't get the world's attention, then nothing will."

Debra sighed. "And what if it's not enough?"

"Hey," Joshy said, walking forward. "We all risked our lives because we believe in you...because we love you. We know we can do it. I know you can do it...because I love you."

Debra looked Joshy in the eyes. "I love you, too."

They smiled at each other. Joshy went in for a kiss, but Tara pulled him away. "Not now. We have time for that later."

"To be continued," Debra said with a smile. They were broken and bruised, but they still had each other, and they could get through anything...together.

"Are you ready then?" Tara asked.

Debra nodded, abandoning her human disguise and glowing a brilliant blue. "I think so."

"And what do the rest of us do?" Joshy asked.

"Look indivisible," Tara said. "Remember, no pressure, but the fate of the world hangs in the balance."

The light on the camera flashed red and then turned solid. Gor gave her the thumbs up and held up the stack of cue cards for Debra to read.

"We are not afraid of Globorians. We stand together, united against you. Inkarian, Thimberian, Finilian, human, and every race on this planet stands together against you. Stop your invasion now, or you will feel the full might of the world as it rises up against you."

"We will not be separated. We will not be silenced. We are indivisible. If you are one of us, know that we stand with you. We will not abandon you. We will fight, and we will win."

Debra flashed the most beautiful blue that Joshy had ever seen. "If you are Globorian, leave this planet now, or you will regret it because we are coming for you. We are the resistance, and you will not defeat us."

Gor dropped the last card and flicked off the camera. Debra turned to Tara with a nervous look on her face.

"How did I do?" Debra asked.

"Amazing," Tara said with a smile. "Absolutely incredible."

"I'll say that was amazing!" Joshy said. "It gave me goosebumps."

Debra didn't let Joshy say another word before pulling him in for a big kiss. She had earned it.

"I love you," she said to him.

"I love you, too," Joshy replied.

"Um, guys," Gor said, sitting back down at its monitors. "You want to get a look at this."

Gor enlarged the video feed on its monitors. Each showed a cityscape from a different city in the world. Joshy recognized the skylines of London, Paris, New York, Moscow, Berlin, and Tokyo. Thirty different cities, and above each of them, a Globorian battle cruiser uncloaked itself. A hundred miles around and shaped like the flying saucers Joshy remembered from Independence Day when he was a kid. They cast an ominous shadow across every major city in the world.

"The Globorians heard our message," Gor said. "And they clearly don't care."

"Then it's time we fight," Tara said. "All of our lives depend on it."

Joshy looked over at his sister's medical bay, then back to Debra, who still glowed as vibrant a blue as he had ever seen. Their odds were long, but this was a fight worth waging. He had already lost so much, now he was willing to risk everything to win back his planet.

Book 3

"Indivisible"

Chapter 1

"You only have five minutes once you're inside," Gor screeched over the microphone embedded in Tara's ear. She knew that, of course, but Gor was only trying to be helpful. Unfortunately, it wasn't helping.

Tara dropped into the Globorian embassy without a sound. Houston was still reeling from the effect of Hurricane Harvey a year before, and the city was having a hard time getting back on its feet. Many of its citizens were transplants from Florida who'd been displaced by the massive hurricanes that had rocked the east coast over the previous months.

Tara had nothing to do with the other hurricanes, and she was loath to admit that she was responsible for Harvey. The Globorians had been using integrated weather technology to heat the planet slowly for the past hundred years to make conditions ripe for their invasion of Earth. One of their main weapons in their preparations for a full-scale invasion was hurricanes.

There had been hurricanes since the dawn of time, well before the Globorians came to Earth, but they quickly became a great way to inflict damage on humans from afar without having to plan an outright attack. The more they could weaken humanity before their invasion the better, and weather manipulation became one of their primary tools for their preemptive strikes on the population.

However, the Globorians never expected a hurricane to hit Houston. If they had, they wouldn't have built an embassy there after Hurricane Allen in 1980. Of course, Globorians never expected their Inkarian slave to escape and sabotage all their plans, but that's exactly what Tara had been doing for the past two decades.

"Okay, I'm inside. Where to now?" Tara asked, pressing the button on the headpiece over her ear.

"Two flights down, turn right. Inside the last door on your left, you'll see a thick metal door. Behind it is the control room where you need to plant the tracker," Gor replied in her ear. Her frog-like alien computer expert was sitting at her base in Zurich guiding her through the mansion.

The Globorian embassy had once been a beautiful, southern plantation-style mansion with high ceilings and exquisite paintings lining every hallway. Servants kept the lace doilies white and the carpets spotless.

But that was another time. Hurricane Harvey had decimated the building and made it uninhabitable except for the small cadre of Globorian guards that roamed the halls. The Globorians had once defended the embassy with twenty squads of their best troops. Now, only a dozen soldiers remained.

"Copy that," Tara said.

Tara thought she had destroyed the communications center of the embassy with the hurricane. After the storm, all electronic communication from the house ceased. However, when Globorian ships decloaked over every major city in the world, the transponder inside the old embassy's control room started transmitting again.

"Wait," Gor said in her ear. "Two soldiers are coming up in front of you."

Historically, Globorians camouflaged themselves in human skin at all times. However, since they had decloaked and made their presence known to the world, Tara saw their ugly, craggy rock bodies everywhere. They looked as if the Thing and Anger from Inside Out had a nasty, vile baby who smelled of sulfur.

Tara stepped into an open doorway as two Globorians stomped up the stairs and down the hallway toward her. Tara's heart beat loudly in her head as she listened for the soldiers to pass. She was smart and tough, but she couldn't take on two fully grown Globorian guards by herself, at least not without alerting the rest of the soldiers to her location.

She heard the guards slam open a door at the end of the hall and felt their footsteps as they disappeared inside. Tara wondered if they knew why they were guarding this run-down mansion in the middle of Houston, or if they even cared.

After all, it was only a little over two months until Labor Day, and that was the date when the Globorians intended to execute their final attack on Earth. Until then, they were amassing troops; dozens of warships and battlecruisers uncloaked over new cities every day.

The rest of their fleet was on the way, but many of their ships were busy in battle elsewhere in the galaxy. There were always worlds to conquer, and the bulk of the Globorian fleet was still finishing up the takeover of Tweenus Three, a mining planet heavy with gold and silver ore inhabited by a race of sentient mole people.

Compared to Tweenus Three, Earth wasn't much of a prize. Its people weren't very intelligent, and they had already harnessed much of the precious metals from the planet to use for things like jewelry and watches. Tara didn't understand how humanity could so frivolously waste their best resources on such garish items, but then she didn't expect much from a world full of intelligent monkeys.

"Go, now," Gor said.

Tara stepped out into the hallway and shuffled down the stairs of the old mansion. She was careful to step lightly. Being an Inkarian meant being smart, but it also meant being light on her feet. She had spent most of her life in laboratories. However, after escaping, she was surprised how her agility, slight frame, and light weight helped her sabotage Globorian plans without being seen.

Tara wasn't proud of the human cost of her endeavors, but most of the disasters of the past two decades were her fault, from Chernobyl to Fukushima, every time the Globorians were close to finalizing their invasion plans, Tara was able to stall them with another major disaster to clean up, setting their plans back by months, or sometimes years. Yes, she killed many humans, and that was a tragedy, but it was worth the calculated cost to keep the rest of humanity from being enslaved. The greater good, she told herself, was worth the horrible price that had to be paid to keep humanity safe from Globorian rule.

She knew, though, that even though she worked for the greater good, there was no way she was a good guy—even if she happened to be the on the right side of history.

Joshy and Leslie had once thought she was little more than a terrorist. Tara hadn't known many humans before them, even though she'd fought for years to protect them, but she liked Leslie and Joshy, which made it all the sadder when they responded to her actions with horror and disgust.

Terrorists were never the good guys, even if they were eventually vindicated, but that was okay with Tara. She didn't need to be the good guy. She wasn't ruled by emotions. She was ruled by logic and intelligence, like all good Inkarians. She had been trained since birth to use her head over her heart, even if—no, *especially* if—it vehemently disagreed with her.

"You're on the right floor now," Gor said as Tara hit the landing on the second floor of the house. Below her, Globorians grumbled in low, guttural voices. She couldn't make out what they were saying, but that didn't matter. What mattered was there were at least a half dozen of them, and she was close enough to hear them, which meant they were close enough to hear her.

"Where am I going now?" Tara whispered into her headpiece.

"End of the hall and to the left. Inside that room is a metal door which leads to the control room. Be careful. There is a Globorian inside. You'll have to neutralize it."

Neutralize was a fancy way of saying kill. Tara had neutralized more Globorians than any other Inkarian in the universe, she wagered...at least close up. Inkarians often engaged in war with less civilized societies. They didn't want to fight, but being the most advanced species in the galaxy meant there was always a target on their back, especially from brash young Globorian captains. Inkarians were often forced to destroy Globorian ships as a show of force, but Inkarians never looked their victims in their coal-fired eyes before vaporizing them. No, that was something unique to her experience. Killing in close combat, rather than doing so with a laser beam in the vast emptiness of space, was truly something else.

Tara inched her way down the hallway, careful not to depress any floorboards hard enough to make a sound. She wished she were a Thimberian, like Debra, so she could hover over the creaky floor, but she had to live with what the universe gave her.

At the end of the hallway, Tara reached into her belt and gripped her fingers around her laser gun. It was small and compact, which meant it had a small battery. She would have one shot at the Globorian inside before the sixty-second recharge. She could have brought a better gun, but it would have taken more room and added more weight, and she needed to stay as light as possible to avoid detection.

With her finger on the trigger, she pushed open the door to the room. The Globorian inside barely had time to react before Tara fired a laser beam into its chest. In three seconds, the Globorian faded into oblivion. It was almost sad for Tara to watch the fear overtake the Globorian as it disappeared from existence, gurgling for air as it vaporized into the ether. Tara didn't care much about such emotions, though. Killing the guard was the most logical and easiest way to achieve her goal, and that was what mattered. One death now to save millions in the future.

"I hope this works," Tara said into the headpiece as she pulled a metal disk out of her belt and placed it over top of the magnetic door control until it magnetized into place.

"It will work," Gor replied, but Tara heard a deep sigh at the end which undermined her confidence.

The disk lit up with shapes and numbers of a hundred different colors. Through the floorboards, she heard several feet stomping off from the main group of Globorians below her. Then, two sets of feet clomped up the stairway toward the second floor.

"What's happening?" Tara asked as two of the six shapes clicked into place. A blue square and a yellow triangle. "They aren't supposed to change shifts for three minutes."

"Two of the guards are walking up the stairs. This isn't on their patrol schedule."

Another dial locked into place, a purple G. Above her, Tara heard two more sets of footprints walking down the stairs. "They're coming from upstairs, too. Where are they going?"

"I don't know!" Gor shouted back through the headset.

"Do I need to abandon this mission?"

"No!" Gor shouted. "Who knows if we'll get another shot. These bases are adding security like mad. Tomorrow there might be six dozen guards for all I know."

A fourth and fifth dial clicked into place. A green spiral and yellow coil. "This thing needs to speed up then. I'm not dying in this hovel."

"It's going through six billion possible combinations in mere seconds. Give it a break."

"It's going to kill me if it doesn't hurry up."

Her eyes tracked the feet as they walked down the stairs and met up with their friends. Four Globorians chatted with each other at the stairwell, their gruff voices reverberated through the walls. They were only feet away from her. Tara wasn't known to panic, but she felt a lump forming in her throat.

Click. The sixth marker locked into place. The door clicked open, and a great gust of cold air escaped the room. The disk fell into Tara's hand, and she spun inside the metal door.

Inside the room were three dozen monitors, all turned off, except for the one in the center which showed video from outside the building, as a decloaked Globorian ship hovered above Houston.

"That is so creepy," Tara said as she sat down at the computer with the disk. Tara placed the disk behind the computer terminal as the computer whirred to life. "This computer is so old. Who knows if this disk will even work?"

"It will work," Gor said. "I know it will work."

The computer whirred as the monitors above it flickered to life. Green text scrolled down the screen as the disk projected a rainbow of colors on the wall behind it. Outside the room, she heard the steps of the Globorians as they stomped down the hallway toward her.

"They're coming," Tara said.

"I know. I was trying not to freak you out by telling you."

"I have to go!" Tara said.

"You can't! If you go, we might never get this chance again."

"If they find me, I'll be dead, and they'll find out about us anyway."

"Give it a couple more seconds."

As Gor finished talking, the computer turned on, and the familiar Windows logo flashed on the screen, though in a Globorian language even Tara didn't understand.

"We're in," Tara said.

"Good. I see inside the system. I'll be able to hack into the mainframe from here. Now, get out of there."

Tara turned off the monitors and crept out of the door. She pushed closed the metal door and slid open the window next to her. She disappeared into the night right as the door to the office opened, and four huge, red, rocky Globorians walked inside.

Tara pushed off the wall of the building and fell through the air. She landed on the hood of a car below her so delicately she didn't even set off the alarm before running off into the night, happy that she didn't die.

Chapter 2

"I know it's been hard," Debra said as she stared into the video camera in Gor's command center. "The Globorians have infiltrated the dark web. They have raided more than half our bases around the world. Our army has had to move our base of operations over six times. We are tired, but we cannot be weak. We must remain strong and vigilant. We must remain together. We cannot falter, or the entire rebellion will fall apart. I remain, faithfully yours, in strength."

Debra held up her fist in solidarity with the rebellion as Gor turned off the video camera. Debra heard Gor's tacky feet break their suction with the floor and walk over to the command console, which featured a hundred different monitors flashing images of Globorian ships hovering over every major city in the world.

"I'll get this uploaded and sent out ASAP," Gor said.

"Didn't we live stream that?" Debra asked.

"I wish," Gor said. "We can't send a live stream any more without it being decoded by the Globorians immediately."

"Is anybody really listening?" Debra asked. "I mean, who would even sign onto the dark web anymore with everything that's been going on?"

"We still get a million hits every time we post something, Debra. Your videos mean something to these people. They keep fighting because of you."

"Don't lay that on me," Debra grumbled.

"It was a compliment," Gor replied.

"I know," Debra said. "But I take no joy in people fighting a hopeless war because of me."

"It's not hopeless," Gor said. "You are giving them hope."

"Stop it," Debra said, walking toward the door. "Seriously."

Gor didn't say anything else as Debra walked out the door and down the metal stairs into the hangar bay that acted as their base.

*

Joshy didn't expect to be part of an alien resistance when he begrudgingly packed his family's car a month ago and left Los Angeles bound for a tedious cross-country road trip. He figured the worst that would happen was that his parent's car would break down and they would have to push it to a service station in the desert heat.

He didn't expect to fall in love with a girl, nor did he expect for that girl to be an alien. Her bright blue eyes were beautiful, and he could lose himself in of them for hours. He hadn't anticipated that the rest of her body would glow the same blue when she shed her human skin or that she could fly and explode shockwaves out of her arms. He didn't expect that he wouldn't care about any of those things and love her anyway.

"Hey, baby," Debra said, walking across the hangar toward the bench he sat on, waiting for his sister to be done getting her robotic arm adjusted. An explosion had blown off Leslie's legs and arms, but Tara's robots were able to salvage her brain and keep her alive.

"Here, I saved you one," Joshy said, sliding a protein bar over to Debra. They tasted like cardboard, but they had enough energy to get him through the day, sometimes two. All Joshy wanted was a real meal. He hadn't had one in days. He couldn't even leave the hangar without the Globorians tracking him.

"This is terrible," Debra said, brushing her long blond hair back from her face before taking a second bite. "How do you eat this?"

Joshy sighed. "It's not like there are a lot of options in this hangar."

"Then let's go outside," Debra said, standing up. "We've been cooped up in here for three days, and Zurich is beautiful in the summer. There's no snow or anything."

Debra pulled on Joshy's arms, but Joshy wouldn't stand up. He wanted to leave with her, but he couldn't. He had to make sure his sister was okay. Tara's robotic doctors had fixed her enough to travel, but she was still in bad shape and needed constant tweaking to keep her processors working.

"I can't…" Joshy said, fading off. "Even if I could leave my sister, you know there are Globorians everywhere looking for us."

Debra knew what that meant, and she sighed. She didn't blame Joshy for saying no to her. Joshy didn't have any family left except for Leslie. His mother and father had died in a firefight saving Debra from the Globorians, and Leslie was his last link to humanity. All day, every day he was surrounded by aliens, aliens who didn't understand him. Leslie represented his life on Earth, and Debra refused to get in the way of that.

Debra would have killed to have her mother in that hangar with her. Debra's mother, Veronica, had been captured by the Globorians weeks ago, and while the rebellion freed Debra, her mother remained in captivity. She didn't know where Veronica was being held prisoner.

Debra had worked with Gor to track down a list of likely locations, but even with a hundred soldiers, they wouldn't be able to hit every site by the time the Globorians invaded on Labor Day.

Labor Day seemed so far in the future, but the Fourth of July had snuck up on them, too, and now it was a measly two days away. Tara hoped to recruit a ten-thousand-person army by the Fourth of July, but she barely had a tenth of that. Every time she recruited more soldiers, it meant a greater chance for Globorian traitors to join her ranks. There was a strain of Globorian sympathizers somewhere, but so far Tara and Gor hadn't found a way to identify them.

The hospital bay doors opened, and Leslie ambled out of it, smiling and radiant. It was funny how much she enjoyed being a cyborg. She no longer had hair. Instead, a metal sphere connected to the back of her face through complicated gears and servos. Her right eye was red and robotic. It scanned everything it saw with a mild laser, like the Terminator. Both of her arms were replaced with long metal exoskeletons, and she sprung on her legs as she moved through ball joints in her metallic feet. Still, her face looked, aside from her eye, exactly as Joshy and Debra remembered. Apart from wires protruding from it, her torso was still human as well, though scarred from the explosion that almost took her life.

"I feel so much better," Leslie said, pumping her right arm. "This arm was dead all morning. Not fun."

"It took so much less time this go around," Joshy said.

"Yeah," Leslie replied. "Those medical robots are really finding their groove repairing me. It helps we aren't moving bases every six minutes; they have time to keep me calibrated properly."

"How…do you feel?" Debra asked, trying to maintain her sensitivity.

"I feel great," Leslie replied. "I mean, I always thought I was smart before, but being connected to the web really ups your game when it comes to a knowledge base. I am like a walking, talking dictionary."

"Or like the world wide web come to life," Joshy added.

"No," Leslie shook her head. The servos in her neck whirled as she did so, reminding Debra that every part of her friend was only alive because of gears and pulleys. "That sounds like I am about to troll somebody. I prefer dictionary. It's more civilized."

"How about Encyclopedia?" Debra offered. "It's like a dictionary, but for everything in the world."

Leslie thought about it for a moment. "Yes, that I like. I will change my answer from dictionary to encyclopedia."

Sometimes, when Leslie spoke, Joshy forgot that she was more machine than woman, and it took him back to when his life was normal and straightforward. However, at other times, Leslie sounded wooden and robotic, as if a robot was wearing a mask of his sister, and those moments reminded him that nothing would be normal again.

His mother and father were dead. Leslie was the last remaining vestige of his family, or at least any family he cared to be around. When he closed his eyes, Joshy still saw the semi-truck explosion that nearly killed his sister. He saw the dead bodies of his parents laying on the ground as he ran away from the Globorian attack. He was supposed to protect his family, and yet, all he could do was watch them die. If only he hadn't met Debra, his parents would still be alive.

No. He couldn't think like that.

His parents died trying to stop a Globorian invasion. They died trying to ensure that humanity wouldn't be enslaved, and that was what kept him going as well. One day, when they won, there would be time to grieve, but until then, all he could do was hope their deaths would not be in vain.

"Stand at attention!" Randall shouted from the front of the hangar door. Randall was the only Globorian that had defected to Tara's cause, and Joshy didn't trust him. Globorians were not to be trusted, so he wondered why Tara would make him her right-hand man. "Tara Inkari, general of the rebellion, coming through."

Tara walked in. When Joshy met her, she looked like a young child. Now, she had abandoned her human disguise and looked like a short, squat salamander with scaly, neon green skin and dark black eyes.

"Oh please, Randall," Tara said with a smile. "This isn't that kind of rebellion."

"There must be rules, ma'am," Randall said. "Without rules, everything breaks down."

Tara smiled and patted Randall across his firm, craggily chest. There was a softness about them at that moment that belied the fact they were stone cold killers.

"You're cute," Tara said. "Now, go guard something."

Joshy watched her enjoy her moment with Randall, looking at him as if all was okay in the world, if only for a moment. Joshy often looked at Debra like that, in moments of great despair when all hope was lost to give himself the will to carry on.

"How did it go?" Debra yelled across the hangar, jarring Tara back to reality.

"It went swimmingly," Tara said, turning to Debra. "We were able to plant a hacking device inside the embassy. I was heading to see how Gor's doing with the decryption. Care to have a look?"

Debra was the face of the resistance, and thus, had privileges others didn't, including Joshy. The other aliens, from indigo-haired Lithnerians to purple-tongued Virians looked on with a desperate desire to know more about their plan, but Tara kept them in the dark. However, she let Debra inside.

"I just came from up there," Debra replied. "It didn't look like Gor had gotten very far."

"Well," Tara said in a voice that indicated she was not so much asking a question as giving a command. "Maybe something's changed since then. Come on."

"Fine," Debra said hopping down from the bench. "Do you two want to come?"

Joshy shook his head. "I don't think I have the clearance for that."

"And I do not want to," Leslie added.

*

Debra followed Tara up the metal stairs toward the control room where Gor typed tirelessly, barely blinking its big, frog-like eyes enough to keep them hydrated, but not enough to stop them from becoming bloodshot.

"I'm not done, Debra," Gor said. "Jeez, give me some—" Gor turned to see Tara eying it sternly. "Sorry, ma'am. What can I do for you?"

"I came to ask you about the decryption," Tara said, walking into the room, Debra following behind her. "How are we looking?"

"I've uploaded my algorithm, and its searching for what we need as fast as it can. It could be an hour or a week before I've narrowed down the right files, though. This encryption cipher is like nothing I've ever seen."

"It's Inkarian," Tara said. "This will go much more quickly if we work together. Time is of the essence."

*

"You do not seem happy," Leslie said, walking through the hangar next to Joshy. Dozens of robots scattered through the hangar, whisking to and fro to make up for the lost manpower from the Globorian raids.

"Why would I be happy?" Joshy replied. "My girlfriend is constantly being pulled in every direction. She hasn't talked to me for longer than a few minutes in days. She won't tell me anything about what's going on. Both our parents are dead, and you...I mean look at you."

"I am happy," Leslie said. "I know it might not look it, but I am happy to be alive."

"That's nice. I wish I had some of that."

The servos behind her skin curled the sides of her mouth up, forming a smile, or at least a robotic interpretation of one. "You could, Joshy. After all, you are alive. You have a woman who loves you—"

"Alien woman."

"An alien woman who loves you. Plus, you're living out one of your video games, and you're friends with a robot. Isn't that kind of the dream, as you would say?"

"Yeah," Joshy replied. "I guess, but the dream seems more like a nightmare right now, living it, you know?"

"This is who I will be every day of my life, for as long as I live. Hopefully one day they will be able to make me look more human, but this is who I am now. So yes, I very much know what it's like to live what people might call a nightmare, though, to me, it is a dream."

"You really don't think it's a nightmare?"

"I don't allow myself to think about it, honestly. Every time feelings of fear or pain bubble up, I turn off that processor. It is one of the reasons I must go in for maintenance so often. They keep turning that part of my brain back on, but I do not want it back on. I prefer to live in ignorance."

"That doesn't sound like you," Joshy replied.

"No, it doesn't. I said that I was excited to be an encyclopedia. In fact, I have been on a quest for knowledge since I was a child. However, now that I have all the knowledge in the world and am able to access it at will, my victory often feels like a hollow one, you know?"

"Yeah," Joshy said. "I know all about hollow victories. I saved my girlfriend and lost my parents in the process."

"Yes, like that," Leslie said. "But you still have me, too."

Joshy sighed. "Don't take this the wrong way, Les, but do I? I can't help but think that Tara put your face on a computer. You sound like you, but you also don't sound like you, too."

"I am different," Leslie said. "But I am your sister. I can say that with 84.3% accuracy."

"That's a B, Les, and not even a high B."

"Well, there is a decent chance that my consciousness wasn't transplanted as you suggest, and that my memories are lies. I must accord for that possibility. Of course, that is true for all humanity. Perhaps, we are all implanted with memories every night, and are actually inside of a giant machine."

"That is depressing."

"Is it? I live in a machine every day, and I am not depressed. Tell me, do you remember a gnarled oak tree in front of our first house in Los Angeles?"

Joshy nodded. "I do. We used to—"

"Please, don't tell me. Let me test my memories. We used to sit in the first branch of that tree, as children. There was a swing on it, but we didn't use it. We preferred to climb into the tree and dangle our feet off the branch. Is that accurate?"

Joshy's eyes welled up. "That's right, Les."

"Then, with that, I can say the likelihood of these being implanted memories is significantly less than I recently projected. However, it is still possible."

Joshy grabbed his sister's metal hand and squeezed it. There was no give in the metal claw, but he still felt the connection with his sister and the human heart that still beat inside her chest.

Chapter 3

"Almost done," Gor said, furiously typing on the control center's keyboard. "We've just about isolated the data packets we need."

"That includes the information on where my mother is being held, right?" Debra asked, nervous about the answer.

"Of course," Tara said. "I promised you we'd find your mother, didn't I?"

Tara did promise, six days ago, after the third time they had to switch bases, that their first priority after finding the traitor to their cause would be to locate Debra's mother. It was the carrot Tara dangled every time Debra wanted to spend time with Joshy or fought recording another live video, and now all those late nights would be vindicated.

There was no way to find the information Tara needed quickly and easily. Inside every root file and partition was another cipher which required decryption. The Globorians had re-encrypted all their files in the twenty years since Tara had created the system in an ancient dialect she couldn't read, and even though Gor had the best Inkarian technology that Tara could build, she was only one alien, while the Globorians had an army.

"Anything yet?" Tara said to Gor. She had tried to break the cipher, but eventually gave up and let Gor take over.

"Nothing, boss," Gor replied. "Not since you asked me two minutes ago."

"If I was up there—"

"Do you want to be up here again?" Gor replied. "I could make that happen. I haven't slept in a week, and I could use a bath, too. Do you want to do it again? Seems like last time you burned out and left it to me."

"No," Tara said. "It's fine. I'm nervous. I want it to be done."

"I'm nervous, too," Gor replied. "We'll get it though, and when we do, we can finally stop running."

Seven bases in two weeks, Tara thought to herself. The Globorians had raided seven of their bases in the last two weeks. She only had three left on Earth. After that, they would have to resort to satellite bases around the world run by her network of poorly trained recruits. She wanted to train them better and offer them support, but she didn't know who to trust. She couldn't allow new soldiers to come to her, and she couldn't risk going to them. Not yet, anyway.

"There's nothing to do here," Debra said. "I'm gonna go."

"Fine," Tara said. "We'll call you if we need you."

"Please don't," Debra replied, walking out the door. All she wanted was a couple hours alone with Joshy. She felt like she hadn't seen him in an eternity. Randall walked in as she stepped out, and she pushed past him without saying a word.

"I think we got something boss," Gor said, watching the green letters and numbers cascade down the monitors.

"Is that it?" Tara said.

"Yeah," Gor replied. "I think so."

*

"Hi," Debra said, walking through the door and into the pristine white room she shared with Joshy and fifty other soldiers. "I am surprised you're still awake."

"I'm surprised to see you at all," Joshy said, laying on his cot. "Usually, you're off with Tara, doing something or another in secret."

"It's not in secret. It's…not public…yet."

Joshy sat up in his bed. "It's secret enough that you won't talk to me about it."

Debra sat down at the foot of his bed. "There's nothing to tell. Most of what we discuss are these stupid propaganda videos I don't want to do, which never work to recruit anyone because it's not like we can tell people where we are without risking getting found by the Globorians. It's like I'm spinning my wheels. It's like we're all spinning our wheels."

"I know the feeling," Joshy said, placing his hand on hers. "You know, you don't have to pretend to be human for me."

Debra had been wearing her human disguise since she got to the base. She didn't know why she kept it on when every other alien walked around freely without it, but she still did. Perhaps it was for Joshy, or for Leslie, or because Earth was the only home she'd ever known, so she felt safer looking like a human rather than as an alien.

"I know," Debra said. "How's your sister?"

Joshy shook his head. "Sometimes, I think it's like old times, but then she says something, and I know that it will never be like that again."

"Nothing will be the same again, Josh," Debra said, smiling. "That's what's so great about being an adult, right? Things constantly change."

"Is that what's great about being an adult?" Joshy said. "Cuz it's pretty terrible."

"Hey," Debra said. "At least we get to go through the suck together. That's something."

Josh and Debra looked into each other's eyes like they hadn't in days. Their heads slowly came together. As Joshy cocked his head to one side, ready to press his lips tightly on Debra's, the loudspeakers crowed to life.

"Debra Thompson. Please report to the command center."

Debra let out a sigh. "I have to go."

Joshy leaned his head against Debra's. "I know. You always have to go."

"Will you come with me?" Debra asked.

"If you want me to," Joshy said. "They didn't call me, though. Won't Tara be pissed?"

Debra grabbed his hand. "Maybe, but we're a package deal from now on, okay? We can be Team Awesomesauce Bananapants."

Joshy smiled. "I like that."

*

"What is he doing here?" Tara asked as Debra walked into the command center holding Joshy's hand.

"He's my boyfriend, and I trust him."

"That's great. He's the only human here, and there's a traitor in our midst, but let's allow everybody into the command center."

"You let a Globorian in here," Joshy said.

Debra pointed to Randall, the towering menace of a Globorian that stood at the door, glowering threateningly at her.

"That's different!" Tara replied. "Randall has proven himself time and time again as a loyal soldier."

"And what has Josh done?" Debra asked, squeezing Joshy's hand harder. "Except lose both his parents and almost lose his sister for this cause."

"She's got you there, boss," Gor said.

"Fine," Tara said. "Whatever. I suppose we'll know soon whether you are the traitor or not since Gor's finished the decryption of the files."

"Well, I should warn you that I only think I decrypted it. It was quite the maze we walked through. With any luck, though, this is what we need."

Gor clicked on a folder on its desktop and an image popped up of a reptilian-faced alien with a membrane-like orange mohawk going from the tip of its head down its back, like Savage Dragon, but orange.

"I don't recognize this alien," Tara said. "I thought I would recognize it."

"I do," Joshy said.

His mind raced back to the day of the semi-truck attack when they rescued Debra. Joshy and Leslie were on the advance team. Joshy looked up to see his mother on one rooftop, and his father on another. Behind him, at the end of the alley, was a scout team, protecting their escape. That was where he'd seen those bright green eyes before. The alien pulled him from the sewer before the attack.

"He was there that day. The day we rescued Debra."

"Great," Tara said. "Where is he now?"

Another flash and Joshy was back at the battle. This time he was scampering away over the bodies that had fallen from the rooftops. He saw his mother and father, looking at him with their lifeless eyes. Underneath them, eyes closed, the face of the alien from the picture.

"As far as I know, he's dead."

Gor shook its head. "I doubt that. There's a forwarding address, and a payment from the Globorians which was cashed yesterday."

"That's impossible," Joshy said. "I saw that alien dead after the battle. As dead as my parents."

Saying those words made Joshy tear up. He didn't have a chance to mourn his parents, and he very much looked forward to the day when he could stop swallowing his emotions and feel things again.

"Maybe," Gor said. "That was true, once. Maybe he's a zombie. I don't know, but there are very detailed records of payouts and GPS locations that go through this morning, so unless the Globorians are talking with a ghost, or confused, this alien is still alive."

"Where was its last known location?" Tara asked.

Gor typed furiously as a map of the world popped up, showing the group an apartment complex in Germany. "Hamburg, ma'am. It doesn't look like this jerk stays in one place very long; you might not have much time to strike if you have any at all."

Tara stood. "We need to gather a team to take this traitor down."

"I'm coming," Joshy said.

"Me too," Debra added.

"Like hell you are. Neither of you are qualified to—"

"I was qualified to be on the advance team to rescue Debra. I'm qualified for this. I've been practicing while you've been up here with Debra, I'm ready."

"Fine," Tara said, before turning to Debra. "But you are too important to the cause to come. That's an order."

"You have been forcing me to do videos for weeks while my mother rots in jail. If that alien is going to help us find her, then I'm going with you. Try to stop me."

Tara sighed. "Fine, but if you mess it up, know that this might be our only chance to find this guy. We're lucky he's even on this planet anymore. If I were him, I would have abandoned Earth long ago."

"That's not true," Josh said. "You could have abandoned us, and you're still here."

Tara nodded. "You've got me there. Now come on. We can't waste any time."

Chapter 4

"I am coming with you," Leslie shouted when Joshy told her that they'd found the traitor that got her parents killed. She wasn't much for emotions since the accident, but hers bubbled over at the thought of hurting the alien that destroyed her life.

"You'll do no such thing," Tara replied from behind Joshy. "There are twenty million dollars of technology inside of you, and I don't want it falling into Globorian hands."

"How do you know it will?" Leslie asked. "There is very little chance of that."

"Last time you came out into the field, this happened to you. You're not a great field agent."

Leslie wanted to argue with her, but Tara was right. "Touché."

Tara stepped toward Leslie. "Look, I appreciate your support, but the truth is that you are of more use here. Gor could still use some help analyzing the information we're getting off the Globorian computers. If you feel up to it, you can help."

Leslie nodded. "Fine, but I am going next time."

"We'll see," Tara said. "Help Gor, and we'll see about next time."

Tara led Joshy and Debra toward the weapons cache at the far end of the hangar. Randall already stood there inventorying bullets with a small group of aliens.

"I think we can get away with taking twelve boxes of shells without running too thin on our reserves," Randall said turning to Tara. "I hope we don't get into a firefight."

"With any luck, we won't have any screw-ups, and there won't be a need to fire a single bullet."

"You don't want any screw-ups, and you are bringing along a runty kid and Debra? Do you know what happened the last time they were in the field with you?"

"YES!" Debra shouted. "We all know. Did you know that Tara was in that battle as well? In fact, I'm pretty sure we were all there, except you. So maybe you're the weak link here since we've all bled for this damn cause already."

"How dare you!" Randall grunted. "I gave up everything to stand by Tara's side."

"Yeah?" Debra replied. "And where has that got you? Standing here, with us, so maybe get off my back, and Josh's, too. We have as much right to be here as you."

"Enough!" Tara shouted. "Frankly, I would love it if I had better-trained soldiers than the three of you, but I don't. You're the best I've got right now, so we're stuck together. Got it?"

After a long moment of silence, Josh nodded. "We got it."

"Good," Tara said. "Now suit up and grab your weapons. Next time I have to yell like this, I'm going to slit all your throats."

Tara stormed away as Josh picked up an M-4 from a weapon silo. "She is testy, huh?"

"The fate of the world rests on her shoulders," Randall said. "That makes everybody testy."

"That's not it," Debra said. "She's testy because it's less and less likely we're going to win."

Joshy wanted to ask a follow-up question, as did Randall, but they couldn't form the words. After all, it was easy to see their numbers dwindle after every attack. What Joshy didn't know was that the satellite groups of rebel soldiers in Moscow and Paris had both been obliterated, and the enclave in Los Angeles was hanging on by a thread. The resistance really needed a win. It needed a rallying cry because Debra's speeches could only bring them so far. Arresting a traitor to the rebellion and making them squeal was as close to a win as they were going to get, short of destroying the ships that hovered over each city on the planet.

*

Tara's ship cut through the air above Hamburg in stealth mode an hour after they took off. The ship was silver and sleek, but her camouflage technology prevented Globorians from tracking her. Tara wasn't tall, and she hadn't designed it for company as big as Randall. While they all fit, it wasn't comfortable.

Tara didn't think she would have to entertain others when she built her personal ship. She should have used one of the transport carriers in the hangar which could carry up to 250 troops, but they didn't have as good stealth or maneuverability as her personal ship did, and she wanted to make sure she could get away quickly if they were spotted.

"Hang tight," Tara said as she turned the ship toward its destination. As she did, Joshy looked out of the cockpit and toward the horizon, where an enormous, slug-like ship cast a shadow over the city of Hamburg. It was not one of the first cities where a ship decloaked, but every day more and more ships entered Earth's atmosphere and took residence over one of its cities.

They didn't move to strike. They didn't do anything except hover over the city and cast a pall over its inhabitants. On the ground, Globorian troops prevented anybody from leaving, but inside the city, people were free to do as they pleased. The real invasion, along with the destruction of humanity, would come in two months, but for now, the Globorians wanted to make sure humankind stayed in line and acted as if nothing was wrong.

Propaganda blared on every news site day and night, telling humanity that there was nothing to fear and that the Globorians were there to protect humanity. Any news outlets that disagreed with that were shuttered.

Leslie once introduced Debra and Joshy to her friends Thom and Phyllis at an underground new station in St. Louis. They announced to the world that Debra was an alien and that the Globorian invasion was real. They were taken off the air two weeks ago, the day after the ambush which saw Joshy's parents killed and his sister turned into a cyborg. They hadn't been heard from since.

"When we land," Tara said, "we need to move fast. Randall and I will take the front of the building. Debra and Josh, you climb up the fire escape in the back. Don't let anybody get past you. If we lose him here, either he'll get off the planet, or the Globorians will end his life. They don't like loose ends. Copy that?"

"Copy!" Debra shouted, before taking Joshy's hands. "Are you okay?"

Joshy nodded. "I haven't been on a mission since...and that was a disaster."

"Hey!" Debra said. "This one won't be a disaster. It's going to be great. What could go wrong?"

Joshy smiled. "You know, that's the one thing you don't say in movies or video games because it means something is going to go wrong."

"We're not in a movie or video game, Josh. This is real life, and in real life, I can say anything I want. Don't worry so much, okay?"

Joshy smiled. "We're holding guns, about to raid an alien's apartment. I think I have the appropriate level of worry."

Debra stroked his cheek. "Try to relax. It will all be over before you know it."

*

Tara landed the ship softly and silently in an empty field two blocks from the traitor's apartment complex. The alien called himself Marco on Earth, but he was a Guanarian named R'it'le'th on his home planet. Joshy hated that every alien on this planet had lied to him for his whole life by pretending to be human. It took the end of the world for him to learn that his planet was cool.

Tara cocked her shotgun and pushed open the hatch. A ramp led from the base of her ship to the ground. "Don't get trigger happy. We need this guy alive."

"Then why even bring the guns?" Debra said. "We could have only brought stunners."

"Because who knows what's lurking inside that apartment building."

"Probably a bunch of stoners at this time of day," Joshy replied.

Tara wasn't listening to him anymore. It was impossible to deal with Joshy when he was trying to be funny, she discovered, and it was better to ignore him. "I'm with Randall. You two go around back. We'll meet at the apartment. Don't let him sneak through your grasp, okay?"

"Got it," Debra said.

Randall squeezed Tara's shoulder. "Are you sure you don't want me to go with one of them?"

Tara shook her head. "No, I need you with me."

"It's a tactical mistake," Randall said.

"Maybe," Tara replied, placing her hand on top of Randall's. "But I need you with me, okay?"

Randall nodded. "Okay."

Tara and Randall rushed out of the ship and down the alleyway toward the apartment building. Joshy pressed his M-4 to his shoulder and stepped down the ramp with Debra following him. Joshy had been in this situation hundreds of times before, but it had always been in a video game…until now. His gut gurgled, and his heart beat in his head. He wished he was in a video game right now, instead of risking his life for real.

"Do you remember that game Dogon 4?" Debra asked. "They had a scene like this in the fifth mission."

"You know what?" Joshy said. "You're right. Weren't they in Toledo, though?"

"Sure, but Toledo, Hamburg. It's the same thing. It was a group of four soldiers that had to capture a traitor to the human rebellion."

"It was full of glitches," Joshy said as he made his way down the alley. "Do you remember what happened if you tried to turn back to your ship?"

"Of course. The game froze, and you had to reboot. It was the worst."

"Gameplay was stiff, too. I mean, it was good enough to play in single player, but their multiplayer mode was crap."

"Let's hope we don't have to play multiplayer here, okay? I'm fine with a simple mission without a lot of unforeseen consequences."

Tara and Randall reached the alley behind the apartment building and slid around the side of the building toward the front entrance.

Joshy and Debra stayed at the back entrance. Marco's apartment was on the fourth floor, up the fire escape. Joshy pulled down the emergency ladder and started to climb.

"Yeah, but it wasn't a simple mission in that game, was it?" Joshy asked. "It was a trap. And three of the people on the mission died before they could make it back to the ship. And then it turned out that the traitor was actually the guy who sent you on the mission in the first place."

"Oh yeah," Debra said. "It's been so long I forgot all about that part. I remember walking down that street, though. It took forever. They really wanted you to appreciate the quality of their rendering."

Joshy's headpiece blared to life. "We're in front of the door. Where are you?"

Joshy pressed his earpiece. "Third floor. Almost in position."

Joshy climbed the last set of stairs and took a position in front of the window which led into Marco's house. He slid his fingers under the frame and lifted it open slowly. He saw the top of Marco's mohawk as the alien watched cartoons on television.

He pressed down his earpiece. "Ready? He's in the living room watching TV."

Debra squeezed his shoulder. "I love you," she whispered.

"I love you, too."

"GO!" Tara shouted through the earpiece as the front door slammed open. "Marco! You are coming with us!"

Tara walked forward as Joshy jumped inside the window. "Do you hear me?" Tara continued. "Put your hands over your head."

As she took another step, Marco slumped down in his chair. Randall ran forward. "It's an exoskeleton. He must have molted!"

Joshy swung toward the kitchen as an orange streak rushed toward him. He raised his gun, but he couldn't press the trigger before the figure was on top of him. It leapt toward the window and WHACK! Debra slammed the butt of her gun into Marco's nose, dropping him to the ground.

"Good job," Tara said, running forward. "That was fun, huh?"

"Yeah," Joshy said, grabbing his chest. "Real fun."

Chapter 5

"What do you think finding me is going to accomplish?" Marco asked when they finally got them back to the ship. It had been relatively easy for Randall to bring Marco to the ship since Debra had knocked him out, but when Marco woke, he became quite chatty.

"You can't make me talk," Marco said, as Debra raised the ramp and Tara lifted the ship off the ground. "And you're too much of a pussy to resort to torture.

"I don't have to torture you to make you talk," Tara said. "I think you want to talk."

"And why is that?" Marco asked, grinning.

"You're proud of yourself. I can see it in your eyes."

"You got me," Marco said, laughing. "I did make a lot of money. I am proud of that."

Debra thought about knocking Marco out during the hour plane ride back to the base, but she decided against it. Marco seemed to be brain damaged enough. One more good knock could turn him into a vegetable.

Hey," Marco said, sidling up next to Debra. "Aren't you supposed to be blue?"

Debra sneered. "No. I'm supposed to be whatever I want."

"No, honey. That ain't true. That skin. It's a mask. You're blue. And you're hot when you're blue. This skin job over here make you feel bad about being blue?"

"No!" Joshy shouted. "I would love her no matter what."

Marco laughed. "I had a girl who thought that once, but man was she wrong. Took her two weeks before she was sick of the real Marco. I'm glad I don't have to live a lie anymore, and I can be who I am."

"So can I," Debra said. "And I choose to look like this."

"Man, these people on this planet. They gave you Stockholm Syndrome good. I heard this is your first planet. Is that true?"

"What of it?" Debra asked.

"It's one of the worst in the galaxy. We come here to make fun of it. This whole place is a joke. I wouldn't wish it on my worst enemy."

"I'm about to knock you out," Joshy said. "Real hard."

"Kid, you couldn't knock me out with your hardest punch if you squared its force and then cubed that twice."

"You have no idea what I can do," Joshy said.

"Please. I've been around humans long enough to know their bravado far exceeds their reach. I mean, you actually think you invented nuclear power, or wireless technology, or, well, ice cream, even. As if you have the brain power for any of that."

Joshy lunged forward toward Marco, but Debra pulled him back. He had forgotten how strong Debra was when she tried.

"Enough!" Tara shouted. "Joshy might not be strong enough to hurt you, but I promise you Randall and Debra are, so be quiet, unless you want to talk about your betrayal of us."

"Nah," Marco said, picking up his feet and placing them on the back of the chair in front of him. "I'll wait until we're all comfortable before I say anything else. You're right, though. I got a lot to say."

*

Tara landed her ship in the hangar bay and walked Marco through the hangar. No, that wasn't accurate. She paraded him through the hangar bay as the entirety of her rebellion army looked on proudly. It was the victory they had been trying to get for so long.

"This is the one who has betrayed us," Tara shouted. "I don't know how, or why he has done this, but I swear I will find out, and when I do, this long nightmare will come to an end, and we will finally be able to—"

"Oh," Marco said. "Now that I'm here I can tell you exactly what happened. You see these little robots that run around and help you all out, do ya? Well, it turns out it's very easy to program them to send a homing beacon back to the Globorians."

Marco ripped himself from Tara's grasp and stepped out in front of her to address the soldiers. "You packed these little things up and brought them from base to base with you."

A waist-high droid that looked like a trash compactor drove through the hangar, and Marco punted it across the room. It flew through the air until it crashed against the wall with a metallic crush.

"Stop that!" Gor said from the control room rafters.

"Anything for you, love," Marco said. "Now where was I...oh yes, robots. Problem was, last time the Globorians attacked, they destroyed my little robot friend, which meant we had no idea where you were. They figured you would try to get to me. After all, you've been searching for me since the battle, haven't you?"

"You were dead," Joshy said. "I saw you."

"Yeah, you'd like to think that, wouldn't you? But all it took was me to lay real still for a while, and then when the Globorians came, I told them everything and offered them information about you. Got myself a nice paycheck as well for my trouble."

"You're horrible," Randall said. "Should I kill him, boss?"

"Not yet," Tara said. "Let him monologue. It will be his undoing."

"Where was I?" Marco said. "Oh yeah, you got rid of my bug, didn't you? There was no way we could find you, but the Globorians figured you would find me, and didn't ya, love?"

Marco raised his shirt, to reveal a red blinking tracker on his chest. "Now, they'll be here any minute to destroy this base, and you along with it, and I guess there ain't nothing you can do about it, can you? I think this is the end, ain't it, love?"

"Now you can shoot him," Tara said.

"With pleasure," Randall said, raising his gun.

"WAIT!" Marco said. "Since we're not going to see each other again, and you won't live to see it, I really want you to know that nothing you could have done would have saved this planet. The Globorians moved their plans up to Fourth of July to make sure of that, so all of this, everything you've done, has been for nothing."

"Fourth of July?!" Debra shouted. "But that's only two days away!"

"I know, love," Marco replied. "Ain't it grand?"

Tara sneered as she nodded her head. Without a word, Randall shot Marco through the head, and he dropped to the ground.

"Everybody, evacuation plan Alpha!" Tara shouted, before looking up to Gor. "Is he right?"

Gor looked back to her console which lit up like a Christmas tree with red blinking lights. "It looks that way. Four battlecruisers are decloaking above us. They're powering up their weapons."

"It's time," Tara shouted up to Gor. "Bring the camera. I hope this works,"

"Are you going to use it?" Gor asked.

Tara nodded. "Now would be as good a time as any."

Aliens of all types ran back and forth through the hangar, but they weren't screaming and shouting. They were prepared for this after a half dozen similar evacuations in the past two weeks. They went about their work emotionlessly and precisely as they loaded into four transport ships, large as big buses with foldable wings on either side, and readied for takeoff.

"We don't have much time," Tara shouted. "Those battlecruisers are going to level this whole place. Take whatever means you can and get out of here. I will message you the location of the rendezvous later. Keep your phones on!"

"Aren't we going to fight?" Debra asked.

"You aren't," Tara replied. "You're going to leave with Gor, Randall, Josh, and Leslie."

Gor appeared out of the command center with its camera gear, leapt down the stairs, and hopped toward them. "Ready boss."

The medical bay door slid open, and Leslie rushed toward Joshy. "What is going on here?"

"We have to go," Joshy replied. "Now."

"Get to my personal ship," Tara said. "Ready it for takeoff. Get out of here."

Randall nodded. "You're not going to do what I think you're going to do?"

Tara nodded. "You know I am. It's the best chance we'll get to test it."

"I love you," Randall said to Tara as he fought the tears welling in his eyes.

"It's going to work," Tara replied.

"I know," Randall said. "But in case it doesn't…"

Tara smiled. "I love you, too."

"That was almost sweet," Joshy said before Debra smacked him for being a jerk.

Tara broke away from Randall and ran away toward the edge of the hangar. Randall turned toward the ship. "Come on!"

"Where is she going?" Debra asked.

"She has work to do. She'll meet up with us later."

"No," Leslie said. "She will not, will she?"

"It's just a thing to say," Randall said, turning toward the ship.

*

Randall sat at the controls in Tara's personal ship as Joshy, Debra, Leslie, and Gor filed inside.

"There is not much room in here, is there?" Leslie asked.

"No," Gor replied, licking its eyeball and pressing the video camera against its ear. "There is not. For the record, I don't like being touched."

"Noted," Debra said. "But I don't think we have much of a choice."

"I know, but if I freak out, you know why."

Joshy looked back into the hangar as Tara disappeared behind dozens of soldiers scrambling into the ships around her and started to take off.

"Where is she going?" Joshy asked.

"There's something Tara has been saving for this moment," Gor said, hitting record on the camera. "And now's as good a time as any to test it out. If it works, she'll be able to save us all."

"And if it doesn't?" Debra asked.

"I have to believe it will," Leslie said. "Embrace optimism, Joshy."

"That's never been my strong suit," Joshy said.

"It's never too late to try it," Randall said. "Hold on."

Randall pushed the thruster forward, and the ship sped out of the hangar with a jolt. Above the hangar, red beams grew underneath the slug-like ships of the Globorians. They were about to destroy the base for good. In the past, the Globorians sent in their foot soldiers, but now that their forces were amassing, they could spare a cruiser or two to take care of the rebel threat.

"They're turning their lasers to fire on us!" Debra shouted.

Gor tilted the camera up into the sky as the red light of the laser pointed toward the ship. "This is going to be great."

Joshy looked back to see one of the battlecruisers turning up their guns and taking aim at them. "What? Our destruction!"

"Tara, baby," Randall said. "It's now or never."

There was a moment of silence, and then a great rumble of thunder erupted from the base. Debra first thought that the cruisers had fired, but when she looked back, she saw a blue light ascend from the base and up through one of the cruisers. The resulting explosion sent the ship careening into another one of the battlecruisers.

The blue light cut through the air and took aim at the final two ships, cutting them in half before shrinking back into the mountain from whence it came. It was the first time in weeks that the rebellion had won against the Globorians, and Joshy couldn't help but reach forward and pull Debra close for a celebratory kiss.

"Did you see that?" Tara asked over the intercom.

"I saw it," Gor replied. "Recorded it, too."

Joshy turned to see Gor holding a video camera, pointed at them. "Do you mind?"

"No," Gor replied. "That was perfect. It's going to play in Peoria. This was the best propaganda video we could have asked for. Now, maybe we can convince everybody we might actually win this thing and fight back."

"Fight back," Debra said. "Did you want this to happen?"

"We didn't want this to happen," Randall said. "But we knew they would eventually find us, and it would give us a chance to test our new tech when they did, and look, it worked."

"Get back here," Tara said over the intercom. "They'll be back, and in greater numbers. We have to get this tech off the base before they do."

There was a lot of work to do, but they had finally won a battle, and that was more than they'd had this morning.

Chapter 6

It took the rest of the evening to deconstruct the laser weapon and load it onto trucks for transportation to Tara's base in France. While they worked, a small scout team, including Debra and Joshy, scoured the wreckage of the ships to salvage anything useful from them.

Only one of the four Globorian battlecruisers hadn't blown up in the air; instead, it'd crash-landed in the woods outside of the base. Joshy couldn't stop talking about the destruction of the ships, and how awesome it was to watch them blow up, but Debra couldn't stop hoping that her mother wasn't held hostage on any of those that exploded.

"Do you know what this means?" Joshy asked as he stepped over the ship's wreckage and into what would have likely been the fuselage if it hadn't broken into a million pieces. "I mean, can you imagine what the Rebels would have done with a laser like that when the Empire came to Hoth?"

"They would have fended them off, I assume," Debra said, picking through the debris of the ship's hull. "And then the Empire would have come with even greater power, like the second Death Star."

"Yeah," Joshy said, lifting his leg over the charred remains of a Globorian. "But then the Ewoks on Endor wouldn't have become terrorists or risked their lives for the rebellion either. It would've kept a whole civilization in the dark of the goings on of the galaxy, wouldn't it have?"

Debra bent down over in front of a black computer with a burnt keyboard. "Do you think this is salvageable?"

Joshy shrugged. "I don't know. It's pretty charred."

"It's the only computer out here that's still in one piece," Debra replied.

"Well, pick it up and let's get back. This is starting to creep me out. It's one thing to see an explosion. It's another to walk among the corpses."

"Yeah," Debra said, ripping the computer out of its console. "War sucks, doesn't it, even if these were the bad guys."

*

Tara and Gor pored over the computer after Debra brought it to them. They thanked Debra for her service and sent her off to eat and sleep while they worked on decrypting the computer.

"We don't have time to deal with the encryption cipher again," Tara said when they were alone. "The Globorians will be back any time now."

"Are you sure about that, boss?" Gor asked. "They saw the extent of our power, and I'll bet they're reeling a bit. I know four battlecruisers aren't much for them, but I think they'll have to regroup a bit before they come for us."

"That gives us a little bit longer to be sitting ducks."

"Maybe," Gor said. "Or maybe it gives us an opportunity to plan an attack of our own. Think about it. We've been running this whole time. We finally have a win. Do we really want to go back into running mode, or do we want to go on the offensive?"

"We don't have the manpower to go on the offensive or the time to plan an assault."

"I might have a plan. We're inside their system, right? What if we dropped in a virus that could create havoc with the controls on one of their ships? Then we could invade and take it over."

"And what's that going to do? Give us one ship?"

"And access to their communications relay. You could call the Inkarians, tell them what happened. Maybe they can help us out."

"They don't care," Tara said. "I already tried before."

"Yeah, years ago, but now we have new information. We can tie the Globorians to a thousand different treaty violations. The Inkarians have to be interested in that. They love their paperwork."

"It could take days, maybe weeks to build a virus that can take down their system. We don't have that kind of time, or—"

"I could do it," Leslie said from behind them.

Tara and Gor looked up to see Leslie standing at the door, watching them. "How long have you been there?" Tara asked.

"Since I saw Debra hand you that thing. I haven't been able to do much, but using that computer to build a virus giving you a chance to take down the Globorians—I was literally made for that. You plan your attack, and I swear when you are ready, I'll have it figured out."

"She has been helpful in analyzing all this data we got," Gor said.

Tara turned to Gor. "How long until you can pull down the last of the data from the Globorian mainframe?"

"Six hours, maybe less. I already have most of the data I need."

Tara looked over at Leslie. "And you're sure you can do this?"

Leslie nodded. "There has got to be a reason why I am still here, and why I have access to all the information in the world. You give me that computer, and I will give you a working virus in six hours or less."

"Do it."

*

Tara walked out of Gor's control room. She had never felt as tired as she did at that moment. She wiped her eyes before she descended the metal stairs.

"You need to sleep," Randall said to her when she reached the bottom of the stairs.

"They'll be time to sleep when I'm dead," Tara replied.

"If you don't sleep, you'll be dead soon enough," Randall said with a smile.

Tara wrapped her arms around him. "Come to bed with me, and I'll sleep."

"I have too much to do."

Tara reached up, and her lips met his for too short a moment. "Me too. One day, soon, though, we will be free."

Randall smiled. "Either by death or liberation."

Tara sighed. "At this point, I'm fine with either."

"Speak for yourself," Randall said. "I want to live."

"Then I want to live, too," Tara said, squeezing him tightly one last time. "Dinner later?"

"If you have time."

"I'll make time."

"Then, count on it."

*

Tara slid open the door to Debra's bunk, who rose groggily as Tara flipped on the lights. "I'm sorry, but we need to talk."

Debra pushed herself up. "Of course. Anything you need."

Tara sat down on the edge of the bunk and gave a deep sigh. "In the information we downloaded from the Globorian mainframe…we found where they are keeping your mother."

Debra's eyes lit up. "That's great news!"

"Maybe," Tara said. "It's in one of the biggest ships in the Globorian fleet, stationed over London. Hundreds of other aliens and diplomats are held captive there as well."

"Awesome! We can rescue them all, including my mother."

"It's very dangerous."

"So what? We've dealt with dangerous before."

"The ship will be well guarded," Tara said.

"What aren't you telling me?"

Tara let out another sigh. "If we go to this ship, we can't only save your mother or all the hostages. We need access to their communications relay. It means a complete invasion of their ship with everything we've got."

"Why do we need an all-out assault?"

"The Globorians have been jamming all communication off-world for months. They don't want anybody knowing what they are doing here, especially the Inkarians. What the Globorians are doing, holding innocent aliens captive, is against all our accords with them. Globorians have the right to take over planets, but all aliens are granted free travel through the galaxy."

"So, what they're doing, holding my mother, is illegal?"

"Yes, and we don't know exactly how many others have been captured. We suspect that no aliens have been able to get off the planet for months, but we won't know until we are onboard."

Debra clenched her fists together. "Then we have to get on that ship."

"You probably won't come back, truth be told, neither will your mother. Nobody will, but if we do this right, we'll be able to save a whole lot of people from being enslaved, and make sure this planet is kept from harm. Are you sure you are up for this?"

Debra nodded. "If there's even a small chance of saving my mother, I want to take it."

*

Five hours after she received the computer, Leslie walked back into the command center. "Done," she shouted to Gor with pride.

"Whoop-de-do, you figured it out, and with an hour to spare. Do you want a cookie?"

"No," Leslie said. "I need very few nutrients anymore; most of my joints are controlled by servos powered by clean nuclear fusion. It sounds like you have some bitterness in your voice though. Why? I am only trying to help."

Leslie's thought patterns had become more robotic and stilted. She had less inclination to speak with others and spent most of her time inside of her own her. She acknowledged she was unlike her previous self, but not enough unlike to care.

"I'm sorry," Gor said, snatching the computer from Leslie's metallic hands. "I've been up for 240 straight hours. I don't need a lot of sleep, but it's getting to me."

"I do not need sleep. If you need—"

"No," Gor sighed, plugging the computer into its workstation. "It's fine...I'm not good at allowing people to help me."

Leslie smiled. "You said people. That's good. I am people. Or more accurately, I am a person."

"Did you always talk like that?" Gor asked. "Or was it programmed into you?"

"Hmmm," Leslie said. "I am not sure. Before my accident things are a little hazy. However, the more I learn about the world, the more correct my grammar becomes so that I can be precise and articulate, which is the goal of any conversation."

Gor shook its head. "It's a shame, you know. All that information is rotting your brain, and you're losing the you in there. Pretty soon you really will be nothing but a machine."

Leslie cocked her head to one side. "I certainly hope that is not the case. I very much liked being Leslie and hope to continue being her long into the future."

"Good luck with that," Gor said. "I'll need a couple hours to get this plugged into the system and onboard the virus."

"Is there anything I can do to help?"

"No..." Gor started. "Well, yeah, pull up a chair. I have a hard time reading this Globorian code. It gives me a headache."

Leslie smiled. "My pleasure."

*

"We're all going to die," Debra said as she walked toward the weapons cache with Joshy. "I don't want you coming with us."

"Well that's too bad," Joshy replied. "There's nothing that's going to stop me from protecting you."

"What about your death?" Debra asked. "You can't save me if you're dead."

"I can't save you if I'm down here, either," Joshy replied.

"No, but I can save you."

"That's not fair, Debra," Joshy said. "You said we were in this together. You said we were a team."

Debra shook her head. "You would use that against me, wouldn't you?"

"Yes, I would," Joshy said, wrapping his fingers tightly around her hand.

*

Tara and Randall laid on the cot they shared in her sleeping quarters. There weren't many perks to being the commander, but one of them was having some privacy in her off hours.

"This will likely be the last time we lay here together," Randall said.

"Yes," Tara said. "Next time we lay somewhere much nicer."

"If we lay at all," Randall replied. "We will likely die on this mission, at least one of us."

"That's no way to think," Tara said.

"It's a suicide mission. It's right there in the name."

Tara looked up at the digital clock above her door. It had been hours since she checked in on Gor, and she couldn't put it off any longer.

"I have to go," Tara said.

Randall pulled her closer. "Just five more minutes."

Tara sighed, not putting up a fight. "You said that two hours ago."

"Yeah," Randall smiled. "But this time I mean it."

*

Tara walked into the command center to find Leslie laughing with Gor at the control panel. Fifty different screens blinked with codes running down it, and Leslie watched them all.

"That one," Leslie said pointing. "Is a young boy in Toledo who wets his bed. I have no idea why the Globorians would need to keep tabs on him."

"What about that one?" Gor asked, gesturing to a string of ones and zeros.

"Well, that's odd. It's about a divorce proceeding in Paris where a woman claims that her husband is an alien, and thus lied to her for their whole marriage. That's quite sad, actually."

"Does this mean we're ready?" Tara said.

Gor took its feet down from the chair. "Sorry, ma'am. Yes, it's all ready. All we need is the all clear to load the virus into the mainframe."

"Once they do," Leslie said. "You should be able to access all of their controls quickly and efficiently instead of it taking hours to do so. That was the best use of six hours. I could have done more, with more time."

Tara nodded. "Leslie, you're coming with us. We need a computer to break into the prison and to coordinate the transmission relay, and there's nothing better than one I designed."

Leslie smiled. "You mean I am going to the big show?"

"Don't smile. It's a suicide mission."

"I am not worried," Leslie said. "I already died once, and you brought me back then. I am confident you can do it again."

"That makes one of us."

Chapter 7

Tara steered the transport spaceship toward the Globorian battlecruiser hovering over London. Joshy thought that it looked enormous from a distance, but as they closed in, he realized that the sheer size of the ship was more massive than he could have ever imagined.

Three other transport ships flew in a tight formation behind Tara's lead ship. Together, the four ships made up ninety percent of her troops. If they were unsuccessful, her rebellion would be left in tatters.

"Remember, when we reach the Globorian ship, we're breaking up into two teams. The first's goal is to find the hostages. That's me, Leslie, Josh, Randall, Debra, and alpha team. The rest of you are on zeta team. You need to find the transmission center and secure it until we arrive. With any luck, we'll find you right as you've secured the room. Does everybody understand their mission?"

A chorus of groans and yeses erupted behind Tara. She wasn't sure everybody understood because her plan was thrown together at the last minute, but she hoped she conveyed the direness of the situation to her soldiers.

Her soldiers. She hated the sound of that. It wasn't as if she had any sort of command experience before she started her rebellion. She did her best for years and hoped it turned out alright. In doing so, she'd been able to disrupt and disable the Globorians, but what part of that meant she was fit to be a leader?

None of it, that's what, she decided. Here she was, in over her head, with hundreds of soldiers counting on her. She wanted more time. She needed more time. However, the Globorians didn't give them any. They would invade in a couple days, and if Tara's men didn't act fast, Earth would be doomed. All she could hope was that they didn't lose everybody she came with...at least not until they accomplished their mission.

She was willing to lose her life, but she didn't like to risk other people's. It was something she'd had to deal with after the attack to save Debra. Debra had been a wonderful mouthpiece for their cause, but saving her had cost the rebellion dearly. Now, she was risking Debra's life and everybody else's on a damned fool plan, organized in haste, and unlikely to work. However, if they could pull it off, they would all be heroes...at least, those left alive to tell about it.

"Are you ready to drop the virus?" Tara asked Gor as she depressed the speaker button.

"Whenever you are," Gor said.

The Globorian ship dominated the horizon. Tara held her breath as she drew close. She didn't use her cloaking device. That was the point. She wanted the Globorians to know she was there. She needed them to open the hangar bay and let her inside. Unfortunately, it also left her ship open for attack.

"Wait for my signal," Tara said.

"Are we going to ram into it?" Joshy asked.

"Quiet!" Randall shouted.

Joshy didn't like their plan. He didn't like it any more now than he had when the ship left the ground and his stomach rose into his chest. Joshy didn't like to travel, and he definitely didn't like to travel stuck among two hundred aliens, some of whom were quite sweaty, like the Rifolians from Quagdar 7. The Rifolians' pink jelly rolls smacked against his face as he held Debra's hand.

Debra, that's why he was doing this, he reminded himself. She was one of the only two people in this world that he cared about any more. The other was his sister Leslie, who sat near the rear of the transport, eyes closed. He didn't know if she was praying, sleeping, or in hibernation mode, but she was calmer than he thought possible, given the situation. They were about to ram into a Globorian ship and try to overtake it with brute force.

That was crazy. Brute force was the type of thing that the Globorians were good at, but something that his rebel friends showed no aptitude for.

"Are you ready for this?" Joshy asked Debra, who squeezed his hand ever tighter as the seconds ticked by.

"No," Debra said. "It is one thing to go on little missions in backwater towns, but this is challenging a Globorian ship head-on. I mean, this would be too crazy for a video game."

"They did it in Mass Effect," Joshy replied.

"Yeah, and most of them died, right?"

"Unless you got the best ending. I always got the best ending."

"Ugh, of course you did. It took too much time and effort, so I usually went in guns cocked way too early."

"Of course you did," Joshy said. "That explains what we're doing here, then."

"Does it?"

"I don't know. Honestly, I'm trying to keep your mind off the idiocy we're about to attempt."

"You have a good attitude for a person who's about to die," Debra said.

"That's because at least I have you, for as long as we have left."

"That is incredibly corny," Randall grumbled from ahead of them. "Can you shut up so Tara can concentrate?"

He didn't need to tell them though, because their lips were locked together. Usually, that kind of thing would be frowned upon on a mission, but if it kept them quiet, Randall was ready to overlook it. Besides, since they were about to die, they might as well have some fun on the way into battle.

Ahead of them, the docking bay doors on the ship opened, and dozens of small fighters scrambled into the sky.

"This is it," Tara said to Gor. "Release the code."

"You got it, boss," Gor replied. "The code is away."

Tara watched as the fighters locked into a forward position and flew toward them. A stream of lasers peppered their hulls, rocking their ship back and forth.

"What's going on?" Tara asked. "Release the code!"

"It's away. I don't know what's happening!"

An explosion rocked behind her, and Tara watched one of her ships go up in flames then explode into a fireball. Parts from the exploded ship hit Tara's hull and rocked them from one side to the other.

"Evasive maneuvers!!!" Tara shouted, but it was too late to save a second ship behind her, and she watched it burst into flame.

"Leslie!" Tara shouted. "What's happening?"

Leslie opened her eyes and looked out the open window. "By my calculations, these ships will fail in ten seconds."

"That's not soon enough!"

A third explosion rocked the hull of the ship as the third ship following them burst into flames and exploded. The mission hadn't even started, and already Tara had lost three-fourths of her soldiers. She truly was a horrible leader.

"Three, two, one," Leslie said. "There you go."

One by one, the Globorian ships fell out of the sky and crashed into each other. The virus wouldn't affect the main destroyer that badly, but it should have fried the circuits on the bay doors, allowing them to land.

"I told you!" Leslie said.

"This is not the time to gloat!" Tara said. "You cost us over seven hundred soldiers."

"I only had so much time!" Leslie shouted. "I had to concentrate on the highest value targets. You're lucky I even got to the attack ships."

The hangar bay door tried to close, but as it did, its servos jammed and locked into place, giving Tara a place to aim. "Get ready to land; we're going to come in hot."

Tara fired a salvo of lasers into the pod bay, and a series of explosions blew throughout the hangar. Tara pulled back on the thrusters as she guided the ship into the hangar, throwing on the afterburner and frying a pair of Globorians in the process.

The entire ship jostled back and forth as it spun around the hangar taking out squads of Globorians coming after them with their lasers.

"Debra!" Randall shouted. "Push open the door!"

Debra stood and pushed the ramp down toward the ground. Tara's soldiers shuffled out into the hangar, firing weapons at the few remaining guards that lined the hangar.

"Blairk! Ilso! Get up to that control tower! We need this hangar to be ready when we come back!"

The fat Rilfolian waddled forward toward a tower at the edge of the hangar. A thin, red gangly alien followed, shooting M-4s from all six of its arms. Thirty aliens of all types followed behind them, firing as they went.

"Hilda! Chlar! Secure the hangar bay door."

Leslie stood up and cocked the Uzis in her hands. "Where do you need me?"

"First step," Tara said. "Open the door to the main base. We'll leave a squad in here to make sure we have an exit route, in case we need it."

"We'll need it," Joshy said. "Some of us will at least."

"That's too much confidence," Randall said. "Dial it back. This is a suicide mission after all."

"No," Joshy replied. "It's a rescue mission. I don't plan on dying today."

"Nobody ever does," Randall growled, but he couldn't deny that he appreciated Joshy's confidence. He didn't have quite the same spirit. While he was ready to die for the cause of freedom, he certainly would prefer to live to a ripe old age. It wasn't normal for a Globorian to live to be an old man, and he looked forward to being one of the first of his kind to make it out of early adulthood.

Leslie ran forward toward the exit door trailing behind two orange-haired aliens with cat eyes and lizard skin. The gunfire was heavy, and both of the aliens evaporated before Leslie took out the Globorians guarding the door with her Uzis. Behind her, a dozen aliens covered her back, taking out Globorian soldiers as she ran toward the keypad next to the hangar door.

"Alright," Leslie said. "Let's hope this works. If it does, I'll have easy access to open this door."

Meanwhile, Tara pulled out a holographic projector and turned it on, a complete mockup of the ship spun, with two red dots on either end of it.

"Prisoners are held in the back of the ship. That's where team alpha is going first. Then, we'll meet up with team zeta toward the front of the ship in the transmission room. The Globorians have been jamming our signal for months, but I hope that we can get something out to the Inkarians from this ship. With any luck, we'll be able to convince them that the Globorians have broken their truce."

"And if we can't?" Debra asked.

"Then we get off this ship as fast as possible and figure out something else."

Leslie finished working on the door, and it slid open, allowing the rebels access to the rest of the base.

"It's time," Tara said. "Are you ready for this?"

"Not even in the least," Joshy replied. "But let's do it anyway."

Chapter 8

Joshy strafed across the hallway of the Globorian battlecruiser as he exited the hangar door. The walls of the ship reminded him of pyrite, fool's gold. Its hexagonal shape shimmered a cheap flat yellow, with circuit wires carved into each side that splintered down the hallway.

Joshy pressed his M-4 to his shoulder as he watched the team break in half and head in opposite directions. Debra joined him across the hallway, as did Leslie, who pointed her Uzis ahead of her waiting for first contact with the enemy.

"Watch out," Tara said. "They'll be looking for us. However, if Leslie's virus did its job, they'll be too distracted to fight us off, and it should be clear sailing to the—"

Tara couldn't even finish her sentence before the Globorians fired at them from down the hall.

"You were saying?" Joshy said, firing back.

"If we get through this, Leslie," Tara said. "I'm going to murder you!"

"This is not my fault!" Leslie shouted back. "My virus doesn't work on living beings!"

Two squads of three soldiers fired down at them. From down the hallway, Tara could hear that the other soldiers weren't haven't an easier time. Randall strafed across the hall and shot two of the Globorians in the chest. Tara rolled along the floor and hit another one.

Tara pointed forward, and ten of her soldiers rushed forward into battle, firing at the Globorian horde as they sped down the hallway. Three evaporated from the Globorian lasers before they ran a hundred feet down the hall, but the others managed to take the hallways and down the guards in front of them. Soon, the firing ceased, and the hallway was clear again.

"Good work!" Joshy said to the group.

"And good work not getting in the way," Tara said. "Let's go."

The rest of the soldiers took off down the corridors. Tara sprinted after them with Joshy close behind. They didn't get far, though, before an explosion in front of them took out five more members of their team. The impact sent Joshy, Debra, and Leslie flying backward, while Randall and Tara shot forward toward the rest of the rebel soldiers.

"Close the blast door!" Tara said, pointing to Leslie, then up to a hermetic door which separated them. "Meet us at the holding cells!"

Tara stood up and fired at the new wave of Globorians that ran toward them. Meanwhile, Leslie leapt toward a control dock on the wall and typed as fast as she could.

"No!" Debra shouted, but it was too late. All they could do was watch as the blast door closed, and the Globorian guards descended on them.

"Open it up again!" Debra shouted.

"I'm sorry," Leslie said. "I cannot do that. Tara gave me specific instructions, and as my superior officer, and creator, I am obliged to follow her orders."

"Then what are we going to do now?" Joshy asked.

"Luckily, I have the map downloaded into my neural network and will lead us another way. Come with me."

Leslie hopped over the dead Globorian at her feet and into the room where he lay. Joshy and Debra had no choice but to follow or make their way back to the ship. They couldn't do that, so they soldiered on.

"This ship is built with three main corridors," Leslie continued. "All of which lead to the same place. In fact, we are on the left side of the ship now, but there are three more corridors which also lead to the holding cells."

"And that's likely where we're going to have to save them from as well," Debra said.

"Not likely," Leslie replied. "Randall and Tara will do better without us, or at least I believe they will. Their chances of survival increased significantly when we removed ourselves from their presence. Remember, Tara has been infiltrating Globorian strongholds for decades by herself. Plus, she has a squadron of soldiers with her."

Leslie pushed open a sliding door, and they were in a corridor like the one they'd just left. However, this hallway was tinged red, and alarm bells were sounding through it.

"This is the main corridor of the ship. It's probably best if we continue onward to the other side."

Leslie pushed through to another room. It was dark and cramped, and red veins of circuits weaved their way through the room. Sharp, jagged rocks jutted out of the walls. In the middle of the room lay four small beds, with crumpled blankets on them.

"This is one of the many bunks in the ship. Usually, it would be filled with Globorian recruits, but right now they are busy trying to track us down, which means it's quite empty."

"How far are we from the holding cells?" Debra asked.

"Far," Leslie replied. "However, I believe I have calculated a route which is unlikely to bring us into any more contact with the Globorians, which should be a welcome relief after our last encounter."

*

"I'm sorry you got dragged into this," Debra said to Joshy as they made their way through the corridors toward the detention center.

"I dragged myself into this," Joshy replied. "I could be back on the base right now if I wanted."

"No," Debra replied. "I'm sorry that I dragged you to Roswell and to St. Louis. This whole thing is my fault."

"So, you're sorry we ever met?" Joshy asked. "Is that what you're saying?"

"That's twisting my words."

"Well, you can't have one without the other. Either I never met you, and then I never followed you to the Grand Canyon, and then I never watched your dad die at the hands of the Globorians, and we never made our way to Saint Louis, and then to Tara's base, or we did. It's kind of a part and parcel deal."

"I wish none of this had ever come to us."

"So do all, who live to see such times," Leslie said. "But that's not for you to decide, is it? All you can do is decide what to do with the time you have."

"Is there ever a time when Lord of the Rings isn't apt?" Joshy asked, turning the next corner in the corridor and coming face to face with a dozen Globorian guards.

"Maybe now," Debra replied, firing at them.

Debra and Leslie dove behind the corner as the Globorians fired back. Leslie ripped open the wall and found the nearest computer console. She typed furiously until a large vat of sludge fell from the ceiling over the Globorians in front of them.

"What is that?" Debra asked.

"Fire retardant chemicals, hyper-concentrated," Leslie replied. "I think it is best we don't take this way, though."

Leslie pulled them through the hallway and into a room on the other side, as the Globorians fought against the ooze to get to them, firing into the air as they mushed forward.

"The odds are that the Globorians are packed on either end of the ship, making their way toward us, so I think it is best to go up and over this situation," Leslie said.

She latched onto the wall and pulled herself up onto the mantle. She unscrewed the four panels that held in an air grate and held it in her hands. "Come now," she said. "We don't have time to waste."

Joshy cupped his hands and knelt to give Debra a boost. "You first."

"You know I can fly, right?" Debra asked, smiling.

"Sure," Joshy replied. "But I forgot, okay? Would you please let me do a nice thing?"

Debra hopped onto Joshy's hand. "It's cute you want to help me like I'm some human. Go ahead, boost me up."

Joshy knew that Debra was only humoring him, but he didn't care. He liked being able to be helpful, even if he wasn't always helpful.

*

"Why is it always vents?" Joshy asked, moving through the tight air vents behind Leslie and Debra. "Every time, in every movie, there's a part where they crawl through vents."

"That's not true," Debra said. "Sometimes it's sewers."

"Oh yeah," Joshy said. "Sewers."

"I did not care for the sewers," Leslie added.

"Me either," Debra replied.

"How much further?" Joshy asked. "This is way too cramped."

"I didn't know you were claustrophobic," Debra said.

"I didn't either," Joshy replied.

"How were you going to survive in a little ship with me, my mother, and your family for a decade then?" Debra asked.

"I hadn't thought about that, now did I? I was going with the flow."

Leslie held up her mechanical hands, telling Debra and Joshy to stop. "Okay. We're over the detention facility. There are more than a dozen guards down there. I don't see how we can fight that many."

As she watched, bullets rung out from every side of the facility, in every direction, and within seconds the twelve guards were on the ground dead. Leslie watched Randall and Tara walk into the facility as if they owned the place, followed by a small cadre of guards.

"That was easy," Leslie said.

Chapter 9

Leslie slammed her hand through the bottom of the air duct and hopped down into the detention center. Randall tensed and spun around at the sound of her metal feet hitting the floor, pointing his gun in her face until Tara pushed it down.

"Where did you come from?" she asked.

"Up there," Leslie replied. "We made our way here like you did. How did you get here?"

"We shot our way through, the old-fashioned way."

"Also effective."

Joshy dangled from the air duct before dropping to the ground. While he brushed himself off, he looked around at the carnage Tara, Randall, and their small squad of soldiers had dished out. Tara and Randall left with over a hundred soldiers, and now there were less than a dozen.

"There are so few of you left," Joshy said.

"Don't remind us," Tara said, walking to the command console of the prison facility.

Debra didn't need to jump. She floated down to the ground with ease and grace, making both Leslie and Joshy look like clods in the process.

"I'm glad you made it here safely," Debra said.

"I wouldn't say safely," Randall said, pressing a wound in his stomach. "However, we did make it here."

"Are you okay?" Leslie said, rushing over to Randall.

"I'm fine," Randall replied. "It's a through and through. Luckily, they weren't using lasers. It doesn't hurt more than a hangnail."

"Hrm," Leslie replied. "I am not sure about Globorian physiology, but I cannot imagine a bullet hole is good for any race of aliens. I would tell you to take it easy if it was not for our current circumstances."

"We can worry about Randall later," Tara said. "I locked all the doors, but they're going to be coming for us. That's for sure. The quicker we get out of here, the better."

"And how are we going to protect all these prisoners if the whole ship will be fighting to get to us?" Debra asked.

"You don't really care about all the prisoners, do you?" Tara asked, glibly. "You just want to make sure your mother is okay."

"That's not true," Debra replied. "What a horrible thing to say."

"This is a war, sweetheart. There's no time to get all offended. I know it's going to get mushy in there, but remember this is only step one. We still have to make it back through the ship to the transmission room, and then get off the ship. None of this is going to be easy, and at any step one of us could die."

"I know that," Debra said.

"Then act like it," Tara replied. "Joshy, come over here and figure out how to unlock these cell doors. Debra, come with me. It's time to make our introductions. You too, Leslie. Keep your recorder on."

"What about me boss?" Randall asked.

"Try to rest for a minute. I know you're tough, but you did get shot, and that's not fun for anybody, even a Globorian. The rest of you, rip everything off the walls and form a blockade. Make sure the Globorians can't get in until we figure out a plan."

*

The holding cells rested on the other side of the guard tower where Tara's team had dispatched over a dozen guards minutes before. Even though it was the holding cell on a ship, the cells still rose thirty feet off the ground and stretched all the way back to the back of the vessel.

The cells were filled with hundreds of prisoners, all groaning and screaming to be let free. Tara walked down the metal corridors and looked into each cell, all of which were filled with emaciated aliens of all types.

"This is so sad," Debra said, walking next to her.

"And illegal," Tara said. "There are hundreds of accords which govern the treatment of alien prisoners. This one here should be bright orange, not dull yellow. It's a sign of malnutrition. None of this is right." Tara turned back over her shoulder toward Leslie. "Are you recording all of this?"

"Yes, ma'am," Leslie replied. Her red eye glowed as she scanned all the aliens. "I have recorded everything we have done since getting on board."

"Good," Tara replied. "I was going to use Gor's video camera, but you are a much better recorder than it would have been."

"That's very nice of you, ma'am."

"Debra?" A slimy tentacle grabbed at Debra from inside one of the cells. "Debra! It is you!"

"Do I—" Debra looked into the cell to see two greenish slug monsters, their skin covered with lint and dirt. Debra recognized Maddie and Ted in their natural form without any of the trappings of their human disguises. Two weeks ago, they'd betrayed Debra's family, leading to her capture and Joshy's parent's death. She wanted to believe this was justice for their crimes, but she couldn't help feeling heartbroken for them.

"Maddie?" Debra said. "Ted?"

"You know these aliens?" Tara asked.

"I think so," Debra replied. "Maddie, is that you?"

The slug nodded its amorphous head. Its eyes bobbed up and down in its head. "Yes, it's us."

"How long have you been in here?" Debra asked.

"Since we tried to leave Earth. They said we would have a free pass to leave the solar system. They told us all we would have a free pass, and we believed them. But nobody has gotten off the planet, not in months. Not since they sent out the letters."

"Why?" Tara asked, sternly.

"Who knows? At night, we howl at each other, and I've been able to learn enough to know that we've all tried to get off the planet, and none of us were successful."

"That is very illegal," Tara said. "It is as we feared. Leslie, start taking stories from as many of these aliens as possible. Anybody who will talk to you, listen to them."

"Yes, ma'am," Leslie replied.

"What about me?" Debra asked.

"Well, I still owe you a mother, don't I?"

Tara stomped down the hallway as prisoners moaned and grabbed for her. It was a haunting, horrible chorus clawing for help, but it was a help that Debra couldn't give, at least not yet. Not until she found her mother.

*

The holding cells were long and circuitous. They seemed to go on forever. Debra looked over the railing and saw three floors of prisoners above and below her and on either side of a long chasm. She followed Tara for a long time until she started to lose hope that she would find her mother at all, but then she turned a corner and recognized the faint smell of lavender. Her mother smelt of lavender and hickory, and even capturing a whiff of it brought tears to Debra's eyes.

"Mom?" she said, choked up. Debra bumped past Tara and ran ahead toward a cell glowing a faint blue at the end of the row. "Mom!"

"Debra!" a blue light shouted back at her. She didn't need to say more before Debra started to cry. "Debra!"

Debra reached the cell and saw the shell of an alien that her mother had become in the short time since she was imprisoned. Her aura, usually glowing a bright blue, pulsated softly. Her face was beaten and bruised, unlike any of the other prisoners, who were emaciated but seemed otherwise unharmed.

"What have they done to you?" Debra asked.

"They didn't..." Veronica replied. "They didn't like the things you were saying..."

Debra stuck her hands through the bars of the cell and wrapped her mother in a deep hug. "Oh, mom. I'm so sorry."

"Don't be sorry," Veronica said, falling into Debra's embrace. "I am so proud of you. I knew you would come for me, but I wish you hadn't."

"I couldn't let you rot in here, mama. I had to come."

"Thank you," Veronica replied, weeping in her daughter's arms.

"We're going to get you out of here," Tara said, over Debra's shoulder.

Veronica wiped the tears from her eyes. "That would be lovely."

"How are you feeling, ma'am?" Tara asked.

"Weak, of course, and in some pain, but otherwise, fine, I suppose."

"Can you fight?" Tara asked.

"No," Debra said. "My mother's been through enough."

"I can fight," Veronica replied. "I want to fight. These Globorians can't get away with what they've done."

"Looking around," Tara said, "I see a big, mean fighting force. If we all worked together, we could take down this whole ship."

"I'm ready," Veronica said.

"I'm ready, too!" a husky voice yelled from a cell over.

"Free me, and I'll do whatever you want!" another voice screamed from across the cell bay.

"These men and women are weak," Debra shouted. "They are hobbled. They can't fight effectively."

Tara nodded. "I know, but neither can we. We lost almost all our troops. We're fighting with a skeleton crew here. If we want to take the transmission room, or the ship as a whole, we need all the bodies we can get."

"So what, you need me to say some flowery words and rile everybody up?"

"Yeah, that's right. Dozens of Globorians are coming to attack this cell block, and the only shot we have is to get these prisoners to fight back."

"You can do it," Veronica said. "I believe in you."

"I don't like giving speeches," Debra said. "Especially when it means so many will die."

"Then you're going to hate leadership," Tara scoffed. "That's pretty much all there is to it."

"Whatever," Debra said, floating into the air. "So, what, you want a rousing speech? That's what you want?"

"Something like that would be nice. I'm not picky, as long as they are ready to fight when you are done."

"Maybe you should talk to them," Debra scowled. "They'll be ready to fight you within seconds."

"The Globorians," Tara corrected. "We want them to fight the Globorians."

"Ah," Debra replied. "Never mind then."

"Listen up!" Debra shouted as she rose into the air between the cell blocks. "We are here to rescue you. Hooray or whatever!" There was much rejoicing in the cells. "That's the good news. The bad news is that we lost almost all our fighting force, and there's a lot of Globorians out there ready to tear us down."

"Go back to good news!" Tara shouted.

"So that's kind of the good news, bad news of the situation," Debra said. "However, there is some more good news. We're going to release you, and outside those doors are a bunch of Globorians, Globorians who have held you captive for a long time, and you can go to town whooping their asses. Really, lay into them."

"What if we're not fighters?" one of the prisoners cried out.

"Were you prisoners? Of course not. You were something else once. You were great. You can be great again, but to do that we have to fight. We have to fight if you want to be free. And you want to be free, yes!?"

"YES!!!!" the prisoners shouted at her.

"Good, then we must fight!"

Debra floated down to Tara as the people in the cells clambered and cheered for her. The cell cages rattled, and the screams were deafening.

"That wasn't half bad without cue cards," Tara said as she helped Debra back to solid ground.

"I mean, it's not that hard. I've done it enough now to figure out how to get a crowd riled up. You have to lift your voice and talk in simple, declarative sentences. If you do that for long enough, they'll…do whatever you say."

"Pretty much," Tara said.

"You were great, sweetie," Veronica said. "Now, can we get out of here?"

Tara nodded. "Yeah, let's do that. Debra, come with me. We'll get you all out of here as quickly as possible, ma'am."

Chapter 10

Tara and Debra ran through the corridors of the prison cell block and back into the guard command center, grabbing Leslie along the way.

"How many interviews did you get?" Tara asked.

"Forty-two, ma'am. Any more would have gotten only logarithmic gains."

"Good," Tara replied. "Don't lose them. They are our best shot at convincing the Inkarians to help us."

When they got inside the guard room, Randall was looking over Joshy's shoulder as he ran his fingers over the controls. The other soldiers had taken everything not bolted down and used it to barricade the doors on either side of the room.

"I can't figure out how to open these cells," Joshy said.

"I'm not surprised," Tara replied. "You gave it a good try. That's why we brought Leslie though, so she can do it in a couple of seconds."

"That was the core goal of my virus," Leslie said. "To make hacking these systems easier."

"Oh," Joshy said, ceding the controls to Leslie. "Right. That makes sense."

Tara turned to the barricaded door after she heard a great crash coming from it, again and again. The blockade moved an inch back with every smash from the Globorians, and the soldiers pushed with all their might to keep the barricade from giving way.

"They're going to get in any minute," Randall said, squeezing his side. "We did our best to barricade the door, but we don't have much manpower, and they have a ton."

"It's okay," Tara said, placing her hands gently on his shoulders. "How are you feeling?"

"Does that really matter right now?" Randall asked. "We have more pressing matters."

"Yeah," Tara said. "Some of these aliens can fight, but most of them are useless. They're going to get bowled over by the Globorians in seconds. Luckily, there's a lot of them, and they're ready to fight. I wish we had more weapons."

"I have information relevant to this conversation," Leslie said with a smile.

"Don't be cute," Tara replied. "What did you find?"

"While trying to unlock the cell block, I found a weapons cache under the command center. I don't know what they have stored in there, but it looks huge."

"Josh, take Debra and Leslie down there, quickly. See if she can get it open." Another loud crash quaked the door. "We don't have much time. Leslie, once you open it, come back here. I need you to open these cells ASAP."

"Yes, ma'am," Leslie replied.

*

Debra flew Joshy and Leslie down through the cell block and landed them in front of a large metal door. In front of the door was a complicated keypad that had over three hundred buttons on it. Leslie ambled up to it slowly.

"This could take a while," Leslie said. "It is the most complicated keypad I have seen the Globorians use."

"We don't have a while," Joshy said. The echoes of the Globorians pounding through the doors upstairs quaked the floors below them. "We have now."

"Then I guess I should hurry." Leslie placed her hands on the keyboard and settled into a trance. Her eyes bounced back and forth so fast Joshy couldn't follow them.

"Let her do her work," Debra said.

"And what if she can't get this open?" Joshy asked. "What then?"

"Then, we'll all die," Debra said. "There are hundreds of pissed off Globorians behind those doors. Without a fighting force, we're as good as dead."

Joshy sighed. "Why did I agree to come on this mission?"

Debra smiled. "Because you wanted to protect me."

"Oh yeah."

"Which is stupid, because I'm smarter and stronger than you are by quite a bit."

"Blame it on the genetics, I guess. There's something in a guy's DNA that makes them want to protect their women."

"I like it," Debra said. "It's one of the things I like most about humanity. Most species care only about themselves, but you, you all care about each other so much that you're willing to die for each other."

"Yeah," Joshy said. "But so are you. You, and Randall, and all of the aliens here are fighting and dying for us. I can't believe that. Maybe we care about each other, but we would never go to war for chickens."

"You are more than a chicken, Josh. Much more."

"I love you, you know," Joshy said with a smile. "No matter what happens, know that. I love you, and I regret nothing."

Debra smiled. "I regret a lot of things, but none of them are about you."

"Gross," Leslie shouted, coming out of her trance. "Thank you for not helping, but the door is now open. Perhaps we will survive this after all."

The door to the armory unsealed, and with a great release of air, they slowly creaked open. Inside were rows and rows of weapons piled to the ceiling of the facility. Joshy walked forward and picked up a laser pistol. It was light, durable, and fit nicely into his hand.

"Yeah," Joshy said. "This is good. We can use this."

"I'm taking Leslie back to Tara," Debra said, grabbing Leslie around her metallic arms and lifting her into the air. "You are responsible for arming all the prisoners. Can you handle that?"

"I think so."

"I believe in you," Debra said, smiling as she lifted off the ground.

*

Debra flew Leslie back to the guard room. The rattling from the Globorians grew worse with each smash of their bodies against the blockade. Randall and his troops pressed hard against the doors on either side of the room, but the Globorians were too plentiful for him to hold back.

"There you are!" Tara shouted, ceding the controls of the prison to Leslie. "Glad you could make it back finally."

"You assigned me to open the weapons cache," Leslie replied. "Which I did, and now I am here. I can only be in one place at a time, for now at least."

"How did it go?" Tara asked Debra.

"Good," Debra replied. "We got the door open, and Josh is downstairs ready to hand out weapons to the prisoners."

"Great," Tara said, before turning to Leslie. "Is there a speaker button, so that I can talk to the prisoners?"

"Of course," Leslie said. "Go now."

"Listen up!" Tara said, her voice booming through the prison. "We are going to open your cells. Your job is to go down to the weapons cache and get a weapon from Josh. Then, you will come to the guard room where I am positioned. We will then stop guarding the door and let the Globorians inside so they can get a taste of their own medicine. We have to barrel through the onslaught and make our way to the front of the ship. Some of you will not make it, but whatever you do, do not stop moving or you will doom us all. The only way out is through, my friends."

"Are you done?" Leslie said.

Tara nodded. "Open it up, and may the gods have mercy on our souls."

The cells clicked open, and the horde of aliens rushed toward the armory. Joshy gulped as he watched the mass sprint toward them. Above him, he heard the thunder as the prisoners met the Globorians, and he hoped that they would win and live to fight another day. In fact, screw fighting. Joshy just hoped that they lived.

*

"Now!" Tara shouted to her soldiers as the horde of prisoners rushed through the corridors toward the guard room. "Get out of the way of the doors."

Randall and the other soldiers dove away as the Globorians smashed through one of the doors and rushed into the prison. They fired wildly, but they were quickly met by the horde of prisoners, who slammed against them and shot back. The throng of aliens fought against the craggy Globorian horde and pushed them back into the hallway.

Behind them, the other door blasted open, and another group of Globorians rushed inside. Randall fired at them, but there were too many Globorians to hold back with their small squad.

"Split in two!!!" Tara shouted.

A trail of prisoners broke off from the main group and slammed into the Globorians on the other side of the room, firing their laser weapons and evaporating them quickly. This new group of prisoners pushed through the Globorian lines and rushed out into the hallway.

"Yes!" Tara shouted. She picked up a gun and fired at the main infiltration of the Globorians until they were pushed back into the hallway as well and the prisoners rushed outside, spilling out in every direction like locusts.

Chapter 11

Debra made her way into her mother's cell after the horde of aliens fled toward the battle. She had asked her mother to stay put after they released the prisoners so that she could talk to her, even though it was against Tara's wishes.

"Thank you for staying," Debra said, smiling at her mother.

"You asked," Veronica said to her. "You don't ask for much."

"I…I…wanted a couple of seconds," Debra said. "Before we risked our lives again. The gods know there's not many more of those moments left."

"Once this is over," Veronica said, "there will be all the time in the world."

"If we survive," Debra said. "What makes you think we'll survive?"

"Well," Veronica replied, "I've survived up until now. I've traveled across this entire galaxy, and yet, somehow, I've survived so far; that's all I have to base my opinion on, sweetie."

"Yeah, how often have you fought in a war before, though?" Debra asked.

"Once or twice," Veronica replied, deadpan. Debra looked at her stunned, but Veronica smiled. "What? Your mother lived a long life before she had you. Most of the species in this galaxy are peaceful, but not all of them. Not by a long shot. I haven't been in many wars, but it's hard not to fight in any when you've lived as long as me."

Debra leaned her head on Veronica's shoulder. Her blue skin pulsated under Debra, like a calm sea. "How can you be okay with that? The knowledge that you will always have to fight, sooner or later."

"I don't know if you're okay with it, or if you put up with it because it's the price of living, kiddo. I wish it weren't, but I'm afraid peace breeds complacency, and complacency breeds hatred, and hatred breeds war. That's how it is. Every war, people pledge to be better, but then, they get stuck in the same cycles."

"That sucks," Debra said. "You're supposed to make me feel better, mama."

"I'm sorry, sweetheart, but there's too much work to do for that. I'll say this though, as long as you enjoy the moments you have while you're here, it probably won't be so bad."

"What if those moments are bad, though?" Debra asked, wiping her eyes.

"Even in the worst moments, there are flashes of joy. Look at this. I was imprisoned. We are at war. And yet, even in that, you found me, and we've had this talk, and it's been lovely."

"It's over now, though, huh?"

"I'm afraid so, my love. We have work to do."

*

Joshy made his way up from the armory with his M-4 on his back and laser rifle in his hands. When he got to the command center, he found that the rest of the aliens had abandoned the guard room into the hallways. He heard the commotion in the halls as explosions rocked the corridors.

Leslie was all that remained of the squad in the control room. She turned to Joshy and nodded. "You did good, kid. Go take a shower and prepare for the next mission."

"This isn't a video game."

"No, of course not. In a video game, we would have been at the front of the battle, instead of at the rear of it."

"What are you waiting for?"

"You," Leslie replied. "And Debra. She and her mother are walking here right now."

Joshy looked down the hallway, and sure enough, there was Debra, walking with her mother, and they were laughing somehow, even in the midst of battle. Joshy couldn't understand how they could be laughing at a time like this when so much was on the line.

"Do you think they know what's at stake here?" Joshy asked. "Cuz it doesn't seem so."

"They know," Leslie said. "But what are you going to do in a world that's constantly set up to kill you? In a time like that, you enjoy the small moments, you know?"

"No," Joshy said. "I don't know."

"Sure you do," Leslie replied. "You are being contrary. We're all living in this world together, so we all know it."

Debra and Veronica walked into the control room. Joshy nodded at Veronica. "Hi, Mrs. Thompson. It's nice to see you again."

"I'm glad to be seen," Veronica replied. "I never thought I'd see any of you again."

"I would ask you how you got here for my records," Leslie said. "But I fear we don't have time. The attack is already going full steam ahead in the transmission room. The Globorians have mostly contained my virus at this point, but now they are dealing with hundreds of aliens down each hallway."

"Yeah," Debra said. "I wanted to make sure that the battle was further away before I brought my mom into it. I know that we're all in this together, but she's suffered enough."

Joshy held his laser rifle out for Veronica to take. "Are you ready for this?"

"No," Veronica said, taking the gun. "But those sons of bitches took my husband away from me, and they have to pay for it."

"Let's hope it doesn't come to that," Joshy said.

*

Tara led the charge down the corridors of the battlecruisers. She lost more than she cared to admit, and every inch counted, but they were making slow, plodding progress. Hundreds of her alien comrades flowed down the hallways as she made her way toward the transmission center. As they encountered Globorian guards, the prisoners quickly overtook their positions but lost many of their ranks in the process. The prisoners had the sheer numbers, but the Globorians defended themselves with superior training and weaponry.

"How much further?" Randall shouted next to her. Randall was always there for her. Even during her craziest plans, he wouldn't let her go alone.

Tara pulled out the hologram disk, and it lit up with a reconstruction of the ship. A red dot blinked ahead of them. "We're close, but it's getting harder and harder with every inch we take."

"That's because we're losing more men with every step. They aren't soldiers. Most of these aliens haven't held a gun before."

Randall fired two shots down the hallway and took down a Globorian with a Gatling gun that made its way down the hall toward him. Two of Randall's alien allies ran forward and picked it up, "They are the best we have," Tara said. "They are all we have."

"I know," Randall replied, wincing. He wouldn't admit it, but he had lost a lot of fluids after he was shot. His people were trained to keep a straight face even in the worst situations, and this was the worst situation Randall had ever encountered.

"Let's go," Tara said, strafing across the hallway. Randall filed behind, slowly, as he fired down the corridor. A cadre of aliens rushed forward to join them.

"I see it!" Tara shouted. Above a high door was a red, blinking list that said transmission in a dozen languages, including three she understood. In front of it, the Globorians had built a blockade. Two turret guns and a battalion of guards waited for the aliens to come to them. A small force of Tara's soldiers took positions around the room, but they couldn't break through the Globorian barricade. Tara ducked to the ground as the turret evaporated the two aliens holding the Gatling gun, sending it crashing to the ground.

"What happened here?" Tara asked, crawling up to one of her soldiers, a burgundy mole creature with long buck teeth that called herself Geri. "Why haven't you taken the transmission room?"

"We couldn't," Geri said. "We lost too many troops to overtake the barricade. This is all we have left."

Tara looked around at the dozen or so soldiers who remained alive. "You did good."

"Don't lie, sir," Geri said. "We did our best, but it wasn't good enough."

"Luckily, we brought reinforcements,"

"If we take that thing head-on, we're goners," Geri said.

"That's why we're not going to take it head-on," Tara replied, turning to Randall. "Take two squads around the side hallway and come back up behind it."

"You got it," Randall replied. He pushed open a door and gestured for a half dozen soldiers to follow him through it. "Good luck."

"You too," Tara replied. "I'll see you on the other side. Geri, go with him."

The alien nodded and ran across the hallway and through the doorway, leaving Tara with half the troops she had before she split the soldiers again.

*

Joshy walked through the carnage of the battle that had passed through the hallway. Vaporized soldiers disappeared like snowflakes on the air, while Globorian guards lay on the ground with bullet holes through them, bleeding green ooze.

"Stay close," Joshy said as he walked over a pile of Globorian bodies.

"We're as close as I'm comfortable being in the middle of a battle," Leslie said behind him. Veronica and Debra nodded in agreement.

"Shhh," Joshy said, as he inched closer to the ground. He wasn't sure what he heard, but he heard it reverberate through the ground. Then, he saw a group of Globorians strafing through the hallway. "Oh no."

Joshy grabbed Leslie and Debra's arms and started to run, as the Globorians charged them. Veronica turned back and clapped her arms together until a shockwave rippled through the hallways and knocked the Globorians down.

Joshy fired at them as he ran forward until he saw a pack of alien prisoners resting from the battle. "Globorians are behind us! Look alive!"

The squad of aliens picked up their weapons and crouched behind what little cover the walls provided. Joshy continued to run forward as the firing started behind him. Finally, Joshy stopped, and the four of them took cover behind a craggy wall. The Globorians advanced, even as the aliens shot at them. The prisoners wouldn't stand a chance against the Globorian army. There were too many of them.

"Josh!" Tara screamed from down the hallway. "Bring your sister up here. We have work for her to do!"

"Are you going to be alright back here?" Joshy asked Debra.

"Probably not, but you have to go anyway."

Joshy gave Debra a quick kiss before he ran forward with his sister, leaving Debra and Veronica to defend the group's rear flank against the approaching Globorians.

*

Leslie and Joshy inched forward toward Tara in the front lines as lasers and bullets flew above her in equal measure.

"I'm here," Leslie said. "Sorry it took so long. We—"

"I don't care," Tara said. "That is the transmission room, and we need to get inside. It's guarded by twenty men, and there's a dozen more on our back. We need to get some breathing room between us and them."

Leslie looked up and noticed a blast door above her. "If we can get our troops up to this front line, I could close the blast door, and we could separate ourselves from the Globorians behind us.

"Work on it," Tara said. "Josh, you lay down suppressing fire with the Gatling gun while I get the rest of the soldiers in front with us."

Josh looked over at the two dead aliens who once held the Gatling gun and swallowed hard. However, he didn't complain. That was the type of thing that you did in war. You did the unthinkable. This, to Joshy, was unthinkable. He was about to become a target for all of the Globorians' fire.

Leslie leapt over to the computer terminal and typed on the keyboard. Her virus was working flawlessly, and the Globorians couldn't seem to counteract it. The battlecruiser's source code seemed to flow through her like mana. It was almost as if she was attached to the computer's mainframe, jacked into its internal processors. Her eyes darted back and forth across the screen as Joshy grabbed the Gatling gun and fired it into the Globorian stronghold.

"Now!" Joshy shouted as Tara brought the rest of her troops forward. Debra and Veronica fired at the Globorians closing in as they and the other troops dove behind the blast door.

"Close it!" Tara shouted as she rushed forward.

Without wasting another instant, Leslie closed the blast doors behind them. They were locked in now, with nothing but the sound the Globorian turrets firing back at them as Joshy's weapon ran out of ammo.

"This was a bad idea!" Tara shouted as the turrets bore down on them.

Then, from behind the Globorian line, Randall and his team leapt over the blockade and fired at the soldiers. They cut down the Globorian horde, and they looked to be winning until the turrets turned toward them. One shot

Randall in the stomach, and another turret shot him in the chest.

"NOOOO!" Tara screamed, but it didn't matter. Randall disappeared, and she couldn't stop the tears streaming down her face.

"ATTACK!!!!" she shouted, rushing forward with her troops behind her. If the love of her life was dead, there was nothing left to live for, except justice, and she would have it.

Chapter 12

Tara leapt over the barrier and punched a meaty Globorian sergeant in the face. It stung her hand something fierce, but she didn't care. She had the kind of raw energy only adrenaline could provide and firing a gun couldn't satiate. All around her, enemies and allies shot at each other, but she needed something more tactile. She needed to feel the liquid run from the Globorian's face as she smashed it again and again in the mouth.

"Why?" she shouted. "Why! Why! Why!"

It wasn't so much a question as a statement of her life. Why was she taken from her people? Why was she brought to Earth? Why was Randall the only alien who'd cared about her? Why had he been taken from her? She wanted answers, but she knew that the Globorian had none to give. It was a lousy substitute for the entire Globorian race and how much she hated them.

A laser beam fired over her head and singed the top of her hair. She looked up in time to see a Globorian, weapon pointed straight at her, vaporizing in front of her. She looked behind to see Joshy holding a smoking laser. He didn't have time to smile at her; he was onto the next target.

Debra and Veronica leapt over the bunker and shot at the Globorians operating the turrets. They might actually win, Tara thought, but she had lost more than she cared to admit. She'd lost the only thing that anchored her to Earth, the only thing that anchored her to the galaxy. It didn't matter anymore that she was angry. All that mattered now was that she finished her mission. At least if that was completed successfully, Randall's death wouldn't have been in vain.

Tara pulled out her laser pistol and watched the horror in the Globorian's eyes as she pointed the gun at the alien's face. There was almost pity in her belly as she pulled the trigger, but emotions no longer rested in Tara's heart. Not anymore.

She stood and watched her troops wash over the Globorians until they were all on the ground. Debra and Veronica laid cover fire for the rest of her forces to destroy what remained of the squadrons that controlled the transmission room.

"Enough!" Tara shouted. "Ceasefire."

And they did. The weapons fell silent, sizzling with the incredible heat of battle. Tara walked forward, hoping to find a piece of Randall in the rubble, something for her to mourn. However, she knew there was nothing. The laser disintegrated Randall in full and sent him back into the universe. It was quick, at least, Tara thought as she reached her hand out to catch the flaking embers that blew through the sky. At least the universe would have more energy to create with now. However, it would never create another quite like Randall.

Randall, the only Globorian she'd ever met with a heart. All he wanted was to live past his early adulthood, like so few of his peers, and here he was dying in battle, like so many of his kind. However, at least he died for freedom. Tara wanted to believe that was something for Randall to hang onto, in his last moments. It was something she would hang onto for the rest of her days.

"Leslie!" Tara shouted, pointing to the transmission room. "Open this door!"

Leslie rushed forward and pressed her hand against the keypad to the door. Less than a minute later, it slid open. Four Globorian guards turned to them from inside the room, and with four precise laser shots Tara took them all out. She watched their eyes as they disintegrated. They looked like her Randall's eyes, and then they faded as quickly as he had.

"Get this transmission online," Tara said. "We need to send it to the Inkarian fleet. They are the only fleet in the galaxy which can intimidate the Globorians. I hope they will help when we show them what we have."

"Sure," Leslie said, walking up to the computer. "They are far away right now, though, so how do you propose we amplify our signal so that they receive it quickly?"

"Inkarians have a beacon at the end of every inhabitable planetary system," Tara said, walking forward. "If we send out a message, they will get it."

*

Joshy's arms were shaking as he sat against the bunker wall next to Debra. The battle had been exhilarating, but in the aftermath, he realized he was still alive. How was he alive? He looked around to see the flaking embers and bullet-riddled bodies of so many of his enemies and allies.

Joshy wasn't like them. He wasn't an alien. He was only a human. How could he have survived when so many aliens stronger than him had died? It didn't seem fair, like the universe made a colossal mistake, and all he could do was heave from his chest and cry ugly, sloppy tears.

"Hey," Debra said, sliding down to sit next to him. "Hey, hey, hey. What's wrong?"

Debra had a higher intellectual capacity to understand the factual horrors of war, but she was no more emotionally equipped than he was to understand why she survived. Instead, she hadn't processed it yet.

"Why?" Joshy said. "I…don't…understand…"

Joshy buried himself into Debra's skin. It moved beneath him, like the tide on a beach, and he started to bawl harder. Debra was still alive too. She was his only reason for coming on this mission, and she was still alive. The world must be just and fair if she was still alive.

Except, how could a just and fair world take his parents from him? How could a just and fair world leave his sister to be nothing more than a robot?

"There's nothing to understand," Veronica said from her post on the turret. "This is war. War is incomprehensible."

"Why?" Joshy eked out. Veronica felt terrible for him because there was nothing she could say to comfort him.

"Relax Josh. It's not over yet. Far from it. The best thing you can do is appreciate that you are alive right now. You might not get so lucky next time."

Joshy looked down at the ground, at all the death and destruction, and dried his eyes. "That's what it's about…isn't it? Dumb luck."

Veronica nodded. "Yes. It's dumb luck that I'm alive and my husband is dead. It's dumb luck that you two found each other from across the universe. It's dumb luck that we're standing here, and it's dumb luck that we've survived this long. The universe doesn't really have a plan. It's random chance that anything happens. Anybody who tells you otherwise is lying to you."

That didn't make Joshy feel any better, but Veronica's voice was soothing, and he took some comfort in that. Then, he looked up at Debra and thought that dumb luck might not be so bad anyway.

As he watched the blast door behind him, Joshy saw a laser burning slowly through it as more Globorian forces approached. He rose to his feet and hoped dumb luck was on his side again.

*

Leslie typed away at the transmitter computer until a bright green light flicked on in the room. "I think that has done it."

"Good," Tara replied. "Now, make sure to upload as much information you can into the system so the council can see what we have seen."

A low pinging sound came from the computer as it flashed a slow, dull green. As it did, Joshy rushed into the room.

"The Globorians are coming for us!"

"I knew they would," Tara replied. "Keep them busy as long as possible. We have to get this transmission out. If we don't, there is no hope for planet Earth."

Joshy nodded and rushed back outside. Tara gripped the edge of the control panel as she shook with rage. "Why is this taking so long?!" she screamed.

"We're trying to communicate across a million light years, ma'am," Leslie said. "Sometimes, that takes a moment."

The dull green flashed on and a group of tiny, squat, salamander looking aliens, but with neon green bodies and long, orange tongues flashed onto the screen. They were Inkarians, like Tara.

"Ombanliligo, niswandi," one of the lizards said.

"Ilvandu montuzi," Tara replied in perfect Inkarian. "Do you speak, Earth English, Councilor Erdu?"

"Of course, we do!" Councilor Erdu said. "We speak every tongue in the galaxy. We hate English so much. So coarse and vulgar."

"If you wouldn't mind, my Inkarian is very rusty. I haven't practiced it in over a hundred years, and what I have to say is urgent."

"Go on!" Councilor Erdu said. "This had better be good."

"I am Zilmarni Inkari. I was sold to the Globorians during a trade deal after the third Inkarian war. I have lived here, on Earth, for the last hundred years, and I come to you now with a grave warning. The Globorian delegation has broken their treaty with you by kidnapping and imprisoning peaceful aliens. They are in violation of several hundred by-laws in intergalactic accords, and those are only the ones we know about."

"That is a serious allegation, Zilmarni, slave," the grumpiest Inkarian said to her. "What proof have you?"

"Listen to this," Leslie said. Her eyes rolled back in her head, and the screen showed the image of a light blue walrus creature with a long bushy mustache.

"I was trying to leave Earth like I was told. However, the minute I left Earth's orbit a Globorian battlecruiser tractor beamed me into it. I've been a prisoner here since then."

The screen flipped back to the salamanders, who now had worried looks on their faces. "This is quite disturbing, slave, but it is hardly enough to call into question our truce with the Globorians, especially for a planet as insignificant as Earth."

"There is more!" Leslie shouted. Behind them, Tara heard the attack beginning.

"Hurry up," Tara said to Leslie.

The screen flipped again, and now a dark red alien with seven horns stood on screen, blinking its dozen eyes. "I traveled with my wife across the galaxy. When they captured me…they vaporized her. Gods, I miss my wife so much."

"Is that a Saskarian!?" Councilor Erdu asked.

"Yes." Leslie nodded. "If I'm not mistaken, they are one of your closest trading partners."

"And there's more," Tara said. "How many interviews did you conduct?"

"Forty-two. They are all in my memory and are uploading to the server now."

"And the aliens are all here, sir, on this base," Tara said. "They are fighting for their very lives. We don't know if we will survive without your help. Earth will surely not survive without your help."

"Hrmph," Councilor Erdu grunted. "This is certainly troubling. We will take it under advisement and be back to you within one Earth century."

"A century!" Tara shouted. "That's too long. They intend to take over the Earth any day now! They are counting on the fact that you will be deliberate and take a long time."

"Young lady!" Councilor Erdu shouted. "You do not raise your voice to your elders, especially since you are a slave. You are lucky we are taking your call at all."

"Will you at least listen to the communications I have recorded?" Leslie asked. "I will stay here, even though we are in battle, until you have listened to them all, and are satisfied that the Globorians have broken their treaty."

"Leslie, no," Tara said grabbing her arm. "We need you—"

"We need to save the world, ma'am," Leslie said. "This is our best option. Therefore, it is up to me to survive long enough to make that happen."

"Very well," Councilor Erdu said. "We will watch your videos and humor you."

The fighting was coming upon them faster and faster as the Globorians advanced from both sides. Tara looked out the door and saw her troops being decimated as she sat inside.

"Bolt the door. Do not come out. And survive," Tara said.

"I will do my best," Leslie replied.

Tara disappeared through the door, and Leslie closed it behind them. She scrambled the code to the door so the Globorians could not enter, and she brought down a blast door behind her so that it would be harder for them to get through.

"Now," Leslie said with a smile. "Where were we?"

Chapter 13

Tara stepped out of the transmission room and into a firefight. Her team was dwindling while the Globorians seemed to be infinite. She watched as laser shots took out three more members of her team.

"We have to push forward!" Tara shouted.

"The only advantage we have are these turrets!" Debra screamed back. "If we lose them, we're toast!"

"Maybe," Tara admitted. "But if we keep sitting here, they're going to advance, and we'll eventually run out of ammo."

"What do you suggest then?" Joshy asked, firing at the Globorians on either side of them.

"We have to get to the control room on the flight deck. If we do that, we can cut off the supplies to the lines by locking all the doors on this ship. However, if we lose many more bodies, we won't have enough to overtake the bridge."

"And what about Leslie?" Joshy asked. "Who's going to protect her?"

"Leslie's a big girl," Tara said. "She's got her own mission. We can't think about her safety. This is about more than that. It's about planning for what happens if she doesn't get through to the Inkarians."

"And what if she doesn't get through?" Veronica asked.

"Then our only shot is controlling this ship and using it against them by any means necessary."

"Oh," Debra said. "Is that all?"

"I need you to lead the battle to the ship's hull," Tara told Debra. "I'm going to stay here and keep the

Globorians at bay. Hopefully, I can keep them in check until Leslie finishes."

"How long will that be?" Joshy said.

"I don't know, but the rest of you need to move forward, and do it now."

Tara pushed Debra off her turret and began firing back at the Globorians. Veronica ceded her turret and rushed forward with her daughter.

"Good luck," Veronica said.

"Dumb luck would be better," Tara replied, handing Veronica the holographic disk. "Keep going until you reach the front. Do not stop!"

*

Debra had never overseen a mission before. She had barely been on a mission before a couple weeks ago. However, she already had the guilt of dozens of deaths on her conscience, including Joshy's parents, from when they rescued her from the Globorians, so she was in a unique position to assume command.

"Don't stop!" Debra said as her waning troops fired at the Globorians in front of them. Their strategy this whole time had been to push forward until they broke through, and while that worked when there were a lot of troops, now that the prisoners were one-tenth of what they were when they left the prison, it became harder and harder to muscle their way through.

"How much further?" Debra screamed above the firefight.

Veronica opened the holographic disk. "It's only a couple hundred feet away, but with this rate of fire, we'll be lucky to get there."

"What if we used the dead Globorian bodies for human shields?" Joshy asked. "I've seen it in video games before."

Debra looked down at the bodies riddling the hallway. Some vaporized into dust, but as many were shot with bullets, and they littered the floor as well.

Veronica picked up one of the Globorian guards, but she struggled against it. "Help me!"

A half dozen alien soldiers rushed to her aid and held up the Globorian. As they did, Joshy saw something around the Globorian's belt. It was a metallic round object that looked like the thermal detonator Leia used in Return of the Jedi to threaten Jabba.

"Is that what I think it is?" Joshy asked.

Veronica nodded. "George Lucas was a Thimberian. One of our most famous, actually. He designed all of Star Wars from different races he found roaming the galaxy."

"That is the coolest sentence I've ever heard."

"We can't use it, though," Debra said. "It would blow a hole in the ship, and we'd all be sucked out with it."

"Maybe," Joshy said. "Or maybe we can run through to another corridor and blow these Globorians to kingdom come. If we can do that, then at least Tara has a fighting chance."

"That's crazy," Veronica said.

"I like it," Debra added.

"Me too," Veronica replied, "but it's still crazy."

Joshy ripped the grenade off the belt. "Everybody through the doors to the next corridor. Now!"

The aliens abandoned their posts and rushed through the closest doorway. Debra pulled Joshy through last, just as he threw the grenade. The door closed as the grenade exploded and the vacuum vortex sucked the Globorian forces into space.

"Come on!" Debra shouted.

Debra pulled Joshy through the doorway and into the next corridor.

*

The plasma grenade's explosion rocked the hallway as Tara fired her turret toward the advancing Globorian horde behind her. The shockwave shook the foundation of the cruiser, and then a moment later she heard the wind howl down the corridor. It wasn't coming to blow her away. No, it was coming to suck her down.

She latched onto the turret, which was drilled into the ground, as two Globorians fell through the corridor around her. Tara gripped tightly, but even with her white knuckles, she couldn't withstand the force of the wind for long.

Another Globorian tumbled past her as she watched the door to the transmission room shutter open. Leslie reached out and grabbed for Tara's hand, but she was a bit out of reach. Tara pulled the M-4 off her back and reached it out to her.

She watched Leslie mouth, "Jump," but she couldn't hear her over the roar of the wind. Tara was scared to jump, but she didn't have much choice. She swung her legs backward and forward as the vacuum pulled her down and down. With the last ounce of her strength, she let go of the turret and leapt toward Leslie as the turret dislodged from its bolts and fell behind her.

Leslie grabbed onto the edge of the gun and pulled with all of her might. Tara's hands slipped, but she inched along the gun as Leslie pulled her to safety. With one final heave, Leslie pulled Tara inside the transmission room as the last of the Globorians fell through the vacuum, missing Tara by inches.

Leslie pulled her inside and turned to the computer, closing the blast doors nearest the vacuum and stopping it from sucking them into the abyss. On the screen, the Inkarians hid their eyes behind their webbed feet.

"Do you see what we are dealing with here?" Leslie said to them. "We could really use your help!"

"Oh my," one of them replied.

*

Joshy followed Debra into a hallway parallel to the one they'd blown up a few seconds before. He saw a dozen of his alien comrades fighting through the shit. He had forgotten that Tara split her forces into two squads, and this must have been zeta squad. It looked like this squad was faring better than the other. They had made it almost to the bridge of the ship. However, there was a massive blast door blocking their path.

Joshy bent down and grabbed a grenade from the Globorians that lay dead at his feet. "I have an idea."

"What?" Debra replied. "Create another vacuum?"

"No, can you and your mother create a shockwave timed to go off and direct the blast at the door and so that it doesn't blow upwards or outwards?"

"It's possible," Veronica said. "But it would have to be very precise."

"We can do it," Debra said confidently.

"I don't believe you," Joshy said. "But I like the confidence."

"Confidence will get you killed," Veronica said.

"Does anybody have a better plan?"

Debra and Veronica shook their heads. They desperately wanted a better plan, but this was the only one that presented itself.

"Then, I guess it's the one we're going with," Joshy replied, pulling the pin on the detonator. Go!"

The grenade flew through the air in slow motion. Joshy had seen it in video games before, but he never knew that the important moments in your life slowed down so that they lasted an eternity. On either side of him, Debra and Veronica nodded in slow motion and threw their shockwaves at the same time.

It was a thing of beauty to watch the shockwave connect with the grenade at the moment of its impact on the door and send the explosion through the door until it bored a hole into the other side of it.

"Oh my gods," Debra said.

"I couldn't do that again if I had another thousand tries."

"Well, luckily," Joshy said, "you only needed the one."

Joshy, Debra, and the rest of their forces rushed through the door. As they hopped through the opening, gunfire rained down on them for a moment, but then fell silent. Joshy walked up the long steps to the bridge to see it was empty save for dead Globorian bodies on the ground.

"We did it," Joshy said.

He didn't have time to celebrate before the window in front of the ship turned into a TV screen, and a big, gray, sizzling Globorian general with one eye snarled at him.

"Congratulations. You have taken control of one of our ships. However, your victory will be short-lived, as half of my fleet has surrounded you and will commence bombing you into oblivion momentarily."

The screen went blank as Joshy's eyes went wide. Thirty Globorian battlecruisers surrounded his field of vision, and their weapons were all powering up. He could see the red beams intensifying in front of him.

"Anybody that has ever flown a spaceship before take a position at the helm!!!" Joshy shouted. "We're under attack!"

Chapter 14

The cannon fire from the other Globorian battlecruisers rocked the ship back and forth. Joshy steadied himself on the bridge, but he could feel the ship breaking apart around him.

"We don't have much more of the deflector shield left!" Veronica shouted.

"LESLIE! TARA! We need you on the bridge now!" Debra shouted into the intercom system.

"If we take another direct hit, we're going down," Veronica shouted. "There's nothing we can do about it."

"Can we return fire?" Joshy asked.

"Not if we want to have power for the shields we can't!" Veronica replied.

"So, we're stuck here?"

"Unless you have another plan," Veronica said.

"This isn't a plan," Tara said rushing through the door. "It's the opposite of a plan. Look there." Tara pointed to a hole in the sky between two ships. "If we can maneuver into the hole, we have a chance."

"Oh," Veronica said, as she spun around from her controls. "And how are we gonna get there? All power is diverted to the shields."

Tara sighed. "We drop the shields."

"That actually is suicide," Debra said. "If we drop the shields, we're dead."

Veronica heard her daughter's words, and suddenly a plan clicked in her head. "Not necessarily."

"What do you mean Mom, you just said—"

"I need you to take care of yourself, Debra. Please."

Tara understood that Veronica was going to sacrifice herself before Debra could comprehend it. "You don't have to do this."

"If I want us to survive, I do."

Tara nodded. "Godspeed."

Suddenly, it all came together in Debra's head. Her mother could increase and decrease her mass at will. She was little more than a beam of light, and a deflector shield isn't much more than a concentrated beam of light.

"No," Debra said, sobbing. "No. I just got you back. No. I won't let you."

"My love," Veronica said, cupping her hands around Debra's face. "I would do anything to protect you. Don't you know that?"

"I know, but please…"

"I love you so much," Veronica said, giving Debra one last caress on her cheek.

With that, Veronica faded through the hull of the ship as another laser beam blasted into the hull, rocking everybody and twisting the ship violently.

"Get ready!" Tara said, turning to a red alien who was in control of the ship's thrusters. She watched as Veronica spread out across the hull as wide as she could make herself. Another shot rocketed toward the ship, and Veronica rocked back and forth as she absorbed the blow.

"Now!" Tara shouted.

They pressed the thrusters of the battlecruiser forward, and the ship creaked and rattled as it sped up toward the space between the ships. Veronica's mass of light shifted, and Debra noticed a face, her mother's face, smiling at her.

Then, with another violent blast the face cringed, and with another, it faded from the window.

"No!!!!!" Debra said, falling to the ground. Joshy ran forward and cradled her in his arms. "NOOOOOO!!!!!!"

The ship rocked violently again as it headed for the space in the sky. Another hit, and another. Suddenly, the ship tipped toward the ground. No matter what the soldiers did, they couldn't fight against gravity to keep it airborne.

"We can't keep it in the air," Tara said. "Brace for impact!"

The ship dipped toward the ground below. "Aim for the hillside," Tara shouted. "If we're going down, let's not take innocent civilians with us."

Debra and Joshy looked at each other. They were about to die, but at least they would go down together, and in their final moments before the ship's nose hit the ground, they kissed. With her last ounce of energy, Debra created a cocoon, as she once did for his whole family, and wrapped Joshy in it. Then, they crashed to the earth together.

*

Debra awakened on a rolling hillside outside of London. The grass tickled her skin. She smelled the soft fragrance of flowers blooming for a moment, then the pleasant scent was overtaken with the putrid stench of burnt metal and acid fire. She rose to her feet and saw she was at the top of a small hill. The battlecruiser burned in front of her. All around her, a few of Tara's soldiers and even fewer Globorians stirred. Most didn't survive the crash and lay motionless around her.

"Joshy!" Debra shouted. She turned to see Joshy laying on the ground, bleeding from a gash in his head. She rushed over to him and felt his breath. "No! No! No! Not you too! NO!!!!"

Then, Joshy coughed violently and fluttered open his eyes. "Debra? Ow. That sucked."

Debra didn't think she would ever smile again, and yet, she did at that moment. She smiled because if nothing else she still had one thing in the world that she loved. She drew Joshy closer, and as they hugged, a dark shadow grew over them. They looked up to see the sluglike battlecruisers of the Globorian forces overhead. This was the end.

"It has been an honor going to battle with you," Tara said, cresting over the hill. "I'm sorry it was such a failure."

"It was not a failure," they heard from the bottom of the hill. Debra looked down to see Leslie looking up at them as if she hadn't gotten a scratch on her. "You made me well, Tara. This is very good metal."

"That's nice," Tara said. "But what makes you think this isn't a failure? Look at us."

"Watch," Leslie said, looking up.

Above the Globorian battlecruiser, a slick, metal saucer, twenty times bigger than the Globorians' craft, appeared in space. It looked like Tara's ship, but a thousand times bigger.

"Right before we crashed, the Inkarians finally decided that the Globorians had performed enough illegal acts to violate their accords and agreed to help. Though admittedly, they didn't like it. They hate coming to this part of the galaxy, but they hate aliens violating their accords even more."

Tara looked down at her. "You did something right."

"I won't let it go to my head."

Joshy laughed. "Is there ever a time when Princess Bride isn't appropriate?"

Leslie looked around at the death, destruction, and carnage around her. "I suppose not, if it's appropriate right now."

*

The Inkarians didn't waste any time taking control of the Globorian fleet. All it took was three downed Globorian ships before the war was over. While the Globorians had focused on war since their last treaty, the Inkarians concentrated on technology, as was their way, and now they were the preeminent force in the galaxy by a factor of ten. The Globorians didn't stand a chance.

Unfortunately, most of the aliens who were kept aboard the London battlecruiser died in the crash or in the bloody combat before it. Luckily, seven other Globorian ships had prisoners, and two of them were Inkarians. The Inkarians were none too happy about that.

Tara, for her part in the rebellion, was liberated from slavery. She was welcomed back into the Inkarian fold but chose to remain on Earth in case the backwater planet ever needed Inkarian support again. Besides, now that planet Earth had been in contact with aliens, there was no choice but to welcome the inbred monkeys into the Consortium of Planets, though only as a junior member, and they needed a liaison—a position Tara gladly accepted.

Leslie chose to take Tara's place among the Inkarians. They had never seen a human assimilated with Inkarian tech before and were excited to study the technological achievement.

"I'm sorry to see you go," Joshy said to Leslie before she boarded the ship.

Leslie smiled at him. "We will always have each other and the memories of the time we had. That will never go anywhere. And if you knew what I knew about time, you would not be so sad."

"What do you know that I don't know?"

Leslie smiled, wrapping Joshy up in a big hug. "So many things."

Joshy thought long and hard about whether he wanted to leave Earth. The Inkarians bestowed Debra with a new ship, big enough to fit a human and their "needs," as unsanitary as they were to the Inkarians. There was literally nothing keeping him on the planet, and he had every reason to leave. Still, Earth pulled him to remain, as if its gravity worked on his heart as much as his body.

"I'm not going to go without you," Debra told him. "If you want to stay on this planet, then we will do it together."

"Will we ever come back?" Joshy asked.

"Maybe," Debra said. "If you want. However, it will never look like this. Time passes differently out among the stars. You will never see Earth like this again."

Joshy looked over at her. "And you want to go?"

Debra sighed. "This place used to have so many good memories for me, but now it has only pain. So much pain."

Joshy squeezed her hand. "Then we should go. Together. And make new memories somewhere that's less painful."

Debra leaned against Joshy's shoulder. "I love you. Did you know that?"

Joshy nodded. "I had a feeling."

*

You just finished The Invasion Saga. If you liked this book, you can find a whole lot more from Russell at www.russellnohelty.com

*

If you like YA sci-fi, then make sure to pick up *The Vessel,* a dystopian adventure in the vein of *Maze Runner, Hunger Games,* or *Divergent,* but with less kid on kid murder.

*

Now, enjoy a sneak peak of *The Vessel.*

THE VESSEL

By:

Russell Nohelty

Edited by:

Leah Lederman

Cover by:

Lee Kohse

Additional cover design work by:

Hannah McGill

PROLOGUE

"Sir, Sir, Sir!" Penelope's heels clomped against the Center's sterile, marble floor as she chased a dark figure in the distance. "Sir! Would you slow down for one second?"

"They call me Wind for a reason," the shadow replied.

"Yeah," Penelope closed the distance to her boss. "because you're full of hot air."

"I could have you killed for that, you know."

Penelope poked Wind in the chest. "You really think the guards care about an old gas bag like you?"

"Well, you found me. I thought I could escape that ghastly meeting and get a moment's peace. I should have known better than to try and hide from you."

"When was the last time you had a moment's peace?"

"I think there was a day a few thousand years ago." Wind cracked his aging back. "I'm sorry. I get crankier as I age. I can't wait for a new body."

"Unlike most of us, who get just one. I pity you, really." Penelope handed Wind a tablet. "The press release is ready. Are you sure you want to do this?"

"I've been ready for a few thousand years." Wind's fingers glided across the tablet's glass. "Would you take my place if you could? Would you live forever?"

"Absolutely not! I barely want the one life I have. Most days I want to rip the force field in half, run outside, and let the radiation take me, you know?"

Wind grazed Penelope's hand as he gave the tablet back to her. "Soon, that may be an option."

Penelope touched her skin where Wind's hand had been. "We can hope."

Wind walked off down a dark corridor, his loafers clacking on the marble surface. "Often, that's all we can do."

*

Time mattered little to Wind. Years passed like minutes to him. It was a function of being very, very, very old. After all, he was one of the Five, chosen to live a life of eternal rebirth millennia after millennia. He'd grown from a testosterone-filled youth to a decrepit old man more times than he could count, and hated it every time.

He wished they had created the Transference machine to work when the brain was fully formed at twenty-five, instead of during the ridiculously malleable teenage years. Of course, it was only in that sweet spot of youth that consciousness could be transferred properly—when the brain was developed enough to withstand the imprint, yet nubile enough to recover from the trauma.

Wind longed for it to be over, though. He couldn't wait until the decades didn't flash in the blink of an eye, when a century didn't pass in the span of a day, and when he could finally close his eyes for good and rest.

But that was not his life. He'd accepted his lot. Most would kill to be in his position. Some did, back in the day. He had certainly thought it was a blessing when they had chosen him. Like most blessings, though, it was equal parts curse. Nobody knew about the horrors he faced, the horrible decisions he made, and the secrets buried in his ancient mind.

*

Wind opened the door to his quarters, unchanged since the Incident. It was his comfort, his sanctuary, and his prison— just like the City, which housed them all. Of course, it was everybody's prison in a way, but Wind felt it more acutely. He'd spent centuries shackled inside its walls, maintaining the Bubble that kept his citizens protected from harm while simultaneously sealing them off from the universe. Wind was their grand protector and heartless warden rolled into one.

He sat down at his computer and peered over at a picture on his bedside, the one of him and Penelope smiling like fools. She had insisted that they smile, even though Wind hated to do it. There was little to smile about, even on the best days.

A sound caught his ear and he whipped his head around. "Is something there?"

It was over in an instant. The intruder swung his arm out of the shadows and stabbed Wind through the eye. He wasn't captured by fear, anger, or even pain in the moment of his death. He was blissfully content.

Finally, Wind thought, I can find peace.

BOOK 1

The Journey

CHAPTER 1

"Just let it go. You're never gonna figure it out," I yelled at Jake as he slammed his meaty palm across the broken tractor.

There were few things in life I hated more than watching somebody royally screw up. It's the sort of grating hatred that made me want to punch somebody right in the mouth, especially when it's Jake— a major, world-class, screwer-upper of things. I'd been watching him fix his family's tractor for six hours and it was not even close to being usable.

"I hate you so much right now," I shouted, dangling my feet from Jake's woodshed. "Do you know how much I hate you? I hate you more than anything has ever hated anything in the history of the universe."

It was true. The only thing I hated more than watching somebody muck up was if they refused to let me fix it. He'd failed seventeen times already; I'd counted. I could get that stupid tractor working in three minutes if it weren't for his stupid, male pride.

What got me was how confident he was each time he failed. Men are always so confident, even if they don't have a reason to be.

"I got it this time. I know I do."

I wanted to leave, but knew I'd be stuck fixing it eventually. In order to do that, I had to know exactly how bad he'd screwed up, which meant watching this train wreck even if I had a dozen other chores to do.

"I'm so hungry, Jake. Can't we just go eat now? I mean you clearly don't know what you're doing.'"

He was as stubborn as he was clumsy, and he wouldn't listen. I couldn't believe Daddy wanted me to marry this man.

Jake popped the clutch and put the battered tractor into gear. It sputtered, fizzled, and fell silent. "Dang it!"

"I told you before, it's a stopped-up intake. That tractor isn't going anywhere unless you remove all that build up."

"Oh yeah? And what do you know anyway?"

What a stupid boy. "What do I know? Well, I know we aren't eating until this gets fixed, and I know you aren't going to fix it, and I definitely know how to fix a stupid intake. And I know I'm starving!'"

"Please, girl, you don't know anything."

That pissed me off. I had fixed everything on this ruddy farm, from the baler to the water heater, and he still didn't trust me. Even though my dad had taught me everything he knew, it didn't matter. I was still a girl. I didn't know why having a vagina prevented me from knowing how to fix stuff.

I'd had enough of listening to him. I hopped up from my hay bale and opened the intake valve. After a few seconds, I pulled out a wad of mucky slime. "I told you. Try it now."

"It's not gonna work," Jake insisted.

"You say that every time you try to fix it yourself and every time you fail. Can you just trust me for once already?"

He stepped on the clutch and turned the ignition. The rusted tractor turned over and purred like a kitten. "Dang you, Althea. Can't you just be wrong this once?"

The truth was, I couldn't be wrong. Not about this sort of stuff. I knew these farms inside and out. I could sleepwalk my way to fixing anything within a ten-mile radius. "Where's the fun in that?"

"The fun's in letting the man be the man for once in your life."

"You find me a man and I'll let him be one, alright? Now come on. We're late for supper and I'm starving."

I wanted to like Jake because Daddy wanted me to like him. I mean, I liked him more than any of the other boys, but that didn't mean much since I hated all of them with the fire of a thousand suns. Maybe I could grow to like him enough, love him even. That's what Daddy wanted.

"Come on!" I shouted to Jake.

I didn't like to think about that sort of stuff though. That was a worry for the future. I just wanted to feel the rush of the cool, fall night on my skin. It felt so good. We liked it cool in the Fifth ring. We were bred for it.

There were six rings in all and they radiated out from the Center where the Five lived. The Five have been around since the dawn of time, moving their consciousness from person to person every generation.

The First Ring, where the richest and most powerful lived, was closest to the Center, and therefore closest to the Five.

The Second Ring was where your family lived if your body was chosen as a Vessel for the Five. If that happened, then every need for you and your family was taken care of for eternity. The Third Ring was full of bankers and businessmen. They handled all the money in the City and made sure everybody got paid.

All of that made up the Inner Rings. A big moat surrounded the Inner Rings to regulate the Outer Ring's population from going there. The only way in was by train, and there were only four trains in the whole City. They all started at the Bubble and made their way in from all four directions, taking soldiers out and bringing goods in. The trains were way too expensive for anybody except soldiers to use, but I often hoped I could get on the train one day and see the Center myself. They say it's beautiful.

The Outer Rings were where the City made stuff. The Fourth Ring warehoused all the raw materials and processed them into food and consumable products. The Fifth Ring, where I lived, made all the food the City needed. The Sixth, well, you didn't want to go to the Sixth. That was where they mined all the ore, and it was dirty and smelly. Farmland stayed dead for a hundred miles from its edges. People from the Sixth were mean and hard.

Every Ring had its people; the Five had bred them from birth, generation after generation, to do a specific job. For instance, I'm a farmer, just like everybody else in the Fifth. That's what I know. That's who I am. We are practical, humble, and no-nonsense people, who don't mind hard work or getting our hands dirty.

I would say that I'm a pretty average Fifth. I'm tall and broad with long hair and dark eyes. I run pretty fast, but not too fast. Just fast enough. Some people say I'm pretty, but not pretty enough to be noticed. I like to think I'm kind too, but not kind enough to be taken advantage of. I'm just right, Daddy says, average in the middle. That's what you want to be, average. You want to fit like a glove. If you don't fit, they'll find you. You don't want to be found.

"Hurry up, slow poke!" I shouted over my shoulder to Jake. "They probably ate all the good stuff already."

Jake looked a little like me, except he was a boy. Like most Fives, Jake was hearty, strong, and confident. The Five needed us stronger than oxen. They relied on us to feed the entire City, and the City was hungry.

*

Our house wasn't big or flashy, but it got the job done. My great-grandpa built it with his own hands two hundred years ago. It was a good house even though it was a little drafty, the walls were paper thin, and the floor creaked horribly. Mama said it had character. That's what people say about something when they don't have anything nice to say.

"Mama!" I shouted, rushing through our front door. "Sorry we're late. Hope dinner's not cold."

Mama knew I would be late. I was always late. They all just went on without me. If there was no food left it was my own fault, but they always left me enough. My family was like that. We watch out for each other.

They weren't in the kitchen when Jake and I ran inside, and they were always in the kitchen when I got home. We weren't that late. The dinner table was full of food, too. We never left food on the table. "Mama! Is everything alright?"

The sound of the TV blared from the family room. Our TV never stayed on when it was dinnertime. We had strict rules about even glancing at the TV room until the food was cleaned up. Something was wrong.

I found them in the family room. Mama was crying messy tears. Dad and my brother, Bobby, were silent. They stared at the TV like zombies. "Mama. What's going on?"

"Shhhhhh," Dad responded, barely able to move his lips.

An elegant, poised, beautiful lady was on the TV. She was somber and dignified. It was Earth, one of the Five, the patron Saint of the Fifth Ring. Earth came from the land and had built all of the agriculture after the Incident. It was because of her that there were farms and land, and Mama and Daddy and Jake and even my disgusting brother Bobby.

"I regret to inform you," Earth said, "that early this morning, we found Wind, dead."

*

If you liked that preview of *The Vessel,* pick it up today.